&

THE MONDAY MANDATES

THE GUSTAFSON GIRLS

BOOK 1

BECKY DOUGHTY

BRAVEHEARTS PRESS

Juliette and the Monday ManDates
The Gustafson Girls Book 1

First published in the United States of America by BraveHearts Press

ISBN: 978-1517198244
ISBN-10: 1517198240
~ ~ ~

Author Information: www.BeckyDoughty.com

For Sisters and Daughters everywhere.
God knew what He was doing
when He made
YOU.

"May I see your license and registration, please?"

After wrestling with the latch on the glove compartment, she withdrew the paperwork for her car, then reached into the back seat to grab her purse from off the floor. Out of the corner of her eye, she saw him take a step back and put a hand on his holster.

The thought that she might be pulling out a weapon struck her as funny, and she had to bite her lip to keep from giggling. Her hands trembled, making it difficult to slide her license from its plastic casing in her wallet.

"Is everything all right, ma'am?"

"Yes, Officer." The late afternoon sun setting in the sky behind him made her squint. She couldn't tell if he was looking at her or not, but she caught a glimpse of her warped reflection in his sunglasses. "I'm just really nervous, I guess."

"Why are you so nervous?"

"I—I don't know," she stuttered as she handed over her license. "I've never been pulled over before, and I'm trying not to freak out."

"I'm not going to hurt you."

"Oh. Good. Thanks." She grimaced. It sounded as though she'd been afraid of just that. "I mean, I know you're not going to hurt me. At least I think I do. I meant thanks for trying to reassure me. I can't help it, though; I get nervous easily." She should just close her mouth. She wasn't making things better by talking.

"Do you know how fast you were driving?"

"Um, I think so." She wrapped her damp fingers around the steering wheel again. "Actually, I'm not sure."

"Ten miles over the speed limit." His voice remained calm, patient, rattling her even more. "Do you know what the speed limit is here?"

CHAPTER ONE

JULIETTE stared wide-eyed into the rear-view mirror at the red and blue lights flashing behind her. Her palms began to sweat as her heart rate sky-rocketed, and it took her several minutes to pull her little PT Cruiser out of the dinner-hour traffic.

She waited, both hands gripping the steering wheel, as the officer approached her window. Finding it still closed, he tapped on it, and she jumped, letting out a tiny squeal. "Sorry!" she called through the glass, turning the car back on so she could operate the power windows. She worked the knobs, accidentally sending the backseat window up and down twice before she finally managed to get hers open. "Sorry," she repeated, peering up at the very tall officer whose eyes were hidden behind his sunglasses.

"Please turn off your engine, ma'am." His voice was firm, and Juliette scrambled to comply.

"Sorry," she muttered a third time, afraid now to look up at him. She toyed with the keys in her lap, sensing his eyes boring into the top of her head. She was sure she'd smell burning hair at any moment.

"Um, I think so," she said again, a hot flush creeping up her chest and neck. "Actually, I—I'm not exactly sure about that either." Her voice cracked into a whisper.

The officer cleared his throat. "Ma'am, I'm a little concerned. You don't seem to know some pretty important pieces of information that someone who gets behind the wheel of a car should know." His patronizing tone irritated her. "The speed limit here is 35 miles per hour. You were driving 45." He paused, just long enough to make her squirm, before continuing. "Were you in a hurry to get somewhere?"

"No, not really." She shook her head and forgot about keeping her mouth shut. "I was just hungry, and I wasn't paying attention to how fast I was driving."

The officer chuckled, and Juliette's stomach flip-flopped uncomfortably. "You were speeding because you were hungry? That's a first." Her grip on the steering wheel tightened; he was mocking her.

Jerk, she thought to herself. "Well, it's the truth." She tried to glare at him, but the sun made it difficult, and she had to turn away again.

He leaned down to look around the inside of her car while she fumed in her seat. As if satisfied there was nothing suspicious about her, he straightened again, tore off a page from his ticket pad, and handed it to her along with her license.

"Look, Ms. Gustafson. Believe it or not, I appreciate your honesty. But being distracted is a dangerous way to drive, much more so than driving too fast because you *choose* to ignore the speed limit. Did you know that most accidents happen when a driver is distracted? Let this be a wake-up call for you. It's why we give tickets; not necessarily to punish drivers for bad behavior, but to encourage them to drive better." He pointed at the pink form she was holding. "Just follow the instructions on the ticket, okay?"

She couldn't believe it. He was actually *lecturing* her! First he mocked her, then he lectured her. No longer nervous, she was offended. She nodded, her lips clamped shut, afraid of what she might say if she let any words slip out.

He patted the roof of her car. "Drive safely now, Ms. Gustafson."

"Thank you, Officer," she managed to squeeze out, her upbringing forcing her to be polite. "Not for the ticket, of course. Or the lecture." Why, oh why couldn't she just stop talking? "I mean, thank you for wishing me safe driving. Thank you for saying 'Drive safely now.'" Her voice trailed off. She stuck her keys in the ignition, turned on the car, and rolled up the window without looking at him again.

"Imbecile," she muttered, not sure if she was referring to him or herself.

~ ~ ~

A TICKET. Her first ever. She didn't know whether to cry or celebrate. And today, of all days.

Today marked six months of life without Mike.

Juliette tucked her feet up underneath her as she nestled into the corner of her over-stuffed beige couch. This was *her* spot. It had always been her spot, and at this rate, it probably always would be. She maneuvered the TV tray over her knees until it was positioned just the way she liked it.

"Another wonderful meal with me, myself, and I. I can eat whatever I want, whenever I want, however I want, wherever I want. No one can tell me otherwise, and I *like* it this way." She raised her plastic fork in a defiant salute, then stabbed it into the middle of The Green Dragon food on her tray. She spun the utensil until it was loaded with noodles and shoved the whole bundle into her mouth. She couldn't close her lips around the bite, but she didn't care; she just chewed with her mouth open.

"Delicious!" she exclaimed when she could speak again. "It's you that I love, Mr. Chen Yu. Only you." She pointed the remote at the television and pressed play. A terribly-acted romance-novel-come-to-life started up again where she'd left it to go pick up her take-out. The heroine was overly made up and vacuous. The male lead looked like he'd been shellacked from head to toe, not a hair or muscle out of place. Even his jeans were pressed. She actually *wanted* the woman to leave him. The storyline was not making her cry, nor giving her anything else to relate to, and it was sucking all the joy out of her favorite food.

Just as she was debating whether or not she could stand another second of the sappy dialogue, her phone rang.

At first, she tried to ignore it. Then she thought it might be Mike and contemplated throwing the thing out the window. She let it ring instead, and the call eventually went to voice-mail, beeping rudely at her. Sighing dramatically, she turned up the movie, preferring to see it through to the bitter end than to be stuck with her thoughts of Mike.

A few minutes later, the phone rang again. "Are you serious?" She pushed the TV tray away and scrambled for the purse she'd dropped on the floor at the end of the couch. It was Renata. "What do you want," she muttered under her breath, while she considered whether or not she could handle talking to her sister right now.

Either she was calling to make sure Juliette wasn't

drowning herself in the bathtub, or she was calling to try to coerce her into going on another family outing to Pizza Haven or the local dog park. "I don't even *have* a dog! Or a family, for that matter. Or a man." She sighed and brought the phone to her ear.

"Hi, Ren." She knew she sounded miserable, but she didn't care. Regardless of how she answered the phone, Renata believed Juliette was seriously depressed, and if she sounded otherwise, her sister reminded her that she didn't have to fake it with her.

"How are you, sweetie?"

"Why do you call me sweetie?" Juliette voiced the first question that popped into her head, belligerence tattering the edges of her words. She softened her tone just a little. "In fact, you call all of us that."

"Do I?" Renata asked. "It must be because I think you're all so sweet. And actually, I don't call Phoebe that. She'd rip my head off and drop-kick it into outer space."

"Hm. Did you two have another run-in?" Juliette smirked at her own ridiculous question. Renata and Phoebe never had anything *but* run-ins.

As though reading her thoughts, Renata replied, "We don't have run-ins. We just think differently. But I didn't call you to talk about Phoebe. I called to find out how you're doing."

"I'm fine." Juliette opted for cryptic. She'd forgotten to turn down the movie and was having a hard time focusing on what Renata was saying.

"You're fine? Really? What is that noise? Do you have company?"

"I'm fine. Really. The noise is a movie. No, I don't have company. Any other questions?" She rolled her eyes as the two main characters on screen started moving toward each other across a parking lot in slow motion.

"You're starting to sound like Phoebe." Juliette could hear the disdain in Renata's voice and it made her bristle.

"That's not such a bad thing," Juliette said, defending their younger sister.

"Oh relax. I don't mean it's bad. I just mean you don't sound like you, because you're acting like her." She sighed. "Again, I didn't call to talk about Phoebe."

"What did you call about, Ren?" Juliette couldn't decide which was worse; this conversation or her movie.

"We had a G-FOURce yesterday."

All ears now, she grabbed the remote and paused the lovers mid-lunge. "What? Why didn't anyone call me? I didn't know." She didn't remember scheduling a meeting with her sisters.

"Wait." A terrible thought occurred to her. "Renata, why didn't I know there was a G-FOURce yesterday?"

"Because we needed to meet without you. We're having a follow-up tomorrow, though, and you need to be there for that one."

"What's going on? I don't like the sound of this. In fact, I'm not sure I really want to be there." Juliette's mind was spinning. They'd met without her. That meant they'd met to talk about her. "This is another one of your interventions, isn't it?"

Renata didn't deny it. "We're worried about you, sweetie."

"Stop calling me that! I'm not your sweetie, Renata. I'm not your child, and I'm not some empty-headed twit who needs to be called placating names." Juliette pressed her forehead into the palm of her free hand and closed her eyes, immediately ashamed of her uncharacteristic outburst. "Look, I don't need an intervention, okay? Yes, I'm sad. Yes, I'm even slightly depressed. When I think about Mike, I get hot and sweaty, but not in a good way. I get sad, and then angry, and then wonder what's so wrong with me that he couldn't love me like I loved him."

"Wouldn't," Renata interjected. "Love is a decision, Juliette. That's why John and I are still married after all these years."

Ah yes. Mr. and Mrs. Perfect. "Regardless, my reactions are normal. I'm not on the verge of suicide, and I'm not going to go be a hermit on some isolated mountaintop. I just need a little time to lick my wounds and heal up a bit."

There was silence on the other end of the phone. "Ren? Are you still there?"

"Tomorrow. Five o'clock. Your place. That way you can't ditch us. Come straight home from work, Juliette. Don't dawdle." The phone went dead in her hand.

"Yes, Mother," Juliette muttered. She glared down the sofa to her spot at the other end where her food waited patiently, trying not to congeal. Her plastic fork had been knocked to the floor in her scramble for the phone and was nowhere to be seen. She didn't really care; she wasn't so hungry anymore.

"I need a dog," she said. "One that will love me unconditionally. And eat my cold leftovers."

CHAPTER TWO

"I DON'T think she's here." Gia perched on the concrete planter box while Renata rapped her knuckles on the front door.

"She's here. She wouldn't dare ditch us." She knocked on the door again, a little harder this time. "And of course, Phoebe's late as usual."

"Actually, we're both here," Phoebe drawled as she and Juliette came up the walk behind them. "I, darling Ren, got here *early*."

Renata had the decency to look abashed, but there would be no apology coming any time soon. Besides, it was a rare day indeed when Phoebe was on time, no less early.

Juliette hugged Renata and Gia, and unlocked her front door. "We walked down to the market on the corner. Mona says 'hi.'" Her smile didn't quite reach her eyes.

"You didn't have to do that. I brought chocolate chip rice cakes." Renata held aloft a bag and Juliette rolled her eyes at her sister's version of indulgence.

"Thanks, but since I'm being forced to host this event, I get to decide what refreshments we're having. In fact, you two should thank Phoebe. She talked me out of serving canned liverwurst and Vienna sausages. After you all held a G-FOURce without me, I wasn't feeling very gracious toward any of you." She stood back to usher them in. "Besides, I have a feeling I'll need a little comfort food when this is all over. Come in, my traitorous siblings, and make yourselves at home."

"Do you really have some Vienna sausages?" Gia asked as she passed by. "I love those things."

"Please don't admit that in public, *mon cochon,*" Phoebe teased, tugging on one of Gia's corkscrew curls.

"I'll go get the java," Juliette closed the door behind them. "I started it before we left; again, thanks to Phoebe's powers of persuasion."

They settled into their regular spots around the coffee table; Renata in the brown leather recliner, Gia on the floor, leaning up against the front of the television cabinet, and Phoebe on one end of the couch, leaving Juliette's end empty. They all knew better than to sit there.

Juliette returned with her tray of coffee fixings, and they gathered around, preparing their drinks, and oohing over the box of pastries from Mona's Market. Along with an assortment of cookies, there was a chocolate éclair for Gia, a pumpkin spice scone for Phoebe, a slice of glazed lemon cake for Renata, and an enormous cinnamon roll for Juliette.

"What happened to your triple chocolate brownie?" Gia asked, noticing the change in Juliette's selection.

"It occurred to me I never really liked the triple chocolate brownie as much as Mike did. I've always wanted one of these ridiculously sticky, drippy, gooey things, but he was a dentist and didn't approve." She closed her eyes in ecstasy as she bit into the roll. "Oh, you guys. This is divine. I might just die a happy woman." With her forefinger, she swiped a dollop of creamy icing off the top of her roll and stuck it in her mouth. "Who needs a man when I can have Mona's sticky buns?"

"Juliette, you little hussy!" Phoebe smirked.

"Phoebe!" Renata reprimanded.

Gia grinned from behind her éclair.

"Mona," Juliette sighed rapturously. "I love you. You and Mr. Chen Yu."

"Speaking of love." Renata effectively put an end to the frivolity. "It's time to officially start our meeting. Georgia?"

Before she came along, they'd called themselves G-Force3, a name their grandfather gave them. "When you girls get your minds set on something, there's not a thing in this world that can stop you," he declared. "You're like a living, breathing G-force!" When Gia was initiated in at eight years old, they officially changed the name of their sister club to G-FOURce.

As the youngest member, it was Gia's job to begin the pledge. "Welcome Empress Juliette, Empress Renata, and Empress Phoebe." She pressed her hands together in a prayer-like manner and nodded her head to each sister accordingly.

"Welcome, Empress Georgia." The other three spoke just as somberly, nodding back at her.

They clasped hands, then, forming a circle, and began the G-FOURce pledge, a time-honored tradition that had somehow survived adolescence into adulthood.

Let the words of our mouths
Be necessary, kind, and true.
Let the secrets we share

Be kept safe amongst us few.
Let the decisions that we make
Be brave, noble, and wise
Oogie-boogie-doggy-loogie
Wiggly-jiggly-fries!
G-FOURce unite!

They didn't collapse into giggles the way they used to, but none of them was quite grown up enough to give it up. The pledge was like an unbroken cord weaving through their lives, binding them together.

Renata took a deep breath. "Juliette, this is an intervention."

"I *knew* it! No. This G-FOURce is *over*." Juliette stood up and tried to take Renata's plate from her.

"Stop it!" Renata refused to relinquish her half-eaten lemon cake, and a brief tug-of-war ensued.

Phoebe started whooping, her fist in the air, "Cat fight! Cat fight!"

Gia's eyes darted from one sister to another, a mixture of delight and horror on her face.

Then Juliette let go and stepped back. Cake and crumbs went flying up into the air, and Renata shrieked as it all came back down, showering her with sticky lemon dessert. Phoebe cheered, and Gia ducked behind a cushion she held up in front of her.

"You … you *brat*!" Renata sputtered, frantically brushing crumbs from her clothes, fingering them out of her hair. "What is *wrong* with you?"

"What is wrong with me? What is wrong with you? With all of you?" Juliette retorted, gathering things onto the coffee tray. "Go home, Empresses. G-FOURce is *not* united today."

"Jules, come on." Phoebe pleaded, quickly stifling her laughter.

"And you, Gia? Are you actually here by your own free will?" Juliette turned a scathing look on the youngest Gustafson sister. Gia stayed behind her cushion.

"Jules, not cool. She's here for the same reason we all are; because we care about you. Sit down, Big Sister. You too, Ren." Phoebe fixed her gaze on a scowling Renata.

"I don't *want* to sit down if I'm going to be attacked again."

"Oh, please. I didn't attack you," Juliette scoffed. "I a-caked you." She laughed, silently at first, then her whole body began to shake until she had to put down the tray lest she drop it. She clutched her stomach as she stared helplessly at Renata, and the more indignant her sister became, the harder she laughed. In a huff, Renata began to gather her things.

"No wait," Juliette gasped, grabbing at her sister's arm. "I'm sorry, Rennie. Seriously. I don't know why that's so funny." She took a deep breath and blew it out slowly, wiping her eyes. "A-caked. It isn't funny at all, really. I don't even know why I'm laughing."

Renata stood, indecision making her appear vulnerable, and Gia spoke up. "Please, Ren, don't go."

Finally, she turned around, and picking up the bigger chunks of cake off her seat, she brushed the rest into the palm of her hand. "If we don't vacuum this up, it'll be ground into the carpet."

Still going into intermittent silent paroxysms, Juliette opened the coat closet in the tiny foyer, and pulled out the lightweight machine she used almost every night before bed. She ran it over the carpet all around the chair, then using the hose, she vacuumed the crumbs off the cushions. When she was finished, she held it up to Renata, a question in her laughing eyes.

"No!" Renata stepped back, swatting at the offending nozzle. But she was trying not to smile.

When everyone was settled again, Renata began once more. "Jules." The nickname sounded awkward coming from her. "We think it's time for you to wash your hands of Mike. So we've come up with a plan."

Juliette rolled her eyes.

"You're not going to like it."

Juliette sighed heavily.

"In fact, you're going to try to get out of it, but you should know that we've thought of everything."

Juliette moaned and pulled her knees up to her chest.

"You look like a pill-bug," Gia observed.

"Maybe an armadillo," Phoebe quipped, and they both laughed.

"Girls." Renata reined them in again. "Okay. We have a list of eligible men—"

"What?" Juliette interrupted, her voice rising to a near shriek. "Just kill me now!"

"Juliette, listen to me. We are not going to stand by and let you wither away over Mike. Just because he was too blind to see how wonderful you are, doesn't mean every other man is, too." Juliette glared at Renata, but she continued, her chin thrust forward. "So we've made up a list of eligible men, and you're going to out with each one of them until you get out of this slump."

"That is the stupidest thing I've ever heard. What is this? High school? No, junior high!" Juliette held a cushion to her face in an attempt to block them out.

"We aren't expecting you to fall in love with any of them. We just want you to go out and enjoy yourself. Have fun."

Juliette didn't speak. She sat with her pillow over her face for so long that Gia finally whispered, "Did she fall asleep?"

"Juliette, sweetie?"

"Is suffocation that easy?" Phoebe poked Juliette's thigh with her toe.

"I'm alive, unfortunately, and awake. I'm just hoping that if I stay behind this pillow long enough, you three will disappear, and all this will turn out to have been a nightmare." Juliette lowered the cushion a few inches. "Shoot. You're still here." She wished she was somewhere else; anywhere but here.

No, she wished her sisters were anywhere but here. This was *her* spot.

What made them think she'd even consider this ludicrous plan? She didn't feel like dating, and she really didn't feel like forgetting about Mike. At least, she didn't want to forget about being angry with him. She wasn't quite ready to stop feeling sorry for herself, either.

"This is an intervention, Juliette, not a choice," Renata continued. "We'll give you a few days to get used to the idea, but unless you can come up with a really, really good reason not to participate, the first guy will be here a week from Monday to pick you up."

"That's ten whole days, Jules. You can be ready!" Gia was full of encouragement, her copper curls bobbing around her face as she nodded.

Renata held up a paper on which were several names and phone numbers. "Here's the list. We were going to call it The Monday Man-Dates, but we decided that was too cheesy."

"Too cheesy? Ha! I think it's perfect. This is cheese at its finest! And stinkiest," Juliette snorted, grabbing for the paper in Renata's hand. "Let me see that."

Renata jerked it out of her reach. "Oh, no, you don't. This is for our eyes only. We only tell them that we're setting them up with you on a blind date. We only tell you their first names. But you have the benefit of knowing that every guy on the list is a personal friend to one of us. Or to John. They're all close to your age; give or take a few years." Then she added as an afterthought, "I'm coming to pick you up next Saturday to take you clothes shopping."

"I have plenty of clothes."

"How would anyone know that? You wear the same thing every day. Black pants, faded top." Renata pointed at Juliette's pale green shirt.

"I do not," she declared, slightly affronted.

"Hey. Be nice."

"I *am* being nice, Phoebe. She needs to hear the truth, and at least I love her enough to give it to her."

"I'm sitting right here, you know." Juliette had to break it up before any more cake got thrown. "And I like my wardrobe. If I'm stuck going out on a few dates to get you three off my back, fine. But I'm going as me. In my own clothes. My own style." She liked her neutral colors. She thought they made her look soft, ladylike, and steady. She wasn't artistic like Phoebe, or funky like Gia. And she wasn't anything like Renata in her tailored shirts and cropped linen pants. She was just Juliette. Black and white, no surprises, no drama. Steady. Neutral.

~ ~ ~

DURING the course of the following week, she tried on several different outfits from her closet, until she secretly admitted her sisters were right. Her wardrobe wasn't neutral, it was boring. By Sunday night, she'd finally settled on her favorite pair of black pants, with a long, lightweight sweater. Trying it on, she eyed herself in the mirror. The buttery beige knit didn't add any pizzazz to her appearance, but she wasn't shooting for pizzazz.

Then Mike showed up on her doorstep.

He brought tiger lilies.

Red tiger lilies. Her favorite flowers in the whole world.

He remembered.

But she couldn't afford to forget so easily.

CHAPTER THREE

"MIKE." She greeted him flatly, not wanting him to suspect just how flustered his appearance made her.

"Julie." He smiled, his straight white teeth irritating her, while his satin voice soothed her. "It's good to see you again." He paused meaningfully, his lids lowering. "Really good."

"Why are you here?" *Be strong, Jules.*

He hesitated briefly, but it was enough to let on that he'd been expecting a slightly warmer reception. He held out the bouquet. "These are for you. Your favorites." When she tentatively reached for them, he didn't let go. Instead, he covered her hands with his own so they held the flowers between them.

She flinched at his touch and tried to pull away, but he tightened his grip, pulling her toward him. "Don't I get a thank you kiss?" As he bent forward, she turned her face away in an attempt to evade his mouth. His lips brushed her cheek instead.

She jerked back at the rasp of his jaw against her skin. "Stop it, Mike." She hoped her voice sounded stronger than she felt.

He stood so close, that even over the heady fragrance of the lilies, she could smell the familiar Mike smell she had loved for so long. Against her will, she felt herself softening the tiniest bit, just around the edges. He must have felt it, too. He cocked his head.

"I knew you'd be home tonight, missing me as much as I was missing you." She wrenched out of his grasp and took a step backwards, flowers now clutched tightly to her, trying to restore the boundaries between them. He looked her up and down and smiled indulgently. "No wild weekend plans for you, are there, my sensible Julie? Let me in."

He *knew* she'd be home tonight? His Julie? *His*? And how many times had she told him not to call her Julie? There were so many things wrong with what he'd just said. She felt her stomach knot, and her voice quivered. "You can't come in."

"Come on, Julie Baby." He tugged on a strand of her hair that had fallen forward over her shoulder. "I've forgiven you. Can't you do the same for me?"

She scowled at him over the top of the lilies. "You've forgiven me for what, exactly?" Suddenly the deep scarlet petals looked sinister to her; beautiful, but speckled with deceit.

"For walking out on me." He stroked her cheek, but she flinched, and he dropped his hand. "You hurt me, Julie. It's taken me a long time to recover from your little temper tantrum."

A Valentine's Day he'd been too busy to celebrate with her.

Had he come to her with flowers and kisses a few months ago, she might have been swayed. She might have apologized for causing him so much pain. She inwardly cringed knowing she might even have been grateful for his offer to forgive her. But now he was too late. Her heart, though bruised by his nearness, was no longer willing to make excuses for him.

A million thoughts raced through her head in that moment; all the times she'd put aside her own plans to accommodate his, all the times he'd canceled last minute and left her alone. All the times he didn't tell her she was important, worth it, *loved*. She wanted to rage at him, to pour over his head all the poison he'd used to douse the fire that had once burned in her heart for him.

But she didn't.

"Excuse me, Mike. I'm kind of busy right now." She started to close her door, but he thrust his arm out to block it.

"You're busy? What plans do you have, Julie? In your pajamas?" He pushed on the door, but she wedged her foot against it from the other side. He lowered his voice. "Stop pouting. It's not cute. Let me in."

"I'm not pouting, Mike." Her voice no longer trembled. "I really am busy. Go home."

"You're lying, and we both know it. Now let me in." He pushed a little harder, and Juliette saw something shift in his eyes. He was angry. Very angry. A chill went up her spine.

"Go home, Mike." She said it more forcefully.

"I'm not going anywhere, baby-doll." His voice became menacing. "Do you have any idea how much I had to pay for red tiger lilies in September?"

"You need to leave right now!" She shoved the crimson flowers in his face, making him stumble backward. From the edge of her vision, she noticed her neighbor watching them from her own front porch. Mrs. Cork's little dog ran out to the lawn, barked a few times, then sauntered across into Juliette's yard, where it turned around three times and squatted. She slammed the door on Mike, his scarlet flowers, her scowling neighbor, and the defecating dog.

For once, she was thankful for Mrs. Cork's nosiness. She knew Mike wouldn't try anything now that he had an audience. She ripped off the beige top, crumpled it into a ball, and threw it away. Even *he* thought her wardrobe was boring.

"Tiger lilies are still in season, you creep. I hope that florist took you to the cleaners!"

~ ~ ~

JULIETTE stared at the mirror, trying to see herself the way any man other than Mike would. She thought of all the things he used to love about her, from her long, black hair, her gray eyes, and slender neck, to her slightly turned out feet.

"I look like a duck," she muttered. The woman who gazed back at her stood just under 5'6" and weighed just over her ideal weight. Mike always liked the extra pounds; maybe she should lose them to spite him. No, losing weight might make it look like she was pining away for him. Besides, she really didn't think it would be right to abandon Mr. Chen Yu or Mona, and she knew they'd be the first to go if she was going to drop a few pounds.

She'd gone on a whirlwind shopping spree over her lunch break, and the long, empire-waist dress she wore looked good on her, she admitted to herself. The raspberry tones brought color to her pale cheeks, and the drape of the fabric made her feel feminine. She peered down at her toes sticking out below the ruffled hem, and smiled at the iridescent turquoise she'd painted them earlier this evening.

Be bold, she told herself. Be daring. Do something stupid. Like actually going out with the first guy on The Monday Man-Date list.

"I'm a chubby, pink, bold, and stupid duck," she declared. She flapped her way into the kitchen where she stubbed a turquoise toe on a chair as she passed her table.

"Ouch! This is not a good sign." She sank into the offending chair and massaged her throbbing appendage. She wondered again what had gotten into her. This was not like her at all. She liked things organized, sensible, planned out. She didn't do well with change. She was not quick on her feet, and she inevitably made a fool of herself when put on the spot. She certainly wasn't bold. Or daring. And she didn't do stupid, if she could help it.

Okay. Maybe waiting nearly ten years for Mike Wilson to make up his mind about her might fall under the "stupid" category, but she'd been fooled by him. She'd believed the years were gifts of time; time for them to plan and prepare, to sort everything out so they could step into their future with all the details taken care of in advance. She glanced through the arched opening to the living room where she could see a row of 3-ring binders, color-coded and labeled, lined up on the bottom shelf of her bookcase. She rolled her eyes. *My well-planned life.*

One binder held all their wedding and honeymoon plans, another, their home plans. There was a binder filled with travel plans for future vacations, and the newest one was labeled *Wilsonettes.* In it, she collected pictures of babies from magazines, catalogs, and online, as if she had choices when it came to how their offspring would turn out. She squirmed at the thought of Mike paging through it, but knew there was no way he'd ever seen it. Even though they'd only split up six months ago, his unexpected appearance last night was the first time he'd been to her place in over a year.

She always went to him.

She stood and shoved the chair back into place under her rectangular dining table. "He called, I went running." She clenched and unclenched her fists at her sides, her skin prickling with humiliation. "What is wrong with me? I'm such an idiot. I'm a chubby, pink, bold, stupid, *idiot* duck!" She charged into the living room, grabbed her purse off the floor, and dug down to the bottom where she knew there was a small clutch of make-up. Years ago, she used to wear lipstick, but Mike told her once that he didn't like kissing her when she wore it. She never knew whether it was because he didn't like the way it felt, or if he was afraid he'd end up with it on his lips instead. She just stopped wearing it. For him.

"It took me a long time to get used to going naked-lipped, and you still didn't kiss me often enough," she railed. "Or long enough. Or sweetly enough." Her voice trailed off.

"Enough! Put on your lips, Jules, and let's see what tonight has in store." She pulled the cap off the Burnished Plum, a slightly shimmery, somewhat dated color that she loved. It made her eyes look smoky, and it made her *feel* dressed up. It was amazing what a little lipstick and toenail polish could do for a girl.

There was a knock at the door, and Juliette froze. Her doorbell didn't work and she'd hung a pretty lantern in front of it to keep people from using it, but tonight, the rap of knuckles on wood sounded rather ominous. She stared at her face in the mirror over the entry table, her eyes large and overly-bright, her skin translucent in the glow of the chandelier overhead. *You can do this, Jules, you can. Bold and stupid, bold and stupid.*

"No, bold and daring!" She pressed her lips together gently and smoothed her hair away from her flushed cheeks.

Her phone rang from somewhere in her purse, startling her. At a loss, she didn't know which to answer first, and she dug the phone out just as she pulled open the front door.

The man on her stoop wore khaki pants and a white shirt, his hair combed neatly back from his forehead and temples. He had gentle eyes, a wide smile, and an air of confidence in his stance that made Juliette automatically step back and open her door wider. She caught herself before inviting him in, realizing her immediate sense of comfort was due to his uncanny likeness to Mike.

What was Renata thinking?

She glanced down at the phone in her hand. Speak of the devil. Renata. She shoved it back into her bag. She'd deal with her sister later.

"I'm Paul Rudyard. As in Rudyard Kipling."

"I'm Juliette. Um, as in ... Juliet Capulet." She could think of no other renown Juliettes on the spot. "But spelled differently." She stuck out her hand. "Nice to meet you."

The man shook her hand, then offered her the bouquet of mixed wildflowers he'd brought. "And these are for you."

"Thank you. They're beautiful." He let his fingertips drift over the back of her hand as she took them. She couldn't help but think of Mike's last visit and tensed, prepared for flight.

"Juliette. What a lovely name. Very romantic. Maybe I should change my name to Romeo." He chuckled, and Juliette smiled politely, taking a step back. This was all so awkward. She was having a hard time remembering why she had agreed to the ManDates at all.

"Oh, I think Paul suits you," she said, trying desperately to steer the conversation away from romantic notions.

"Besides, if we were *that* Romeo and Juliet, this night would be ending very badly for both of us."

There was an awkward silence that lasted way too long, and the uncomprehending look on Paul's face compelled her to explain. "You know, we'd have to kill each other. I mean ourselves. We'd both have to commit suicide. But first I'd have to take a poison that made it look like I was dead, and then you'd kill yourself rather than living without me, and then I'd come around and find you dead, and then I'd have to kill myself for making you kill yourself. Not a good first date."

In her head, Gia chirped, "Cricket. Cricket."

"You haven't read Shakespeare," she stated.

"Oh. Yes. Shakespeare. Of course." Paul nodded, then he smiled, recovering his composure. "Your sister did tell me you were a little depressed." He winked and his smile broadened. "But I have a much better plan for this evening than a double suicide."

"She told you what?" Juliette stiffened. Renata really *was* the devil.

"It's all right." He reached over and patted her shoulder. "She thought I should know that you were feeling a little down, that's all." His placating tone was beginning to make her skin crawl. "Well, I'm here to change the way you feel. I'm going to take you out, and wine and dine you until you can feel nothing but happy."

Juliette reached for the handle of the door, and Paul mistook her intentions. "Are you all ready to come outside and play?"

"Oh dear," she murmured, looking down at her toes poking their little blue tips out at her. "Oh dear," she repeated, shaking her head. *Bold and daring, Jules. He's already got the stupid thing down.*

"What is it?" Paul asked, hunkering down a little in order to see her face. Finally, she looked up at him.

"I can't, Paul. I can't go out and...and *play*. I'm sorry if you were misled about me. I'm afraid you and I have very different expectations about this evening."

"Oh. I see." He nodded sagely. Then he shook his head. "No, I don't see. That's why I'm here. To change your expectations." Paul's confidence didn't seem to waver at all.

Juliette took a deep breath and blew it out slowly before she replied, setting the blossoms in her hand fluttering their petals encouragingly. She chose her words carefully, but kept them firm. "Paul, I was under the impression this was a blind date, not therapy. I don't mean to be rude, but I don't think this is such a good idea after all. I'm sorry. I'm—I'm going to say good night now." She stepped back and began to push the door closed.

"No, wait!" Paul put a hand up to block it, just like Mike had done, and Juliette felt panic swirl in her belly. The look on Paul's face, however, was not angry, just a bit desperate. "Don't do this, Juliette. I promised your sister I'd—"

"You shouldn't be making promises about me to my sister." She said it so quietly she wasn't sure if he'd heard. Then very gently, she closed the door in his face.

She still held the flowers clutched in one hand, and she was trembling as she waited, listening. She could hear nothing from outside, so she worked up the courage to look through the peep hole. Paul still stood on the stoop, facing the door, as though trying to figure out what had just happened. As she watched, he finally turned, shoved his hands in his pockets, and began to whistle as he walked away, his pants stretched oddly over his backside. She wrinkled her nose in distaste; she'd seen Mike do the same thing a hundred thousand times.

"Juliette!" A muffled, faint voice made her spin around, her heart pounding.

"Who...who's there?"

CHAPTER FOUR

"HEY! Pick up the phone!"

Juliette unearthed the device from the black hole of her purse. She stared down at the screen. Eight minutes and counting. The whole traumatic exchange had lasted less than ten minutes. And Renata had heard the whole thing. "Hi, Ren."

"I can't believe you sent him away!"

"Well, I can't believe you sent him here in the first place!"

"Oh, Juliette! Why couldn't you be polite?"

Juliette stomped her foot, her sandal smacking the entryway tiles. "I *was* polite, Renata. I was so polite that it took him several minutes to realize I'd closed the door in his face. But you," she waved a hand in the air in frustration. "You told him I was depressed? Thanks! I wish you'd warned me. I could have been better prepared. I still have my black sackcloth and shroud, you know!" She was shouting into the phone. "That was insensitive and manipulative, Ren. I don't think I really like you right now." She covered her face with the hand she'd been waving around above her head.

Renata was silent a moment before answering. "Well, I don't like you right now, either. You're not acting like yourself these days, Juliette, and it makes it difficult for me to know how to handle you." Renata's tone warned her that her feelings were hurt, but then, so were Juliette's.

"I don't want you to *handle* me. What I really want is for you to leave me alone! But since clearly that isn't possible, I'd at least appreciate a little respect on your part. I do not need some man showing up on my doorstep offering to help me find my happy place again. Just because you think you can control your little world, Renata Gustafson, doesn't mean you have the authority—or the insight—to control mine, okay?"

"Dixon."

"What?"

"My name is Renata Dixon, Juliette." Renata's voice was tight, and Juliette fleetingly considered warning her about triggering her TMJ. Nope. Grind away, little sister. Grind those teeth down to nubbins.

"Are you serious? Really? After everything I just said, that's the only thing you heard?" Juliette held the phone out in front of her, and shook it as though the other end was connected to her sister's head. She put it back to her ear and said, "I love you, Renata Dixon," she punched out her sister's married name across the line. "But you make me want to do very bad things to you, so I'm hanging up on you now. Good night."

What was it about Renata that could make her behave so irrationally? No one else made her feel so out of control and childish, not even Mike. She kicked off her sandals and sent them skittering across the floor, resisting the urge to pick them up and return them to the empty spot on her organized shoe shelf. She stepped over them with purposeful indifference on her way to the kitchen, where she tossed the bouquet on the table. Her toe still hurt from kicking the chair, and stamping her foot on the hard tile hadn't helped it feel any better. And her hair was starting to bug her.

"Who am I kidding?" she muttered, as she headed to the bathroom. She wasn't the kind of girl who wore fluttery dresses and left her hair streaming down her back. She dug out a clamp from her accessories drawer and clipped her hair up in a knot at the back of her head. All she needed now was a pair of black pants and a tee-shirt—or better yet, an old pair of jammies—in order to feel that everything was as it should be.

She looked down at her pretty pink dress and swished the skirt around her legs a few times. She wished the night had turned out differently with Paul Rudyard. He had a nice name. He had a nice face, a nice smile. But he was just too ... well, too nice. Nice wasn't all it was cut out to be. Mike had been nice once, too.

"Until I got tired of being his little door mat," she fumed. "Then he got tired of being nice." She changed from her dress into her favorite flannel finery, and headed back to the kitchen to dig around in her refrigerator for something to fill her empty stomach.

She was feeling better until her phone rang. She dug it out of the couch cushions where she'd tossed it after hanging up on Renata.

Phoebe. Juliette couldn't imagine Renata calling Phoebe on purpose, but she supposed it was possible tonight. They were in cahoots on this whole ridiculous intervention, after all.

"Hey, Phoebe." Juliette tried to sound casual.

"Hey, Jules." Phoebe sounded just as casual. *"Comment allez-vous?"*

"I'm fine, thank you. And how are you, little sister?"

"I'm fine, too. Whatcha up to?"

"Actually, I'm getting ready for a big night in. I'm in my jammies, and I've put the kettle on for hot chocolate. Now all I have to do is figure out something to eat and find a good movie to watch. Wanna join me? You bring dessert."

"What happened to Paul?"

"He went home," Juliette quipped, keeping her voice light.

"I see." She didn't say anything else, and Juliette sighed. She didn't want to talk about it, but apparently, it was unavoidable.

"I sent him packing." She dropped onto the couch. "He was awful, like some fatherly version of Mike. I'm serious. He even dressed like him. Couldn't Ren have been a little more creative?" Phoebe chuckled on the other end of the line. "It's not funny!"

"I thought about screening her guys, but then she'd make us do the same with ours, just in case I sent over one of my hot, young models, or Gia tried to hook you up with a pimple-faced teenager."

Juliette moaned at the thought of either one. "I will not go out with someone I might have given birth to, got that? In fact, I don't know that I'm up for any more dates at all."

"Were you serious about me joining you?" Phoebe asked after a moment's pause.

"Of course. Even though I know you're going to try to talk me into going out again. But I was also serious about dessert. I won't let you in if you're not packing sugar."

~ ~ ~

JULIETTE and Phoebe sat at either end of the sofa, facing each other, their feet tucked underneath each other's rear ends. They sipped hot chocolate and passed back and forth the bucket of ice cream bon-bons Phoebe brought.

"Am I really so pathetic, Phoebe? I'm telling you, if tonight was as good as it gets, I'm calling this whole thing off. I finally talked myself into being okay with going out for a little fun, and the first one out the chute is Thera-Paul!"

"Well, I can't speak for Gia's guys, but my friend is up next, and he's no Thera-Paul." Phoebe smiled smugly.

"So prep me. And do a better job than Ren did."

Phoebe frowned. "She prepped you? That's against the rules."

Juliette rolled her eyes, her bluff called. "No, she didn't. In fact, she told me nothing. But I think I deserve to know if the guy's a weirdo, don't you?"

"Absolutely! I can tell you that much. My guy's a weirdo." Phoebe popped another bon-bon into her mouth.

"Forget it. I don't want to play anymore."

"He's weird in a good way, though."

"Come on. You gotta give me something." Juliette shoved a bon-bon in each cheek and grinned like a chipmunk.

"No, I don't. That's disgusting."

"Yeth, you do."

"No, I don't."

"Yeth, you do."

"No, I…."

"All right!" Juliette interjected, spitting one of the chocolates into her napkin. "Be like Ren, then." It was the worst insult she could think of at the moment. "And you're right. That was disgusting." She wiped her mouth with a clean napkin.

"So, speaking of Ren, when are you going to make up with her?" Phoebe asked.

"Never."

"Come on, Jules. You know she's trying."

"Trying is right. She's extremely trying. And why are you, of all people, defending her? You two don't even like each other."

"I love Rennie," Phoebe laughed. "She and I aren't as different as she thinks we are. But I can see that better than she can. I know she loves me. She just has a hard time showing it."

"Whatever. You two fight like cats and dogs. You always have."

"It's not real fighting, though." Phoebe swallowed the last of her tea. "I've just made it my job to remind Ren that she's not perfect. I love her too much to let her convince herself that she is." She set her empty teacup on the coffee table and settled back into her corner of the sofa. "And she loves me enough to do the same for me."

Juliette didn't miss the flicker of pain in her sister's eyes, and she poked her in the thigh with her turquoise toe. "Hey."

"Hey."

"Je t'aime, Phoebe Gustafson."

"I love you more."

"Only because there's more of me to love."

"Stop it. You're perfect just the way you are, Jules." Phoebe looked imploringly at her. "You know, I almost feel sorry for Mike, even though he never deserved you." She reached down and squeezed Juliette's ankle. "He let go of the best thing that ever happened to him. You."

Juliette still struggled to imagine her life without the man she'd built it around. What was wrong with her that he didn't want her? Why *did* he let her go?

"But don't you ever let a man take the best of you, Jules. That's no man's right to take. Only yours to give." Something in Phoebe's voice made Juliette stop thinking about Mike.

"Phoebe?" she asked gently. "Did you—did something—someone...?"

Phoebe's vague smile only confirmed her suspicions, and Juliette stretched out a hand to her younger sister, rather shaken by the haunted look usually masked by her beauty. How had she never noticed it before? They laced fingers, the connection tender, and when Phoebe's eyes welled up, hers did too. "Do you want to talk about it?"

Phoebe shook her head and squeezed her hand before letting it go. "Someday, maybe. Not today. Besides, I'm here for you, remember?"

"Oh goodness, Phebes. I'm fine. You know that. But now I'm worried about you." Juliette straightened up and crossed her legs like a pretzel, an elbow on the back of the sofa, resting her head on her palm. "Does this have anything to do with what's between you and Ren?"

Phoebe lifted her shoulders in a dismissive gesture. "What's between us is old history. You said it yourself. We've argued our whole lives. There's always been stuff between us, and if there isn't anything, one of us will make something up just to keep the argument going." She waved a long finger at Juliette. "Which is why you two have to stop fighting. I can't stand the competition."

Juliette studied her sister, a little taken aback by her ability to set aside her pain so effectively; obviously a well-rehearsed habit. Finally, she nodded. "Okay. I won't push.

But...."

"Jules. I'm fine. You need to stop worrying about me."

"Like that will ever happen. Worrying is like breathing to me, Phoebe. You know that."

Phoebe held out the nearly empty ice cream carton. "Well, since I can't ask you to stop breathing, have another bon-bon. Then tell me what you're going to wear on your date next Monday."

CHAPTER FIVE

JULIETTE liked her job. She was a secretary for both the Philosophy and Economics departments at the local University, and she loved the resulting diversity of her daily tasks. The students who wandered in and out of her office were a constant source of joy in her life; as diverse as the programs she oversaw.

Kelly, a senior majoring in Economics, was being pressured by her boyfriend to move in with him after graduation. "What should I do?" Kelly would pace the small floor space in front of Juliette's desk, asking the same question almost daily, then drop dramatically into the chair and throw her arms out wide. "I love him so much, but I want us to get married first. What if I say no and he breaks up with me?" Instead of giving Kelly pat answers, she encouraged her to do what she already knew was right.

Gavin technically had two more years until graduation, but at the rate he was going, a degree was going to take a lot longer than that. He wasn't interested in the process of education. He preferred the social life and the free gym membership, and was struggling to keep his grades high enough to convince his parents and professors that he should be allowed to stay. His major was clearly the wrong choice; he'd based it on the misconception that Philosophy was all about opinions and beliefs, therefore, no learning of new things was required. "Dude, have you ever read Homer's *Iliad*? Or *Odyssey*? That guy was insane! Or he was smoking something when he wrote that stuff. How else could he come up with such a freak show?" Juliette was doing everything she could imagine to keep Gavin from flunking out.

She and Sharon Scoville, the secretary who shared the office suite with her, had been best friends for as long as she could remember. It was Sharon who told her about the university job, and their friendship made their daily tasks much less menial. They carpooled, ate lunch together, and shared many an evening meal together when Chris, Sharon's husband, taught his night classes at the local junior college across town. Tonight, they were going out to dinner at their favorite little Greek restaurant to discuss Juliette's new dating game.

Sharon settled herself into the passenger seat. "I'm starving!" She turned in her seat and smiled at Juliette as they pulled away from the curb. "So? How did it go? What was he like?" She'd had a lunch date with some visiting staff and hadn't got the scoop from Juliette yet.

"He looked exactly like Mike."

"Ugh."

"Yeah."

"So did you wear your new dress?" Sharon had made Juliette model it for her when she returned to the office with it and had given it her vote of approval.

"For about half an hour, yes. But honestly, it just made me look like a chubby, pink duck." She explained the whole duck phenomenon to Sharon.

"Well, it's a good thing it was a blind date, then, right?"

"Ha-ha," Juliette responded sarcastically. Then a silly thought occurred to her. "You know, if all my dates actually were blind, it wouldn't matter if I looked like a duck, would it?"

"In fact, if we were all blind, the world would be rid of a lot of its problems," Sharon concurred.

"Not if I still drove." Juliette swerved wildly, and Sharon squealed and punched her in the arm, making her swerve again.

"Don't hit me while I'm driving!" Juliette hooted. They were laughing so hard neither of them noticed the flashing lights behind them, but the sound of the siren's whine got their attention without further ado.

"Oh no!" Juliette gasped, as they exchanged horrified glances. The only other vehicle on the street was a pickup truck, and it was parked, so there was no doubt that the police car was hailing them. "I can't get pulled over again!" she wailed. "Where did he come from?"

"Again?" Sharon looked aghast at her, trying to get her giggles under control. "When did you get pulled over, and how come you didn't tell me about it?"

"Because it was stupid. I was only driving ten miles over the speed limit, and the officer lectured me, ticketed me, and treated me like I was a little old lady."

"Juliette Gustafson got a ticket? For speeding? No way!" Sharon's eyes were wide with amused shock, and she covered her mouth with her hand, laughing again at the look on Juliette's face.

"Stop making fun of me! I can't concentrate."

She pulled over, resisting the wild-hair impulse to punch

on the gas and lead the officer on a merry car chase. She rolled down her window and turned off her ignition, feeling like an old hand at the procedure now.

"Hello, ladies."

Juliette looked up, up, up into the face of the same officer who'd pulled her over not even two weeks ago.

She had a momentary flashback to a night when she'd been sent to her room for cutting Renata's hair. Hiding under her bed, she waited for Papa to come home, her heart pounding in her chest, until her bedroom door opened, and his feet crossed the floor, stopping directly in front of her face. She slid just her head out from beneath the dust ruffle, and looked up, up, up at Papa, who towered over her, too.

"Hello, officer," she squeaked. Sharon tittered helplessly.

"That was quite some driving," he declared, as he bent down to study them, his forehead creasing above the top of his sunglasses. "What's so funny, ma'am?"

"Nothing, sir." Sharon chewed her bottom lip.

Juliette squared her shoulders, trying desperately to hold on to whatever dignity she had left. She started to explain. The whole talking thing, that was her first mistake. "I was just pretending to drive blind—' She stopped abruptly, and Sharon burst out laughing.

The officer straightened, his shoulders and head disappearing from view, and a desperate Juliette turned to her friend. That was her second mistake. When their eyes met, she, too, began to laugh, and when the man ducked his head again and asked for her license and registration, she could only nod in response and hand them over.

"This is getting to be a habit for you, isn't it, Ms. Gustafson?" Apparently, he recognized her, too.

"Sorry," she hiccupped, afraid to look at him.

"Have either of you been drinking?" He glanced down at the watch on his wrist as if to condemn them for even considering being intoxicated at this hour. He removed his sunglasses, braced his hands on his knees, and eyed them both, searching their faces for evidence of anything criminal. Juliette thought she saw his nostrils flare, as though sniffing the air for fumes.

Sharon leaned forward to see him around Juliette and shook her head. "We don't drink, Officer." The way she said it must have set his mind at ease. He studied them for a few more moments, then nodded.

"Driving blind, huh?"

Juliette did look at him then, in a rash attempt to be bold. His face was rather close to hers as he leaned down at her window, and she was surprised to see he wasn't nearly as old and staid as she'd originally thought. In fact, he didn't look any older than she was. With his glasses off, she could see the humor in his deep-set gray eyes, almost the same color as her own, and she began to relax. She opened her mouth to say something clever. That was her third mistake.

"It gets better. I was pretending to be a chubby, pink duck driving blind."

Sharon laughed so hard, she doubled over in her seat, barely able to catch her breath. Juliette, mortified, stared straight ahead. She waited in silence while her friend got herself under control. The officer waited in silence, too.

Finally, a subdued Sharon reached a hand over to lay it on Juliette's shoulder. "Oh, Juju." She looked past her at the man still standing beside the window. "Officer, please don't give us a ticket. You caught us in the middle of childish fun, and we're sorry if we were being a little reckless. We'll be more careful, we promise."

Juliette nodded silently. Without warning, a tear slid from the corner of her eye, and she swiped it away as quickly as she could.

"Are you all right, Ms. Gustafson?" The officer spoke gently, his voice low.

She nodded again, wishing for all the world she would wake up to find this was just a bad dream, but two more tears betrayed her, forming cool tracks down each flaming cheek. "I...I'm fine. Allergies." Sharon patted her shoulder but didn't say anything.

"I see." The policeman reached into his shirt pocket, then held out his hand, offering her a folded tissue. "Don't worry. I haven't used it yet." Undone by his kindness, she covered her face with the tissue and nodded.

Sharon got out, and she and the officer met at the back of the car. Juliette could hear them speaking in low tones, and at first, she tried to eavesdrop, but after a few moments, she realized she didn't really want to hear what they were saying about her. She thought instead about *moussaka,* and how glad she was that The Fat Greek made one with zucchini, as well as the standard eggplant. She much preferred the color of eggplant to the taste and texture of it. Zucchini, on the other hand, she loved.

The conversation stopped, and Sharon came around to Juliette's window. "Out with you, girlie. I'm going to drive." She spoke gently, but in a way that brooked no argument. Juliette obeyed and walked around to the passenger side where the policeman held the door open for her. Before she climbed in, she paused and looked up at him, in spite of her embarrassment.

"Thank you, Officer. I'm sorry for behaving so badly in public." She didn't think that sounded right. "Not that I behave badly when I'm alone or anything." He nodded solemnly, but she could tell he was trying not to smile. "Oh, never mind," she muttered. "Quack." She plopped her duck butt down on the seat, and refused to look at him again, her humiliation complete.

CHAPTER SIX

QUACK?" He said the word out loud, his brow furrowed as he watched them pull away. Was that supposed to mean goodbye in some secret code? She did say she was pretending to be a duck.

"Women," he muttered, shaking his head as he thought about his own sisters. They drove him crazy with their secret codes and their secret societies, their members-only secret activities designed that way to intentionally exclude him. It was one of his pet peeves; people making secrets out of things that shouldn't be, creating subterfuge for fun at the expense of everyone else. He preferred facts; straight-talking, clear-headed, sure-footed facts. He couldn't count the times he'd wanted to halt someone's tirade with a raised hand, and pull out his best Sergeant Joe Friday; "Just the facts, ma'am. Just the facts."

Victor Jarrett liked things predictable. He liked things in order, and he liked things rational. Emotional outbursts and erratic behavior of any kind made him uneasy, and he found great reward in setting things right. Being a police officer soothed that angst in a way even he couldn't explain. He didn't mind the discomfort of the initial confrontation knowing he would do everything in his power—it was his job!—to bring resolution, to restore peace and order.

The woman he'd pulled over twice in so many weeks was anything but predictable. Or rational. Laughing hysterically one minute, sobbing uncontrollably the next? He thought he'd handled himself pretty well, all things considered, but Ms. Gustafson needed help, and not the kind of help his job description required, or even qualified, him to give.

So why was he standing here worrying about her and the soap opera she was living? Why did he care that, according to her friend, her recent break-up from a man who'd strung her along for years had her feeling vulnerable and a bit off-kilter from her normal self? Off kilter? Unbalanced was more like it. Who pretends they're blind while driving a car?

Yet something about the way she'd looked at him, her eyes traveling up, up, up until they met his, made him want to pat her on the head and promise her everything would be all right. She'd seemed like a lost little girl at that moment, and he had to force himself not to feel sorry for her. He knew better than to fall for that wide-eyed innocence; it never ceased to amaze him the helpless appeal cornered women could project.

He'd seen more than his fair share of it before he was old enough to leave home. His mother had worked her slippery charm on man after man, and then his sisters followed in her footsteps. He knew personally the false promises behind those soft-eyed gazes. He'd hated growing up in a house full of women, especially the manipulative, self-indulgent women in his family, who treated men like they were the latest fashion to be worn a few times, then tossed away.

James Victor Jarrett was named after his father, a man

who came and went so quickly that no one, not even his mother, seemed to remember much of anything about him. When Victor was little, she told him his father was a police officer who swept her off her feet, who loved her with wild abandon for one sweet year, then died in the line of fire, his last words to his partner, "Tell James I love him. Tell my boy…I…love him." Every night he'd beg to hear about his father, and every night Loreena would recount the same story about his valiant life and tragic end, often shedding a tear or two in the telling. He'd heard it a hundred thousand times, but it was the story his little boy heart wanted to hear a hundred thousand times more; that his father was a hero who loved him.

In third grade, when he was eight, his teacher asked if anyone wanted to read to the class what they'd written about heroes in their journals. James shared his precious story about his father, Officer James Victor Jarrett, while his classmates sat enthralled and envious that their fathers—accountants and doctors and construction workers—weren't heroes like James' daddy. Mrs. Hopper called home that evening, and his mother came to his room where he lay sprawled on his bed, fingers laced behind his neck, still basking in the glow of his newly-acquired stardom. She kissed him on the top of his head, then his nose, then each cheek.

"You are *my* boy, Jamie, no one else's. Don't tell anyone else about your father, okay? It's just our story, honey."

That was when he knew it wasn't true. He never asked her to tell it again, and she never offered. He wanted to believe that at least he had his father's name, but he wasn't so sure of that any longer, either. When he turned nine a few months later, he announced from that day on, everyone was to call him by his middle name, Victor.

~ ~ ~

THEY ordered their *moussakas* to go and headed back to Juliette's place. The rest of the evening, Juliette alternated between laughing over her second encounter with Officer Jarrett, and moaning about the fool she'd made of herself.

"You're totally hormonal today, Juju. If I didn't know any better, I'd think you were pregnant!" Sharon eyed her. "Are you sure you're not?"

"Of course not," Juliette bemoaned. "That wasn't in the plan yet."

"You and your plans. Why can't you just let things happen instead of having everything so perfectly planned out? Things don't really work that way, you know." Sharon eyed the row of binders on the bottom shelf behind her friend.

"I know. It's not like I planned to act like an idiot tonight. In fact, every time I opened my mouth, I *planned* to sound intelligent, maybe even witty. But that's certainly not what came out."

"Uh...no. You made a complete ninny of yourself," Sharon teased, then sighed dreamily. "He was so cute, too."

"I know." Juliette cringed, remembering the moment she'd noticed. "See? This is why my sisters are worried. It wouldn't matter if men *were* blind; I'd still open my mouth and send them running scared."

"Officer Jarrett didn't seem scared."

"Officer Jarrett? Well, I don't ever want to see Officer Jarrett again in my entire life."

"Don't drive blind then," Sharon quipped, glancing down

at her watch. "Or speed. He's got your ticket now, pardon the pun." She stood and stretched. "Take me home, Juju. I need my man. I need my bed. I need my man in my bed." She offered Juliette a hand up. "Are you going to be okay?"

Juliette nodded. "I'm glad you're not ashamed to be seen with me. Thanks for putting up with my charming social graces."

"Put up with them?" Sharon squeezed her tightly. "I *live* for them! You make me laugh more than anyone else I know, including Chris, and he's pretty funny."

Their conversation was easy in the car on the way to the Scovilles' little home a few miles away, and Juliette parked in the driveway behind Chris' car. They were still talking when he came out to meet them, and Juliette greeted him with a hug, and thanked him for loaning her Sharon for the evening.

Then she climbed in her car, backed out onto the street, and waved to her friends who stood together on the front lawn of their beautiful little world.

Home again, she took a quick shower, donned her pajamas, and made a cup of chamomile tea to settle her still buzzing nerves. It wasn't quite ten o'clock, and she knew if she tried to fall asleep this early, even as weary as she was, she'd toss and turn for another hour.

Juliette flipped through the channels on television, but could find nothing she wanted to watch. Finally she switched over to a music station and perused the bookshelves for a good read instead. Her eyes fell on the row of binders, and she bent over to pull out the largest one, labeled *Wedding & Honeymoon.*

Returning to the couch, she opened it to the first section where she'd collected sample wedding invitations. On impulse, she tore one out of the book and shredded it into a neat pile on the floor at her feet. Then she did the same to another, and another. It was like cleaning out an old wound; although painful, relief came with each empty page.

She turned to the next section; wedding dresses. It was a little more difficult to destroy them, but she did anyway, albeit with a few tears. The last one she stared at for a long time. It was her favorite. Leaving the neck and chest bare in an old-fashioned square neckline, the dress fell from a slightly elevated waistline in yards and yards of shimmery fabric. The skirt wasn't full and poofy, just fluttery like a fairy dress, and feminine in every way.

She ran her fingers over the page as she imagined herself walking down the aisle in the gorgeous dress. Waiting on stage was Sharon, her matron-of-honor, and each of her sisters, all beaming at her. On the bride's side of the church she found John, Renata's husband, and their four boys, in white shirts, black pants, and slicked-back hair. Granny G sat beside them, and next to her, was an empty seat where Grandpa would join her after giving Juliette away.

In front of them sat Papa and Maman, Simone with her head covered in a stylish black hat and birdcage veil, the netting muting the contours of her face. She never wore a veil in real life, but as Juliette's memory of her mother's features faded over the years, the veil made her feel less ashamed of not being able to recall every detail. Her father, who should have been walking her down the aisle, was seated beside the beautiful Simone; Juliette could only imagine Papa and Maman together ever since that terrible day almost fifteen years ago.

~ ~ ~

IT WAS graduation day, and she and Sharon could talk of nothing except the trip they were taking to Hawaii together in a week. Their families had combined resources and purchased the girls a four-day vacation, just for the two of them, and they thought they were the luckiest eighteen-year-olds in the world.

As the last of the fireworks flared in the sky, Juliette looked out over the friends and family gathered to celebrate their graduating seniors, anticipation for the future bubbling up inside her. As she scanned the crowds, she spotted Ren and Phoebe, jumping up and down, waving frantically and cheering loudly, while people around them covered their ears and leaned away. She laughed, pointed at them, and blew kisses. She grabbed Sharon's hand and started tugging her in their direction.

"Where's Maman and Papa?" she asked, hugging the two girls simultaneously.

"We were hoping you might have seen them," Renata squeezed her in return. "They were supposed to meet us at the back before the ceremony, but we waited until the pomp and circumstance started and finally just sat down."

"I haven't seen them," Juliette said. "Why didn't you come with them?" Sharon had located her family nearby and was caught up in her own set of congratulations.

Renata rolled her eyes. "Maman was running late as usual, so we came in my car."

Juliette looked over at fourteen-year-old Phoebe who was back up on the bench, looking out across the crowds, her hand up to shield her eyes from the brilliance of the outdoor amphitheater lights overhead. Juliette hopped up next to her and looked in another direction.

"They're not here," Phoebe said in her carefully careless drawl, but the flicker of concern in her voice made Juliette's heart beat a little faster.

"I'm going to the back to look," Renata said, reaching up to squeeze Juliette's hand, a proud grin on her face. "Congratulations, Juliette." She turned to walk away, but Phoebe grabbed a handful of Renata's long hair and pulled her to an abrupt stop.

"Ouch! What are you doing?" Renata smacked Phoebe hard on her exposed thigh below the mini-skirt the younger girl wore.

"Wait," Phoebe barely flinched at the sting of Renata's hand. "Come up here, Rennie. Look." Juliette helped Renata up onto the bench, and they both turned to look where Phoebe was pointing. Pushing against the crowd streaming out of the amphitheater, were their grandparents. In Grandpa's arms, little Georgie squeezed her baby doll tightly.

They weren't supposed to be here. Georgie had a terrible cold and ear infection, and Grandpa and Granny G had offered to stay home with her.

"Something's wrong," Renata murmured, stating the obvious. They watched as their grandparents made their way slowly toward the stage, searching the faces of the people milling around. The girls weren't difficult to find standing above the crowds, but they didn't wave or shout. Juliette reached for both her sisters' hands, and Renata, in turn, grabbed Phoebe's free one. They stood in a tight circle and waited.

Sharon, from three rows over, turned as though she'd heard her name, and her eyes met Juliette's. Then somehow, she was up on the bench beside them, her arms around her friend, just as Grandpa spotted them.

From her perch on the bench, Juliette read the pain in his eyes; she saw the suffering on her grandmother's tear-stained face. And she knew with a certainty that felt like ice in her blood that Papa and Maman would never see any of their daughters graduate.

CHAPTER SEVEN

ANGELA Clinton started drinking hours before, and by the time she got behind the wheel of her car to get to her high school graduation, she was plastered. And late. She never saw the Buick Park Avenue pulling into the intersection in front of her. She did see the light turn red, but not soon enough to stop for it.

The sound of metal clawing and screeching against metal seemed to come from down a long tunnel, and she slumped into the ride as her car spun around and around, the steering wheel jerking out of her hands. She hit her head hard against the window and watched in confusion as the world outside swirled together like taffy, twisting her down, down into darkness.

With consciousness came pain, and she avoided both with every fiber of her being. Somewhere in the back of her mind, she knew something horrible had happened, but she didn't think she could bear to know what it was. She forced herself to float in that place between dreams and wakefulness, keeping reality at bay for as long as she could.

~ ~ ~

BECAUSE of where her birthday fell in the calendar year, Angela was to be tried and sentenced as an adult. But everything moved in slow motion as the Gustafson family was made to wait for what little justice a trial could bring, while Angela lay unconscious in the Intensive Care Unit at St. Jude's. The doctors could give no reassuring time frame, because there was no clear reason for her delayed recovery. The days turned into weeks, and then months, while she continued to drift somewhere just out of reach.

Those months proved to be almost beyond endurance for everyone, especially Grandpa and Granny G, who not only had to deal with the loss of their only son and his wife, but were left with the four devastated girls to care for. Their burden was overwhelming, but somehow, they managed their grief in a way that allowed the girls to learn how to manage their own.

Little Georgie, too young to understand the finality of death, slept on a mattress in her grandparents' bedroom, her homesick tears in the middle of the night breaking their hearts.

For a time, the three older sisters slept together in the big bed in the guest room. They never talked about the accident, but they whispered to each other their memories of Maman and Papa long into the night. Granny G woke them each morning with hot chocolate, warm hugs, and soft words of comfort to push back the despair in their eyes long enough for them to face another day.

When the news came that Angela was finally able to go to trial, an eerie stillness settled over the household as they prepared for the coming ordeal. Juliette was the only sister who could attend, as the others were in school, but she promised to relay everything exactly as it happened.

Facing the teary-eyed, sallow-skinned girl who looked so fragile on the stand, it was all Juliette could do to remember that Angela had murdered her parents, leaving her and her sisters orphans. She held her own tears at bay until she got home that first day. After filling her sisters in on all that had been said in court, she disappeared into the bedroom. Burrowing under her covers, she stayed there until the next morning.

She surprised everyone by returning to the courtroom. She sat beside her grandparents, still as a stone, staring through Angela, willing her shattered heart to harden against her old classmate.

On the final day of the trial, as one by one, the jurors stated their guilty findings, Angela kept her head down, tissues pressed to her eyes. Somewhere in the stillness of the subdued courtroom, a woman wept quietly, and a man, in harsh whispers, demanded she get a hold of herself. Juliette wondered if they were Angela's parents, but she didn't care enough to turn around and look.

Then Angela murmured something to the judge, who nodded his assent, and stated for the record, "Miss Clinton would like to address the family of the victims."

Angela looked straight at Juliette and began to speak, her voice hoarse, but sure. "Juliette, I can never undo the horrible thing I've done. I deserve whatever sentence I receive and so much more. I should be dead instead of your parents. I am so sorry. I can only hope that someday you, and your sisters, and you, Mr. and Mrs. Gustafson," she glanced briefly at the elderly couple, "will find it in your hearts to forgive me. I'm sorry." Her voice caught on the words and broke.

Juliette stared at her, eyes dry, unwilling to acknowledge her speech with even a nod.

It wasn't long after the trial that Juliette decided getting up was no longer necessary. One morning, she turned away from the smell of hot chocolate. She refused the warm hug and covered her ears when the soothing words came. Granny G let her stay in bed that day. And the next. And the next.

But on the fourth day, the others were sent out of the room to drink their hot chocolate with their little sister and grandfather in the kitchen. Granny G sat down on the edge of the bed and smoothed back the tangled hair from her eldest granddaughter's face. "Sweet Juliette, you must get out of bed today. And if you do nothing else, take a shower, because you smell like hopelessness. Your sisters are worried, and Georgie is wondering if you're going to die as well. She won't believe me when I tell her no. She wants to hear it from you."

Juliette stared blankly at the wall as though her grandmother wasn't there. Granny G tried again. "Your sisters need you, Sweetie. Ren and Phoebe. Georgie needs you." She sighed, a sound that rested on Juliette's chest like a boulder. "Grandpa and I need you."

Juliette finally turned and swept her empty eyes over the old woman's face. After a long pause, she said, "I need Maman and Papa. Who will give me what I need?" Then she slid her feet out over the edge of the bed, pushing herself up into a sitting position. More to herself than to her grandmother, Juliette spoke again. Her tone was lifeless, but her words were full of something else. Granny G flinched when she heard the gentle girl say, "I hate Angela Clinton. I wish she was dead."

But she did get out of bed that day. And the next. And the next. Something from deep inside of her, however, stayed behind, buried beneath the blankets of grief and anger, and the Juliette that rejoined what was left of her family seemed somehow hollowed out to the others.

Her whole life had changed that night; the night it was supposed to have begun. She didn't go to Hawaii with Sharon, even though Sharon was willing to wait; in fact, she avoided her friend altogether. Sharon was devastated, Juliette knew, but how could she understand that the sympathy and compassion in her eyes was more than Juliette could bear?

She didn't go away to college with Sharon either, but instead found a job at a local bookstore so she could stay close to her sisters. They were her life-lines, even though she knew it was hard for them to tell. She pushed them away more often than not, but the thought of leaving, even for a semester at a time, terrified her.

Her life became ordered, routine, predictable. She got up in the morning before any of the others, showered and dressed, then woke Phoebe and Renata so they could get ready for school. While they were primping, she played with Georgie and helped Granny G with breakfast. Then after Renata and Phoebe ran out the door, she headed to the bedroom to pick up after her sisters. She straightened any beds that weren't made, scooped up discarded clothing, and organized items on the dressers, making sure everything was as it should be before pulling the door closed behind her.

By 9:45 every morning, she was unlocking the doors of Bountiful Books, and by ten, she was ready and waiting for the first customer. She kept the shop spotless, the books in order, and the cash register balanced. She always had a pot of coffee brewing in the tiny back office for Wendy, her boss, who showed up around 10:30, having learned quickly that she could depend on the young lady with impeccable manners and ethics. Juliette graciously greeted each of her customers, and they enjoyed conversing with the unpretentious clerk who knew something about every book in the store. She was creative in her displays, patient with the shoppers, and never left anything undone that she could do herself.

At seven o'clock in the evening, Juliette was home, often with a new book to read to Georgie, or, for Phoebe, the latest release in the series all the high school girls were reading. Renata's favorite author was Agatha Christie, and since Granny G had every Hercule Poirot and Miss Marple book ever published, she already had an unlimited source on hand. But Juliette also knew she had a secret penchant for Vikings, and every once in a while, when she stumbled across a piece on Norse mythology or Viking romance, she'd tuck it into Renata's backpack for her to discover on her own. For the grandparents, Juliette brought hugs and quiet conversation; it was all they wanted from her, evidence that she was doing all right.

And she was. With her routine in place, Juliette was beginning to put back together bits and pieces of her life. The day she called Sharon, Granny G secretly wept with relief. The restoration of their friendship was a giant step toward Juliette's recovery.

Even so, she had changed. Control became a domineering factor in every decision she made. Juliette knew it, and she wished she could be less constrictive, but she didn't know how to let go. She tried to write down her thoughts, but even her journals were columned, and labeled;

precise. She and Sharon, or her sisters, would go clothes shopping, and inevitably, Juliette came home with another pair of black pants or straight-cut blue jeans, or a pair of black shoes and white underwear. The few times she ended up with something colorful or trendy, it sat in her closet untouched until she returned it or gave it away.

When Juliette met Mike, everyone was happy she'd found love. He didn't pressure her to be anything she wasn't. He encouraged her to take her portion of her parent's life insurance and put a sizable down-payment on a place of her own. She finally did so with a real sense of accomplishment. That act of independence spurred her on to look for a better job, one with benefits, and Sharon convinced her to apply for the secretarial position at the University. It was perfect for her, because it left her available to continue helping out Wendy on weekends and during the two months of summer break, and her schedule coincided perfectly with Mike's.

A knock on the door interrupted Juliette's reminiscing, and she was relieved. She did not want to be thinking good things about Mike right now.

The relief only lasted until it occurred to her who it was. Renata. Juliette gritted her teeth and glared at the door. She still didn't want to talk to her, and she was not happy with being forced to do so, especially so late.

She laid the binder down on the coffee table and headed for the door. "I don't want to talk to you right now," she called out, knowing that Renata probably had her ear pressed to the paneling.

Juliette waited, expecting her sister to holler something along the lines of not being so childish. Nothing. She stood up on tiptoe and looked out through the peephole.

Officer Jarrett?

CHAPTER EIGHT

WHAT was he doing here? She looked down at her oversized t-shirt and worn pajama pants, the pattern so faded in some spots, it was difficult to make out the cute little puppy faces all over them. She wasn't wearing a bra, and her hair was pulled up into a messy ponytail on top of her head.

"Just a minute!" she called, racing back to her bedroom for something to cover herself with, pulling the rubber band from her hair as she went. She shrugged into her pink terry-cloth robe and ran her fingers through the haystack of hair she'd just upended.

"Why is he here?" she wailed, eying herself in the mirror. The robe didn't make her look any more attractive, but at least it covered her childish night clothes, and made her feel slightly more secure beneath the additional layers of fabric. Besides, if the man was going to show up on her doorstep after ten o'clock at night, then he would just have to take what he got.

Juliette turned the entryway light off to minimize what he'd be able to see, then thought it might look suspicious, so she flipped it back on. She pulled the door open a few inches and eyed him from behind it, the security chain still in place. "Yes?"

Realizing how ridiculous that looked—he was a police officer, after all—she closed the door before he could respond, unlatched the chain, then opened it again, still only wide enough to be civil, if not exactly polite.

"Good evening, Ms. Gustafson. We received a request to come by and check on you." He smiled politely and indicated a printout he held in his hand. "Is everything all right?"

Was he trying not to laugh at her?

"I'm fine," she said, feeling a little defensive. Did he honestly expect her to still be all dolled up at this hour? "Who called you? Was it Renata Dixon?" That would be just like her overbearing sister to notify the cops because Juliette wouldn't take her calls. "I'll kill her."

"That's probably not something you want to say in front of a police officer, ma'am." He *was* mocking her!

"She's my sister. I'm allowed to threaten her life with no recriminations." She could almost hear Phoebe applauding her snappy comeback, and Juliette straightened her shoulders, rather proud of herself. Here she was, facing off with an officer of the law, and *not* making an idiot of herself this time. She sounded witty *and* confident. Let him laugh. His derision would roll off her back like water off a... "Off a duck," she chortled out loud.

Officer Jarrett cocked his head. "What was that?"

Why couldn't she just keep her thoughts inside her head these days? "I like ducks," she muttered.

"Ducks. You mentioned them earlier today, too."

"I know." She changed the subject. "So, did Renata call you?"

"The caller asked to be kept anonymous." He folded the printout and slipped it into his breast pocket, then hitched both his thumbs over the black belt around his waist.

"How convenient." She knew she sounded cranky, but it was awfully late for reticence.

He studied her openly. Something about the way he looked at her made her pulse quicken just enough for her to notice. It wasn't inappropriate; in fact, he looked genuinely interested in the state of her well-being. But there was something more, too. It was almost as if she was being measured, and she had little doubt she'd be found lacking.

He, on the other hand, didn't seem to be lacking in any way. There was just a hint of silver at his temples and in his neatly-trimmed sideburns, and she thought it suited him. It softened his otherwise pronounced features; his high forehead, his squared-off jaw, his large nose. Large noses on men were a secret weakness of hers, and his, even she had to admit, was a big one. But the way it divided the angles of his face seemed to work, to draw one's attention to his eyes. His eyes, almost black under the spotlight of her front porch, were deep pools of—

Whoa. Did she just compare his eyes to deep pools? She cleared her throat, and stared at his chest instead, certain the flat planes of the bullet-proof vest beneath his uniform would keep her wayward thoughts in check. Instead, she found herself wondering how much was vest and how much was chest. With his height and wide shoulders, she was sure he wasn't lacking in the muscles department, either. Her gaze drifted up to his neck, his chin, then his mouth…before she caught herself again.

"Well, like I said, I'm fine. See?" She pulled the door open a little more so he could look inside to the quiet order behind her. Flustered, she kept talking. "But thank you for coming by, Officer. It's good to know how our tax dollars are being spent. Do you also get kitties down out of trees or is checking up on the crazy old maid as ugly as it gets for you?" She tried to keep the sarcasm out of her voice, reminding herself she was angry at Renata, not this unsuspecting man who was just doing his job, but it squeezed itself in between her words anyway. It had been a very long day and she couldn't imagine a worse way to end it.

He lifted a hand, drawing his thumb across his lower lip, as though trying to erase the grin settling on his mouth. "Look, Ms. Gustafson, I'm relieved to find you whole and healthy. Calls like this one often end quite differently."

He was lecturing her again, but this time she knew she deserved it. Feeling contrite, she hung her head a little. "I am grateful. I'm glad there are people looking out for me, and I do appreciate you coming to check on me." She wasn't quite ready to go as far as apologizing—he *had* laughed at her—so she offered him her hand instead. "Thank you."

His grip was solid and gentle at the same time, and she found herself wondering if his embrace would feel the same way. Blushing, she averted her gaze again and withdrew her hand quickly. Where on earth were these thoughts coming from?

"My pleasure," he said warmly. He pulled a card from his pocket and handed it to her. "I don't think we were properly introduced earlier. I'm Officer Jarrett. Victor."

She took the card and studied it. Officer James V. Jarrett, it said, and she wondered why he went by Victor. She looked up at him and smiled ruefully. "I'm Juliette Gustafson. But then, you already knew that."

"Yes," he nodded, his smile broadening. "But it's good to

officially meet you, Ms. Gustafson."

"It's good to officially meet you, too, Officer Jarrett."

"I'm glad all is well here. If anything changes, please don't hesitate to call the station. Your neighborhood is part of my beat, by the way, so I'll be watching out for you."

When he reached his car, he turned and saluted, flashing her a grin that made a ribbon of heat swirl up inside her. She slipped inside her home, closed the door gently, dropped the security chain back in place, and sighed rather femininely.

~ ~ ~

VICTOR worked the swing shift because he preferred it. He liked the evening crowd of civilians; it seemed people were generally more relaxed and better-behaved than they were during working hours, or in the middle of the night, at least in this small Southern California town.

In contrast, on the day shift, he issued speeding tickets to disgruntled drivers who were already late to work, and during the lunch hour, folks were even angrier at him for cutting into their precious break time. By two o'clock, the end of the shift, still an hour away, seemed forever in coming.

Graveyard was worse. There was no reasoning with alcohol, and when the bars shut down around two in the morning, he never knew what to expect. Something about the dark of night seemed to trigger a surge of human depravity, and Victor had seen the worst of his cases while working graveyard. He understood it was called that because it made the person working the shift feel like the walking dead, but he believed it had more to do with the fact that death had a vested interest between midnight and the early hours of the morning. Because of his clean record and seniority, he didn't have to work graveyard often, but when he did, he put on prayer like he put on his uniform, and he didn't say 'amen' until he was back home again.

His uniform gave him the authority to participate and intervene if necessary, but always with a degree of detachment that allowed him the space he needed to keep a clear head. Yeah, he knew there were some real psychological issues in that way of thinking, but by the grace of God, he'd come a long way from the angry little punk he'd been when he left home, and he simply preferred things black and white.

Someday, he was certain, the right woman would come along who understood his level-headed nature and respected his need for order. They'd get married, have a few kids, and grow old together.

He just hadn't met her yet.

It wasn't for lack of trying. In fact, just over a year ago, he'd quietly proposed to his girlfriend, but Amanda turned him down, explaining that she was "somewhat bored" with their relationship. Well, so was he, and he liked it that way. He didn't want drama. He didn't want emotional highs and lows. He wanted to be able to count on the woman in his life to be who, and what, and where she said she was going to be, and in return, he would do the same for her. He and Amanda parted ways with one last dinner at her favorite restaurant, followed by a warm hug and a cool kiss.

He shook his head as he compared the gentle, rational Amanda to Juliette Gustafson.

"It's no wonder the boyfriend bailed," he muttered to himself. The myriad of emotions he'd witnessed on her face in just three encounters made him grimace. He wasn't interested in emotionally unstable or unpredictable women.

He'd had enough of them to last him a lifetime.

Victor left home a month before his eighteenth birthday under the barrage of his mother's weeping, and then cursing when the tears had no effect on his decision to leave. He crossed the little lawn he'd neatly mowed and trimmed the day before, tossed his duffel bag in the bed of his pick-up, folded his lanky frame into the driver's seat, and pulled away, leaving behind the houseful of women; free at last.

He made a point to visit a few times a year. Loreena laid a guilt trip on him every time, even as he walked in the front door bearing flowers and gifts, and of course, cash. The money always seemed to appease her enough to allow him to stay for a few days.

During those visits, he did his best to tolerate his older sisters, twins, who moved in and out of the house between boyfriends. Darlene and Sasha were still just as manipulative and obnoxious as they'd been growing up. From the time he was old enough to care, they'd taken every opportunity to humiliate and embarrass him, especially in public, and they still hadn't grown out of it.

Victor loved his family. He especially loved the fact that they lived nowhere near him, because truth be told, he didn't like them very much.

So what was it about this Gustafson woman that had him thinking of his sisters? When it came right down to it, they had nothing in common but the fact that Ms. Gustafson's behavior unsettled him. She dressed modestly, she didn't wear her make-up like she was in an 80's girl band, and once she calmed down, she seemed almost reasonable; nothing at all like Darlene and Sasha.

Maybe it was that unexpected desire in him to make sure she was okay that disconcerted him. Even though they weren't close, even though they drove him absolutely mad with their antics, Victor still felt responsible for restoring order to his mother and sisters' lives whenever things got out of control for them. Even if it just meant showing up with money, the only love language they seemed to understand. Although he barely knew her, something about Juliette Gustafson stirred the same desire in him to rescue her, to set things right for her.

And he didn't like it one bit.

CHAPTER NINE

"GUESS who stopped by for a visit last night?" Juliette tried in vain to spear a piece of broccoli with her plastic fork, chasing it around the plastic bowl until she gave up and picked it up with her fingers.

"Not Mike! Did you call the police?"

Juliette rolled her eyes at the irony of Sharon's question. "Funny you mention the police. No, I didn't call the cops. The cops called on me."

"You lost me there, Juju." They were eating lunch at Sharon's desk, having opted to pick up food from the cafeteria and return to their office to visit.

"So you don't know anything about it?"

"About what?" The curiosity in Sharon's eyes seemed sincere.

"Officer Jarrett came by to check on me last night."

"No way! THE Officer Jarrett? The gorgeous hunk who pulled us over yesterday?" Sharon leaned forward, her eyes round with questions. "Is that even legal? Was he on the clock, or was this an after-hours kind of visit?" She wiggled her eyebrows suggestively. "Was he still in uniform?"

"Whoa!" Juliette sat back in her chair. "Do you ever breathe? And do people still even say 'hunk' anymore?"

Sharon sighed dramatically. "I can't believe it! What did he want? Wasn't that a little weird for you?" Then she put a hand up to cover her smile. "What were you wearing? Please tell me you weren't ready for bed when he came."

In answer, Juliette glared across the desk at her friend. Sharon guffawed and clapped her hands. "Not your puppy-face jammies?"

"Yep," Juliette shrugged. "But I dressed them up with my pink robe."

"Oh, Juju! That's awesome! But what did he want?"

"I don't really know. He just said someone called wanting the police to check on me." She eyed Sharon, but her friend shook her head.

"Wasn't me, girlfriend. If I was that worried, I'd make Chris drive me over. Besides, I'd just spent the last several hours with you, *duckie*. I knew you were fine, albeit a little psycho." She leaned back in her seat and chortled with delight. "I can't believe you wore your pink robe to the front door! Well? What did he say? Was he nice?" She wiggled her fingers at Juliette. "Details! Give me details!"

Juliette filled her in on the conversation she'd had with the officer. She didn't tell her how his smile made her knees wobbly and her fingertips tingle, nor did she tell her how good it sounded when he said he'd be watching out for her.

"I know Ren sent him. I still won't answer her phone calls."

"I can totally imagine her filing a Missing Persons on you. But if it was Ren, you need to call her and thank her," Sharon teased.

"I was planning on calling her tonight anyway. She's a

pain, but she is my sister."

Their conversation meandered from one subject to another, until Sharon commented, "What's up with you? You seem really distracted. Are you thinking about your policeman?"

Juliette smiled but shook her head. "He's not 'my' policeman, but he certainly didn't make last night any easier for me. I didn't sleep much, I guess. I pulled out the stupid binders and started shredding sample invitations."

"You let Mike keep you up."

"No, I barely thought of Mike at all last night." She sighed heavily. "Angela kept me up." For some reason, she'd been consumed by thoughts of Angela, and even when she finally did fall asleep, she dreamed of being in a car with her, Angela driving wildly, out of control, tears streaming from her eyes as she screamed, "I can't stop! I can't stop! Help me, Juliette!" What disturbed her most was that when she awoke, trembling from the vivid dream, the only thing that seemed to settle her was the thought of Victor Jarrett standing in front of her house, promising he'd be watching out for her.

"Angela Clinton?" Sharon leaned forward, brushing tender fingers along Juliette's forearm. "Oh, Juju, I'm sorry. Where did she come from?"

"I was thinking about the wonderful wedding I had planned for me and Mike. That's why I was shredding the stupid invitations. It's time to get rid of that whole plan, you know? But in my mind, I pictured what it would be like to walk down the aisle, with all my favorite people in the world around me."

"How does Angela fit in?"

"Papa and Maman were there, too, sitting together." Juliette's eyes began to well up. "Sharon, I can't seem to get

Maman's face right anymore. I look and look at her pictures, and I know that face like it's my own, but when I try to bring it up in my mind, I can't see it. I've started imagining one of those cute little French birdcage veil thingies so I don't have to get her features right."

"It's been a long time, Juju," Sharon half-whispered.

"But I don't *want* to forget Maman. I *want* to forget Angela, but for some reason, her face I can see clearer than ever. It's like I have these images of her burned into my brain. In U.S. History, laughing at some stupid thing Mr. Hanson said. On stage at Baccalaureate, singing like an angel with that incredible voice. I can even conjure up an image of her lying in a hospital bed, all broken and bruised, tubes and wires going everywhere, even though I certainly never visited her there. And I can still see her, plain as day, on the stand, begging me to forgive her." Juliette shook her head vehemently. "But I can't, for the life of me, see my own mother's face! Angela is still taking things from me, even after all these years."

Sharon reached over and pulled a couple tissues from the box on her desk. She kept one for herself and handed the others to Juliette.

"I just want my Maman today. I feel very lost, and I haven't felt like this in a long time." Juliette dabbed at her tears, careful not to smudge her make-up. "Sorry to unload on you."

"Oh, please." Sharon snorted. "You always carry way too much on your shoulders. Unload already."

"Then there's this whole Monday ManDate thing. My sisters are trying so hard to cheer me up and get me past this 'getting-over-Mike' stage, but they don't understand how stressful blind dates can be to someone like me. It really,

really stresses me out. I'm sure that's why my emotions are all over the place these days." She blew her nose and reached for another tissue and patted her damp cheeks with it.

"I'm trying, Sharon. I really am. But Mike was everything to me for so long. Even though I'm totally convinced splitting up was the best thing for me, there's always this horrible little 'but maybe' whispering in the back of my mind. *But maybe* he might change. *But maybe* he's missing me and realizing how wrong he was to let me go. *But maybe* I can convince him that it can work again." She wadded up the tissues and threw them at the trashcan against the far wall, missing it by miles. "What is wrong with me? Why do I even entertain that little voice?"

Sharon listened while Juliette ranted, refilling their tissue supply as needed. By the time lunch was over, Juliette had a headache, a red nose, smeared make-up in spite of her best dabbing techniques, and some relief from being able to talk through her feelings.

"Are you going to be okay?" Sharon asked.

"Yes. Thanks to you." But the rest of the afternoon, Juliette had a difficult time concentrating on her work. Something seemed to be waking up in her, something she didn't understand. Life had been so straight-forward, so *neat* before she left Mike. She didn't know how to deal with messy, and that's how things were beginning to feel.

~ ~ ~

JULIETTE stood in front of the mirror and examined her appearance, something she seemed to be doing a lot of lately. Tonight she wore a layered linen skirt the color of flax—she needed the security of neutral—and a brick red blouse with a ruffled neckline. Her hair was swept back off her face in a loose French twist with a few tendrils whispering against her neck, and she had on a clear lip gloss, having decided to tone down her makeup, too. A pair of garnet earrings sparkled prettily when she turned her head, but that was all the bling she wore. Even her shoes were sensible; she slipped into low-heeled linen sandals and headed for the living room to wait for Frank Clapson.

Five minutes before seven, someone knocked on the door. Feeling much more prepared this time, she quietly crept to the peephole, not letting her shoes clip the tile.

"Hm," she mused, pleasantly surprised by what she saw. The man outside her door was very handsome, definitely someone Phoebe would be seen with, and he was armed with a beautiful bouquet of green—*green!*—roses. She watched him for a few more seconds, but he just patiently waited, not checking his watch, not looking around, not turning to stare longingly over his shoulder at his car, wondering if he could make a mad dash for it and get away unscathed. He didn't seem nervous at all, and that made her even more so. She straightened her shoulders and pulled open the door.

"Hi," she said. "You must be Frank."

"I am," he agreed, and took her proffered hand in his. He pumped it once, very aggressively, and released it, and Juliette had to resist the urge to rotate her shoulder a few times, to make sure it wasn't out of joint. Strike one. "And you must be Julie."

"Juliette." Strike two.

"Juliette. My apologies." His smile faltered for just a moment, but then he remembered the flowers. "This whole blind date thing is new to me, so I wanted to find flowers that were new to me, too. I've never seen green roses before, have you?"

Juliette buried her nose in the blooms, breathing deeply of the delicate fragrance. "They're beautiful, Frank. Thank you. And what a nice sentiment."

"I'm glad you like them," he beamed. "Are you ready?"

"Let me put these in a vase first. Please, come in." She wedged the door open with a rubber door stop, just in case Phoebe didn't know the man as well as she thought she did, and pointed at the sofa. "Make yourself comfortable. I'll just be a moment." Besides, she'd seen Mrs. Cork's door open and heard her little dog yapping furiously from the front yard. She was certain her neighbor would be paying close attention to what was going over here.

They decided to wander around a local estate sale shop to pass the time before their dinner reservations. The store was segmented into individual booths, so the options were endless. Frank, as it turned out, was a collector of old stringed instruments, and this was one of his favorite stomping grounds. He pointed out where he'd discovered old mandolins, ancient lutes, even a rare Martin guitar he'd purchased for a mere pittance of what it was worth.

So far, between the green roses, the way he opened and closed doors for her, and his unique interests, Frank was quickly making up for his first two strikes. Juliette was actually enjoying herself.

In one booth she found a hammered copper cuff bracelet that had a beautiful marbled patina. She picked it up and studied it, ran her fingers over the chunky curve of it, then returned it to the tray. She turned to leave, then hesitated. She'd never wear the thing, but Phoebe would in a heartbeat. "I think I'll take it after all," she said to the lady who was getting ready to slide the tray back inside the glass counter.

She made her purchase and it was time to go. While they talked amiably in the car, she noticed Frank kept eying the paper bag that held her bracelet. Finally she asked, "Do you want to see what I bought?"

"I saw it," he grinned. "I'm just curious why you aren't wearing it."

"Oh. Well, it's a gift for Phoebe. It's totally her style." She pulled it out and studied it, then slipped it over her wrist, and held it up for him to see.

"For Phoebe? I thought it was for you. For tonight."

She shook her head. "I don't wear stuff like this. It's totally *not* my style."

He laughed, and cocked his head to look at her, as they pulled up in front of the restaurant. "What do you mean? You're wearing it, and it matches the shirt you've got on. I'd say it totally is your style." He mimicked her, but in a nice way.

"But I ... I got it for Phoebe," she insisted lamely.

"And how will she ever know? I won't tell her. Will you?"

Juliette stared at the bracelet where it encircled her wrist. It did look like it belonged there. She turned to find Frank grinning mischievously at her. "It was never hers," he said. "It was yours the moment you laid eyes on it. I saw the way you touched it." He reached over and ran his fingers over the back of her hand. "The same way I do when I come across something I want."

Juliette flinched visibly under his touch, and suddenly the air in the car was stifling. Oh no! Was that strike three, or did she start back at strike one again? Frank withdrew his hand, aware of her reaction, and turned off the engine. *Please, oh please, don't apologize. Just pretend it didn't happen. Don't apologize, please.*

"I'm sorry. I shouldn't have said that. Your sister told me that you didn't—"

"Um," Juliette interrupted, holding up her hand. "I don't really want to hear what Phoebe told you about me." Strike two. Or four. But who was counting anymore?

Frank cleared his throat. "Are you hungry? Shall we go in and eat?" Juliette nodded and he came around to her side to help her out.

It was awkward at first, but she sensed he was really making an effort, so she tried a little harder herself. "I've wanted to eat here for years. I'm glad you chose it." Mike didn't like Japanese food.

He helped her order, and they laughed at her bad pronunciations, but the food, when it came, was delicious. Once they got past the discomfort of the incident in the car, they got along fine the rest of the evening, sharing small talk about work, favorite vacation spots, and hobbies.

After dinner, he took her to a local movie theater. Juliette was a little disappointed; it seemed rather cliché, and it all but eliminated the chance to get to know each other any better. The movie they watched, however, was not a typical date night movie, and when it was over, they headed to a bookstore that was open late, and enjoyed a stimulating discussion about the independent film over coffee and pastries.

When he finally saw her to her front door, she could tell he wanted to be invited in, but she was ready to call it a night. After the movie, she'd sensed a shift in his attention, a closing in. She'd been able to ignore it in the bookstore, and enjoyed herself in spite of it, even though he made his intentions more and more obvious, but in the car he'd been the perfect gentleman, and she assumed he'd gotten the message.

Apparently not. When she attempted to go inside, he reached for her hand.

"Juliette, I want to kiss you. I've wanted to kiss you since you put on that bracelet. No," his voice turned to dark chocolate. "Since the moment I picked you up. You looked so beautiful holding those green roses. Come here." He pulled her toward him, but she resisted, never having been very keen on dark chocolate.

"No, Frank. Thank you for the wonderful time tonight, but I'm really not ready for that."

He stopped pulling but didn't release her. "I know you felt it too, when I touched you in the car. You don't have to be afraid of me, Phoebe."

Strike three and you're out.

"My name is Juliette, not Phoebe." She pulled her hand from his grip, and marched inside, closing the door on her date just a little harder than she'd done the week before.

CHAPTER TEN

PHEBES, I'm so sorry. I've done it again." Juliette wailed into the phone when her sister answered.

"Jules, calm down. What happened?"

"I closed the door in Frank's face. I'm sorry. But he called me Phoebe."

"He what? What a moron!"

"And things seemed like they were going so well." She flopped backward on her bed and kicked her sandals off, rolling to the side quickly to avoid one that flipped out of control and landed on the pillow where her head had been a moment before. She grabbed it and threw it on the floor in frustration.

"Do I need to come over?" Phoebe sounded tired; it *was* almost midnight.

"No. I just wanted you to hear it from me before you heard it from him." She groaned. "I do *not* want to tell Renata that I failed again."

"Then don't. You spent the whole evening with him, right?"

"Yes." Juliette rolled onto her side, bunching her pillow

under her head.

"So you don't want to marry the guy. That's all right. Doesn't mean you failed. In fact, this means you get to go out on another Monday ManDate. Ren will be thrilled!"

"Oh, say it isn't so!" Juliette couldn't bear the thought of another disastrous date.

"Go to bed, Jules. This will all be funny in the morning."

"Then you're not mad at me?"

"For what? For putting old Frank in his place? Are you kidding?" Phoebe laughed. "Any man who calls a girl by her sister's name should be drawn and quartered. He's lucky to get off so easy." Then she paused. "Is that all he did, or did Frank cross a line? He's a little touchy-feely, but harmless, or so I thought. If you tell me otherwise, I'll kill him."

"He was fine." Juliette's eyes roamed over the items on her bedside table, lingering on the Police Department card resting against the base of her lamp. "Yeah, a little touchy-feely, but nothing I couldn't handle."

"Just getting frisky, was he?" Phoebe chuckled.

"At one point I had to cut him off at the pass with a trip to the little girl's room."

"The oldest escape route in the world," Phoebe drawled. "I didn't know you knew that one. Did it register?"

"I thought it did, because he was slightly more reserved for the rest of the time we were there. But there was this one thing he did that really started to get to me." Juliette ran her fingers through her hair, massaging her scalp as she relaxed, relieved beyond measure that she hadn't disappointed Phoebe. "He'd rest his hand on my low back to usher me in or out of doors, and then he'd leave it there until we were at our table or at the car, or even in line to purchase something. At first, it was kind of nice; gentlemanly, you know? But as the night wore on, I noticed he would press his hand in a little more firmly, making me walk closer to him." She grimaced as she remembered the weight of his palm against her spine. "I could feel his fingers spreading out, like an octopus, like he was trying to touch as much of me as possible."

"Ew."

"Yeah. Ew."

"So? Did he try to kiss you?"

"Ugh. You had to ask." Juliette groaned. "Yes. He told me that he *knew* I wanted to kiss him, too. How would he know that if I didn't know it myself?"

"What a toad." Phoebe sighed on the other end of the line. "Bummer. I'm sorry things didn't end well. Did you at least have some fun tonight? Were you able to *not* think of Mike?"

"Yes, I had some fun. I did think of Mike, but I didn't miss him. I was angry at him. Does that count? I was angry because *he* didn't take me to that restaurant, the Japanese one I've been dying to go to in forever. I was angry because it wasn't *his* hand on my back. And I was really angry because if he had married me, I wouldn't have to be working my way through the stupid Monday ManDates."

"Hm. Not exactly what I was hoping for." Phoebe sighed. "You know they say that love and hate are two sides of the same coin. You're not still in love with him, are you?"

"No. I didn't say that I hate Mike. I said I was angry with him. Kind of like I'm angry at the professor who just dropped a request on my desk for seventy semester workbooks to be made up for him by Wednesday, or like I'm angry at my backside when I happen to catch a glimpse of it, or like I'm angry at my neighbor who lets her little yapper-dog poop on my lawn and never picks it up. Why can't it poop on her lawn?"

"*You* could always poop on her lawn."

"Phoebe!" But it was just what Juliette needed to cheer her up. She chortled gleefully. "You never know. Maybe I'll do that one of these days."

"Just don't tell me about it, okay? I refuse to be an accomplice to a crime like that."

"You won't tell Ren, then?"

"That you're going to defecate on your neighbor's lawn? Why would I tell her that?"

"No! That my date with Frisky Frank was a flop!" Juliette rolled to her back, crossed her ankles and propped an arm behind her head.

"Nope."

"Thanks. Sorry I called you so late."

"No problem, Jules. *Je t'aime.*"

"I love you, too, Phebes." She felt a little better about the evening, but she couldn't help wondering if perhaps she was too stiff, too conservative. Maybe she should have let Frank kiss her. Maybe she might have enjoyed it.

She closed her eyes as she tried to imagine being kissed by Frisky Frank. His arms went around her, he dipped his head toward her, but when she tilted her face up, his features shifted. His hair darkened, his jaw filled out, and as his lips touched hers, she sighed pleasurably, a sound that ended in a little gasp as her eyes flew open.

She'd just been kissed by Officer Jarrett. And she'd enjoyed it immensely.

~ ~ ~

SHARON toyed with Juliette's new bracelet. She brushed her

fingers over it the way she imagined her friend had done and laughed again. It really was a beautiful piece of jewelry, and Sharon thought Frisky Frank was right when he convinced Juliette to wear it.

"I wonder what your sisters are telling these guys. What are they saying to them that would convince them to take you out?"

"Thanks. You make me sound like a freak." Juliette snatched the bracelet from her friend, returning it to her wrist. She turned it this way and that, loving the way it looked against her skin.

"You know what I mean. And I'm serious. First dates are hard enough. Blind dates must be worse by far." Sharon leaned back in her chair and tipped her head slightly. "Take Frank for instance. He's known Phoebe for years, right?"

"Mm-hm," Juliette said around a mouthful of pasta.

"Well, was it really so terrible then that he would call you Phoebe? He must have had her on his mind all night, hoping he wouldn't let her down by letting you down. He had the pressure of trying to make *both* of you happy. And Thera-Paul? I almost think it was better that Ren told him something about the state you're in. At least he knew what his purpose was. But then, is that really fair to a guy?"

"What do you mean?" Juliette frowned.

"Well, doesn't that kind of demoralize them? It's a bit like slot-machine mentality. Put in a quarter, see what you get. If you don't like it, put in another quarter. There might be a keeper in there somewhere."

"Ugh. I hadn't thought about it that way." What Sharon was saying did make some sense. "Do you think I should stop?"

"Maybe that's what I'm asking you. There's something

about this list thing that isn't sitting well with me. So," she shrugged. "I've been praying about it." She sat forward, took another bite of her sandwich, then a few moments later said, "If you decide to back out of this whole thing, I'll support you. I'll stand up to the G-FOURce for you."

"Wait a minute. You just took me out clothes shopping last weekend." When Sharon talked about praying, or going to church, or any other aspect of her faith, Juliette's discomfort usually came out as belligerence.

"I know. But I've thought about it a lot the last few days. Do these guys know they're just one of many on a list? And if they did know that, would they still agree to be on it?" Sharon took a quick breath and kept talking. "Are you really giving any of them a fair chance? Isn't this all about finding something 'better than Mike,' or at least taking your mind off him?"

"You're using up all the oxygen again," Juliette muttered, taking a gulp of her iced tea. She didn't want to think of the feelings of the men on the list. They were there to make her feel better, not the other way around. But then, how selfish was that?

Sharon reached over and tapped on the bracelet on Juliette's arm. "Look, Juju. I like that you're open to trying new things again. I don't want to discourage you from going out, okay? But it isn't like you not to consider the feelings of others. These guys are real people with real feelings. They may, in fact, be just as vulnerable as you are right now."

"Do you think I should stop?" Juliette asked again.

"I don't know. I guess I want you to think about your motivation, what you really want from this. And I'm a little worried about your heart, too. You still seem kinda vulnerable to me, Juju." She looked imploringly across the desk at Juliette. "Just don't fall in love with a guy before you know anything about him. Talk to his friends. Find out what you can about his family life. If he won't share his life with you before you marry, there's no reason to think he'll share it with you after the vows tie you to him." Sharon leaned back in her chair again, hands up in a sign of surrender. "There. Now I *have* used up all the oxygen so I'll shut up. I know you've heard it all before, but I can't tell you how glad I am that Chris and I were friends first. It made room for God at the center of things."

"You never would have let a man come between you and God." Although she said it with some alacrity, Juliette couldn't help the twinge of jealousy darkening her thoughts. Not that she cared about God so much, as that she would have been happy with only half of what Sharon had with Chris.

"Wrong, Juju. I would have put Chris there in a heartbeat, if I could have gotten away with it. Believe me, I tried." Her brow furrowed at the memory. "Chris wouldn't let me. He wouldn't marry me until he knew I was more committed to loving Jesus than I was to loving him."

"How could he possibly know something like that?" Juliette scoffed at her friend's words. They reminded her of Frisky Frank insisting he knew she'd wanted to kiss him. "What did you do to prove it to him? Go to church with him? Read the Bible in front of him? Only listen to religious music around him? Because I know what you were listening to when you were with me, and it wasn't songs about Jesus."

She saw the hurt in her friend's eyes, but the subject of God always made her want to lash out. At Sharon, of all people, though?

"You're actually right, you know. I was trying to be a

good little Christian girl, because it was the only way I could have Chris." She shook her head and smiled softly. "But there's no fooling God. He knew I still didn't really believe I needed Him, at least not as much as I thought I needed Chris. Somehow Chris figured it out, too. That's why he broke up with me right before the wedding, remember? He said he needed to make sure that we were following God's plan for our lives and not just our own."

"We made that dart board out of his face."

"Yep. And we made good use of it, too." Sharon chuckled. "Do you know what happened to it?"

"You still have it?" Juliette was surprised to hear that.

"I gave it to him for Christmas the first year we were married. But it looks a little different than it did the last time you saw it. Now it's so covered in little round bandages you can hardly see his face at all. Just one big brown eye peeking out from beneath a blanket of spots." She cupped a hand around her left eye like a telescope.

"Bandages?"

"One morning I woke up and started getting ready for my day. I tried to read my Bible, looking for answers in it, treating it like a magic lamp, you know? But I couldn't concentrate. So I just sat there, crying, begging God to make Chris choose me again. Then I heard something." She leaned forward, an intensity in her eyes that made Juliette want to squirm. "It wasn't a sound; just this instant awareness of a thought. *'But I want Chris to choose Me. And I want you to choose Me.'*" Sharon had a faraway look on her face as she relived that morning in her memory.

"I realized at that moment that I had never really chosen Christ for myself. I was just going through the motions, thinking that was good enough. Something in me shifted, like a trapdoor or a skylight opening." Her voice got quiet, intense. "And there was this overwhelming desire to do just that; to put Sharon aside, and put Christ in her place." She took a deep breath, then met Juliette's eyes. "Instead of *asking* for Chris, I began to *pray* for him; that he would do the right thing no matter what the cost, even if it meant walking away from me forever. I didn't want to stand in the way of God; that became very clear to me." She smiled; her eyes bright with unshed tears. "And every time I prayed for him, I put a new bandage on his poor, punctured face."

"And, poof! God gave Chris back to you." Her voice dripping with brutal sarcasm, Juliette cut her off, finishing the story for her. Sharon's words just confirmed to her what she'd always thought of God; He was cruel and selfish, fickle. "God, in His kindness and goodness, bribed you with the man you love. He took him from you so He could break you, then gave him back, but only after you sold out." This was the God she knew; the one who didn't play fair, because He didn't have to. He made the rules, so He could break them any time He wanted.

"No, Juliette. No." Sharon shook her head emphatically, her voice pleading. "God didn't take Chris away from me. Chris made the decision to leave. And it wasn't because God made him do it; in fact, God gives us so much room, so much grace. We might have been all right had we not split up for those few months. But Chris just knew we were bound for trouble if we weren't both on the same page. He loved me, but he loved—loves—Jesus more. When I finally realized that, realized how much strength of character it took to choose God over me, it changed the way I saw myself." She shook her head, clearly trying to come up with the right words to explain her experience.

"I know it doesn't really make sense, but God didn't come to me in condemnation. He came to me in—in revelation. He showed me the condition of my heart and asked me if I was okay with it. When I saw how selfish I really was, especially when it came to Chris, I *wanted* to change. And do you know what? He answered both of our prayers, Juju, both mine and Chris's. The whole time I was asking God for Chris," she pressed a hand to her chest. "Chris was asking God for me, begging God to change my heart so he could come back to me. Remember that skylight I talked about? Now, it's like the whole roof has been ripped clean off. It's not perfect; it won't be until Heaven. But things are so much clearer when seen through the light of His love, instead of my own selfish love." She reached over and squeezed Juliette's hand. "Just don't settle, Juju. Okay? Hold out. Hold on."

CHAPTER ELEVEN

"IT SOUNDS to me like this Frank guy might have been a winner. Are you sure you don't want to go out with him again?"

They sat companionably at Juliette's table, having made up over coffee. She couldn't tell if Renata was digging for more details or sincerely curious. "He was all right. He just wasn't really my type."

"How will you know if someone's your type when you won't spend time getting to know him? How can you tell in just one date?" Renata sat with her legs crossed, one white-sneakered foot swinging back and forth, back and forth.

"Hey. I only committed to working my way through The Monday ManDates. I never agreed to date any of them more than once, and I certainly never agreed to get to know any of them." Her acerbic answer made Renata's eyebrows arch, but Juliette ignored the perfectly-tweezed little things.

"Okay, okay. So, next week's guy is one of Georgia's friends. I don't know much about him, except that he's in a rock band."

"A rock band? Seriously?" Juliette stared aghast at her

sister. "I'm afraid to ask. How old is he?"

Renata shrugged. "I don't know. Georgia doesn't know either, but she assured me he's plenty old enough for you."

"Ren! He could be twenty! Gia's just out of high school! Anyone over eighteen seems old to her. What are we going to do together? Hang out in his padded garage, and watch him and his band rock out, dude?" She drew her words out like a surfer. "Maybe I'll call Frisky Frank after all."

"Frisky Frank?" Renata's leg stopped pumping. "What are you not telling me? I warned Phoebe not to put any of her trashy boyfriends on the list."

"Leave Phebes alone, Ren. Frank wasn't trashy. And he wasn't really that frisky, either. He just wasn't very *anything*, as far as I was concerned. Kinda like a Ken doll. Nice to look at, but missing some important bits."

"Juliette!" Renata rose to the bait every time and all three sisters knew it.

"Hey. He lasted longer than Thera-Paul." She snickered, fairly certain Renata hadn't heard that nickname, either.

"Thera-Paul?" To Juliette's surprise, Renata smiled. "That's very clever. And I have to admit, it sort of fits him. Well, I'm hoping you survive Mick Jagger so you can go out with Tim. I think you'll like him."

"What if I do fall for Mick Jagger? What if he's my type?" Juliette wiggled her not-so-perfect eyebrows at her sister.

"You won't fall in love in only one date, Juliette." Renata stood and carried her mug to the sink. "I need to get home. Thanks for the coffee."

Juliette followed her into the living room, then stopped abruptly when Renata did.

"Where are your binders?"

"I'm destroying them. One page at a time. It's my

grieving process."

"Well, good for you. I think that's healthy." Renata put an arm around Juliette's shoulder and gave her a quick, sideways squeeze. "I'm proud of you." Then she grinned. "One more thing. Your Monday man's name is Taz. As in Tazmanian Devil, I presume." She leaned closer and whispered dramatically. "You might want to see if you have any leather in your closet." Then she traipsed off down the walkway to her minivan.

Juliette closed her front door and leaned back against it. Taz? Seriously? What kind of full-grown man chooses to be called Taz? This whole blind date thing was beginning to get on her nerves.

Besides, Sharon and Ren were right. How could she possibly get to know someone in one date; in three or four hours?

Granted, there most definitely was such a thing as chemistry, and *that* you experienced immediately. She'd felt it with Mike the afternoon the young college student wandered into Bountiful Books and smiled at her with his perfectly white teeth. When their fingers brushed reaching for the same pen, it was like electricity, and Juliette had jerked her hand away in surprise. Mike came back at closing that day, and for the first time in the five years she'd worked there, she didn't go straight home.

He won everyone but Phoebe over from the very beginning. Even shy little Gia warmed up to him, and Phoebe eventually came around because he made Juliette smile.

But Mike had been different back then. He was young and athletic, a cyclist who competed whenever he could. He was excited about school and worked hard to get the best grades in his class, to stand out in every way. He looked forward to his future with great plans for a successful career, and he was completely taken by Juliette.

Over the years, however, he became distant and busy, consumed with his education and the financial strain he was under. By the time he graduated, they saw each other maybe once a week, and more often than not, it was only briefly, because of the pressure he was under to stay on top. He was no longer excited and hopeful; he'd become driven and detached.

After graduation, Juliette had expected things to change, for the old Mike to resurface. However, he went from being obsessed with perfect scores to being obsessed with landing the perfect position in the perfect location with the perfect salary and pension plan. Nine months after graduation, Mike still had no job, and he often took out his frustration in arguments with Juliette, especially when she suggested he start smaller and work his way up.

"You have no idea how much money I owe in school loans! I can't just take any old dentist job. I worked hard to get where I am, and I deserve the best. Don't you want the best for me? For us?"

"We could get married. Joining forces might help out financially. One home, one—"

"You don't get it, do you?" He cut her off, his hand slicing the air like a guillotine. "I'm not marrying you or anyone else until I have the job I want. I won't settle for less, do you hear?" His words drove spikes into her heart. Did he think he was settling for less with her?

It was one week after another lackluster Valentine's Day, one he'd been too preoccupied to remember. It had taken her that long to work up the courage to face him, to ask him what his intentions were, but she did, palms sweating, voice shaking, knees wobbling. He stared at her for a long time with emotionless eyes.

Finally, he said, "Honestly, I don't know what I want with us anymore, and I suppose it's not fair to ask you to wait around until I figure it out, is it?" He shrugged, as if to shirk off any responsibility for all the years she'd already waited for him. "I just want to be sure, Julie, and right now, I'm not."

She stood there, rooted to the spot, staring at the floor as his words churned her insides to liquid. Finally, she lifted her eyes to meet his, feeling as cold as he looked. "I have given up nearly ten years of my life waiting for you to make me your wife, and all you have to say is that you're not sure I'm what you want? You have taken, and taken, and *taken* every single one of those years, Mike. Shame on you for being so selfish, and shame on me for being so blind." He just sat there, sprawled on his sofa, his eyes flitting back and forth between her and the movie he'd muted when she came in. It took every ounce of her willpower to walk out the door, her legs threatening to give out every step of the way. She climbed in her car, turned on the engine and pulled away, her heart pounding like a kettle drum in her chest.

~ ~ ~

"THERE'S a concert tonight at our church. A Christian musician. He's fantastic and he's a local boy. Would you be interested in coming?"

"Um... sure." Sharon rarely invited her to church anymore, mainly because Juliette almost always declined the invitation. She used to go with them when Chris and Sharon were first getting to know each other before seriously dating. Then Juliette began to feel the pressure from them to consider their faith as her own. She finally sat down with her friend and explained to Sharon that although she was happy for her and Chris, and hoped they wouldn't be disappointed by God, she was not interested in serving an unpredictable deity. Besides, she saw how hard Renata worked to be a good church lady, and still seemed miserable all the time. Although she couldn't imagine Sharon ever becoming like that, if it took misery to make God happy, she wasn't interested.

It had been awkward for a while, but the friendship had seen much greater difficulty in the past, and they quickly got through it. The Scovilles remained open and genuine with their faith, but they no longer tried to win her over.

So when she readily accepted Sharon's invitation, her friend was understandably surprised. And delighted. "I thought maybe I'd scared you off all church with my sermon last Tuesday."

"You can be pretty scary when you get on one of your God-kicks." Juliette spoke gently, taking the sting out of her words.

The weekend had been lonely for Juliette so far. Saturday morning, she'd stopped by her sister's yard sale for a while, and took the boys out for breakfast and an hour at the park so Renata could deal with the mid-morning rush without them underfoot. They were so different one from the other, and she loved each of them to distraction, maybe because they reminded her so much of her and her sisters. But she was always glad to take them home. They were Renata's boys, not hers, and they somehow made her feel the empty places in her heart. That evening, she grieved her way through the last of the wedding and into the honeymoon, even going so far as to cut up a lingerie store gift card she'd bought to be used when the time came. She didn't care that she was throwing away money. The amount was insignificant compared to everything she'd wasted on Mike over the years.

To Juliette, Sunday night church attendees were always surprisingly informal, but the congregation seemed even more amped up than usual. Looking around, she realized a large percentage of the crowd was her age and younger. Then the musician came out on stage wearing torn jeans and a leather jacket, a beat-up acoustic guitar slung over his shoulder. People were on their feet, clapping and cheering, as he broke into the first song.

He was incredible. His singing was melodic and full, with a rasp around the edges that he used to his advantage when his lyrics got gritty. His guitar never over-shadowed his voice, but she could tell he was very comfortable with both instruments. About halfway through the evening, Trevor played a love song so poignant and sweet, it brought tears to her eyes. She thought his eyes glistened, too, as the song ended with whispered words of hope.

Then he shared a story from the Bible about betrayal, about a man who loved a faithless woman who kept going back to her old ways. Over and over the husband welcomed her back home, and loved her unconditionally. Over and over she wandered, until finally, she ended up on the slave block. He found her, and bought her, paying full price for her, and he covered her with his own cloak and took her home.

"That is what God does for us, my friends. He welcomes us back home over and over again, forgiving us, loving us, giving us hope. All we have to do is respond. You are His bride. I am His bride. And just like Hosea did for Gomer, Jesus paid the full price to free us from our slavery to the things that would keep us bound up in sin." He continued to finger intricate chords on the guitar, the music ebbing and flowing with the passion in Trevor's voice. "Fear. Bitterness. Anger. Pride. Unforgiveness. He wants us free! But He doesn't beat us over the head with a big stick, or force Himself on us. No!" He shook his head emphatically. "He doesn't tell us to go get cleaned up first, and only then can we come to Him. No! He rescues us, He cleans us up and dresses us in the finest threads. He just loves on us, and gives us hope. Receive Him. Receive His love. He loves you so much." He kept repeating the words as he strummed, the music a throbbing heartbeat, and Juliette couldn't stop her tears from falling. His music tore holes in walls around her heart, walls she didn't even know existed, and the tightness in her chest made it difficult to breathe.

Juliette didn't understand why Trevor's words and music touched her in such a raw place. The way he talked made her want to believe in a love so deep, even though it didn't line up with what she knew of God. Was it possible that she was wrong? Was He really this loving, forgiving, pursuing God who wanted to cover her and offer her hope? It didn't make sense, but it didn't stop her heart from longing for it to be true.

At the end of the service, the pastor joined Trevor on stage and led the whole congregation in a prayer of repentance. Juliette was instantly on guard, feeling manipulated, set up by an expert salesman. She wasn't ready to take a step like that, and she didn't like feeling pressured into it. She bowed her head out of respect, but didn't repeat the words the pastor spoke. When he finished the prayer, he handed the microphone back, and Trevor sang one last song.

"Wasn't he wonderful? I could listen to him forever!" Sharon gushed after the service. They were in the car, making their way out of the parking lot. Chris reached over and squeezed her hand, then brought it up to his lips to drop a kiss in her palm. Behind them, Juliette watched the exchange with longing.

"Was that story about Hosea for real?" It didn't sound like a typical Bible story.

Sharon smiled and turned in her seat so she could see her. "Yes, it's for real. That's one of the most bittersweet love stories you'll ever read. He was an Old Testament prophet. God told him to marry Gomer, a very worldly woman who went astray many times, giving birth to children that were not his, sharing gifts from him with her lovers. But God told Hosea to take her back again and again as a model of how God takes His people back again and again."

"Sounds like a raw deal for poor Hosea." Juliette wasn't so sure she liked the story after all, feeling a deep sympathy for the man who gave, and gave, and received only pain and betrayal in return.

"I know," Sharon agreed, hugging her well-used Bible to her. "But it ends so beautifully. Filthy, naked, and utterly hopeless; can you imagine how Gomer felt when she heard her husband's voice offering to pay full price to buy his own wife off the auction block? Then he loads her up in his wagon, and takes her out to the wilderness where he loves on her, like Trevor said, and she finds restoration. 'No longer will you call me Master, but Husband,' Hosea tells her. It's such a beautiful picture of how Christ loves us. He doesn't want us to come to Him in fear or obligation, but in love. He wants us to call Him 'Husband.'"

God wanted her to call Him Husband? The words were like a balm to her soul.

The two in the front seat were silent, allowing the message, and the music from the night, to sink into Juliette's heart, seeping into all the parched places where fear, and bitterness, and unforgiveness had left her gasping for breath.

CHAPTER TWELVE

ONCE again, for the third Monday in a row, Juliette stood in front of her mirror sizing herself up. Tonight, she didn't look like a duck. *That* she could say in all confidence. Tonight she looked like a thirty-three-year-old trying to look twenty. She wore a new pair of jeans, one she'd bought months ago to motivate herself to lose ten pounds. They weren't very comfortable, but only because they were a style she wasn't accustomed to wearing. They sat low on her hips making her feel like she constantly needed to pull them up, but when she did, she ended up with a wedgie. She wisely put them on the instant she came home from work; it took an hour to make up her mind whether or not she could tolerate them the rest of the night. They did look good, she admitted, turning around to look at her backside, pleasantly surprised.

She wore a sheer, black and turquoise blouse over a black tank top, and with her hair down, she looked a little wild, a little mysterious, like she could handle a night of loud music and greasy pizza, and come out in one piece when it was all over, eardrums intact.

The boots made the outfit. Gia brought them by work at lunchtime. "You're going to need these," she grinned mischievously. "I can't tell you why, but wear jeans, not your work pants." She wouldn't divulge anything else.

Juliette had seen Gia with them on before, usually paired with leggings and some kind of funky skirt, and she liked them on her little sister. But they didn't belong in her wardrobe. Black, loaded with buckles running up the outside of each calf, the soles were thick and deeply treaded. She pulled her jeans down over the top of them, but the buckles bulged oddly under the denim, making her legs look deformed. She tucked her pant-legs inside the boots instead, re-buckled everything, and decided that was the way to wear them. If you've got buckles, flaunt 'em. She grinned at the sound of a loud motorcycle driving by.

"I'm wearing biker boots," she mused. Those were words she never thought she'd utter in her entire life. "With buckles!"

Juliette didn't think ducks wore biker boots. With or without buckles.

There was a knock at the door. Either he was way early, or one of her sisters was here to stress her out.

She peered through the peephole. He was early. He had his back to the door as he peeled off a pair of fingerless gloves. He wore a leather jacket over a pair of tight blue jeans, and beyond him, parked on the street in front of her house, was a Harley.

"Oh, Gia!" she cried, in a sheer panic now. "You didn't!" She glared down at the boots that should have been a red flag.

Maybe she could duck out the back. Or she could say she was in the shower, and didn't hear him knocking. That would teach him to come early.

No, she was ready, he was here, and besides, if she bailed, she'd never be able to face Gia. Well, at least there were no flowers this time. They seemed to be a harbinger of doom when they accompanied men on her front stoop. She pulled open the door.

"Hi." Her voice shook a little as he turned around, then splintered off into silence when she recognized him.

"I'm Trevor. You must be Juliette." Tucking his gloves into a back pocket, he thrust his other hand toward her. When she didn't immediately reciprocate, he chuckled. "If you're feeling half as awkward as I am about tonight, then we might just survive this."

She finally put her hand in his, and he shook it confidently. "I know I'm a little early. Sorry about that. I had to make a stop by my cousin's on my way over, and it didn't take as long as I thought it would. I figured if you were ready, maybe you'd like to start out the night with a little spin on the bike. It's perfect weather for it." He turned and glanced proudly at the Harley on the street, then back at her again. "What do you say? You ever been on one before?"

His voice sounded just the same when he spoke, throaty and rhythmic, and she tried to gather her discombobulated thoughts enough to answer him intelligibly.

"Um." So far, *not* so good.

"Okay. I think I'm doing this all wrong. Let me start over. Hi. I'm Trevor Zander." He held out his hand again. Juliette smiled back. If the man who wooed a whole crowd last night was feeling flustered, too, then she was in good company. She thought she could do better than 'um' this time. She shook his hand a second time.

"And I'm Juliette Gustafson. Nice to meet you. I, um, I

saw you sing last night." Ugh. An 'um' *and* a bit of gushing groupie. *Stop talking, Jules.*

"You were there? Wasn't it a great night? Did you feel it, too?" His eyes lit up as he spoke, his nervousness evaporated in the fire of his passionate response. Juliette nodded. She'd certainly felt something moving through that room. She hadn't been the only one in tears.

"I'm so glad you're a believer, Juliette. I was having a hard time with this whole blind date thing, but wow. God works out the details, doesn't He?" Trevor turned and pointed at the bike. "What do you say? It really is a beautiful time of day for it. We can watch the sun setting over the hills if we go now."

She eyed the bike dubiously, but before she could say anything, he continued. "I have to admit, I'm still a little high from last night, and I don't know exactly what we're going to do tonight, but I just figured I'd let God direct things for us. So what do you say? Shall we ride off a little of this nervous tension? I brought an extra helmet."

The man was so alive, so exuberant, and expressive. He was like a tamed wild man, and Juliette was trying not to be overwhelmed by him.

"You look amazing, by the way. Great boots." He tapped her toe with his own booted foot. "Do you have a jacket? Maybe some gloves?"

Juliette made up her mind. "Okay," she said decisively. "I'm game. I do have a jacket. And gloves. Hold on." She yanked open her tiny coat closet and grabbed an old leather bomber jacket that had been her dad's. She rarely wore it, but she took it out periodically, and put it on like a hug, or just buried her face in it and breathed deeply. Even after all these years, it still smelled like him, and she smiled as she imagined what he would say about her climbing on the back of a big, black motorcycle with a complete stranger.

Trevor stepped forward and took it from her, then held it as she slid her arms into it. "Nice jacket. Looks really old."

"Thanks." She nodded, smiling. "It was my father's."

"Nice," he said again. "Speaking of fathers, let's start this night out right. Can I pray for us?" He took her hand in both of his, and bowed his head without waiting for her answer.

"Father, You already have a plan for us tonight, and even though we don't know exactly why You brought us together, we do know that You're in charge. You've already gone ahead of us, preparing the table for us, and now we invite You to join us. Let everything we say and do tonight be honorable to You. I want to make You proud, Father. Amen." He let go of her hand and grinned at her. "Ready?"

Juliette's head was spinning and she stared blankly at him, at a complete loss. He was so different from Thera-Paul or Frisky-Frank. Or Mike. He was so different from anything she'd seen on television or in the movies. How could God *not* be proud of a man like this?

"Is there something wrong?"

She shook her head, feeling a blush color her cheeks. "No. Sorry. I'm just..." she faltered. "I'm just trying to figure out a purse for tonight."

He laughed. "I don't carry a purse, so I'm cool if you don't. Just tuck your license and keys into a pocket in your jacket. Your hair, though; you should tie it back. Otherwise the wind will tangle it so badly you'll hate me."

She grabbed an elastic band from a little ceramic knick-knack dish on one of the book shelves and quickly braided her long hair.

"Perfect," he approved.

She followed him down the walk to his bike, but the closer she got, the larger it looked, and the more trepidation she felt. "I…I've never been this close to a motorcycle before. This one is really big. Are you sure it's safe?"

Trevor laughed. "Safe?" he asked, spinning around so he was walking backwards in front of her. "Nah. But then again, nothing is safe in this world, is it? That's why it's so great to know this world isn't all there is. I don't want safe. Then I wouldn't long for Heaven." He chuckled at the look on her face. "Relax. I am a pretty safe driver, for what it's worth." He unclipped a helmet from the back seat and handed it to her. "It's my cousin's—that was the stop I made on my way over. It fits Gia. Hopefully it fits you, too."

After she had it on, he reached out and gripped it with both hands, moving it around on her head. "Does it feel like there's extra room in there, or is it snug? You don't want it too tight or you'll have a headache in minutes, but it can't be loose, or it's almost more dangerous than going without." He gave her chin strap a little tug.

"It's fine," she said, not even sure what it was supposed to feel like. She tried to keep her voice from trembling. "I guess Gia and I have the same size head. Has she ridden with you?" She tried to imagine her shy little sister throwing a leg over the back of this monstrous machine. How did Gia even know this guy?

"First time a few weeks ago. It took some convincing, but I could tell she really wanted to." He winked at her. "She said you'd like it, too, if you'd just give it a chance."

At first Juliette tried not to think about Trevor and Gia discussing her, but then she got curious. He seemed like a face-value kind of guy.

"Can I ask you something?" Her voice was a little muffled

and Trevor reached over and pushed up her face guard.

"Absolutely. Ask me anything." He waited attentively for her question.

"What exactly did my sister say to you about tonight?"

Trevor slid his own helmet over his head and buckled the chin strap snugly before answering her. "It was the strangest conversation, really. I think that's why I agreed to it. Your sister is good friends with my cousin Ricky. Do you know him?"

"Ricky Nolan? Yes. Huh. Small world." So this was Ricky's helmet. He was in on this, too.

"Yep. Well, they come by sometimes just to hang out. She's a good girl, your sister. And she's a good friend to Ricky, too. I keep thinking the two of them might get serious one of these days, but he assures me they're just friends. Anyway, one day we were talking about plans for the future, and your sister mentioned you. She said you were really good at planning things, but something had happened recently that had changed everything for you." When he noticed her frown, he reached over and tugged on her chin strap again. "She totally respected your privacy, don't worry. But what she did say touched a chord with me. She said that it seemed like you were just learning to swim even though you'd already been in the water for so long everyone assumed you knew how already. I asked her if I could use the concept in a song, and she agreed, but only if I would meet you. I was totally up for that."

"Meeting me is one thing. Taking me out on a date is another thing altogether."

"Yeah, well, I don't know what happened to you, but I do know what it feels like to have the earth ripped out from under my feet. That whole swimming metaphor summed up some stuff I went through a few years back, too. It took a while for me to learn to swim on my own, and I guess I just felt the Lord nudging me to bear witness to you."

"What does that mean? Bear witness?" She tried not to sound belligerent but this Jesus jargon, as Sharon called it, bugged her.

"Yeah, that's one of those Christianese phrases," he replied, as though he'd read her mind. "Sorry. To me, it means to be living proof of what God can do and does do in our lives." He looked down the road in anticipation. "It wasn't about a date, Juliette, no matter what we call it. Dating to me is purposely choosing to pursue a relationship with someone. This may be even bigger than that. Call it a divine appointment if you need a label, but if I turned down the opportunity to speak a little hope into your life, then I'd be walking in disobedience. I've tried that before and it doesn't work, not for very long anyway." He stopped talking a moment, letting her mull that over.

"I see," she said, more to fill the silence than because things were suddenly clearer.

"So, Juliette Gustafson." he grinned, settling onto the bike. "Here we are. Are you game to spend an evening with me? I'm the guy you saw last night. That's the real me, on stage, off stage; I live it every day."

This was the most confusing night of her life. Here was a man who believed the way her best friend did, who spoke like a religious zealot, who dressed like a rebel, and sang like an angel. And he wanted to take her to the edge of town to see what kind of sunset God had up His sleeve. She was way out of her league. And scared. And intrigued.

"I'm game," she said again, her voice as shaky as her confidence.

He flipped down the foot pegs for her and showed her where to put her feet. With one hand on his shoulder, she awkwardly got her leg up over the back, and sat behind him. He turned so he could see her. "You'll have to trust me, okay? Lean with me when we take the corners, not against me, and hands around my waist, but not too tightly. I'm ticklish." He grabbed at his belt and wiggled it. "You can hold on to my belt. It's not going anywhere."

Juliette could feel her cheeks warm inside the helmet, glad he couldn't see her blush. He was refreshingly candid about everything. She nodded and tentatively rested her hands at his waist, her fingers curling slightly around the wide black leather belt threaded through the loops on his jeans. He glanced down at them, grinned at her like he knew something she didn't, then continued.

"When you're a little more comfortable, you can lean back against your backrest, but you still need to keep your hands on my waist at all times. Don't let your feet drag; keep them on the pegs. When we stop, I'll support the bike. You keep your feet off the ground, okay? The bike heats up and certain parts will sizzle your skin right through your clothing, so be very careful, especially of the mufflers. Can you remember all that?" She nodded, her heart pounding furiously in her chest. "Think of it this way. Riding on the back of a motorcycle is a bit like being in a relationship with God. It could be the ride of your life, if you'll just trust Him."

She nodded again, not quite sure how to respond to that, bumping her helmet against the back of his. "Sorry!"

He just grinned. "Feet up, windscreen down, Juliette. Let's go!"

The rumble of the bike as it came to life beneath her both terrified and exhilarated her. She let out a little squeal as he revved the engine a few times, and threw her arms around him, abandoning all traces of dignity.

"Not too tightly, remember," he called out. She tried to relax her grip, but she closed her eyes as they pulled away from the curb.

At first the intimacy of being wrapped around a stranger, and the adrenaline rush of flying down the road with no protective metal framework around her, made her so tense she forgot to move with him, and he had to remind her several times. Once she even put her foot down at a stop light. He reached back and patted her knee. She returned the errant appendage to the peg with another shouted apology.

Ten minutes later, she was one with the bike, one with Trevor, one with the world. She leaned back into the padding behind her and felt her toes uncurl in her boots. It was one of the most freeing experiences she'd ever had.

It was even better than shredding wedding invitations.

CHAPTER THIRTEEN

JUST AS the sun was preparing for its grand exit, they pulled into a well-maintained rest stop. "Come on. We have to hurry or we'll miss it." Trevor grabbed her hand, pulling her along in his enthusiasm.

They followed a trail meandering up the hillside until they reached a small clearing. One bench sat alone on the edge of the slope, over-looking the valley where the town nestled.

"I didn't realize we'd come up so high," said Juliette, her voice hushed. "This is amazing." She slid onto the bench beside Trevor, and they sat in silence as the sky unfurled its dazzling twilight colors for them.

"Wow," Juliette whispered.

The sky subtly swayed and shifted before beginning to fade. Finally Trevor spoke too, his tone reverent. "And they say there is no God."

Then he began to sing, his eyes closed, a love song, a prayer.

"In a sunset's glory, in the awakening of dawn, when I see Your handiwork displayed across the sky. I am amazed, I am in awe. I am in wonder of who You are, that You would love one such as I."

He sang softly, the words seeping from every pore, and Juliette sat beside him, barely breathing, letting his voice wash over her. How she longed to see God the way he did.

Suddenly he stood and stretched out his arms. His voice rose, and that perfect rasp at the edges of it went to work on the walls around her heart all over again.

"How can I do anything else but praise You, thank You? Hallelujah. Hallelujah."

The echo of his song rolled out over the valley and back to them, and Juliette bowed her head under the power of her emotions. She felt his hand rest companionably on her shoulder.

She was glad for the shadows; she didn't want him to see her face. She'd shed a few tears but not enough to be embarrassed. It wasn't that. It was because she knew that everything she was feeling—the doubts, the wonder, the pain, the confusion, the longing—it would all be there, exposed for him to see, and she simply didn't want to put on any masks right now. She wanted to stay vulnerable to whatever was going on inside her for a little while longer.

They waited until the last of the light faded from the sky.

"We should go, Juliette." He spoke quietly, gently, squeezing her shoulder. "It's dark, and I promised to feed you."

Even though there were a few lampposts along the trail, Trevor pulled a flashlight from his pocket and turned it on. "Take my hand. I'll get you there safely." Once again she was pulled along by him, by the things he stirred up in her heart.

They agreed on a popular burger place, and Juliette was surprised to find she was ravenous. He teased her mercilessly about ordering so much, but she didn't feel guilty when she saw the mammoth burger he got for himself. Their conversation was relaxed and aimless; they talked about Ricky, about her sisters, and about Trevor growing up an only child.

"I hated it when I was younger, but by the time I was a teenager and totally into my music, I was glad not to have the distraction of other siblings. That sounds pretty narcissistic, doesn't it? But it's true. My folks one hundred percent supported me and encouraged my dreams. My dad, man, he totally empowers me to be the best man I can be. I think the only down side of it all is that I left home feeling pretty entitled. I learned the hard way, repeatedly, that it wasn't always about me. But then, I always had Mom and Pop to pick me up, dust me off, and kick me in the butt, until I got back in the saddle again." He took a long swig of his soda and leaned back in his chair. "Dessert?"

"How can you even think of dessert right now?" Juliette groaned, very unladylike. "I'm so stuffed I can hardly breathe! And these stupid jeans don't help either. Why didn't I wear stretch pants?" She was still working on the last of her seasoned French fries. Trevor had convinced her to mix ketchup and mustard and the house dressing together as a dip, then made a huge scene when she admitted she liked it. Everything about Trevor Zander seemed bigger and bolder than normal.

"Well? What next? Do you want to go home? For another ride?" He leaned back in his chair, stretching his legs out under the table, and nudged her calf with one of his feet.

"Can we ride for a while?" She felt the flutter of anticipation in her belly.

He grinned and grabbed her hand, pulling her to her feet.

"Let's go. Hit the bathroom and I'll pay the bill. If you're not out in two minutes, I'm coming in after you. If I don't get to touch up my make up, you don't either."

They rode for another hour. Trevor knew all the back roads, and scenic routes, and he periodically pointed out things he thought might be of interest to her. Most of the time, however, they didn't try to talk. She was glad because it gave her time to think about the last twenty-four hours, and all she'd experienced with him.

She was drawn to him, but it wasn't necessarily because of his looks, or his charisma, both of which he had in boatloads. She couldn't put her finger on what it was exactly, but she thought perhaps it had less to do with him, and more to do with what was going on inside her heart. She was on the verge of something, and she wondered if this was what Sharon meant about the skylight opening.

When he finally pulled up in front of her little home, she was prepared to invite him in. She didn't want him to leave until she'd gotten some of her thoughts sorted out. There was no shame, no fear, no rigidity in his faith like she saw in Renata's. There was freedom and joy, even when he talked about pain in his life, and she wanted to understand.

She looked up at him while she dug in her jacket for her keys. "Will you come in?"

He shook his head. "But if you want to talk, we could sit out here on your front steps."

At her curious look, he explained. "I try to avoid anything that could be misconstrued, or that might lead somewhere that it shouldn't; like being alone with you, a beautiful woman, in your house late at night. Riding a bike together is pretty intimate already."

Juliette shook her head again at his lack of pretension,

appreciating him even more. "Then allow me to welcome you to my front porch. I'm going to get a couple of cushions because I know for a fact this concrete gets hard. Would you like some coffee?"

"Coffee sounds good." He dropped down to sit on the top step and turned to lean his back against one of the concrete planter boxes on either side of the stoop. "I'll be right here when you get back. I promise."

Juliette returned shortly with a stack of cushions and a box of treats from Mona's. She'd stocked up just in case the night turned out badly.

"Nope." She flicked his hand away when he reached for a cinnamon roll. "That one's mine. I already licked it."

"Did you lick this one?" he asked, pointing at another icing-covered pastry.

"Probably." She picked up the cinnamon roll he first tried to take and broke it in half. "Here. You can have the unlicked side." She handed him the bigger chunk. "Actually, I bought these with the intention of eating every one of them all by myself," she admitted, feeling a lack of guile, herself. "So as far as I'm concerned, I'm being really grown up and generous with you." She took a bite and sighed with pleasure. "I do love Mona, Trevor." She tapped the box where Mona's logo was stamped. "You need to know that up front."

He spoke around the bite in his mouth. "Mm. I can see why."

Juliette brought the coffee tray out shortly and poured them each a cup. She sat facing him with her back to the opposite planter, and they chatted for a while, until finally, Trevor asked, "So what's really on your mind?"

Now that the question was voiced, she had no idea

where to begin. Trevor didn't push her, just sipped his coffee in silence while she stumbled over her words. She saw his lips move silently at one point and wondered if he was bored by her babble. The thought made her feel even more uncertain, and she pulled the edges of her dad's jacket tighter around her.

"Sorry," she muttered. "I'm not being very clear, am I?"

"That's okay. Take your time. I'm in no hurry." His reassurance made her feel a little better, and she sat quietly for a few moments, gathering her thoughts. From the corner of her eye she noticed a patrol car coming down the street. Her heart rate sped up again.

Officer Jarrett.

He was looking right at her, and she waved hesitantly while trying to ignore the small lurch in her stomach.

"Hey, it's Vic," Trevor said, pushing himself up and brushing the crumbs off his lap. "You know him?"

"Um, a little." Any other time, she would have been thrilled to see his car pulling up. At least he'd get to see her in something other than tears or her pink bathrobe. But right now, she felt vulnerable and maybe even a little resentful at the inconveniently-timed interruption.

"He pulled you over, didn't he?" Trevor's eyes widened, alight with humor.

"Um, yes." What else could she say?

Trevor laughed out loud and loped down the walk to the curb, where he waited until the officer was out of his car. Then he embraced him affectionately. From the porch steps, Juliette could clearly hear their conversation.

"I wondered if I'd get a chance to see you while you were here." Officer Jarrett briefly glanced over Trevor's shoulder in her direction. "Is everything all right here?"

"You bet. So you know Juliette, do you?" Trevor beckoned to her to join them.

She stood up and came down the steps; hesitantly, because she was beginning to feel really uncomfortable about the way the policeman was watching her. Why exactly was he here?

"How are you, Officer?" She smiled, and stuck out her hand in greeting. He paused briefly before he took it, his grip not nearly as gentle as the last handshake they'd shared, and there was no accompanying smile either. In fact, there was nothing warm about this contact, and she withdrew her hand quickly, squeezing it into a tight fist at her side. Oh, the zing was still there; at least it was for her. But it was obvious that any response on his part had all been in her imagination. She felt inexplicably bereft by his cold shoulder. It must have shown on her face.

"Look, Vic. You scared her." Trevor punched his friend in the arm. "But then, you scare me, too."

"Careful, man. I could arrest you for assaulting a police officer." Victor Jarrett was joking, she knew, but when he looked at her, his gaze had an edge to it that made her want to hide behind Trevor.

CHAPTER FOURTEEN

THE CALL came in as Victor was winding down for the night. He'd already processed all his paperwork, and he was starving; the pastrami sandwich he'd eaten on his break had not been sufficient to get him through his shift.

With a population of nearly 70,000, Midtown wasn't much bigger than a small town, but the crime rate was low, and the police station looked like something right out of a classic Hollywood television show. The building was an historical landmark, with pillars framing the huge oak double doors that opened into the foyer. The receptionist sat at a heavily-scrolled information desk in front of a Wall of Fame with portraits of officers who'd come and gone through the years. The dispatch office was off to one side behind security glass paneling, and depending on the time of day, there were at least two or more people sitting at the long counter taking calls.

"Hey Romeo! I know you're getting ready to head out, but you might want to take this one." Sarah waved a paper at him as he passed by the door that was propped open. "It's your girl, Juliette." She teased him relentlessly about Juliette

Gustafson. After he pulled her over the second time, he'd come back to the station and regaled her with the story of their encounter. When Sarah found out he'd gone to her home to check on her at the end of the night, she wouldn't let it go, teasing him about going above and beyond the call of duty, even though she knew he'd never take advantage of his authority that way.

He didn't mind Sarah's jabs. She was level-headed, good-natured, and always remained calm under pressure. It's what made her such a great dispatcher. She knew how to get the facts and keep her wits about her, even when she was dealing with weeping mothers, terrified children, or worse.

He took the printout and read over it quickly. When he looked up, his brow was furrowed. "Is this a joke?"

Sarah shrugged. "I asked the woman twice. She swears it's true and is demanding someone come shut the place down. She seemed legitimately concerned for her personal safety. Maybe you should take a back-up."

Victor kept glancing at the words in front of him. A call-girl service? Juliette Gustafson was a call-girl? Nothing about her indicated to him that she might be involved in anything so seedy. Her neighbor's words, however, left little to the imagination. Juliette had different men over every week. Once, the woman claimed, there'd even been a fight in front of the house, one that involved some physical violence.

"Why didn't she call us then? About the fight?"

"She did, remember? Granted, it was a few days late, but that's why you went out there in the first place. It's a little confusing to me, but from what I gather, at first she really didn't want to get involved. She thought the guy was the boyfriend, that it was just a lover's quarrel. But now this Mrs. Cork believes the boyfriend is really Juliette's pimp-daddy."

"Pimp-daddy?" It all seemed so absurd, right down to the terminology.

"Her word, not mine," Sarah chuckled. But the humor didn't reach her eyes. Victor was clearly disturbed by the information, and he could see she was having second thoughts about giving him the call rather than handing it off to someone on the next shift. "She says the latest guy is a Hell's Angel, and he's disturbing the peace with his loud motorcycle."

~ ~ ~

"WHY DO I even care?" Victor asked himself as he drove slowly from the station to her home. But that was exactly why he was taking his time to get there; he was trying to figure out why he was so stirred up by the notion of Juliette Gustafson being paid to entertain men. Was it really because it didn't seem possible, or was it because he didn't want it to be true?

Frustrated, he thumped the backrest of the passenger seat with his closed fist. "Get it together, man. She's a woman. It doesn't have to make sense." And like an on/off switch, his blood began to cool. "That's right, Vic," he nodded, breathing himself out of the closed-in sensation that accompanied any emotional flare up. "Did you really think that wide-eyed innocence was real?" He rolled down his window, letting the night air cool his flushed cheeks. "Man, red flags! She changed on a dime, remember? Hissing and clawing like a barn cat, then purring like a kitten, waving sweetly from the front steps." He shook his head over how easily he'd been fooled. "Fell for it hook, line, and sinker, didn't you."

By the time he turned down Juliette's street, he felt in

complete control of his emotions.

When he saw her sitting companionably with a man on her front porch, he was glad for the opportunity to study her behavior and body language without her realizing.

When he recognized Trevor Zander, he felt something tighten in his gut, and he hoped and prayed that the neighbor was wrong; that his friend had a completely different reason for hanging out with Juliette Gustafson than what her neighbor claimed.

When Juliette rose and came toward them, Victor became absolutely certain the neighbor was right about her. She looked nothing like she had the other night, and he found it difficult to swallow as he watched her approach.

Maybe it was the boots that made her walk that way, but he was not prepared for the tantalizing sway of her hips that her tight jeans only served to accentuate. He forced himself to lift his gaze to her face, but her features were back-lit, and he couldn't read them. He did notice, however, the way her leather jacket slipped off her right shoulder as she walked, taking the fabric of her shirt with it. The pale curve of her neck and shoulder glowed like a beacon, and he clenched his teeth to keep the accusations from spilling out of his mouth. She stopped in front of him, sidling a little too closely to Trevor for Victor's comfort.

When he looked down at her face, now illuminated by the street lamp behind him, he almost cringed. There was that vulnerable uncertainty in her smoky eyes again, a look that made his blood run faster. But this was no longer the weepy girl in the pink bathrobe and messy hair. Tonight she was mesmerizing, a terrifying combination of fragility and mystery. He would not fall for it. And if he had any say about it, neither would Trevor.

When he took Juliette's soft hand in his, the warmth in his belly became a blaze, and he had to resist the impulse to jerk his hand away, clasping hers tighter and more firmly instead. He saw her bewilderment over his rough handling, and scowled in response.

Nothing about this night was lining up; nothing. He didn't like the way he was feeling, and he didn't like that he was struggling so hard to keep his emotions in check. He didn't understand his reaction to her, and, for the life of him, he couldn't figure out what Trevor Zander was doing in the company of the likes of her. He had the grace to feel slightly abashed when his friend reprimanded him for being so gruff, but he wasn't going to let down his guard any time soon.

~ ~ ~

"LET ME guess. Our man, Taz, took you for a ride. That will leave you pale and shaking every time." Victor crossed his arms and stared at her, his expression unreadable.

"I'm fine, really." She brightened at the memory of the ride. "It certainly wasn't because of the bike. I've never been on one before tonight, and it was amazing!" Then she turned and poked Trevor in the arm. "But, Taz? I completely forgot about that! When I heard your name was Taz, I was expecting something a little different. Then you introduced yourself as Trevor and it slipped my mind." She smiled as her voice took on a teasing quality, and she shot a quick glance up at the policeman. "Thank you, Officer Jarrett, for reminding me. Now fess up, Mister. Taz, as in Tazmanian Devil?"

"Trevor Aidan Zander, at your service," he said, with a bow and a flourished hand. "I suppose I was a bit of a mad thing when I was a kid. Comes from being an only child, right?" Juliette could easily imagine a miniature version of Trevor bouncing off the walls, driving everyone around him crazy.

"So what exactly *did* you expect?" He eyed her quizzically; so did Officer Jarrett. She stood straighter, suddenly in the spotlight again.

"Well, you're my little sister's friend. I was picturing a pimple-faced, boy-band type. Or maybe a Mohawk haircut and a studded collar?"

Officer Jarrett smirked, but she could tell his ridicule was directed at her, not at Trevor. "You haven't heard any of his music, have you?"

"Actually, I was at his concert last night." She didn't mention that her heart still ached from hearing Trevor sing again tonight. For whatever reason, this was not the man who'd come to her door a few weeks ago, asking if she was all right, promising to look out for her. What was wrong with him? What had changed? "It was amazing," she finished lamely.

"Amazing? Just like his ride?" The policeman's question dripped with sarcasm, mocking her words.

"Dude," Trevor cut in, looking from one to the other with a curious expression.

Victor looped his thumbs in his pockets and shrugged. "Surprised you liked it, that's all," he said by way of explanation. The obvious disdain in his voice cut her deeply.

She blinked away the sting behind her eyes and hugged herself against the chill that had nothing to do with the late September evening. Enough. If he wasn't here on business then maybe it was time for him to leave. "Was there something you needed to see me about, Officer?"

"See you?" His eyebrows rose as though even the thought was beneath him. "No. Just doing my rounds." He turned to Trevor, his expression not softening. "I need to get back to work. Touch base with me before you leave town, okay?"

Juliette knew it wasn't a suggestion. Trevor nodded and the two men shook hands. "Good night, Vic. I'll call you in the morning."

Officer Jarrett turned and saluted her. "Good night, Ms. Gustafson." She only nodded in response. They watched from the sidewalk as he climbed into his patrol car and drove away.

Finally, she turned to look at Trevor. He was deep in thought, concern etching shallow lines into his forehead. Afraid he might want to talk about what had just happened, and not prepared to discuss it, she spoke first. "You're leaving town?"

CHAPTER FIFTEEN

YEAH." He nodded, coming out of his reverie. "Last night was the kick-off for my first West Coast tour. I'm heading out in a few days." When he saw the look on her face, he frowned. "I mentioned it a few times last night."

"I'm sure you did, but last night I didn't know you, so…." She smiled ruefully. A tear slid from the corner of her eye and she turned away so he wouldn't see it. Too late; he reached over and wiped it away with his fingertip.

"Hey." He took her hand and led her back to the steps, pulling her down to sit beside him. He waited patiently while she cried, shoulder to shoulder, otherwise, not touching her, but handing her napkins from the coffee tray as needed.

"I'm so sorry, Trevor. I really am a mess. Gia's worried for good reason. I feel like I'm doing everything I can possibly think of just to hold my head above water, but nothing I do seems to work. I keep going under, and I'm so afraid I'm not going to come back up." She paused, remembering his songs, his voice, and the things he shared about love. "Last night, you sang into places in my heart that haven't been reached in a long time. So long, in fact, that I didn't even know they were still there. You talked about being a slave to stuff and that's how I feel. I feel like those locked places house parts of me that are chained to anger and bitterness, to fear. I don't want to look at them, I don't want to face them, but they've been let out now, and I can't shut them up again."

She told him then about the night her parents were killed; about Angela Clinton, and the consuming anger she felt every time she thought of her. She told him about her years of tight-fisted control, of her perfectly laid plans, of the last near-decade she'd spent waiting for a man who didn't know if he wanted her.

"Oh, how I long to be loved unconditionally, the way God seems to love everyone but me. I would give anything to know that kind of love. To know He thinks of me that way. I wish I could see Him the way you do, the way my friend does. But I can't, Trevor. To me, God is cruel and unpredictable, and He doesn't like me any more than I like Him. Is…is it me? Is there something wrong with me?"

Trevor didn't answer her right away, and she saw his lips move silently again. She realized then that he was praying and she looked away, giving him privacy. He wasn't going to give her some flippant, easy answer to her deepest pain. He was going to handle with care what she'd entrusted to him.

Finally, he spoke. "Juliette, there are so many things that happen to us, things we can't control, both good and bad. Whether you believe in God or not, bad things are going to happen to us because we live in this imperfect world in these imperfect bodies with these terribly imperfect minds and hearts. Some of us will endure stuff far worse than others. What happened that night with your parents changed everything for you and your family. I can't even imagine what you've gone through." He poked her knee. "And you let me go on and on about how wonderful my parents are and how I couldn't have survived without them. But you somehow did just that, didn't you? I'm sorry."

"Don't be silly. You didn't know." She poked him back. "I could have spoiled the mood and said something like, 'Cool. My folks are dead.' Wouldn't that have been a downer?"

"Okay, yeah. That would have sucked a little. But I could have handled it. I'm a big boy now. Passed that pimple-faced stage years ago." He stood up and stretched, then crouched down in front of her so he could look her in the eyes.

"Listen. I don't have all the answers for you. Only God does. But this I can promise you." He reached over and lifted her face with a hand cupping her chin. "Are you listening?"

"Yes," she murmured softly, hoping her nose wasn't running.

"Remember the motorcycle ride? Remember how I said it was like being in a relationship with God, that you have to be willing to trust Him, and let Him lead, let Him be the One in control?" He rubbed away tears with his thumb then lowered his hand to her hands where they were clenched together in her lap.

She nodded, but didn't look away.

"If you will give Him all those hidden places, those chained up parts of you, He'll release you. It won't be easy, I can assure you. Daily, you'll have to choose to hand Him the keys to your heart. Daily, you'll have to choose to follow Him into those dark rooms and let Him teach you how to be a new you. He doesn't let us just sit around while He does all the work. He's a much better Father than that! But He'll let you know what it is you must do to air out those rooms, and

He'll go through it all with you." Trevor brushed her cheek with the back of his knuckles and stood up again. "He loves you, Juliette, far more than any man ever could. He's not some cruel master. He wants you to call Him 'Husband.'" He said it just like Sharon had, and Juliette lowered her gaze, her breath catching at the intimacy in his voice. He placed a hand on the top of her head. It felt like a blessing. "All you have to do is get down off the slave block and into His wagon—or on the back of His Harley—and go home with Him so He can set you free from all that stuff keeping you enslaved."

Warmth flooded over her, from the top of her head where Trevor's hand rested, all the way to the tips of her toes, where they were still ensconced in Gia's boots. She knew, without a doubt, that he was right; she just had to let God take over. Something inside of her sprang open, like a skylight, and she smiled to herself, imagining how Sharon would react when she told her.

Right there on the front steps of her home, she and Trevor held hands while he led her in a prayer similar to the one the pastor prayed the night before. "Father, You know my broken heart even better than I do." Juliette repeated the words, forcing them out past the tightness in her throat. "I need You, Jesus, to wash me clean. I need You to break the chains of sin in my life. I'm sorry for my anger and bitterness toward You. I'm sorry for running from You again and again. I want You to live in me. I give You my heart, Jesus. Help me to see You as my loving husband. Teach me how to love like You do. Amen."

Trevor stayed with her a little longer to make sure she was okay, and she promised to let Sharon know about her freed heart first thing in the morning.

"It's really important you don't try to go from this place

on your own. You need to have other believers supporting you, helping you understand. Do you have a Bible?"

"Somewhere, yes." Renata had once gifted all her sisters with a Bible. Juliette thought it might be out in a box of books in her garage.

"Read Hosea chapter six, verses one through three. Just those three verses for now. Ask God to show you something in them, something just for you. He will. He'll meet you in those verses." Trevor helped her to her feet. "Do you want me to write that down?"

"I'll remember." She hadn't been able to get the story of the prophet out of her mind for the last twenty-four hours. She tucked back a few strands of hair that had come loose from the braid and looked up at Trevor. "I don't know quite what to say now. I've never had a date end like this before."

"Ah!" Trevor grabbed her shoulders and brought her close in a fierce hug. "Remember what I said? This wasn't a date. It was a divine appointment! How much bigger can you get than redemption and hope and salvation? Yes!" He whooped loudly, and she put out a hand to shush him.

"My neighbor is going to call the cops," she giggled.

"It'll just be Vic. He'll cover for us." Officer Jarrett's name threw a damper on things.

Trevor slid his hands down her arms until he held both her hands in his, and dipped his head to meet her eyes, his tone suddenly still and serious. "Hey. I don't know what that was all about; Vic's little visit. I've never seen him be intentionally rude before. I'll apologize for him because I know him, and that was totally out of character for him." He frowned, more to himself than to her, obviously concerned for both Juliette and his friend. "But I don't want his behavior to mess with your head, especially tonight. That's how the devil works; he likes to wander into the middle of things and throw cold water on the fire of the Holy Spirit, and he'll use whatever he can to do it, even the good guys if they're all he's got available to him. And I can assure you," he squeezed her hands to emphasize his words. "Victor Jarrett is one of the good guys. Apparently, it was a bad night for him, but that doesn't mean it has to be a bad night for you, okay?" He waited for her nod, then dropped her hands and picked up the coffee tray.

"Now, I'm going to brave the house because I need to use your bathroom." His tone was again light, teasing. "Can I trust you not to take advantage of me once I step inside your lady-lair?"

"I'll try to restrain myself. In fact, I'll wait outside for you," she promised, his words making her smile. "It's the first door on the right down the hall. You can't miss it."

She sat back down on the top step, toying with one of the boot buckles. She eyed the bike, and sighed as she thought again of how alive she'd felt sitting behind Trevor, giving him full control, trusting him—quite literally—with her life. That's what God wanted too, for her to trust Him with her life. No, it wasn't safe, and it wasn't going to be easy, as Trevor had said. But the freedom that came from leaning with, instead of against, of keeping her feet up and out of the way, it all made sense to her on a much deeper level now. She giggled at the thought of Jesus pulling up on a Harley and asking her to ride with Him.

Then she remembered how loud the bike was. She'd hear about it in the morning, she was sure. Yappy-dog would come out, and Mrs. Cork would ignore its activity while she complained aloud to herself about noisy neighbors. Then she'd scoop up her dog and go back inside, leaving the little brown pile behind.

"Grrr." Juliette grumbled.

"Are you growling?" Trevor asked from behind her, startling her.

"Can you just pretend you didn't hear that?" Juliette peered up at him from the corner of her eye. She gave him her hand, and he pulled her up.

"Of course," he laughed. Then he brought her fingers to his lips, and pressed a quick kiss to her knuckles. "Farewell, Miss Juliette. Thank you for the lovely evening." He released her hand, loaded her arms with the four cushions they'd used, then said, "Remember: He sought you out tonight, and you were paid for. In full. Now it's all about learning to live in the freedom of His love. Don't give up."

"I won't," she assured him.

He took the three steps down to the sidewalk. "And don't believe the devil when he whispers to you that it isn't real, or that it didn't happen, or that it's not worth it. He'll try to convince you. He'll work every angle he's got. That's why it's so important to plug in right away, you understand? Call your friend. Don't put it off."

"I won't," she said again.

Halfway down the walk he turned around and repeated what he'd said earlier. "I know he acted like a jerk, but Vic really is a good guy. I'd trust him with my life. If you ever need anything, he's the man to call."

"I won't." This time she only muttered the words under her breath, smiling beatifically.

Juliette shuddered at the thought of intentionally facing Officer Jarrett again. His unkind treatment tonight had really hurt, and she didn't think she could handle any more of his aggression. She was far too vulnerable these days.

Trevor's bike rumbled to life, and she watched until he disappeared around the corner. When she could no longer hear him, she went inside and closed the door.

CHAPTER SIXTEEN

TREVOR didn't wait until the next day, but came straight from Juliette's place, banging on the door until Victor got out of bed and let him in.

"Do you want to tell me what that was all about?" There was no apology for the late hour; he simply walked in, dropped to the sofa, and started demanding answers.

"Maybe you should tell me," Victor replied, not bothering to turn on any lights. He was not in a hospitable mood. "Do you know anything about her?"

"I took her out to dinner and a ride. Yeah, I know something about her."

"How did you hook up with her? Are you seeing her now?" Victor's blood began to boil at the thought, and his scalp tingled.

"What's this all about? You're acting like I'm doing something I shouldn't." Trevor leaned forward and set his helmet on the floor between his feet. He indicated the chair on the other side of the coffee table. "You're pacing, man. Sit down and talk to me."

Victor glared at him for several seconds before sitting.

For the last several hours, he'd been tormented by thoughts of what was going on at Juliette Gustafson's home. He'd returned to the station, documented that the call was just a disgruntled neighbor, and clocked out, all under the watchful and curious eye of Sarah. He knew she was dying to ask questions, but he didn't give her the opportunity; he was too full of questions himself, and in short supply of answers.

When he got home, he headed straight for the shower, hoping to wash away some of his confusion. By the time he went to bed, however, he was even more unsettled. If he closed his eyes, he saw her; sashaying down the sidewalk in her clever jeans, peeking shyly up at him with those luminous eyes, then turning them adoringly on Trevor, as she called him 'amazing.' He punched his pillow; he could feel every lump.

None of it made sense. Trevor Zander, of all people, out with a girl like that in the middle of the night? Call-girl or not, she was obviously pretty wild in those ridiculous boots of hers. Victor didn't know what bothered him more, the surprise of finding his friend there, or the familiarity between them.

He wasn't even close to being sleepy when Trevor showed up, but that didn't mean he felt like talking to the guy. Here he sat, though, in the shadows cast through the windows by the streetlights outside, waiting for explanations.

"You don't date randomly, not unless you seriously want to pursue someone. Isn't that your rule?"

"You don't have to tell me my own rules."

"Then what were you doing with her?"

"Maybe I'm pursuing her. What's the problem?"

"What do you know about her?" Victor asked again.

"Why, Vic? Is there something you think I should know?"

"How did you meet her?"

"Her name is Juliette. And why are you answering my questions with questions?"

"I *know* her name," Victor growled, standing up and crossing to the window.

"Dude, this is the most worked up I've seen you in a long time. You want to tell me what this is all about?" It was the third time Trevor had asked the question.

Victor spun around and ground out between clenched teeth, "You want to know why I showed up tonight?" He scrubbed his hands through his hair as he tried to get a grip on his frustration. "I got a complaint about her, that she's involved in some seedy stuff. Having to do with men." Why couldn't he just say it? "Can you imagine my surprise when I pulled up and *you* were the man she was with?"

"What exactly are you implying?" Trevor's voice had a new and dangerous edge to it.

"If the rumors and complaints are true—and I'm going to be doing a little research on your Ms. Gustafson—you just spent your evening with a call-girl, my friend. Or even worse, the kind of girl who gives it away for free."

Now Trevor was on his feet. "Watch yourself, man."

They stood facing each other across the room, feet firmly planted, and Victor was momentarily swept up in the out-of-time-feeling of an old western gun fight. His trigger finger even twitched.

Finally, Trevor spoke again. He didn't sit. "You're wrong about her, Vic. And you do her a serious injustice with your accusations. You're acting like a blind fool. I don't know what's gotten into you, but whatever it is, it's got you by the throat." He leaned over and picked up his gear. "I suggest you take it up with the King. Ask Him about her. Juliette's wild, but not in that way."

He crossed the room and put a hand on Victor's shoulder. "Father, Your son needs Your peace tonight. Give him discernment. Open his eyes with Your wisdom. Amen."

Victor had tried praying tonight, demanding that God let him sleep, but his prayers seemed to bounce off the ceiling. Trevor's words, on the other hand, crashed through the plaster above them, and Victor sensed the sought-after peace pouring down, washing over him. His shoulders relaxed as he realized God had just answered him; He'd heard his prayers through the plaster after-all, and sent his friend to put him in his place.

Even after Trevor's visit, however, Victor couldn't get Juliette Gustafson off his mind. He realized how ridiculous the whole call-girl thing was, but an urgent curiosity about who she was still poked and prodded, and he felt compelled to find out.

Thank goodness she lived on his beat; driving past her house at all hours bordered on stalking, but he had the law on his side, and he was going to use it until he managed to clear his head about the whole thing.

~ ~ ~

FOR THE first time since she'd taken her university job, Juliette called off work for no reason except that she needed a day off. Whatever showed up in her inbox could either wait a day, or—novel idea—the professors could learn how to use the copy machine themselves. Preferably without breaking it.

Today, all she wanted to do was revel in her divine appointment—not date—with Trevor Zander—not Mick Jagger. If a certain cop happened to wander into her thoughts the way he'd wandered onto the scene last night, well, maybe she would see things a little clearer in the light of day. Maybe she'd figure out what had turned him so sour.

Her first order of business was to uncover that Bible. She found it in the second box she unpacked, brought it inside, wiped the cover down with a damp paper towel, and quickly gave up trying to locate Trevor's verses just by flipping through the pages. Even with the table of contents, finding Hosea was a challenge. It was a short book, stuck in the middle of a lot of other oddly-named short books, and she wasn't accustomed to the thin, crinkly pages that kept the Bible from being a tome.

"Come, let us return to the Lord," she read aloud the first three verses of chapter six, listening to the cadence of the words. Holy poetry, she thought to herself. "For He has torn us, but He will heal us; He has wounded us, but He will bandage us."

"That's me, God," she closed her eyes and whispered, "Will You heal me? Will You bandage me? I'm so tired of being torn and wounded."

She continued reading. "He will revive us after two days; He will raise us up on the third day, that we may live before Him. So let us know, let us press on to know the Lord. His going forth is as certain as the dawn; And He will come to us like the rain, like the spring rain watering the earth."

The words fell on her like rain, watering the parched soil of her heart. She read the verses again, then tried to read on, but the passage got confusing really quickly, so she returned to those three, short, but over-flowing verses. Everything her heart needed was in those words. Again and again she read them until she knew the words by heart.

When the phone rang a few minutes after eight, Juliette laughed to see Sharon's name pop up on her screen. "What's wrong, Juju?" No greeting, no polite phone etiquette. No games. She loved being Sharon's friend.

"You know Trevor Zander, the musician from Sunday night?"

"I took you, remember?"

It all sounded a little fantastic, even to her own ears, and she was the one who'd experienced it, but by the time she finished relaying her Monday ManDate adventure, Sharon was in tears.

"I'm crying like a blithering idiot, and I'm at work, Juliette Gustafson! How could you do this to me?" But she was ecstatic and wanted to know every detail of the night. "Imagine! Trevor Zander! Are you going to see him again?"

"That's the weirdest part. We didn't click. I mean, he's an amazing guy. Perfect in every way. Seriously. Like, the ultimate perfect guy. But that *zing* just wasn't there." Juliette forced herself not to think of Victor Jarrett's hand around hers.

"Makes sense to me. That's probably why you were finally able to really hear God's voice; because there were no emotional entanglements between you and Trevor, you know?" Sharon continued, her voice filled with excitement. "Isn't it crazy? God used something as ridiculous as the Monday ManDates to reach you. Think about it, Juju. All this stuff with Mike, and the bad dates with the other guys, it was all leading to last night. Trevor showed up with his shameless passion for Christ, and you were already primed from his concert the night before. Wow. Just wow."

"Oh, Sharon," Juliette sighed. "It was just like you said; like a skylight bursting open. Suddenly, I could see things from a whole new perspective."

"So how do you feel today?"

"I feel incredible. I feel light-headed. I feel scared. I know I have a lot of work to do. I have a few people to deal with, and Mike is one of them. I've got a lot of anger and bitterness in me over what he's done right now, and thinking about letting that jerk off the hook makes me a little sick. I kinda liked holding on to the anger, so it's going to be tough to give it all up."

"Good girl. How can I help?" Sharon was still sniffling, but Juliette could hear the excitement in her voice.

"You can pray for me."

"Of course."

She got up to pour herself another cup of coffee and headed out to sit on the front porch steps in an effort to recapture some of the euphoria of the night before. "I need to learn to forgive people, Sharon. Now that the walls are being torn down, it seems there's a whole roomful of folks who've been trapped inside the dungeon of my little, shriveled heart, just waiting to be forgiven and set free."

They talked for a while longer before Sharon had to get back to work. "Oh! What about the Monday ManDates?" Sharon asked.

"I'm done. And now I have a good reason, thanks to Trevor."

"What are you going to tell your sisters?"

"I don't know. Maybe that I've found true love, and no one on their silly little list could ever compare to Him."

"That'll go over well." Sharon's sarcasm did not go unnoticed.

"I know. But I also know I can't do it any longer. Just pray they understand."

Sharon giggled.

"What are you laughing about?"

"You just asked me to pray for you, not once, but twice, in the same conversation."

"Don't gloat, Mrs. Scoville. It's not what Jesus would do."

When the phone rang later that morning, and she saw it was Renata, she let it go to voice mail. Around noon, when Phoebe called, she let it go to voice mail, too. When Gia called right as Juliette was sitting down to a light supper and a glass of orange juice, she didn't answer the phone either. But she did text them all at that point, letting them know that Monday night had been the greatest night of her life, and if they wanted details, they'd have to join her for a G-FOURce on Thursday evening, 6 o'clock, her place.

Dinner will be served, she added.

Needless to say, she got three texts right back. Two of them were short, congratulatory, and anticipatory. The third one, in all caps, just said, "WHAT HAPPENED? CALL ME RIGHT NOW!"

She didn't. Nor did she answer the phone when Renata called an hour later, and twice more before bed.

CHAPTER SEVENTEEN

RENATA showed up a half an hour early, just as Juliette knew she would. Juliette only smiled and told her she'd have to wait to hear about Taz, but she could go to The Green Dragon with her to pick up dinner.

"This whole thing was my idea," Renata berated. "You owe me something."

"Not going to happen, Rennie. Hot mustard?" Juliette grabbed a handful of packaged condiments and dropped them in the box of Chinese food. "This stuff smells so good, doesn't it? Thank you, Mr. Chen Yu!" She hollered over her shoulder and waved at the proprietor, who beamed and waved back.

Juliette was not going to let her sister's pouting get to her. She just grinned, and put an arm around Renata, who was carrying the box of food.

"Careful!" Renata exclaimed, but a small smile lifted the corners of her mouth. "Oh, dear. You've got it bad, haven't you?"

Juliette just nodded. Let her meddling sister think she was in love. They'd all know the truth by the time the G-

FOURce was over.

When they got back to the condo, both Phoebe and Gia were sitting together on the front porch, an open box of cookies from Granny G between them.

"Hey! Don't eat those now," Renata scolded, playing right into their hands.

Phoebe shoved a whole cookie into her mouth and stared belligerently up at them as they approached. "Mwhasha gah air?"

Gia translated. "Whatcha got there?"

"What do you think?" Renata asked, rolling her eyes. "Green Dragon. Fine dining by Juliette."

"Rummy!" Phoebe declared.

"Yummy," Gia echoed.

They headed inside and set the table with paper plates and forks. Gia poured Ginger Ale for each of them, the traditional drink of the Gustafson family when dining on Chinese takeout, and Renata made sure everyone had napkins and their fair share of hot mustard and soy sauce packets. Renata prayed a blessing over the food and their time together, then Gia began the G-FOURce pledge. As the last word died out, Gia leaned forward and let out an impassioned plea.

"Tell us, Jules. Tell us everything!"

"Well," Juliette began, her eyes sparkling. At the anticipation in Gia's eyes, she almost felt badly about the little game she was playing. She took a deep breath and plunged in anyway. "I've fallen in love."

Renata scoffed. "In one night? Please."

"I really have."

Phoebe ate her noodles in silence, not taking her eyes off her oldest sister. Juliette was fairly certain she wasn't buying the love at first sight bit, either.

Gia, on the other hand, could hardly contain her excitement. She clapped her hands and bounced up and down in her seat. "I knew it! I knew you'd like him. He's so amazing, right?"

"No. You didn't fall in love in one night," Renata stated matter-of-factly, laying her chopsticks down after dropping the same piece of chicken three times. She picked up her plastic fork instead. "Maybe you're attracted to this Taz guy, but you're not in love with him. Now tell us about your date."

So she did. Juliette started with Sunday and the concert she'd attended.

"I was there, too!" Gia exclaimed. "I wish I'd known. We could have sat together."

She told them all the way up to Trevor bringing her home at the end of their night out together. Then she stopped to eat. The other three were finished and sat watching her, varying degrees of uncertainty on their faces. Finally, Renata spoke up.

"You mean, he just started singing, out of the blue? Weren't you embarrassed?"

"It wasn't just singing, Ren. He was…I don't know…communing with God! I didn't really think about being embarrassed."

"But wasn't it awkward for you?" Renata looked rather skeptical about the whole thing.

"No, no, no. It was very cool. I've never seen a guy be that *transparent* before. It's one thing to do it on stage, where you're supposed to put on a good show, but to do it like that? He's the real deal." Juliette took another bite of orange cashew chicken.

"You rode on a motorcycle?" Phoebe finally spoke. She pushed her empty plate away and leaned forward across the table. "Okay. Fess up. What have you done with our Jules?" She held up a plastic fork, pointy end threatening Juliette.

"I didn't just ride on a motorcycle, Phoebe darling. I rode on a Harley." Juliette said smugly. "Three times. It was amazing."

Phoebe grinned lasciviously. "I bet it was."

"So when are you going to see him again?" Renata asked, redirecting the discussion back to the white-washed zone.

"I'm not."

"You're not?"

"What?"

"I thought you loved him!"

Juliette shook her head. "I never said I fell in love with Trevor. Or Taz. I haven't gotten to that part yet."

Renata released a huff of breath and stood up. "This is ridiculous. Give it to us straight, Juliette. I have a husband and four boys waiting for me at home, and I don't have all night to play your little guessing games."

Juliette finished her last bite and pushed her plate away. Just in time, too, as Renata plucked it off the table, along with everyone else's dishes, and carried them to the trashcan. She turned on the kettle for hot water and stood apart from them, leaning against a counter.

Juliette took a sip of her ginger ale, and picked up her story where she'd left off. "Trevor wouldn't come in. It's one of his dating guidelines. He tries to avoid temptation, or even the appearance of it, like going into a single woman's house late at night."

"Good for him," Renata said.

"Hm," Phoebe murmured. Juliette couldn't tell whether it

was a good murmur or a bad murmur.

"So we sat on the front steps and shared a box of Mona's pastries." She didn't tell them about Officer Jarrett. "And we talked about God." She leaned forward, her voice soft. "It was as though Trevor turned on a light and shined it on a completely different picture of God, one I'd never seen before."

No one said anything. They just stared at her as though she'd suddenly grown a third eye. "Stop looking at me like that."

"Sorry," Gia apologized.

"Go on," Phoebe prompted.

Renata's silence carried far more meaning than any words she might utter.

"I've been such a mess lately; because of Mike, yes, I admit. Not because I'm not getting over him, though, but because I was putting my hope in him and our future together. I was putting my hope in the wrong thing. So when we ended, well, my hope kinda ended, too. Like Granny G says, it was like I'd died already but just hadn't had the good grace to lie down somewhere." She smiled tenderly—their grandmother loved her colloquialisms—and continued. "Trevor introduced me to hope again, you guys. Hope in God. I—" She laced her fingers together to keep them from shaking, suddenly nervous about telling them. "I fell in love with Jesus."

Phoebe sat back with shrouded eyes; Juliette recognized the look instantly. It was the same way she used to watch Sharon when her friend's words had been like nails on a chalkboard to her ears. *Oh Phoebe.*

Gia had tears in her eyes as she listened with rapt attention to Juliette's story, but she didn't speak either.

Renata pulled mugs from the cupboard and let them clink loudly on the counter top. Finally, she turned, and pointed an accusing finger at Juliette. "You tricked us. You led us to believe you'd fallen in love with Taz. Or Trevor. Or whatever his name is. You *lied* to us."

Juliette was taken aback. It was remarkable the difference between the ecstatic response she got from Sharon, and the way Renata was reacting. It didn't even appear to register that Juliette was now officially a believer, something Renata had tried convincing them all to become for as long as anyone could remember.

"No, Renata. I never lied. Maybe I manipulated the G-FOURce in my favor tonight, and for that, I'm sorry. But you're missing the point, the amazing, miraculous, wonderful point. I met Jesus on Monday night. Trevor showed me, Rennie! I thought you, of all people, would get it, would be thrilled." She pressed a palm over her heart. "I'm like you now."

Renata smacked her hand on the counter. "You are *nothing* like me, Juliette," she stated between clenched teeth. "You have no clue what it means to live day in and day out as a Christian. You're still high on your come-to-Jesus emotions, and I can't tell what part of the night you liked best; the motorcycle rides, Trevor serenading you, meeting Jesus, or Mona's sticky buns. They were all amazing, according to you." Juliette cringed as her sister's words echoed Officer Jarrett's taunts in her mind.

"Renata Gustafson!" Phoebe interjected, reaching over to cover one of Juliette's hands protectively. "Get a grip, sister!"

"Dixon! My name is Renata Dixon; *not* Gustafson! Why do you people keep calling me that?"

"You people? Do you mean us, your Gustafson sisters?"

Phoebe was standing up now, too, palms flat on the table as she leaned forward. "Listen, Mrs. Dixon. I don't care what you want to call yourself, but you have always been, and will always be a Gustafson girl, got it? That's what binds us together; the fact that we're Gustafsons. It *certainly* isn't because we have anything else in common." She pointed a long, red-nailed finger at Renata. "And that's something *you* make sure none of us forget." She raised her hands in question. "What is wrong with you, Ren? Can't you just be happy for Juliette? So what if you don't like the way she went about telling us her news. Be glad she did tell us at all. I don't think I would have had the guts to face this firing squad."

Phoebe turned to Juliette. "Jules, I, for one, am happy for you. I don't understand it all, and I'm not really sure I want to, but you're absolutely radiant, and I haven't seen you like this in a very long time. Whatever it is that's got you all lit up, I support it. Burn, baby, burn." She sat down abruptly and gulped the last of her ginger ale. Her hands were trembling.

Gia raised her own glass in silent support, and drank her soda until it was gone. Juliette followed suit.

Renata fumed a while longer until the kettle whistled. She turned it off and filled the four mugs with hot water, then delivered one to each sister. She set a basket of assorted teabags in the middle of the table, along with the sugar bowl, the carton of organic whole milk that Juliette loved, and the honey bear. Then she sat down. They fixed their teas in silence.

Juliette finally spoke. "We also need to talk about The Monday ManDates."

There was no rebuttal.

"I'm sorry, but I have hated them from the very beginning. For various reasons, I agreed to go along with the whole plan anyway. I've tried, you guys. I really have. Granted, I didn't give Thera-Paul much of a chance, but I made a valid effort with Frisky Frank, and I certainly invested in Trevor this week. I know you meant well, but I don't want to do it anymore. It's not me." She held up her hand, palm out. "I motion to cancel The Monday ManDates."

There was a brief silence, then Gia raised her hand. "I second the motion. Oogie-boogie."

Phoebe put her hand up. "Oogie-boogie."

They all looked at Renata. Finally, she sighed heavily, and put her hand up, too. "Fine. Oogie-boogie. We can cancel The Monday ManDates."

Juliette closed her eyes in relief. "Thank you," she whispered.

"Now what?" Phoebe eyed Renata, an eyebrow raised in question.

"Why are you looking at me?"

Phoebe shrugged. "I thought maybe you might have a backup plan for getting Juliette married off."

"That wasn't what the intervention was about," Renata snapped. "It was about getting her mind off that idiot ex of hers. Besides," she shot them all a smug look. "It worked, didn't it? She's not pining over Mike anymore."

"Yes, it did work, Ren. So thank you." Juliette lifted her tea in a toast. "Here's to The Monday ManDates Intervention. May it go down in G-FOURce history as an unparalleled success."

The other three joined her in raising their mugs. "Oogie-boogie!"

"So," Gia spoke up. "You really aren't going to see Taz

again? Because I think he's awesome, and I wish you guys could at least be friends."

"We are friends, Gia. In fact, he called me his sister in Christ. Weird thought, isn't it? A brother. I wouldn't know the first thing to do with a brother." She wrinkled her nose. "And actually, I won't be seeing him again for quite a while. Neither will you or Ricky. He's going on some kind of a tour for the next several months."

"Yeah, I know. Cool, huh? I just thought you two would hit it off, and he could leave his heart here with you. Wouldn't that be romantic?"

Renata rolled her eyes, then asked pointedly. "So what's the deal? Is there someone else?"

Juliette took a sip of tea as Officer Jarrett popped into her head. She tried desperately not to blush.

CHAPTER EIGHTEEN

"THERE IS!" Phoebe sat forward, setting her own mug aside. "Look at her! She's blushing!"

"No, no! There's no one, really." Juliette shook her head, her eyes down.

"You're keeping something from us, Jules. You're a rotten liar." Phoebe scrutinized her with narrowed eyes.

Juliette pushed back her chair and stood up, gathering up the teabag wrappers and used napkins scattered around the table.

"Oh, no you don't." Renata reached out and snatched the trash from her hands. "Sit down and give us the scoop. You know we'll find out about him soon enough."

Juliette shook her head. "No, you won't. I doubt you even know him." Then she cringed as she realized what she'd just admitted.

"Ha! I told you!" Phoebe leapt up and spun in a circle, her flowery skirt fluttering around her legs. Gia joined her, and the two of them waltzed around the kitchen together, hooting like children. Renata was grinning, too, and she didn't even roll her eyes at the other girls' antics. Juliette sighed and sank back into her seat in defeat.

"Why do I even let you in my house?"

"Because you love us so much," Phoebe and Gia swept around behind her. "Even Renata." Phoebe planted a kiss on the top of Juliette's head. "And we love you more. Now tell us all about him." She grabbed her chair, dragging it over until she was sitting elbow to elbow with Juliette, and Gia slid back into her own seat, her cheeks flushed from the romp.

All three sisters stared at Juliette, expectant, determined.

"Fine. But you're going to be disappointed," Juliette grumped. "I got pulled over several weeks ago." There was a round of confused glances. "I got a ticket."

"Were you speeding?" Renata asked.

"Yes. Ten miles over the limit."

"And?"

"Then about ten days later, I got pulled over again by the same officer. I made a total fool of myself, and he thought I was a freak, but Sharon talked him out of another ticket, and he let us go with a warning."

"Were you speeding again? You didn't learn from your first ticket?"

"I wasn't speeding, mother." Juliette gave Renata the evil eye over her mug, sipping her hot drink carefully. "I was pretending to drive blind."

Phoebe started to snicker. Then Gia. Then Renata. Finally Juliette joined in too, laughing at her own expense.

"I'm sorry, Jules, but only you would pretend to drive blind." Phoebe wiped her eyes, moist from her laughter.

"So what does this have to do with your new man?" Renata asked when everyone had calmed down. "Wait!" She held up a hand. "The police officer?"

"You fell in love with a cop because he pulled you over twice?" Phoebe elbowed her, but not hard enough to slosh the tea. "Desperate, Jules."

"It's not like that." Somehow, the direction of the conversation was changing, and Juliette felt a little befuddled, not quite sure how to explain her connection to Officer Jarrett. "Someone called the police and sent him over to check on me. He's a friend of Trevor's and—"

"He's been here? Juliette! You have an officer hot on your tail!" Renata laughed at her own joke. No one else did.

Juliette filled them in on the rest of her encounters with Victor Jarrett, and by the end of her story, they were all a little subdued.

"Something must have happened. Guys aren't fickle like we women are. They don't go from being sweet and gentle to mean and rude without a reason." Phoebe shook her head in consternation. "Are you sure you weren't just reading too much into his behavior the other night?"

"No. Even Trevor said it wasn't like him at all. I don't know why it upset me, anyway." Juliette shrugged. "He's not my type at all."

"What do you mean, not your type?" Renata snorted. "I don't think you even know what your type is."

"Well, I knew Frisky Frank wasn't my type. Or Thera-Paul. Besides, I really mean he *can't* be my type. I can't be interested in a police officer."

"Why not?"

"Because his whole life is too unpredictable. I couldn't stand the uncertainty and danger." Juliette straightened in her chair. "So see? It's all worked out for the best. I don't want a police officer anyway."

"Or a Frank. Or a Paul. Or a Trevor." Renata frowned.

"Maybe you should start thinking about what you *do* want, instead of always ruling out what you don't want."

"Let's make a new list!" The suggestion came from Gia, and the other three turned to look at her. "What?" she asked.

"Good idea, Georgia." Renata nodded. "It might benefit all three of you."

"All four of us, lest you get lax in your expectations, and John slacks off," Phoebe teased.

"Not possible," Renata shook her head. "He's perfect in every way."

Now it was Phoebe's turn to roll her eyes. "Oh my. Let's make a list of Mr. Perfect's attributes. Go, Ren."

"Wait!" Gia exclaimed. "What should we call this one?"

Juliette sighed and covered her face with her hands.

"We'll call it The Champion List." Renata tore a page out of her agenda and handed it to Juliette, along with a pen. "Here, Juliette. You write. We're going to find you a new man, yet."

"But I don't need a new man right now!" she wailed.

They decided to make the list anyway. "You'll be ready someday," Renata stated. She started it off with words like loyal, faithful, and committed. Phoebe winked at Juliette and added hot, impulsive, and daring. Gia's first word made them all stop and listen as she explained her contribution.

"Patience is really important to me. I don't want a guy who will push me into things I'm not ready for just because he thinks he's ready. I want my relationship to grow at a pace that lets me learn to really appreciate it. Love needs time to take root and grow strong before it blossoms, right?" When no one responded she tried to further clarify.

"You know Granny G's giant sunflowers? Sometimes one will get planted too close to another one, and it ends up too tall and skinny to support the weight of the flower head at the top. Then it falls over and can't survive. I don't want to be in a relationship like that where all the glory is in the flower, only to have it fall on its face because we didn't put our energy into the roots and stalk first."

Much to Gia's delight, her word had been moved to the top of list. She also added brave and gentle, along with funny and kind.

Although the reason for The Champion List was still a little ambiguous to Juliette, it didn't come with the same pressures of the Monday ManDates, so she stopped arguing and start contributing. She had a few things she would add to it in private; traits her sisters might dismiss, but traits she decided she wouldn't do without in a man. *Believes in God* was going at the very top.

That night as Juliette lay in bed perusing the new list, she admitted that the character qualities were wonderful, but she seriously doubted there existed such a man. No one could be that perfect. Okay. Maybe Trevor Zander was. But if Trevor had the market on perfection, then perfection apparently wasn't what she was looking for. And really, the thought of being with someone so flawless intimidated her.

Sleepy, she lay the list down on her Bible on the nightstand. Reaching over to turn off the light, her eyes fell on the card still propped against the base of her lamp. Officer James V. Jarrett.

She was so confused over the change in his behavior toward her. Before Monday, she might have thought he was a good candidate for their new list, but now she wasn't so sure.

She switched off the lamp and almost turned away, when she realized she could still see his name in the blue glow from the oversized numbers on her alarm clock. She stared at the tiny letters as though the key to his strange behavior might be written there. Victor, not James. Trevor had called him Vic. Vic Jarrett. No, she preferred Victor. Victor Jarrett. Victor and Juliette. Juliette Jarrett.

"James and Juliette Jarrett? Oh no!" She grabbed a pillow and put it over her face.

But the more the names played over in her mind, the more musical they sounded to her ears.

~ ~ ~

IT WAS Monday again, and she couldn't believe how nice it was to have the evening to herself. Juliette had gone to the grocery store on her way home from work and stopped at her favorite little Italian bistro for take-out dinner. She showered, changed into her pajamas and robe, and passed the mirror with only a wave and a light-hearted "Hello, Ducky!" in her best cockney imitation. Her plans included relaxing, eating, watching a little television, and whatever else she could do without moving off the sofa.

Juliette sat down and pulled her tray toward her. On it was her dinner of tortellini pasta in a sun-dried tomato sauce, a chilled bottle of sparkling water, and a huge square of Tiramisu. She was starving.

She unfolded her napkin, picked up her fork, and jumped when someone knocked on her door. She wasn't expecting anyone, and having discovered a darling new BBC sitcom that started in ten minutes, she hoped it was just a case of a wrong address, although she couldn't imagine why anyone would want to visit Mrs. Cork.

Through the peephole, under the glow of her porch light,

she saw a man. He had a freshly-scrubbed look about him, and was obviously nervous; he kept tugging at the tie around his neck and repeatedly smoothing his already slicked-back hair.

"Oh no," Juliette moaned, her thoughts creating a traffic jam inside her head. Was there a Monday ManDate scheduled for today after all? Had she agreed to this? And would he go away if she just ignored him?

No, that would be cruel to the poor man standing outside. Opting for honesty, she opened the door. His uncomprehending look made her feel terrible, but she squared her shoulders and smiled up at him.

"Hello," she said, her voice already laced with apology.

He tugged on his tie and smoothed his hair. "Hello." He cleared his throat. "I'm Tim Larsen. Uh, are you…" he cleared his throat again. "Are you Juliette?" His eyes darted over to the house numbers on the plaque beside her door.

"I am." She smiled weakly, wishing for an easy way out for both of them. "Are you a friend of Renata's?" Wishing for an easy way to mortally wound Renata, too.

"Uh, Renata, yes. And John."

"I'm so sorry, Tim. I'm afraid there's been a mix-up. I wasn't expecting you tonight."

"You weren't expecting me?" He was a big man, quite a bit taller than she was, and he looked nice, albeit ill at ease, in his black pants and pale blue shirt. He wore a lightweight tweed sports coat that made him look almost professorial, but the tie seemed more like a noose than a fashion accessory as he stuck his finger over the knot at his throat and tugged.

"Not tonight, no." She stepped away from the door and indicated her outfit.

"I see."

"I'm sorry," she apologized again. She saw movement at the corner of her eye, and glanced over to see Mrs. Cork come out her front door carrying her dog. She didn't put the fluff-ball down as she usually did, but instead, stood there with her free hand on her hip, watching them. She was not smiling, and she did not return Juliette's polite little wave.

Tim cleared his throat again. "Uh, we have dinner reservations at seven."

"Oh dear. Right. Reservations." What could she say? This was terrible.

"Did I come early? Would you like me to wait?" He reached inside his coat and withdrew a cell phone. "I can call the restaurant and move the reservation back."

"No, Tim." She held up a hand to stop him and apologized yet again. "I'm so sorry. Somehow, somewhere along the line, wires got crossed. I—I'm not prepared to go anywhere tonight."

He had the disconcerting tendency to watch her lips when she spoke, and she resisted the urge to cover her mouth with her hand.

"Okay. I see." She couldn't be certain, but she thought she heard a trace of relief behind the disappointment in his voice. They both stood there for a few more awkward moments, Mrs. Cork unabashedly glaring at them.

In her head, Gia was back with her crickets.

"Well. Uh, I'm…going to go then." He wasn't quite mumbling, but she had to lean forward to hear him. "I'm sorry to have intruded on you like this."

"You didn't intrude. It was just a mix-up." Everything she said sounded placating, rather than comforting.

"Right. A mix-up. Okay." He nodded. "Uh, goodnight." And he turned and made his way down the steps and out to the street where a large black truck was parked. She knew nothing about trucks, but despite its shiny paint job, it looked old, maybe a classic, with its rounded hood and wheel wells, its narrow bed.

She waited until he pulled away before she went back inside, waving once more at her disgruntled neighbor. She wasn't surprised when the woman only scowled in return.

While she waited for her pasta to reheat, she dialed Renata's number. Her sister answered the phone in a distracted manner, obviously in the middle of some family activity.

"Hey, Ren. Do you know a guy named Tim Larsen?"

"Yes. He's one of John's friends. A hunting buddy. How do you—" Then she gasped. "Oh no!"

"Oh yes. He just left my house."

"Oh no!" Renata repeated. "I completely forgot to call him and cancel." She shushed a kid who was trying to get her attention. "What did you say to him?"

"I just told him it was all a misunderstanding. Don't worry. I didn't blame you."

"I can't believe I did that. I need to call him." Renata sounded genuinely worried.

"It's all right, Ren. He'll be fine, I'm sure. He's probably relieved, now that he's seen me in my pajamas." She braced the phone between her shoulder and ear as she pulled her food out of the microwave.

"I told him he had to wear a tie. Did he?"

"He did. But anyone could tell he hated it." Juliette set her hot plate on the tray, turned the television on but kept it muted, and sat down on the edge of the sofa to finish the conversation while the opening credits of her show flashed soundlessly across the screen in front of her. "You should have called him, Ren."

"I know. I blew it. Poor Tim." She paused a moment, then asked, "Are you sure you don't want to go out—"

"No, Renata. Don't even think about it."

A heaviness settled around her shoulders. Why did her sister seem so insensitive to others? Why did she feel like she had to control everyone?

What about her faith? Where did that come into play with her control issues? Juliette always struggled to line up her sister's actions and attitudes with the way her friend, Sharon lived. It was one of the reasons Juliette had such a hard time trusting God; how could He be so different to different people?

Perhaps, though, Renata didn't have it right, in spite of her insistence that she did. Juliette shook her head. It was all still a little confusing to her, this whole Christianity thing, and she certainly wasn't the one to judge her sister who'd been a believer for years.

Another knock interrupted her thoughts. Now what? She got up and headed back to the door, dreading the thought that Tim might have returned.

Officer Jarrett? What was *he* doing here?

CHAPTER NINETEEN

GOOD EVENING, Ms. Gustafson." The officer stood on her front porch looking better than anything her imagination had drummed up over the last week. His hair was uncharacteristically messy tonight, as though he'd run his fingers through it, and the intense look in his eyes made her toes curl inside her socks.

"Officer Jarrett," she said flatly, glad he couldn't read her thoughts.

"We've received reports of suspicious activity in the neighborhood, and I'm here to investigate." He was very serious.

"Really? Should I be worried?"

"I suppose that depends on what's going on. Are you alone?"

"I—I'm sorry? I don't understand."

"Are you alone, Ms. Gustafson?" he repeated, a little louder, a little slower, as though she was hard of hearing, or slightly dense. "Do you have company?" His gaze darted past her shoulder.

"No. It's just me." She reached back and pulled the door

nearly closed behind her, blocking his view into her home. She didn't like the way he was speaking to her, and still feeling a little bruised from his behavior last week, she wasn't going to stand for it again. "What exactly can I do for you?"

He ignored her question and asked one of his own. "Have you had any unwanted or unsolicited visitors lately?"

"What? No." The memory of Mike trying to push through her front door a few weeks ago intruded on her thoughts, but she didn't think that was any of this man's business.

"Are you certain?" His tone irked her.

"I think I would know." Out of the corner of her eye, she could see Mrs. Cork's partially-opened front door and the woman's silhouette back-lit from inside. The dog was yapping away from somewhere behind her. Nosy old poop. Then another thought suddenly took shape.

"Wait. Are you here because of her?" She tipped her head toward her neighbor's place. "Did *she* call you about this supposed suspicious activity?"

He didn't respond.

"Look at her, Officer. Which one of us is behaving more suspiciously?" It had to be. It just *had* to be! "I don't know how long you've been a policeman, but I'm sure you know about busy-bodies, nosy neighbors, and meddling gossips. Well, *that,*" she pointed with an arm fully extended. "Is a prime example of all of the above." She grimaced with satisfaction as Mrs. Cork's door closed abruptly and the dog went silent.

"What is she complaining about? Is that why you were here last week? Because of her?" Her eyes got wide as she put two and two together, and she gasped indignantly, then glared at him with squinted eyes. "You were extremely rude to me that night. You were expecting something very different than what you found, weren't you? Suspicious activity? Ooh!" She stomped her foot. Then her eyes got wider. Her mind was working overtime now, and the pieces were falling into place like the inner workings of a combination lock. "Wait! This is the third or fourth time you've been by to check on me now. It was her all along, wasn't it? She's been calling the police on me!"

He held up a hand, interrupting her rant. "A call from one neighbor asking questions about your integrity is not enough to send an office—"

"Questions about my integrity?" Her voice was rising along with her heart rate and her color, she was certain.

"Please calm down, Ms. Gustafson."

"Calm down?" The condescending jerk! "I'd like to know what I've done to make my neighbor complain!"

When he raised a hand in a calming gesture, she had to resist the urge to smack it away. "In fact, since you're here, maybe I should file a complaint of my own. That woman lets her dog out front without a leash, and I *know* there's a leash law in this town. Then she stands there and watches as the little rat comes over here and dumps on my lawn. She has yet to pick up one pile in the four years I've been living here. Why don't you go harass her?" She knew she sounded vindictive and petty, but she couldn't help it. Something about the way he stood there, watching her come unglued, made her want to lash out at him.

Officer Jarrett referred to his notes again, ignoring her tirade. "The caller," he said, emphasizing the term as though he thought he could convince her of its anonymity. "Reports that there has been a string of strange men in the neighborhood over the last several weeks."

"Strange men? Strange men?" She felt like a parrot. "Could you be more specific? Were they, by any chance, standing on my front porch, holding flowers?" Apparently, Mrs. Cork spent way too much time standing on her own front porch.

"Do you know anything about strange men in the neighborhood?"

"Oh, Officer." She smacked a palm to her forehead, then spoke in a syrupy tone. " I can explain. You see, I've been trying out a new man every Monday night, hoping to find myself a husband." Amazed at how ridiculous the truth actually sounded, she continued, oozing sarcasm with every syllable. "Well, all those men have worn me out, and I needed a rest. I had to send tonight's man away, poor thing." She flapped her hand in the air as if shooing off a fly. "It's just little ol' me and a quiet evening of rest and recovery."

He said nothing, just studied her, his expression unreadable. Juliette could only imagine what was going through his head. She took a deep breath and let it out slowly through her nose. Her shoulders sagged and she leaned her head back against the door jamb, closing her eyes.

"What more do you want from me, Officer Jarrett? It's the truth, okay?" She ran a hand through her untidy hair and opened her eyes to peer up at him, but his head was down now, and his face was in shadows. "My sisters thought I was turning into a weird old maid. They've been setting me up with blind dates over the last couple of weeks. Let's just say it hasn't gone well, not even the night Trevor took me out. But that wasn't *his* fault." She kicked the edge of her doormat in frustration. "No, it was because *you* showed up and insisted on making me feel like a criminal." She turned away to look down the street where she'd last seen Trevor riding off into the night. She wished with all her heart she could be on the back of that bike at this very moment, instead of talking to this insufferable man.

When he still didn't speak, she continued, no longer caring what he thought of her. "I spent way too much time last week trying to figure out what I'd done to make you treat me so unkindly. I get it now. I know your type only too well. I'm just a silly little woman to you, so it's okay for you to think the absolute worst of me. I'm not even worth you giving me the benefit of the doubt, am I?"

Straightening, she brought her gaze back up to meet his. His eyes were still in shadows, but his brow was creased, his mouth tight. "Well, Officer, it's over. No more men. No more blind dates. In fact, no more dates, period. Finished. Done. The end. The fat lady sang, okay? Tonight was just a misunderstanding. My sister forgot to call the next guy on the list and he showed up." She snorted and put a hand up to cover her eyes that were suddenly prickling with unshed tears. "And why, oh *why*, am I telling you this? I sound as pathetic as you think I am."

Spent, her anger having boiled over and evaporated, she asked, "Are you going to arrest me? Or can I go back to my take-out pasta-for-one that's already been microwaved twice?" She rolled her eyes. "At this point, I'll probably die of radiation poisoning before my sisters find me a husband."

Then he grinned. Oh, there it was; that beautiful, heart-stopping smile.

No! She would not respond to it! She glared instead at Mrs. Cork's front porch, wondering if the woman could feel her eyes burning her flesh through the closed door.

"Really? Is all that true?" His voice was surprisingly gentle, and she could hear no trace of mockery in it.

She stood in her doorway, embarrassed by her lack of self-control, demoralized by the circumstances, and pathetic by her own admission. "Would it be possible for anyone to make something like that up?"

"I don't know," he chuckled. "I hear some pretty good stories in my line of work. In fact, I recently pulled over a lady who claimed she was just pretending to be a blind duck driving."

He was trying to be kind. Juliette snorted. "I bet she cried like a baby when that excuse didn't work."

"She did." He nodded sagely. "I must admit, that *was* one of the more terrifying encounters I've had. I even considered therapy after that."

"I bet. She sounds crazy."

Victor cleared his throat. Twice. "My friend said something like that about her. He called her wild." Juliette recoiled at the thought of Trevor talking badly about her. Victor must have noticed her flinch, because he reached out as if to touch her arm, then withdrew his hand quickly. "But in a good way. He calls his bike wild, his parents wild; he even calls God wild."

Juliette smiled up at him in relief, glad he'd explained. "Really? Well, I guess she doesn't sound so bad, after all."

"No. She doesn't sound so bad, after all," he echoed her words, his tone making her blush. "Ms. Gustafson, I owe you an apology." He actually dropped his gaze and stared at his toes for a few moments. He spoke quietly, almost sheepishly. "I have been imagining all sorts of things about you, and apparently, none of it's true. I don't know why I let my thoughts get away from me." He looked up, and waited until she met his gaze again. "My job doesn't allow for assumptions, or snap judgments, yet that's exactly what I've done. Then again," he grinned. "I've never come across someone quite like you before."

She caught herself staring at his mouth the same way Tim Larsen had stared at hers, and she blinked, then darted her eyes over to Mrs. Cork's for something else to look at.

"All kidding aside, I'm sorry. It sounds like you've had quite a month, and I certainly haven't helped. Will you forgive me?" He held out his hand, palm up, as though offering more than just a handshake.

She felt the rush all over again as she placed her hand in his. Solid and gentle, secure and warm, it was all she could do not to close her eyes and sigh. She pulled away as quickly as she could without being rude, uncomfortable by her lack of restraint. She crossed her arms, hugging herself, unaccountably shy now. "I'm sorry, too. I was very rude to you tonight. I think I even stomped my foot at you."

"You did." He chuckled. "Although that was pretty wild."

If she didn't know any better, she might think he was flirting with her. The notion sent a tingle all the way from the top of her head to the tips of her toes, and she quickly changed the subject.

"Poor Mrs. Cork. She probably thought I was running some kind of escort service."

Officer Jarrett looked away, but not before she saw his guilty grin.

"No way! And you believed her?" Juliette clapped her hands gleefully. "No wonder you were so mean to me! You thought I was leading Trevor into debauchery, didn't you!" She started laughing as she recalled the events of the night from this new perspective; the look on Victor's face as he pulled up behind Trevor's bike, his hesitance to even touch her, the stern request for Trevor to call him before he left town. "Did you tell Trevor any of this?"

Victor nodded reluctantly, his mouth a crooked smile. "And he refused to believe you were running any kind of shady operation. He defended you, informed me that I was a blind fool, and called you wild. In that order." His gaze turned serious. "I don't like being called a blind fool, but I only have myself to blame for it."

"It seems that I'm not the only one who's been driving blind around here."

"Ah." He wrapped a hand around the back of his neck and nodded, his smile back. "Touché, Juliette. Well played."

Heat swirled in her belly at the sound of her name on his lips. She smoothed back her hair and tightened the belt of her robe. "I really did plan on a quiet, boring, uneventful night, sitting in front of the television with my bowl of pasta, you know. Nothing seems to go the way I plan these days, but I'm kinda getting used to it." She shrugged resignedly. "I don't mind as much as I used to."

"I'm sorry I kept you from your dinner."

"It's one of those dishes that gets better with age. Kinda like me." His eyebrows shot up and he laughed; she blushed at her forward response. *Stop talking, Jules.*

"Then I'm glad I could be of service to you. Go eat. I've got things under control out here. Suspicious activity eliminated." He actually sounded a bit flustered.

"Thank you," she nodded. "And on behalf of myself and the neighborhood, especially in regards to the preservation of Mrs. Cork's virtue, I thank you too."

"You're welcome, Ms. Gustafson."

"I liked it better when you called me Juliette." It was out before she could catch it.

"Well, then, Juliette, you're welcome." He descended the

three steps on her stoop, then half turned back. "Goodnight, Juliette."

She watched him walk away and knew that Trevor was right. Victor Jarrett was a good guy. The night could have gone a lot differently had he been a man of lesser caliber. He climbed into his car, and she waved as he drove off, the second—and hopefully the last—man she was sending away for the night.

She'd missed her whole episode, but her pasta was surprisingly good.

CHAPTER TWENTY

VICTOR didn't get back to the station until the end of his shift. There'd been a break-in at the local high school, and the security guard managed to catch one of the students responsible for it. Unfortunately, in the scuffle, there were minor injuries, and tempers flared when he and a few other officers arrived on the scene with parents. By eleven o'clock, he was weary of people and their unchecked emotions, and ready to call it a night.

He folded his long legs into the driver's seat of his Camry, a vehicle he was incessantly teased about because of its "married-with-children" status. All he cared about was its "excellent-gas-mileage" and "never-breaks-down-ever" status.

Pulling out of the station parking lot, he let his mind drift back over the evening. Actually, it raced through the evening, straight to Juliette's front door, and stayed there. He smiled at the memory of her clenching her fists and stamping her foot, then poking fun at her own behavior later. His thoughts sobered as he heard the resignation in her voice when she told him about her sisters' plans to get her married off. He shook his head—he could relate to scheming sisters.

And her laugh when she realized he'd thought of her in the worst way possible....

When she laughed at him, however, it didn't feel like when Darlene and Sasha laughed at him. In fact, rather than frustrating him or angering him, which was exactly what his sisters intended, Juliette's teasing made him want to join in, to come up with reasons to keep her laughing. Her eyes sparkled, her nose scrunched up, and she showed all her teeth, something his mother declared to be crass, vulgar.

Victor liked it. He thought it was charming.

The more he thought about it, the more he realized it wasn't just her laughter that charmed him. Juliette came across as an odd combination of vulnerable and brave, of naive and brash, of ridiculous and serious at the same time. He couldn't pin her down, but for some reason, he didn't feel like he had to. In fact, he was beginning to enjoy the surprises that came wrapped up in the package of Juliette Gustafson.

His relief over her explanation of the call-girl accusations was remarkable, considering he already knew in his heart they couldn't be true, and he owed Trevor a real apology. It was Monday night. Even if he had a performance tonight, the musician would surely be done by now.

As he pulled into his driveway, he glanced over at the front door, and saw Juliette standing there in her pink, fuzzy bathrobe. He blinked hard, and she disappeared. He shook his head and scrubbed his eyes with the heels of his hands. Wow. He was really tired.

But the image kept returning, and the more he thought about it, the more he wanted it to be real. Wouldn't it be nice to come home to her standing on his doorstep? Waiting for him with her eyes all lit up in welcome?

"Oh, man. Get it together. She's too unpredictable, remember? And she's got crazy sisters." But his thoughts defied his words, and his heart kept whispering her name. He parked in the garage and went inside, heading straight for the shower. He'd call his friend as soon as he was out.

Trevor answered on the second ring. "Vic! How goes it?"

"Just home from work. And you?"

"Had a great show tonight. Just winding down. What's up?"

"I owe you an apology. My accusation about you and Juliette Gustafson was way off, and I'm sorry. I spoke to her tonight, but I wanted to follow up with you, too."

It's cool, Vic," Trevor replied after a moment of silence. "I'm not sure I understand the whole situation, and I don't really need to. But what about the Big Man? Did you take it to Him, too? You accused one of His girls of some pretty vile stuff."

Victor cringed. No, he hadn't even considered apologizing to God. But when Trevor put it that way, he felt conviction all the way to his toes. "I'll do it as soon as I'm off the phone."

"Nah, let's go together now. Jesus, You're awesome and overflowing with mercy. Please receive my brother's heart."

Victor picked up after a leading silence. "Forgive me for believing the worst of Juliette and Trevor, both. Help me to see people through Your eyes and not my own. Thanks for giving me a friend who will stand beside me even when I'm a fool."

Trevor echoed, "Thank you, thank you, Jesus."

Being friends with Trevor was often a challenge, not because Victor didn't know what to expect from him, but because Trevor's consistency never ceased to surprise Victor. There was no guile in the man. He wore his heart on his sleeve, connected everything back to God, and did so shamelessly. He included prayer in everyday conversation as though Jesus actually stood in their midst.

Victor was much more reserved in all his relationships, particularly with God, but a part of him longed for the authenticity Trevor had. "Thanks. I didn't realize how much I needed that."

"Absolutely." There was a moment of silence, then, "Hey, I know I said I didn't need to understand it all, but this question won't go away. Why were you so willing to believe the worst about little Miss Juliette? It's not like you to pass snap judgments."

The question barreled through him like a freight train, and he resisted the impulse to deny it. He thought for a few more moments before answering. "I'm not really sure, to be honest."

"Okay. Well, what makes you so certain she's telling the truth now that you've talked?" He wasn't going to let this go.

"I don't know. I suppose because I want to believe her."

"So you changed your mind about her because you *want* to? Just like that?"

Victor let Trevor's words sink in. His friend didn't say things just to be cruel, but he did feel like he was being goaded. "Sounds pretty bad, huh?"

"You still sound like a blind fool to me."

"What's that supposed to mean?"

"Look, Vic. Juliette's a good woman. She's desperate for the Lord and has finally let Him in. Maybe she's got you all stirred up because God's using her to do something in you. Don't you think it's odd how often you're being sent to her side? I don't believe in coincidence, my friend. But divine appointments, absolutely. And the fact that she's got you acting like a fool, tells me there may be more to it than just a little life lesson to be learned. I sure didn't turn into a raging idiot when I was around her."

"Hey. I just went from blind fool to raging idiot. And who says I'm all stirred up?"

"And back to blind fool again," Trevor chuckled. "Dude. I've known you for more than ten years, and I've never seen you stirred up like you are now over any woman. Not even Amanda."

"So cut to the chase," Victor grouched, not wanting to discuss his ex-girlfriend. His pride was still recovering from her rejection. "What are you saying?"

"Go back to the King, Vic. Find out what He wants from you. Seems to me He's hooking the two of you up. Maybe you should consider it."

"Are you playing matchmaker?"

"Call it what you like. This may be a home-run for you, dude. You might want to pick up the bat and jump in the game before God sends someone else along to take your place."

"What on earth does all that mean?" Victor's impatience was quickly turning to frustration. "I hate analogies."

"Fine." Trevor yawned over the phone. Victor tried not to be offended any more than he already was. "You want my advice? Ask her out."

"What?" Victor's voice actually cracked on the word, and he heard Trevor chuckle.

"Pray about it first. Then ask her out. Divine appointment."

~ ~ ~

IT WAS like discovering a long lost treasure in the book she held in her hands. Juliette poured over the Bible in every spare moment, more and more able to understand what she was reading. The New Testament was full of letters to the early churches teaching them how to love God and live as Christ-followers, and she was amazed at how timeless the advice was, applicable to this modern day, to her own life.

She read about Jesus, as told by His followers, and wondered what it must have been like to witness the radical Christ in person. Would she have believed back then, or would she have thought He was a rabble-rouser and an upstart, too?

She tried to decipher the stories of warfare and plunder, of kings and queens, and the adventures and misadventures of the people of Israel in the Old Testament, but it was often overwhelming.

"It'll happen, Juju. The Bible isn't going anywhere anytime soon." Sharon assured her that God understood, and was making things clear to her a little at a time.

Juliette went to church on Sundays with Sharon and Chris, hanging on the words taught from the pulpit. Sometimes she even went on Saturday night, even though she knew the same message would be preached the next morning. She always got something new out of it. It had only been a month, and she couldn't get enough.

It was Saturday, and her plans to go to church that evening gave her the courage to make the overdue phone call to Mike. Although she felt it necessary to follow through with it, she'd put it off yet again. She didn't want to think about him at all.

In fact, the only man she wanted to think about was Officer Jarrett. She could close her eyes and see him standing on her front step, thumbs in his pockets, grinning down at her, making her feel like they were the only two people in the whole world. And the memory of his deep voice saying, 'Goodnight, Juliette,' still sent shivers down her spine.

Just a few weeks ago, she'd practically hated the man. Now she was mooning over him like a sick puppy because he'd smiled at her, and said her name. More than once, she'd even contemplated what kind of petty crime she might commit so she could call the cops on herself. Without risking going to jail, of course.

"You really are pathetic, Jules," she muttered. But call Mike, she must, and that meant thinking about him, instead of the man in the dark blue uniform.

Her hands were shaking, but she was curiously relieved when Mike answered. He seemed eager to have dinner with her until she explained the circumstances under which they would be meeting. He accused her of trying to manipulate him, and she tried to explain her motives.

"I don't want us to have this ugliness between us. We don't have to be friends, Mike, but I don't want to leave things unresolved. We spent too many years together to walk away angry."

"Then don't walk away at all. I don't want to have dinner with your friends; I want to have dinner with you." His voice became softer, cajoling, the way it used to when he wanted something from her. "Come on, Julie. Let's start fresh, okay? You're right. We need to talk, but just you and me."

"Mike, I'm not coming back. That's not why I called you."

"You're being selfish now. I know what makes you happy, and I already love you like no one else can," he declared, as if mere words could change her mind.

"Don't do this. Please." The conversation was moving in a direction she wasn't prepared to go without some support. When he said things like that, she could feel the ground give a little beneath her feet. "I know you'll find your way, and that you'll make a terrific dentist. I'm sure whatever job you get will be just exactly what you deserve. You've worked so hard, and I'm proud of you for all you've accomplished." As she said the words, she realized a huge part of her actually believed what she was saying. She *was* proud of him and his determination and his zeal.

There was a much smaller part of her that was curled up in a miserable little ball of regret over the way things were between them, over what would never be. "I also believe that the right woman is out there, waiting for you to be the right man for her. But it's not me." Her voice caught a little on the words. "Things have really changed for me, and we're going in very different directions now." She took a steadying breath. "What we had isn't enough for me anymore."

"Not enough for you? What do you mean? I have a great career and can offer you a lifestyle far beyond your wildest dreams. A home, closets full of clothes and shoes, vacations, even kids, if you really want them. Anything you want, Julie. How can it be not enough?"

As Mike listed all the things he had to offer, her stomach began to churn. He sounded like he was trying to bribe her into coming back to him. "Do you believe in Jesus?" she whispered when he'd finished.

There was silence on the other end of the line, but she didn't try to fill the empty air space. Finally, he spoke, his venomous voice searing the newly exposed places in her heart. "Jesus, huh? You couldn't find a real man to replace me with, so you opted for an imaginary one?"

Juliette pulled the phone away from her ear for a moment; his blasphemous words repulsing her spirit. "Wow, Mike. I'm not even going to be offended by that, because I don't think you understand what you're saying."

He grunted derisively but didn't speak.

"I…wish this had gone differently. I was hoping…well, I have to go now."

He laughed cruelly. "Do you have a date? Are you going out with Jesus?"

"Actually," she smiled at his question, an inner joy she couldn't explain deflecting his verbal attack. "I am. I'm going to church tonight."

The silence at the other end of the line was different, empty, and she knew before she looked at her screen, that he'd already hung up.

Well, she'd kept her cool and hadn't attacked him, even when he tried to goad her into a fight. "Thank you, Jesus," she murmured. She thought of something Trevor had said. "I hope I made You proud."

CHAPTER TWENTY-ONE

BY THE time she was ready for church, Juliette was late, but she had no one to make excuses to, so she went anyway. Tiptoeing in, she sat in the first empty seat she came to. She tucked her purse under the chair in front of her and glanced down at the Bible on her lap. It was becoming her most faithful companion. She carried it everywhere, even to places where she knew she wouldn't be reading it, but she found comfort in just knowing it was at hand.

The music was loud tonight, and she liked it that way. She was still learning the songs that everyone else seemed to know, but she followed along the best she could. With the volume up, she could sing out loud, and not worry about disturbing anyone else's worship.

As soon as Pastor Eric began to speak, Juliette knew he was speaking directly to her. "You've heard it before; forgive and forget someone who has done us wrong. But no! That's not what the Scriptures tell us. In Luke 6:27, Jesus tells us we are to love, and forgive, and to *pray* for those who do us wrong, who hate us. How can you pray for someone you've forgotten? No matter how much we think a person may deserve it, we are not to condemn anyone to a life of misery. Jesus knew what He was saying when He put all three action steps in the same statement. Love, forgive, pray. In order to love your enemy, you must forgive your enemy. In order to forgive your enemy, your heart must be changed toward him or her. In order to have a changed heart, you must ask God to do a work in you. And guess what? That means prayer."

Juliette felt utterly convicted and she was struggling to understand why. Tears slipped unchecked down her cheeks as she sat in stillness, her head bowed during the closing prayer. Why did Pastor Eric's message make her heart ache so badly? Was she still harboring unforgiveness toward Mike? She shook her head at the thought, certain she was truly free of the anger she'd felt just a few short weeks ago. Granted, before tonight's message, she'd hoped to be able to forgive and forget Mike, but she was okay with forgiving and forgetting what he had done to her instead, and praying for his heart.

"What am I not getting?" she whispered. In her mind she heard Trevor adamantly urging her to give God her hidden and chained up places. "Please show me, Lord. Walk through these air-tight rooms with me."

Juliette stayed seated as people made their way out of the sanctuary and off into the night. She sat, head down, focusing intently on the tips of her shoes. "Oh Lord. Help me. I can't do this alone. I feel so alone," she whispered.

"Excuse me." For a moment Juliette thought she was going to be asked to leave, or to make way, but then she recognized that voice. "Juliette?"

She couldn't look at him. She didn't want him to see her like this, all tear-stained and weak again. She slumped even lower in her seat, wishing she could vanish into thin air.

~ ~ ~

VICTOR noticed her the moment she slipped in the back door of the church. He had just turned to say something to his friends who were sitting in the row behind him, and stopped abruptly when he recognized her tiptoeing in. He couldn't stop staring; what was she doing here?

When he broke off mid-sentence, Michelle turned to see what had distracted him. "Who is that?" she whispered, elbowing her husband, Tom, to make him look, too.

Victor was a part of Tom Peterson's discipleship group, and the three of them had become good friends over the years. Between the Petersons, Taz, and a handful of other friends he'd made since moving to Midtown, Victor had found a new family.

Michelle Peterson certainly treated him like a kid brother. She teased him mercilessly about women, or the lack thereof, in his life, and no one was more thrilled for him than she, when he and Amanda started seeing each other. She and Tom took them under their wings, spending time with them, getting to know the woman he'd finally chosen to date.

So when he showed the older couple the ring he'd purchased for Amanda, Michelle surprised him with her questions. She didn't ask him if he was sure it was what *he* wanted, but if he was sure it was what Amanda wanted.

When he informed them the next day that Amanda had turned him down, Michelle shook her head sadly, but she obviously wasn't surprised. Victor took it all in stride, chuckling humorlessly. "Funny thing is, I would have been just fine with her boredom. Beats drama any day."

"Ahem!" Michelle cleared her throat from behind him.

"Vic?"

He blinked hard and turned back to her, a schooled blank look in place. She eyed him sharply; he hoped he wasn't blushing. "What?"

"You were saying?" she prompted.

"Um...." He looked right at her, but his thoughts were already back on Juliette.

"Oh, never mind, you big lug. But you've got some 'splainin' to do after the service."

Victor's thoughts were all over the place. Did she attend church here? Why didn't Trevor tell him? Was this one of those divine appointments his friend had talked about? Was he supposed to ask Juliette out tonight?

The idea settled on him like a warm blanket. Yes, tonight. Tonight he would speak with her. Tonight he would take the step his heart had urged him to take since the first night he'd stood on her doorstep, Juliette dressed in that ridiculous pink bathrobe, threatening to kill her sister.

She'd paraded right past him, a divine appointment if he'd ever seen one. Tonight was definitely the night.

He stole glances at her during the rest of the music, grinning when he realized she was singing her heart out and hardly knew the music. He almost thought he heard her at one point, when the worship leader changed keys and moved right into the next song.

Every time he looked at her, he felt confirmation about pursuing her. She seemed so genuine, so sincere in her offering. Watching her worship reminded him of a conversation between him and Michelle about women doing everything in groups. She laughed and told him he'd never really understand the psychology of it because he was a man, but to pay attention when a woman did something on her own. "If she's not waiting for an entourage of friends, then it's something really important to her, and you'd better take note of it."

But halfway through the message, he saw her tears. At first it was only a few slipping down her cheeks; then she was crying for real, crumpled tissues in her clenched fists. He felt helpless sitting there, watching her weep. He couldn't just get up and cross the aisle to her; that would be presumptuous of him. Besides, she might not want his attention.

"Just give me the facts, Friday." Michelle poked him in the shoulder when the service was over.

"I...I don't know much about her, to be honest. She's a fairly new believer, I think." He stumbled over his words, quickly categorizing what little he did know about her. University job, interfering sisters, best friend named Sharon, PT Cruiser. It was all the facts, but none of those things really said anything about Juliette. "Taz likes her," he finally said, rather lamely.

"Trevor? As in, he *likes* her, likes her?" Victor couldn't help grinning at the juvenile phrase coming out of his friend's mouth.

"I don't think so," he said. "He told me to ask her out."

"What?" Michelle's tone was incredulous. "He *told* you to ask her out? Who *is* she?"

"Her name is Juliette. She went out with him a few weeks ago, and I guess he thinks pretty highly of her."

"But what does any of this have to do with you? How do you know her? I can see that you're...interested."

"Michelle thinks you *like* her, like her." Tom, always quick with the one-liners, interjected with a chuckle.

"Let's just say that I...uh...met her on the job. Which

means mine may not be her first choice of shoulders to cry on, and I think she might need that right now." He turned back to watch her again, suddenly worried that someone else might sweep in and offer her comfort.

"Victor Jarrett, what are you not telling me?" Michelle eyed him, head tilted. "I'm getting the feeling yours are *exactly* the shoulders she needs right now, and you're the resistant one, not her." She turned to her husband beside her. "Help me here, Tom."

The older man rubbed his chin and eyed Juliette. "Do you think your friend would like to join us for pie?"

"Tom! What kind of help is that?" Michelle elbowed him. "She's not a man. Food isn't always the answer."

"I was actually thinking about asking her to join us when I saw her come in. But not now." Victor shook his head. "She's crying."

"So? Everybody cries in church sometimes." Tom winked at his wife.

"Absolutely," chimed in Michelle. "And there's nothing to be ashamed of when you do."

"You might want to reassure her of that," Tom prodded, thrusting a chin in Juliette's direction.

"Me?" Victor shook his head again. Dealing with crying women while on the clock was a piece of cake. There were no strings attached, no ulterior motives, only that of restoring order. Off the clock was a whole different story. "I'm not so good with tears. Or women." After a brief pause, he admitted, "Especially *that* woman."

"Maybe you should learn to be," Michelle said around a curious grin.

Tom wasn't going to let this one go either. "A woman needs to know her man isn't going to be embarrassed of her tears." He slid a protective arm around his wife's shoulders. Michelle smiled and nodded, her eyes warm and tender.

"Her man?" Aghast now, Victor stared at them both. "Uh, I'm not *her* man."

"*A* man, then," Tom corrected. "A woman needs to know—"

"I got it the first time. But I don't think I'm that man right now. And I doubt she wants to go out for pie, either. At least not tonight."

"Nothing wrong with tonight. I'd like to meet her." Tom spoke nonchalantly, but Victor heard the challenge in his voice.

"Tonight isn't the night," he reiterated firmly, ignoring the little voice in his head that was trying to remind him of his earlier decision; *tonight is the night!* "Don't push it, Tom."

It was the tears. He hated it when his mom and sisters used their tears to get what they wanted from people, and he could feel a building resistance toward Juliette as long as she kept crying. Unlike Darlene's or Sasha's, he thought hers were genuine, but it still elicited the same response in him; to push her away.

"She needs a shoulder before she needs pie," Michelle stated, her brow furrowed.

"I agree." Victor crossed his arms. "That's why I'm recruiting you."

"A man's shoulder. A man's strength." Now Michelle was getting pushy.

"How do you know she hasn't got a man already?"

"Because she's sitting in church alone and crying, Victor!" Michelle wasn't joking any longer. "If she had a man—a good one—he'd be sitting there with her, and she'd be crying on *his* shoulders."

He glared at his friends; they stared back with their own stony challenge.

"Oh, good grief! I'll go talk to her!" He thrust himself up out of his seat.

Tom stood up, too. "Come on, Michelle. We'll wait for Vic and—what's your friend's name?"

"Juliette," Victor growled.

"Juliette. We'll wait for you two out front." He tipped his head toward the woman across the aisle. "Take your time. We're in no hurry."

And now, here he stood, awkwardly hovering over Juliette, not sure what else to say to her. His formal 'excuse me' had been pitiful at best, and he was pretty sure her silence meant that she wasn't very excited to see him.

"I'm not trying to be nosy," Victor began. He slid into the seat beside her and stared straight ahead, trying to figure out how to not embarrass either one of them any more than he already had. "I just want to make sure you're all right."

"I'm fine," Juliette sniffed, holding her soggy tissue to her nose. "I'm just a little emotional. But I guess you figured that out already."

"That's all right. Everyone cries in church sometimes. It's nothing to be ashamed of." He cringed as he heard Tom's words come out of his own mouth. Grasping at straws.

"I'm not really ashamed of crying," she muttered. "Only of being *seen* crying."

"Oh." What does one say to that?

"I'll let you sit there if you don't look at me, okay?"

Victor chuckled, relief flooding through him. Humor. This he might be able to handle. "I promise not to look at you." After a pregnant pause, he continued. "Is there anything I can do to help?"

"No. Yes. I mean, probably not." She sighed. "I don't know."

"I see." Although he didn't. At all. "Well, why don't we start with the 'yes' part."

"Okay. I could use some dry tissues, but I don't want to go out there where everyone will stare at me."

"That, I can do for you." Easy enough. "I'll be right back. Don't go anywhere." He stood up and stepped out into the nearly empty aisle, then paused. "Would you...would you rather talk to a woman? I can send one of my friends—"

"That's all right," she interrupted him. "I'm already embarrassed enough. At least this is nothing new for you." She still held the tissue to her nose but did finally look up at him. "But could you hurry? It's like someone turned on a faucet in here."

He found Tom and Michelle waiting for him in the foyer as promised, chatting with a few other couples. He pulled Michelle aside. "Hey. It may be a while. You don't have to wait. I, uh, have to get back." He felt like a schoolboy, trying to come up with excuses to justify staying behind with her. "She needs some tissue."

"Don't be silly. We'll wait." Michelle's eyes were sparkling with humor. She poked him in the chest. "Because I want to know what's going on, and why you haven't said anything about her before tonight."

Victor grinned self-consciously. "There's nothing to tell." He turned to go, but threw a quick glance back over his shoulder at her. "Yet."

He grabbed a box of tissue off the information counter and hurried back inside. He slowed as he approached Juliette, his chest tightening at the sight of her hunched figure sitting so forlornly in her seat. There were very few people left in the sanctuary; they might not have a lot of time, but at least they had some privacy.

"Here you go," he said, dropping into the seat beside her again. She took several tissues from the box he offered her and held them up to her face.

"Will you please go...somewhere else?" Her voice was muffled behind her hands, but he understood her words perfectly, slightly taken aback.

"Oh. Sure." He began to rise, but she reached out to stop him.

"I'm sorry. That sounded awful. I didn't mean for you to *leave,* leave. I just need a moment of privacy, if you don't mind. At least let me blow my nose without you in ear shot. And don't watch. In case 4-ply isn't thick enough and I have a blow-out or something."

By the time she was done explaining herself, Victor was smiling. "Of course. I forgot about the not looking thing." He glanced around, momentarily at a loss. "Okay. I'll go wait for you in the foyer. There's no hurry, just come out when you're ready." He tucked the tissue box into the seat he'd vacated and headed back up the aisle.

CHAPTER TWENTY-TWO

AS SOON as his back was turned, Juliette scrounged around in her purse for a mirror. The guy was staying to talk to her—to her!—and she could not face him with swollen eyes, streaked mascara, and a drippy nose.

"Oh no!" she wailed when she saw her tiny reflection. She fanned her face with the bulletin, willing her swollen lids to deflate. "Please, oh, please unpuff!" she pleaded, alternating between patting and fanning and staring mournfully at her distorted features.

Five minutes passed, then ten, and the longer she stared at herself in the mirror, the more convinced she became that she could not go out there and face him again. Maybe if she hid in here long enough, he'd get the hint and go home.

"Excuse me." This time it was a woman's voice breaking into her thoughts. She looked up and smiled at the stranger, trying to act natural. "Juliette?"

"Yes."

"I'm Michelle. I'm a friend of Victor Jarrett's. I just want to make sure you're okay."

"Oh. Well." So much for taking a hint. Juliette just

shrugged.

"I see." Michelle slipped into the row of seats in front of Juliette and turned around to face her.

Finally, Juliette sighed and said, "Would you mind doing me a huge favor? Do you mind letting Officer...Victor know that I'm okay, but that I'm just going to hide out in here until he's gone?" She snorted. "I'm not really good company right now!"

Michelle smiled broadly, apparently enjoying Juliette's transparency. She paused only incrementally, then reached over the seat back and placed a hand on Juliette's knee. "Listen, Juliette. I'm going to be a meddling busybody, but I think you should know that Vic couldn't keep his eyes off you the whole service. I don't think he's going to agree to that."

Juliette's belly flip-flopped, half in happiness, half in despair. He'd been watching her throughout the whole service? But that meant he'd witnessed her embarrassing breakdown, too.

And he came to her rescue anyway.

He didn't run.

"You know, most men would have ducked out the back door once the tears started," Michelle said, as though reading her thoughts.

Juliette sighed. "I know. But, look at me. How can I face him looking like this?"

"He's already seen you, though." Michelle looked a little bemused.

"I know!" Juliette wailed, putting her face in her hands. "This is how he always sees me! I think I've cried every time he's been around! Just once—once!—I'd like to look all put together around him, not soggy and..." She looked up forlornly, her gray eyes tearing up again. "Psycho."

"Psycho? Goodness, it can't be that bad."

"You have no idea," she retorted, but didn't expound.

Michelle reached over and patted Juliette's knee again. "Listen. Why don't you take a few more minutes, and I'll take Vic out to the parking lot to wait for you. Moonlight softens everything, even tear-stained cheeks."

"What if I sneak out the back door?"

Michelle grinned as she stood to go. "I'll just send the cops looking for you. I've got connections, you know."

Now Juliette smiled too.

~ ~ ~

THEY WERE waiting, just as Michelle promised, out in the parking lot, strategically positioned between lamp posts where the light was lowest. Juliette had a brief moment of panic and actually considered making a run for it and never coming back to this church again. But then she'd have to explain to Sharon and Chris, and they'd make her come back anyway. Might as well get the humiliation over with. She approached them quietly, her fingers locked around her Bible in an attempt to quell their shaking.

"Hi." Her voice cracked with nervousness, and Victor, who'd been listening intently to something Tom was saying, jerked his head up, and turned his gaze on her. He took a quick step toward her, then stopped.

Michelle had no such reservations and hurried to her side, slipping an arm through Juliette's, drawing her into the circle. "Perfect timing. The boys were just getting into an argument about cars."

"Juliette, is it? I'm Tom, Michelle's husband." The older

man stuck out a hand and shook hers warmly.

"Nice to meet you. I'm Juliette. Hi…uh, Victor."

"Juliette." It was just her name, but there were a hundred unspoken words crammed into that single sound. It made her want to sigh, and smile, and cry again, all at the same time.

"Okay, you two." Michelle spoke into the electric silence, her voice offering a firm footing under Juliette's shaky legs. "Would you like to join us for pie and coffee?"

"I…I don't know if I'm up for going out in public tonight." She'd thought through this before coming out. "Can I take a rain check though? I do like pie."

"Of course. I'll hold you to that. Victor?"

"Actually, I…" He glanced over at Juliette.

"I'm fine, Off—Victor. You go have pie." Juliette could tell he was waffling because of her.

"No." He shook his head. "I mean, I— "

"Spit it out, man." Tom thumped him on the back, grinning broadly, and Juliette bit down on her bottom lip when she saw Victor's blanched face.

"I'd really like you to come, Juliette." He hadn't come any closer, standing three feet from her with his thumbs hooked into his pockets, but his words seemed to cross the space between them, wrapping themselves around her.

Michelle jumped in. "Here's an idea. We can get pie to go and take it back to our place."

"I suppose that would be okay." On the spot, Juliette couldn't figure out how to back out gracefully at that point. "Do you live close by? I'd like to stop by my place first. Freshen up a little, if that would be okay."

"Actually, Tom and Michelle live only a few blocks away from your neighborhood." Victor was studying her, a question in his eyes.

"We do? That's perfect! Why don't you stop by your house, drop your car off, and Vic can pick you up from there. We'll get the pie and meet you two back at our place in about a half an hour. Will that work?"

"I can do that," Victor agreed. Juliette nodded, feeling a little short of breath, and she didn't think it was all because of her terribly stuffed up nose.

"Perfect. And when you get to our place, you can explain to me why you, sir, know where this young lady lives." Michelle winked at Juliette and took her husband's hand. "One French Silk and one Key Lime pie coming up. Any objections?"

"Nope."

"Sounds delicious," Juliette agreed.

"Are you sure you're okay with this?" Victor asked quietly, once the older couple was out of hearing.

"It's fine," she replied. "Especially since I can go home first and make myself a little more presentable. You don't need to pick me up, though; I can drive myself. If you give me the address, I'll meet you there."

"But I'd like to pick you up." He said it quietly, but it sounded to Juliette like he really meant it.

"Oh. Okay. Well, that would be nice." She smiled shyly and turned away. "Um, I guess you know where I live."

"Where are you parked?" Victor scanned the parking lot for her little PT Cruiser. "I'll walk you to your car."

When he fell in step beside her, Juliette felt a smile tugging at the corners of her mouth. Things were turning out far differently than she'd imagined when she'd decided to attend church that evening. The parking lot was large, and the elongating silence between them made them both begin talking at the same time.

"So how long have you been coming to church here?"

"Have you been a policeman for a long time?"

"You go first," Victor laughed, reaching over to place a hand on her back as he steered her between two vehicles. How different the careful weight of his palm felt compared to Frisky Frank's octopusing fingers. It was the first time he'd intentionally touched her, other than a handshake, and she secretly hoped it wouldn't be the last.

"I just started coming here about a month ago. In fact, I just started coming to church, period. My friend, Sharon, the one you met when you pulled us over, this is where she and her husband go, so this was the obvious choice for me. I usually come with them on Sunday mornings, but I needed to be here tonight." She tucked a strand of hair behind her ear and glanced up at him. "It hasn't been an easy Saturday for me."

"I'm sorry. Is there anything I can do to help?" His voice was gentle, sincere, attentive.

You can marry me. The thought startled her so that she stumbled, and he reached out to steady her. This time, his hand lingered a little longer.

"You're doing it now," she said, referring in part to his palm sending a delicious current up and down her spine. "Thanks for not letting me go home to drown my misery in a tub of chocolate ice cream."

"My pleasure. The misery part, not so much the ice cream. Especially since there's probably ice cream involved anyway, if I know Tom. And I've been on the police force in this town for twelve years." He changed subjects so seamlessly that it took a moment for her to remember that she'd asked him about his work.

They arrived at her car, and she dug in her purse for her keys. "That's a long time. Do you like it? I mean, is Midtown a good place to be a policeman?"

"The salary isn't great for Southern California, but the benefits are. I like what I do, I like the folks I work with, and I like this town. That's worth far more to me than a couple extra bucks on my paycheck."

"So are you the good cop or the bad cop?"

"You'd have to endure the hot seat to find that out." She could hear the smile in his voice.

"Actually, I think I've already been on the hot seat with you. Let me just say that the verdict on you is still out." She turned and looked up at him just before unlocking her car door. "I think I'm going to enjoy listening to you try to explain how you know me to your friends."

"Yes. That. Maybe we should compare stories first?" He reached out and opened the door for her.

"No way! You're on your own, Officer." She slid into her seat and dropped her purse and Bible on the passenger side floor. "These are your friends. I'm just showing up to defend myself, should you try to throw my fuzzy pink duck butt under the bus."

"What is it with you and ducks?" He asked, bemusedly, peering down over the open door at her.

"Ah." She clambered back out, stood straight, and gestured at her turned out toes. "Ducky."

He laughed, and waited until she was comfortable behind the wheel before closing the door. Then he headed back the way they'd come, his long legs quickly covering the distance to his own car.

She sat still for several moments, both hands wrapped around the steering wheel, just breathing, willing her heart to slow its pace. Could this really be happening? Was this a kinda-sorta date? Did he ask her out tonight? Or was it the Petersons' idea? Did she dare get excited?

Unable to contain it all, she let out a tiny "Squee!" Turning the key in the ignition, she murmured, "Okay, God. Whatever this is, *help!"*

She pulled into her garage, waited for the door to close completely, just as her grandfather had taught them, before heading inside. She'd just dropped her purse and Bible onto the kitchen table when she heard the knock on her front door.

Opening the door wide, she found Victor standing on her doorstep, grinning down at her, looking just the way she'd imagined him over the last several weeks. Except tonight, he wasn't in uniform. And he looked even better not in uniform, she decided. The pine green, long-sleeved shirt he wore followed the contours of his torso. Chest. Definitely more chest than vest. Closing her eyes briefly to curtail her wayward thoughts, she stepped back and held a hand aloft. "Do you want to come in? I just need a minute."

He stepped inside, and her entry instantly shrunk.

"Please make yourself comfortable," She pointed into the living room before hurrying down the hall toward her bedroom.

~ ~ ~

VICTOR could hardly believe he was standing inside Juliette's home. Over the last few weeks he had waited in vain for a call that would send him here again, but Mrs. Cork seemed appeased by the cessation of Juliette's blind dates. He still felt like a stalker as he slowed his car in front of Juliette's condo while driving his route, hoping to catch her coming or going. Once, he'd made eye contact with Mrs. Cork, who was out front. She'd quickly scooped up her unleashed dog and waved. But now, here he was, inside, at her invitation, not on the job.

"Lord, help me not to make a fool of myself tonight." His muttered prayer was heartfelt. He hadn't planned any of this, and he wasn't accustomed to winging things, especially when it came to relationships, and in particular, relationships with women.

He glanced around, appreciating her simple, sensible furnishings. There were a few feminine touches of color and texture here and there, and the books on her shelves were definitely not what he would read, but all in all, he liked how comfortable he felt in her home. The walls were painted a soft caramel, the furniture in varying shades of earth tones, and the lighting was pleasant; soft, but not too dim. The bookcase and picture frames matched, all painted a low-sheen black.

He peeked into her kitchen, his appreciation growing. There were a few dishes in the sink, and her coffee pot still had the remains from earlier in the day. A soup pot was upside down on a towel beside the sink, evidence she'd recently cooked something. He was glad to see she used her kitchen, unlike so many single people he knew. Amanda, as gracious as she was, hated to cook, and she referred to her kitchen as the room where she kept the refrigerator and microwave. Juliette's refrigerator was covered in magnets, photos, and handwritten notes.

"I'm ready," Juliette said from the doorway, startling him. He turned; embarrassed that she'd caught him wandering.

"I'm sorry. I didn't mean to snoop."

"I told you to make yourself at home, Officer. Besides, I have nothing to hide," she quipped, spreading her arms wide. "No illegal gambling club, no hotbed of iniquity, no secret smuggling ring. What you see is what you get."

"Well, if it makes any difference, I like what I see." He meant it, too. He liked what he'd seen of her little home, but he also liked seeing her in it. He could hardly tell she'd been crying. Her eyes were bright, her cheeks flushed, and she had put some shiny stuff on her lips that made him notice how pretty they were. Her hair was swept up in a clip at the back of her head, leaving her long neck exposed, and she wore all black, except for a silver choker encrusted with chunky stones, all blues and greens, making her eyes look like deep waters. His gaze drifted back to her lips and stayed there.

"What?" she asked, bringing a hand up to her mouth. "Is there lipstick on my teeth?"

"No." He reached over and drew her hand away from her face, letting her fingers slip slowly through his. He saw something in her eyes, a flicker of uncertainty. "No, Juliette, your lipstick is perfect." He suddenly wanted to taste those lips; to kiss the shimmery pink right off of them. He had to stop looking at her mouth. He had to get out of her house. Now. "You look…great." *Edible.* "Let's go eat some pie."

He waited while she locked up, noticing the slight tremble of her hands, and he wondered—hoped—it was in reaction to his touch, because he was certainly a little shaken up himself. His eyes drifted along the curve of her neck, and he thought he could see her pulse fluttering in the hollow just above her collarbone. His fingers ached to touch her there, and he swallowed hard.

He felt like a live wire around her. Every sensation was

heightened, standing this close to her. He could smell her hair, the soft floral fragrance she wore. He could hear her shallow breaths, even though the sound of his own heartbeat thundered in his ears. And he couldn't stop looking at her, her skin, her eyes, her mouth, the slope of her shoulder, the arch of her back where he wanted to test the fit of his hand again.

Shake it off, man. Slow down.

But he rested his hand on her back anyway as they walked down the sidewalk to his car. Perfect fit. Even the way his fingers curved toward the indentation of her waist was just right, as though his hand belonged there. He held the door for her, and hurried around to his side.

Ten minutes later, they were pulling up in front of the Petersons' home.

CHAPTER TWENTY-THREE

THEY SAT around the square dining room table, having indulged in pie, ice cream, and too much coffee, while Victor regaled them with his version of how he and Juliette met. He described pulling her over, not once, but twice in so many weeks, and when he teased her about quacking at him the second time, she explained her recent duck obsession to all of them, right down to the fuzzy, pink bathrobe part.

"It's my favorite outfit on you," Victor remarked. Juliette rolled her eyes.

"Only because it's practically the only outfit you've ever seen me in."

Beneath the table Victor's knee kept bumping hers, and she thrilled at the sensation that swept through her every time it did. She wondered if she'd be able to stand on her own two feet by the time the evening was over. Perhaps she'd just float instead.

"Aren't you glad we didn't let you talk us into leaving you at church?" Michelle toyed with her fork, making swirling designs in the remains of the chocolate mousse on her plate.

"I was pretty pitiful, wasn't I, all curled up in a fetal position, crying like a baby."

"Church is a good place to cry, Juliette." Victor reached over to brush her cheek with the back of his fingers. She froze at his unexpected gesture, and a brief silence fell around the table.

"Okay, then." Michelle laughed and pushed her chair back, preparing to rise. "I think I'll wash up these dishes."

"Oh! Let me help," Juliette said, pushing her own chair back. Her heart was pounding in her chest, her cheek felt singed where he'd touched her, and she could tell by the look on his face, that he was just as startled as she was over his caress. Michelle carried the pies, while Juliette gathered up the plates and forks and took them to the sink. She was glad to put a little space between her and Victor. She needed to catch her breath.

"So Juliette," Tom called from the table. "Victor tells us you have sisters."

The sink was in the kitchen island, so she stood facing the men while she rinsed the dishes. "I do. Three of them. I'm the oldest, then there's Renata, Phoebe, and Gia, in that order."

"Any brothers?"

"No brothers. Just us Gustafson girls."

"Hear that, Vic?" Tom raised his wiry brows at his friend. "Victor here is afraid of sisters. Especially his own."

"The big brave policeman is afraid of a couple of girls?" It was easier to talk at a distance, she decided.

"Sisters in particular," Victor clarified. "My sisters, your sisters, even sisters in habits and head gear. They all scare me."

"Oh dear." Juliette wondered if he wasn't just a little bit serious. She could imagine the G-FOURce might intimidate a man.

"He also mentioned that you know Trevor Zander," Michelle said from behind her. Juliette glanced over at Victor in surprise, wondering how much he'd told them before tonight. His just smiled and shrugged.

"Yes, my sister, Gia, is friends with Ricky Nolan, Trevor's cousin."

"Your sister introduced you two?"

Juliette blushed, wondering just how much Victor had said. Why was Michelle asking about her connections to Trevor? "Well, not exactly." She didn't know how to explain the Monday ManDates; it was a subject they'd skirted around all evening, but now she didn't see how to avoid it. "She kind of set us up on a blind date."

"A blind date? With our Trevor Zander? Really?" Michelle questioned, her tone laced with disbelief.

"Is there more to this story than you're telling us?" Tom was taking his cues from Victor now, who was nodding and rolling his eyes.

"Okay. That's good enough, ducky," Michelle teased, taking the dishrag from Juliette. "Come sit. If this story is half as good as how you two met, then I want to hear it."

So over the dregs of the coffee, Juliette told them very briefly about the termination of her relationship with Mike and the subsequent forced participation in her sisters' family trips, date nights, and parties. "It would have been much less awkward if I had children, or a date of my own, right?"

By the time she had explained the Monday ManDates intervention plan, and was indulging them with details of her evening with Frisky Frank, they were laughing uproariously.

When she got to her date with Trevor, however, she

became shy, not sure how to describe one of the most pivotal nights of her life.

"It was one of the nicer dates I've had in a long time," she explained lamely, trying to come up with a word besides 'amazing' to describe it. "I rode on his motorcycle, and that was a first for me. It was very exhilarating. Anyway, at the end of the evening, we went back to my condo to share a box of desserts I had stashed just in case it was a lame date."

Victor was eying her, the look on his face incomprehensible.

"We were sitting outside on the front steps. Just…just talking. About stuff. About Gia and Ricky. About his music. And then…." She faltered.

"Then I showed up and sparks flew." Juliette had opened her mouth to continue, but snapped it shut at his admission.

"Oh my!" Michelle murmured, her eyes wide with interest. "Did you two boys duel?"

"Unfortunately, no. I wasn't honorable enough. I had made some assumptions about Juliette." He slid a reassuring hand over to rest on her knee where it warmed her flesh through the fabric of her pants, but this time his expression assured her the gesture was intentional. "And I made a fool of myself. Trevor came by later that night. Needless to say, it was a pleasant time had by all."

"Well, Victor, you really know how to ruin a party, don't you?" Michelle reached across the table and patted his cheek. "I'm glad to see you've eaten some humble pie, not just French Silk and Key Lime. And I'm glad you, Juliette, decided to forgive him his bad behavior. Otherwise, we might never have met you and that would be the biggest disaster of all. We already like you a lot more than we like him," she said, tipping her head toward Victor.

Juliette smiled and tentatively placed her hand on top of his where it still rested on her leg. He turned his over and laced his fingers with hers, and she held her breath as a delicious sensation coursed through her.

"I like her a lot more than I like me, too," Victor agreed.

Half an hour later, Juliette noticed Tom yawning. She and Victor said their goodbyes to the Petersons with the promise of future pie-fests, and as Michelle gave her a quick hug, she tucked a slip of paper into her hand. "This is my phone number if you feel like you need to talk to someone. I'll be praying for you, for wisdom about the things that the Holy Spirit was whispering to you tonight in church."

Juliette thanked her again, and Victor helped her into his car. She smiled to herself at the sensible charcoal interior, thinking how well it suited him.

He pulled up along the curb in front of her place and turned off the engine, then shifted in his seat to face her. "Juliette." How she loved the way he said her name. "I had a great time tonight."

"I did too. And I like your friends. They're good people."

"I'd like to see you again," he said, without further preamble. He reached for her hand, twining his fingers with hers, tracing small circles on her palm with his thumb.

"I'd like that, too." She thought she should say more, but she couldn't concentrate while his thumb was doing that.

"I work nights, so it's not very convenient for dinner dates."

"That's good."

"What do you mean?"

Juliette tugged her hand out of his. "I—I'm sorry. I can't think when you're doing that," she admitted, fumbling for the door handle. "I think I need some air."

Victor grinned and came around to her side of the car, locking it up once she was out. "You okay?" he asked, standing a little too closely for comfort, but she nodded. There was more room out here, more air.

Then he reached for her hand again, and together they walked to her front door. When she began fumbling with her keys, he took them from her. "Let me."

She waited silently while he unlocked her door and pushed it open. He didn't move though, but stood blocking the entrance with his large frame.

"Listen, Juliette." His tone was suddenly serious. "The Petersons are like family to me, so the fact that you liked them means a lot to me." He reached up and brushed her cheek again the same way he'd done earlier, but this time he turned his hand around so he was cupping her face. She closed her eyes, relishing in the feel of his roughened palm against her skin. "It would also mean a lot to me if I thought you liked me a little, too."

His words and his touch gave her courage, and she stepped forward to place her hand on his chest, her fingers lightly brushing across a white button near his collar. "I do like the Petersons, but I was there tonight because of you, Victor." She looked up into his eyes and smiled, bold and shy at the same time.

Victor let go of the door and covered her hand with one of his, pressing it hard over his pounding heart. "Can you feel it? That's because of you, Juliette." His voice was husky as he echoed her words. He dipped his head and rested his forehead on hers, his eyes closed. She smiled to herself, feeling the pulse of his body against her palm. Victor slid his free arm around her, his hand pressing into the dip at the base of her spine, pulling her the last few inches toward him.

Heat spread through her body as she let herself relax against him, and she sighed, a soft exhalation of the breath she hadn't realized she'd been holding. He held her there, one arm around her, the other still pressing her hand to his chest, as he swayed a little, back and forth, moving to a melody only he could hear.

Finally he spoke, softly, gently. "I'm going to leave now." His abrupt words surprised her at first, but then she realized they were at an impasse. Neither wanted the night to end, and both knew it had to. She was glad to let him take the lead.

She stepped out of his embrace and put her hands up to her warm cheeks. "Good night, then, Officer Jarrett." She nodded, a happy smile on her face.

"Good night, Ms. Gustafson." His expression was a mirror of hers.

She went inside, closed the door and leaned against it. Her chest was so tight it almost hurt to breathe, but it was a wonderful pain, and she sighed, reveling in her suffering. She crossed to the window to watch him leave, and her brow furrowed in confusion.

Victor stood on the sidewalk beside his car, twirling his keys on his finger. He stared at her house for the longest time, then turned and made his way around to the driver's side of the car and opened the door. He stood inside the open door for a few moments, looking back at the house, then stepped away from the car, and let the door swing closed again. Back up on the sidewalk he came and started up the walk a few steps, before turning around again, and going back to his car. This time he climbed in and pulled the door shut behind him. But he still didn't start it up; he just sat there in the parked vehicle.

For the life of her she couldn't figure out what he was doing. She was just beginning to think there might be something wrong with the car when he started it up and pulled away.

Suddenly, the car swerved back toward the curb in front of Mrs. Cork's place, jerked to a stop, and Victor threw open the door and climbed out. He slammed it behind him and marched up the sidewalk, up the walkway toward her door, his long strides covering the distance in record time. He cleared all three steps in one leap.

She pulled the door open and they stood, facing each other, her eyes large with uncertainty, his intense, almost fierce.

Then he moved, stepping into her, his hands cupping her face, drawing her body up against him as he lowered his mouth to hers.

She didn't resist, not even for a moment, as he kissed her, gently at first, his lips pressed against hers, then with more fervor, as he felt her lean into him, opening to him.

When she let out a soft sigh, he abruptly released her as though she'd reprimanded him. He stepped back, his hands hanging limply at his sides. He stared at her, his face pale.

"Juliette." His voice broke off, like his throat was being squeezed. She stood in the middle of the entry, afraid to move lest her legs give out from under her, and stared back at him. Then she felt her own throat tightening, and heat beginning to creep up her neck. Her nose started to tingle and she knew she was going to cry.

"Juliette," he groaned, realizing it too, and he moved toward her once more, taking her in his arms again, and cradling her to him, one large hand at the back of her head, holding her against his chest as her tears fell. "I'm so sorry," he muttered. "I'm sorry."

Finally, without pulling away, he whispered, "Did I hurt you?"

"No." She felt his relief as his body relaxed, and he rested his cheek on the top of her head.

"I don't understand what's happening to me, Juliette. I couldn't leave. I tried." He stroked her back absentmindedly, comforting them both. "I can't seem to find my footing when I'm around you. You make me act a little insane, and that's not fair because it sounds like I'm blaming you for my lack of self-control. I know it's not your fault, but I don't act like this around anyone else. I didn't mean to scare you, but I'm a little scared myself."

"You didn't scare me," she murmured.

"Then why are you crying?"

She paused. "I'm embarrassed to say," she finally replied.

"Come on, Juliette. Tell me what I did to make you cry." He tipped her face up with a finger under her chin. "Please."

"You didn't do anything wrong, believe me. I cry when I'm happy, too. It's just that you make me feel—I feel—I don't know. I feel *beautiful* tonight, and I haven't felt that way in a long time." Her words faded to a whisper and she pulled her chin out of his grasp, pressing a burning cheek to his chest again.

Victor leaned back a little. "Juliette, look at me." He waited until she lifted her eyes to his. "You *are* beautiful." He brought one hand back up to cup her face again. "You are so beautiful." His thumb rubbed gently along her cheekbone, his long fingers tangled in the hair behind her ear, and his eyes stayed open, watching her as he lowered his head again, and kissed her ever so sweetly on the lips, on the nose, on each eye, then back to her mouth, where he whispered, "You *are* beautiful."

She submitted to his tender assault, kissing him back when he let her, nibbling at his lips when they lingered long enough on hers.

Finally, he lifted his head, his gaze heavy in a way that warmed her blood even more, and he stepped back, taking her hands in his. He brought first one, then the other, to his lips, and placed a tender kiss on the knuckles of each. His voice vibrated when he spoke. "I should leave now."

She nodded, not trusting her own voice.

"Goodnight, Juliette."

"Goodnight, Victor."

He turned and made his way down the walk to his car, climbed in, and drove away. She closed the door and locked it, knowing he would not return tonight.

CHAPTER TWENTY-FOUR

SUNDAY morning dawned gloriously but Juliette stayed in bed. She pulled the blankets up to her chin and covered her face with one of her many pillows, blocking out the brilliant sun trying to force its cheer in through the tilted blinds.

"Go away," she muttered to the morning.

When she'd gone to bed last night, she was sure she'd lie awake for hours, playing over and over the incredible evening with Victor. She must have been completely worn out, however, because she fell asleep before she got to the kissing part.

"I didn't even dream about it," she whined to the empty room.

She did dream about Angela, though, and that's what had her wanting to bury her head. In the dream, instead of Angela, it was Juliette who'd been at the wheel of the out-of-control car. It was Juliette who drove faster and faster, careening through the busy streets of Midtown. But it was still Angela's terrified cries echoing through her memory long after she was awake.

Juliette concentrated on Victor, trying to recapture the intensity of his gaze, the feel of his arms around her, and the firm lines of his body against hers, but her thoughts kept stumbling over Angela.

Angela, Angela, Angela.

Finally she gave up, dug herself out of her burrow, and trudged grumpily into the kitchen to put on some coffee. She toasted a blueberry bagel, slathered it with too much strawberry-flavored cream cheese, and licked the knife rebelliously. Then she headed back to bed with both. She was overdue to wash her sheets anyway.

Propped up against her plethora of pillows, caffeinated and fed, she felt herself begin to relax a little. She considered going to church, but she wasn't quite ready to hear again Pastor Eric's message about forgiveness and carrying each other's burdens.

Angela. Forgive her? Forgive and forget her cataclysmic collision into their lives? Yet that was what God seemed to be asking her to do. She knew it like she knew what color pants she'd wear to work on Monday.

"But how, God? How?" she asked into the air. "How do I forget my graduation and the look on Grandpa and Granny G's faces, the shock on Renata's? Or the stillness in Phoebe's eyes? How do I forget Gia crying for Maman and Papa to come and take us home?" Her throat was tight and she slid down beneath the blankets again, burrowing under the pillows until she felt completely cocooned. Protected by the muffled silence, she allowed her mind to wander unchecked as she imagined what her parents would be like today.

I wonder what Angela is like today.

The thought came unbidden, intruding on her memories, and she tried to push it away. She didn't want to think about

Angela, not now, not here in Pillowland. But try as she might, she could not make the girl leave. No, the woman. Her classmate would be a thirty-something-year-old woman now, just like Juliette. Did she still have corn-silk hair and laughing brown eyes? Had she gained a hundred pounds on prison fare or could she still wear her cheerleader uniform?

Did she still sing?

Angela Clinton performed at almost every school event during their last two years of high school. She had pipes that stunned people into silence the moment she released her first note. It was a natural gift, one that had been discovered by a fellow cheerleader in tenth grade, and had catapulted Angela to small town stardom. She sang the National Anthem at every sports activity. She won awards for the school's choirs in state-wide musical competitions, and she held lead roles in all the drama department's musicals. Angela's face was on the cover of many a local newspaper, and she had an online presence that would make most politicians green with envy. She was funny and personable; her gift had not made her prideful or unapproachable. It helped that she was absolutely adorable in a svelte, pixie-like way. People liked to look at her, to be around her, and they liked to be considered one of her friends.

Juliette always wondered, with so many friends, why Angela had been driving to graduation alone that day.

The Gustafson girls never talked to each other about her anymore. After Juliette's post-trial melt-down, the topic of Angela became taboo.

Well, maybe it was time to drag the girl out of the deep, dark, locked-up place of pain and silence, and finally face her again. Could she do it? Could any of them?

The relationships the sisters shared were rather

unorthodox. They were so different, each girl, and had they not been related, they would likely not have been close, if friends at all. This was something they'd often discussed and were proud of in an odd, inverted way. Their bonds went deeper than simply liking each other or getting along. They were joined by blood and bone, first and foremost, but also by that fateful day that changed the direction of their lives in one defining moment.

And somewhere in her heart, Juliette was just a little afraid that if they opened up that moment, if they freed Angela from her solitary confinement, then they'd be freed from one another, too. The cords that bound them together would be loosed, and they would no longer need each other with the same under-lying desperation as they did now. Was she willing to take that risk?

When she finally emerged from Pillowland, she was no nearer a solution to her dilemma. She knew it was time to deal with Angela; she also knew she wasn't strong enough to do it on her own.

"Victor," she whispered, wishing she could call him, but knowing that burdening him when this new thing between them was just beginning to unfurl would be disastrous. "Victor," she murmured again, warmth spreading through her at the thought of him. "Victor." She wrapped her arms around herself, longing to feel his strength instead of her weakness.

She thought about calling Victor's friend, Michelle. The woman seemed so sincere last night, but in the light of day, she might feel differently. And to be honest, Juliette wasn't very enthusiastic about calling a brand new friend and unloading on her. What a downer of a phone call that would be!

She sighed and leaned over the side of her bed to pick up the Bible that had slipped to the floor last night. Michelle also included a verse on the little piece of paper and Juliette had read it several times, letting the words sink in.

"Come to Me, all who are weary and heavy-laden, and I will give you rest. Take my yoke upon you and learn from Me, for I am gentle and humble in heart, and you will find rest for your souls. For My yoke is easy and My burden is light."

The thought of sharing her burden with Jesus, the idea that He wanted to come along side her and walk through life connected to her, was more than she could comprehend. She longed for the rest for her soul He offered, and she knew all she had to do was accept it, just like Trevor had said. "Receive it, receive His love. He wants to love you." But how? There seemed to be no answer to that question.

Finally, she climbed out of bed and headed for the shower. She couldn't lie there all day, waiting for answers that weren't coming. She had to get out and do something, anything.

It was, after all, a glorious day, and she had something to celebrate.

Victor Jarrett had kissed her last night. For real.

~ ~ ~

ARMED with her Bible and a notebook, Juliette walked the two blocks to the neighborhood park. She hoped the crisp October morning would help clear her head a little. There were a few parents with children around the playground and a young man walked a brindle-coated Great Dane on a short lead, but the park wasn't very busy, and she was grateful.

She located a secluded bench where she could watch the comings and goings and made herself comfortable, stretching her jeans-clad legs out in front of her.

As she sat in the cool of the shade, her mind wandered back over the puzzle of Angela. Once she'd allowed herself to consider what she was like today, Juliette could think of nothing else. When Angela was sentenced, she'd gone to a correctional institute for women only a few hours' drive from town. Was she still there? Did they move long-term prisoners from jail to jail? Did her parents visit her? Had the Clintons stayed here in Midtown all these years, not wanting to be too far from their daughter? She had never considered them before; it was as though Angela's family had disappeared behind the bars of her prison cell right along with their daughter.

But the truth was that they, just like the remnant of the Gustafson family, had gone on living their lives. Somewhere, maybe even close by, Angela Clinton's mother and father had continued to get up every day, to face the world with the knowledge that Angela was a murderer; that vivacious, gregarious, inhumanly flexible, and oh, so musical Angela, had recklessly killed the beloved parents of four young girls, forever changing their lives.

The Clintons' lives had forever changed that day, too, she belatedly realized. Juliette had never before considered how the accident might have affected them. She'd never wondered about Angela's mother, how the woman endured throughout the whole horrific ordeal. She'd never given thought to how difficult it must have been for Mr. Clinton to keep his family strong during the public exposure of their personal lives, while his daughter's name was plastered all over the headlines as the worst kind of teenager.

And she certainly had never imagined Angela as an outcast, an orphan in her own right. The girl had been sent to prison, broken and alone, forever condemned and labeled, removed from the life she'd always known.

No! She would not feel compassion for the girl! She was the orphan, not Angela! She, and Renata, and Phoebe, and Gia. Maybe Angela couldn't actually *see* her parents anytime time she wanted to, but she could contact them any time she needed them. Juliette, on the other hand, would never hear her mother's voice again. She would never feel her father's arms around her. She would never again be able to sit across the table from them and talk about life, about boys. About Jesus.

Visit Angela. *No.*

Visit Angela. *No.*

Visit Angela.

"No!" She said the word out loud, her voice cracking on the single syllable. A woman pushing her little boy on a swing across the way glanced up at her, mild curiosity on her face. Juliette smiled self-consciously, sat up straight, and opened her notebook, trying to look like a normal person instead of a crazy freak, sitting in a corner by herself, yelling at no one.

The blank page on her lap stared up at her, its emptiness mocking her racing thoughts. The notion to visit Angela had taken her completely by surprise and her heart pounded in her chest. She had no desire whatsoever to see Angela again. She was perfectly content with not having answers to her questions about the Clinton family.

"What if I just write her a letter?" Juliette whispered, searching for a compromise.

She slipped the pen from the spiral binding of the

notebook and wrote *Angela*. The girl's name seemed to sit on top of the crisp white paper with its water-blue lines, as though even the fibers wanted to push the letters away. Juliette stared at it for several minutes, her pen poised for more, but nothing came.

Sighing deeply, she laid both the Bible and the notebook on the bench, and stretched her legs out in front of her again. She leaned back and looked up into the branches overhead, squinting her eyes at the flickering light filtering through the leaves. "You know," she muttered quietly, not wanting to draw anyone's attention, "I didn't have to make decisions about Angela Clinton a month ago. Why can't things just stay the same, at least regarding her? Why are you making me think about her now; worry about her?"

Instead of the silence she expected in answer to her questions, a pitiful whimper made her sit up and look over her shoulder. Beyond the tree was a row of tall bushes, and the sound came from there. She stood and scanned the greenery for any sign of movement; sure enough, beneath one of the shrubs, a scruffy little dog lay curled in on itself. It gazed up at her with baleful eyes, and its tail flopped pitifully in response to her approach.

CHAPTER TWENTY-FIVE

"HI, PUPPY. Are you okay?" Juliette had never owned a dog and didn't know exactly how to handle the situation, but she didn't want to do anything to make it feel cornered. She couldn't tell if it was hurt or not, but she could see the outline of ribs and the pronounced ridges of each vertebrae running down the dog's back. The shoulder blades and hip bones protruded sharply beneath the skin as well. "Oh, puppy, you must be starving."

Her heart broke as the dog tried to push itself up, then collapsed back into a heap with another whimper, its eyes never leaving Juliette's face. She couldn't just leave it there, but she knew better than to crawl under the bushes for it. "Come on, puppy. You need to come out. Come to me." She knelt on the grass a few feet away from the dog, her heart aching as it dragged itself out on its belly. She stayed where she was, coaxing, pleading, urging, until it was close enough to touch.

"Please don't bite me, okay? I want to help you." She reached out a hand, palm up, and rested it on the grass in front of the dog's nose. The pitiful thing stuck out its tongue and licked her fingers. She eased her hand up and tentatively scratched its ears, stroked its shoulders, and ran her hand down the bony back. "You're coming home with me, okay? Will you do that?"

She stood slowly so as not to startle it but the dog only thumped its tail a few times. It wasn't as small as it had seemed curled up under the hedge, but it didn't look like it weighed much, and Juliette was fairly certain she could carry the creature home without any problem. It didn't even struggle when she scooped it up in her arms. Wrinkling her nose at the smell emanating off the unkempt fur, she headed back along the path that lead out of the park.

By the time she reached home, the dog was like dead weight in her rubbery arms. Inside her garage, she lay the dog down on a rag rug door mat, then stood, massaging her aching limbs. It rested its head on its paws again and watched her intently, but the tail no longer moved.

Juliette dug her phone out of her pocket and dialed Renata's number, hoping she'd be home from church by now, and would pick up her phone. They'd only spoken briefly since their discussion over Tim Larsen, but Juliette desperately needed her sister now. The Dixons had two Labradors; Renata would know what to do.

Renata answered, much to Juliette's relief, and she rushed in. "Hey Ren, I just brought a stray dog home, and I think it's almost dead. It's really skinny, but it's so sweet and trusting, and I just couldn't leave it at the park. I don't know the first thing to do for it, though, and oh, my goodness, it stinks."

"Slow down, Juliette. You brought home a stray from the park? What were you thinking?"

"I know, I know. But you wouldn't have left it there

either."

"Have you given it any water or food?"

"I don't have any dog food." Juliette was beginning to panic as she thought quickly about the contents of her refrigerator and pantry. "Can I give it tuna?"

"No. What about water? I know you have that."

She covered the mouthpiece with her hand and made eye contact with the dog. "Hold on," she said to the animal. "I'll be right back." She hurried into the kitchen for a bowl, then returned to the garage and filled it with water from the laundry sink. She set it down in front of the dog and stepped back. The animal raised its head and sniffed the dish, then began to lap up the liquid until it was completely gone.

"Wow. Poor thing was really thirsty. Should I get it some more?"

"No, not yet." Renata directed her from the other end of the line. "Wait and see if that stays down. If it hasn't had anything to eat or drink in a while, it might gorge itself, and then throw up all over the place. Just give it a little at a time."

The dog stared up at Juliette. She crouched down to stroke the fur over its ribcage, and was delighted to see the tail wag a few times. "Now what?" she asked.

"You need to call the animal shelter and have them come pick it up, Juliette. You don't want a dog, and you certainly don't want a stray."

"Who says I don't want a dog?"

"You?" Renata scoffed. "A dog? Since when have you ever wanted a dog?"

"I've been thinking about it recently," she said, her tone defensive.

"Recently…as in the last half hour, since you stumbled across this one?"

"No, as in the last couple of months. Since I left Mike."

"Juliette."

"What? I have! And this dog needs me. I don't want to call the pound." She rubbed the velvety ears between her thumb and finger, surprised at how soft the fur was there.

Renata took a deep breath and let it out slowly, as if preparing to talk to a child. "You still have to call the shelter. It's for your own good, Juliette. For you and the dog. They'll quarantine it to make sure it's not sick or rabid, give it vaccines if it lives, spay or neuter it, and if no one claims it, then you can take it back for a nominal fee. It's worth every penny."

Juliette rolled her eyes and stood up, wrinkling her nose as she sniffed her fingertips. "Fine. I'll call them when I get off the phone. But this dog is mine." She hadn't realized until that moment that her mind was made up.

"Do you need me to come over? I can bring some dog food."

Juliette couldn't believe what she was hearing. "Really? On a Sunday? What about your guys?"

Renata's voice was like a tire gone flat. "John's taken the boys out to lunch. It's a guy thing, you know; a man and his sons. So," there was a brief pause, as though she was choosing her words with care. "I guess I'm free to do as I please this afternoon. Shall I come over?"

"Oh, Ren, that would be great. I would feel so much better if you were here." Juliette could tell there was more to the story than what Renata was telling her, and she confirmed it with her next words.

"I'd feel better if I were there, too, instead of sitting here staring at the walls. I'll be right over, bearing flea and tick shampoo and dog food." She hung up before Juliette could even say good-bye.

~ ~ ~

RENATA, nose wrinkled THE moment she walked into the open garage, insisted they bathe the dog immediately, and it took a surprising amount of effort to keep the suddenly energetic animal in the deep laundry sink. Once clean and dried, though, the dog looked much more presentable, and he certainly smelled better. Juliette loaned her sister a clean set of clothes, and they took turns showering while the dog slept, exhausted by its bath-time adventure. When Juliette emerged from the bathroom, Renata had lunch ready for them and was filling a bowl with food for Tootles, who was lying on an old blanket on the kitchen floor where they could keep an eye on him.

Renata had confirmed that, yes, the dog was in fact a male. She also didn't think he was very old; pointing out that he still had a few of his sharp baby teeth intact. "He must have been born on the streets, poor guy. I wonder what happened to his mommy. He's just a little lost boy."

And that was how Juliette came up with his name, after one of the lost boys from Never Land.

Renata placed the bowl of food in front of the sleeping dog while Juliette poured a couple glasses of iced tea for them, then they sat down to share their meal. Without really thinking about what she was doing, Juliette grabbed Renata's hand. "Do you mind if I pray today?"

Renata hesitated momentarily, then shrugged. "Sure."

"God, thanks for my sister. And thanks for Tootles. And thanks for the sandwiches. Amen." She smiled shyly across the table, knowing she needed some practice before she could sound anything like her sister. Renata stared at her with raised eyebrows.

"You're really serious about this, aren't you?"

"About what?" Juliette didn't know if she was referring to her prayer or the dog.

"Your faith," Renata clarified. "You're really taking this whole thing seriously."

She nodded, and took a bite of her sandwich. They ate in silence until Renata nudged her, and tipped her head toward the dog. Too tired or too lazy to get up, Tootles had scooted over to the bowl and was eating the food while still resting on his belly.

"He is pretty cute," Renata conceded.

Juliette grinned like a proud parent. "I know." She had called the animal shelter and learned they had emergency staff only on Sundays, so Juliette offered to keep the dog until Monday when there would be more help available.

"So tell me exactly how you found him," Renata asked. In the flurry of activity, there'd been no chance to discuss the details of Juliette's morning walk.

"Well, I skipped church this morning so I decided to take my Bible down to the park—oh! My Bible! I left it on the bench!" Juliette jumped up from her seat. "I need to go back and get it. My notebook, too."

Renata frowned up at her. "I didn't know you had a Bible."

"You gave it to me; don't you remember?"

"You kept that?" Renata's surprise made Juliette smile.

"Of course, silly. I wasn't going to throw a Bible away. I was too afraid I'd get struck by lightning or something."

"Wonders never cease," Renata quipped. "Well, I'm glad you kept it. I'm glad you're using the Bible I gave you." She pushed her chair back and stood up. "So, what are we waiting for? We need to go find that Bible!"

Turning to the dog, she said, "Tootles, you're coming too. We don't know what kind of house guest you are. And no barfing in my car, do you hear?"

CHAPTER TWENTY-SIX

THEY DROVE the short distance to the park and Renata ordered Juliette to stay with Tootles in the car while she went in search of the Bible. She returned quite some time later, books in hand, just as Juliette was beginning to worry.

Once in the car, instead of driving away, she just sat there. Juliette waited, but didn't say anything. She knew if Renata wanted to talk about something, she would. Finally, the younger woman spoke, not looking at Juliette, just staring straight ahead through the windshield.

"I wasn't snooping, okay? But when I got to the bench, your notebook had blown open, and I saw the first page." She took a deep breath. "I have to ask. Are you writing to Angela Clinton?"

Juliette looked down at the notebook where it now rested on the floor at her feet. She hadn't planned on talking to any of her sisters about Angela, at least not yet, and especially not Renata. She didn't want her judging her or bossing her around, but the decision had been taken out of her hands.

"Well, the thought had occurred to me." Juliette shrugged. "But as you saw, I didn't get very far."

Renata snorted. "No, you didn't. How long did it take you to write her name?"

"I don't know. Half an hour, maybe."

"It took me two days," Renata stated, finally meeting Juliette's gaze in the rear view mirror. "Once I even made it as far as 'How are you?' before I realized that's probably one of the stupidest things I could ever ask a girl in prison. Usually, I just stare at her name for way too long, then crumple up the paper and throw it away."

Juliette reached up and put a hand on her sister's shoulder.

"I know. Pitiful, isn't it?" Renata shook her head. "But I keep thinking she probably needs to hear something from us so she can have some closure. I just have no clue what to say to her."

"Oh, Rennie," Juliette murmured. "You're worried about Angela needing closure? Why is that your responsibility?"

"Because it's what I do, Juliette. I…I fix things. I clean up after everyone else. I straighten up the messes so we can all get on with living. Just like I did for you and Tootles today." Renata reached a hand back and scratched one of the dog's ears. "It's who I am."

Juliette let her sister's words course through the filter of her new awareness, and heard, for the first time, Renata's perspective on the way life had been for them all those years ago. She closed her eyes and saw her sister, sixteen years old, stepping up to bat when Juliette stayed in bed. She heard Renata's voice telling the others to brush their teeth, do their homework, put their dishes in the sink, listen to Granny G, when her own voice was silent, absent altogether. She remembered Renata's fingers sweeping her tangled hair away from her face, and kissing her on the forehead, as she whispered, "Goodnight, sweet Juliette." Just the way Maman used to do. The lump in her throat was making it hard to breathe.

"Is that how it was for you? Did you have to clean up after the mess Angela made? Did you feel like you had to fix everything so we could get on with life?"

Renata reached down and turned the key in the ignition. "I don't really know. I don't think I really felt much of anything. I just went into auto-pilot, and that's what came out of me." She checked for traffic and pulled away from the curb, heading back to Juliette's place. "I'm a fixer. I fix things. I organize things. I *do*."

"And what did I do?" Juliette asked, already knowing the answer. "I just disappeared. I shut down. I just stopped living for a while." She caught Renata's gaze in the rear view mirror. "But you. How did I not see what it was doing to you? You just stepped up and filled all of our empty shoes, didn't you?" She shook her head. "That was a lot of shoes for a teenage girl to fill, Rennie; not only Maman's and Papa's, but mine, too."

"Don't say that. I just covered for you while you took care of being at that trial for the rest of us. We couldn't go, remember? You had to carry that burden on your own. I might not have been old enough to sit in court with you, but I was old enough to know it was more than one of us should ever have to go through alone. I couldn't imagine sitting in the same room as that girl, but you did it day after day for us. Your whole life got rerouted; graduation, college plans, your future. Even your trip to Hawaii with Sharon. It wouldn't have been the same with just Granny G and Grandpa there. We needed to know that one of us was representing us. At least I did." Their eyes met in the mirror again. "Don't belittle that sacrifice, Juliette. I saw how it affected you." Renata sniffled, and a single tear made a track down the curve of her cheek. "Someone needed to be strong while you were being stronger. I was next in line." She paused before continuing, a little hesitantly. "I think I did okay, don't you?"

Juliette nodded, unable to speak as she dealt with this new version of things. How could she have been so self-centered?

"You were amazing, Renata. You still are. And I'm sorry it's taken me fifteen years to tell you that."

Renata parked the van, sat very still in the ensuing silence after the car was off, then turned a little in her seat. "Well, thank you, Juliette. It means a lot to hear that from you." It was as if a switch had been flipped and suddenly the familiar, abrasive Renata was back. "I just wish other people in my life would realize that too. I do have some personal worth, you know. I'm not just a label. I'm not just a soccer mom or a church lady or...or a bee with an itch." She wouldn't cuss even if someone paid her to.

"I know that." Juliette was taken aback by the shift in her sister's demeanor.

"You're the only one, then." And Renata climbed out of the car and closed the door, carefully, but firmly, as though closing the door on the conversation. Juliette had seen the look on her sister's face a thousand times before; they were done talking about this subject.

Renata excused herself to make a phone call. When she returned from Juliette's bedroom, there were traces of more tears in her eyes, but her face was closed, her mouth clamped in a look of determination that brooked no argument. It was a face that hurt Juliette's heart.

"I really should get going. Are you and Tootles going to be all right?"

"Of course we are. But are you okay?"

"I'm fine, Juliette." Her flippant tone said otherwise.

"Do you need help with anything? You put off getting your stuff done to come help me. Maybe I can return the favor."

"Don't be silly, Juliette. I only did it for Tootles." She ran a foot down the curve of the dog's back. "You don't tell me I'm too controlling, do you, Tootles?"

It was like a slap in the face. This was the Renata she was accustomed to, but after their conversation today, she'd hoped things might be a little different between them.

Renata scooped her purse off the counter and crossed the room to where Juliette still sat at the table. She reached down and gave her a quick, perfunctory hug. "Don't get up. I'll see myself out."

Juliette stood up and followed her sister out the front door anyway. "Ren?"

"Yes?" Renata paused on the sidewalk and turned around, an overly-bright smile on her face.

"Thank you. If Tootles could talk, I'm sure he'd tell you himself, but I want you to know how much we both appreciate you coming over and helping us out."

"Of course. I'm glad someone needed me today." Then she turned on her heels and practically jogged to her car. Juliette thought she saw her swipe at her eyes as she pulled away.

She wandered back inside, feeling low all over again, but this time for Renata, too.

In the kitchen, Juliette dropped down on the floor beside Tootles, who snuffled and sighed, and looked up at her with shining eyes.

"I'm tired of hurting, Tootles, and I'm tired of watching other people hurting, too." He turned his head and licked her knee with his long, pink tongue, as if to assure her that he was feeling much better, thanks to her. The scripture from Michelle drifted into her head.

Come to Me all who are weary and heavy laden and I will give you rest.

"That's you and me, puppy. We're heavy laden, aren't we?" She was surprised at how nice it felt to have someone around to talk to. She sat back against the cabinets and closed her eyes, listening to the sounds Tootles made; his breathing, the periodic thumping of his tail against the floor. Who would have guessed that a humble little stray would come to mean so much to her so quickly?

Take my yoke upon you and learn from Me, for I am gentle and humble in heart.

"Jesus?" Juliette opened one eye and looked down at the dog. "Are you Jesus?" Then she giggled and covered her face with her hands. "I think I might have just peered over the edge, there, Tootles!" She rubbed the dog's velvet ears again. "But maybe I'm not so far off. Maybe you're a gift from Him. Maybe you're here, not because you need me, but because I need you. Did you ever think about that?"

Tootles rolled onto his back so she could scratch his belly.

"Maybe you're my love gift from Jesus, Tootles. Is that what you are, puppy? Are you a love gift, funny dog?" She caught herself talking in a high, squeaky voice and rolled her eyes. "Oh, Tootles. You've turned me into an old maid!"

By the time the stars were out, Juliette and Tootles were soul mates. They'd read the Bible together, they'd had dinner together, they sat outside on the front stoop together watching the sunset while she told the dog all about Victor Jarrett's kiss. She even admitted she was hoping a certain cruiser might be making its rounds right about then, and she tried in vain to teach her furry friend to wave.

But no police car drove by that night. Or the next. Or the next. There was no phone call from a certain, gray-eyed officer, either. And as the days went by with no word, Juliette began to wonder if the kiss had been nothing more than her imagination after all.

CHAPTER TWENTY-SEVEN

"YOU DON'T look so good, buddy." Tom studied him from across the room. "I got the time if you need to unload." It was Tuesday morning and the other men in the group had already taken off, leaving only the two of them behind. Victor closed his eyes and leaned back into the sofa. He reached up and scrubbed his face with both hands, then ran his fingers through his hair. "Rough night at work last night?"

"Nope." Victor shook his head, not sure he wanted to talk about what was bothering him.

"Is this about that Gustafson girl?" So much for that.

"Yes," Victor growled, not opening his eyes.

"I like her. So does Michelle. And you know she's not an easy sell."

"I like her, too."

"So what's the problem?" Tom settled more comfortably in his favorite armchair and Victor made him wait while he stewed over the words all jumbled up in his head, trying to figure out how to get them out in a semblance of order.

The last two days had been a roller-coaster of emotions

for Victor and he couldn't stand it. One minute he was aching for Juliette; the next he was berating himself for acting like a crazed Don Juan, charging into her house to devour her. What had come over him? When he closed his eyes he could see himself standing on the sidewalk outside her home, torn between the urge to run, and the desire to run back to her.

What a fool he'd made of himself after all! When she opened the door, and stood there looking up at him, those silky eyes large and trusting, her mouth—oh man, her mouth! He'd only slept fitfully the last few nights, waking up time and again to the memory of her pressed against him. He could hear her whisper, "You made me feel beautiful," and he wanted to assure her again and again that she was.

He hated the way his mind wouldn't stop spinning, racing around the moments he'd spent with her, robbing him of sane thought. He couldn't concentrate at work, and his boss actually raised his voice at him over paperwork that wasn't completed properly. He hadn't been yelled at in a long time, and Victor blamed Juliette for distracting him. Even worse, he felt ravenously hungry all the time but nothing sounded good to him and the coffee he was drinking was making his stomach roil in protest.

"She makes me crazy."

"Okay."

"She is so ridiculously emotional. Every time I see her she's either crying uncontrollably, laughing like a lunatic, or hissing like an alley cat! I never know what to expect with her."

"Isn't this a little premature? I thought Saturday night was the first time you'd been out with her."

"Of course it's premature! That's why it's so ridiculous! I

hardly know her and she's already got me tied up in knots! Can you imagine what it would be like to actually date her?" He reached over and grabbed his mug off the coffee table, sloshing a little of the hot liquid on his hand. The pain actually felt good, and he grunted with satisfaction.

"May I join you two?" Michelle poked her head into the living room.

"Come on in," Victor gestured at all the empty seats around them.

"So what happened? This isn't what I was expecting. You both acted like star-crossed lovers when you were here on Saturday," Michelle stated, choosing a chair beside her husband.

"You want to know what happened? I'll tell you what happened. I took her home, told her I wanted to see her again, and she agreed that she wanted to see me again, too. Then I hugged her and I left."

"That all sounds good to me." Michelle smiled encouragingly.

"Yes! It does, doesn't it? But then I had to go and flip out." Victor set his cup down again and laced his fingers together on the top of his head. It felt like his brain was about to erupt like a volcano, and he could just imagine the mess that would make in Michelle's bright, yellow living room. "I charged up to her front door like I was doing a drug bust, and when she opened it, I assaulted her! I tackled her like she was a line-backer!" Then he released an expletive that had all three of them wide-eyed with shock.

"Gah! See what I mean? Now she's got me cursing!" He jumped to his feet. "I'm exhausted, I'm acting like a raving lunatic myself, and my chest hurts. All because of her." He clenched his fists at his sides, pacing the floor. "I need to sleep but every time I close my eyes, I see her looking up at me with those...*hungry* eyes. I can't take it!"

Michelle and Tom exchanged glances. Tom finally spoke. "I'm having a hard time understanding your...hesitation about dating her, Vic. Seems to me your response is pretty appropriate."

"Appropriate? In what way, exactly, is my behavior appropriate? I scared us both! I even made her cry!"

"Were they good tears or bad tears?" Michelle asked.

"How should I know? They were tears!" But he did know. *You made me feel beautiful.* "Good, I suppose," he grunted, dropping back onto the sofa.

"Like I said, I don't understand why this is all such a bad thing. Trevor stands by her. We think she's the real deal. So do you. You said so yourself." Tom was ticking things off his fingers as he spoke. "You're single. She's single. She's apparently got a close, albeit perhaps a little misguided family—"

"Aha!" Victor interrupted, his voice louder than he'd intended. "Her sisters sound like mine! Meddling and manipulating, ridiculous schemes coming out their ears. I'd be crazy to go for that."

"Have you met her sisters?" Michelle prodded. "Maybe they're not so bad."

"No, but from what little she's said about them, I don't really want to."

"You sound like a little boy, Victor. You don't *want* to?" Michelle frowned at the younger man. "Shall I tell you what I think?"

Victor held up a hand and shook his head. "Uh, no, I don't think so. I'm afraid to hear what you think. In fact, I'm not really sure why I'm sitting here discussing this with you.

When did my private life go public?"

"I thought so," Michelle said, as though he'd responded with a compliant nod instead of petulance. "I think you're drawn to her *because* she's so transparent, and you're not accustomed to women being transparent. I think you're confused and befuddled and fumbling and bumbling—"

"Hey," he scowled. Tom just chuckled behind his coffee cup.

"And making an idiot of yourself because you're feeling something that doesn't make sense to you, something you can't control. You're resisting so you can stay in control."

"And what's wrong with wanting to maintain some control? It's worked for me so far."

"Really? Your control bored Amanda right into the arms of another man, Victor Jarrett."

His eyes widened in surprise at Michelle's uncharacteristically sharp words.

"You know what, honey?" She only called him that when he got really stubborn, and Victor felt a strong impulse to cover his ears. "I don't recall you ever feeling this way when you were with Amanda. I don't recall you feeling much of anything with her, in fact. I think this Juliette is waking you up, and you're just being a big grump about it. With bed-head to boot."

Victor scowled and pointed a finger at her. "You know what, *honey*?" he mocked her. "I thought she was waking me up, too, but then I dove headfirst off the deep end, and I don't like the water here. It feels like I'm drowning."

Tom chuckled and reached over to take his wife's hand. "I hear the only way to stay afloat is to stop flailing, and kicking, and resisting. Maybe you should just relax and go with this, Vic. You might actually learn to swim with us big boys. You know, those of us with a good woman swimming alongside us."

Victor shook his head, trying not to look longingly at their entwined fingers, his own hand tingling from the memory of Juliette's tucked into his. "I don't think you get it, Tom. It wasn't about relaxing, that's for sure. It was terrifying. I was actually afraid of what I might do next. I'll tell you what, if that woman had invited me into her home at the end of the night, you'd be dragging me off to confession right now. At this point, I'm not sure I shouldn't be going anyway! She…she gets inside my head, and I can't think of anything else, I want her so bad. It's not healthy." He paused, alarmed that he'd admitted so much out loud. "Besides, she has those sisters. I can't handle any more meddling sisters. I can't do it. I *won't* do it."

"Then you're an even bigger fool than I thought you were," Tom shrugged.

"Why does everyone call me that?" Victor brought his palm down on the top of the coffee table, the smack surprising them all. "Sorry," he grimaced, ashamed of his outburst. "Sorry." He took a deep breath and let it out slowly. "Look at me! I'm in uncharted territory here, guys. Amanda was so…so easy to deal with. Predictable and sensible, calm. Nothing she did ever surprised me, or caught me off guard. I always knew what to expect from her. I wasn't even surprised when she turned down my proposal."

Neither of his friends spoke. They just let his words hang in the air between them. But Michelle's eyes were asking a question.

"What?" he demanded.

She smiled patiently at his impatience. "Well, first, my friend, a word of warning. Don't ever compare a new woman—even a potential one—with a woman from your past. It's tantamount to relationship suicide. Secondly, I'm wondering if you honestly consider all those things you just said about Amanda to be *good* things."

Victor glanced at Tom for support, but he shook his head sympathetically. "You're on your own, man."

"Thirdly," Michelle continued. "I was wondering if you really believed that the success of a relationship is gauged by how easy a person is to 'deal with,' as you so intriguingly put it."

Victor opened his mouth to speak but Michelle held up her hand.

"And fourthly, are you seriously going to let a couple of sisters scare you off? After everything those women you grew up with have subjected you to, you'll just sit back and let Juliette's sisters keep you from her? It seems to me, Vic, that you, of all people, might be just the right man for the job."

"Your logic escapes me," Victor ground out, but only because he wasn't ready to admit that everything she said made perfect sense to him. Why *was* he comparing Juliette to Amanda? It wasn't as though Amanda had set a standard he hoped his next woman would meet.

But she *had* been safe, he reasoned, and that was good, wasn't it? He needed predictable and if nothing else, Amanda had been predictable.

Juliette, on the other hand, had yet to *not* surprise him during any of their encounters, so why would she be happy with predictable? He took a deep breath and let it out slowly. Why would any woman, for that matter, if Amanda, herself, hadn't been happy with it?

But the sisters? That was another story altogether.

"Have you prayed about this, Victor?" Michelle's voice was quiet, serious.

"Yes! Yes, yes, yes! I even asked God to keep me from being a fool on Saturday night!" He shuddered again, remembering how driven he'd felt, how untethered and wild. How foolish. "A lot of good that did me." He rose to his feet again, slowly this time, suddenly weary beyond belief. "I'm tired," he sighed. "I have to be at work in 5 hours. I need to go home and get some sleep."

Tom walked him to the door and put a hand on his shoulder. "We'll be praying for you, Victor. The Lord has already offered His wisdom. All you have to do is ask for it. Go home and rest. We'll talk soon."

CHAPTER TWENTY-EIGHT

TOOTLES did not like the leash.

Tootles did not like being taken for walks.

Tootles wanted to take Juliette for runs.

Tootles had recovered quickly from both his hard life on the streets, and from the subsequent surgery that left him just a little bit less of a man.

Juliette was exhausted. All the time. "He doesn't listen, he doesn't learn," she admitted to Sharon a few weeks after she'd adopted him. "He doesn't even know his own name! I thought he did, the little trickster, because he'd come running when I called him to eat, but he just knows the sound of the cup in the dog food bag. Then last night, he broke down the kiddie gate."

"Did he get out?"

"Yes." Juliette sighed heavily, and let her head fall into her hands, elbows propped on her desk. "He got out of the kitchen and into my bed."

"Oh dear."

"Yeah. Oh dear. Put it this way. No one slept last night."

"You let him sleep with you?" Sharon laughed.

"No! I let him sleep in the garage."

"Why can't you just put him out in your little back yard? It's got a good sturdy fence, doesn't it? Wouldn't it keep him in?"

"During the day, he seems okay with that. I assume he is, anyway. At least he isn't whining when I leave and it seems to me like he only starts barking when he realizes I'm home. But at night, if I leave him outside, he whines, and howls, and scratches at the back door. You can hear him up and down the block. I know because I took a walk one night without him. I needed a break from having my arm ripped out of its socket."

"So the garage, it is." Sharon nodded understandingly. "How did that go?"

"Oh Sharon!" she wailed. "It was awful! I felt like a child-abuser. He cried for hours!"

"Dude, you look like sh—"

"Gavin!" Sharon interrupted the Philosophy major who had just walked into the middle of their conversation. She had a fairly accurate idea of what word he was going to use to describe Juliette's condition.

Gavin grinned and dropped a folder of papers on Juliette's desk.

"What is this?" She picked up the folder and began to thumb through it. "Is this your work?" She straightened in her chair, as she took in the neatly formatted and typed pages of his first quarter portfolio.

"Yep. Paid good money for it, too." His smile turned smug and he dropped into a chair, arms crossed over his broad chest.

"What do you mean, good money? Did you pay someone to do this for you?"

"No, I hired someone to help me."

"Gavin," Juliette studied him, questions buzzing through her mind. "Are you blushing?"

"No. It's hot out there." He jerked a thumb over his shoulder toward the window where the November sun shone in from a crisp, cloudless Autumn sky. But blushing, he most certainly was, and for some reason, it made Juliette feel a little more confident that the papers she had were not illegally come by.

"So this is your work?"

"Yep. I did all the philosophizing, and Kelly helped me make it look good. Thanks for hooking me up with her." His neck went from red to purple.

"I see," Juliette tried not to smile, but she saw Sharon duck down behind her monitor across the way. "I've heard she's an excellent tutor."

"Dude." His satisfied tone spoke volumes. "She's awesome." Then he shoved himself up out of the chair and started pacing the floor.

"Are you okay, Gavin?" Juliette had never seen him flustered before.

"Um, yeah." He paused in front of her desk, "I just…so…um, she has a boyfriend, right? Do you know if it's serious?"

"Yes. And yes." Juliette nodded. "She has a boyfriend. It's serious. But, it's not fatal. Nothing's forever, especially when it comes to true love."

"Juliette!" Sharon admonished her from her desk. "Don't be so cynical."

"Sorry, Gavin. I'm just tired and cranky."

"Yeah, I could tell. You look like…."

"Gavin!" Sharon cut him off again.

"Like an angel of mercy, okay, Sharon? Angels of mercy are always tired because they're always helping everyone else."

"Nice save, college boy," Sharon chuckled.

"Look, Gavin," Juliette drummed her fingers on the desk a few times. "As far as Kelly's concerned, she thinks she's serious about the guy. As far as I'm concerned, I think the guy needs to respect her more. That's all I'm going to say about them. But you? Here's what I have to say to you. Respect her, you might win her heart. Disrespect her, you'll have me to deal with."

"And me," Sharon quipped.

"I can do respect." Gavin straightened his shoulders and grinned. "I come from good stock. My dad taught me that a man always treats his woman like his queen."

"*His* woman?" Juliette rolled her eyes. "The last time someone called me 'his' I was deeply offended, Gavin."

"Really? Then maybe when he called you that he wasn't being respectful. It sounds totally different when your woman is being treated right." Gavin frowned down at her.

Juliette smiled ruefully and nodded. "You're right, Gavin. He wasn't treating me with respect."

"You're also right about the 'his' thing, Gavin. I love it when Chris calls me 'his' because I know he takes responsibility for me. He's got me covered," Sharon added.

"Exactly," Gavin nodded, then turned back to face Juliette. "So. Who's disrespecting you?"

"I broke up with him months ago."

"You sure? Because I could go teach him a thing or two about respect." He began flexing his remarkable chest muscles as evidence that he was up for the task. Juliette had to cover her eyes because he was standing right in front of her desk.

"Gavin! Stop! You're making me feel very uncomfortable right now!" She peered through the cracks between her fingers. "Sharon, make him stop."

"What? Does this make you nervous?" Gavin held up his arm and flexed some more. "Frightened and confused? It'll make that guy you're talking about nervous, too, I'll bet. You just let me know if I need to handle things, okay?"

Juliette rolled her eyes. "Can you see the headlines? Student Defends Secretary's Honor in Front Lawn Flex-off. Oh, the publicity we could generate for this school!"

Gavin smirked and sat down again. "Okay, fine. I won't go hunt this guy down. But I have a question then. Why do you ladies let men treat you disrespectfully? What happened to chivalry and all that knights in shining armor stuff? Isn't that what girls dream about? Someone who will ride into town and fight for them?"

Juliette stopped smiling and stared at him, caught off guard by his direct questions. Finally, Sharon spoke up.

"Wow, Gavin. How did you get so insightful, so...."

"Philosophical?" The young man asked, grinning broadly. "Well, I didn't learn it in school, that's for sure. This place is full of ladies who don't respect themselves, and don't expect their men to respect them either." He shrugged. "You want to hear something funny? When I was a kid, my dad was taking some night classes at college, and for the longest time, I thought he was studying to be a knight. You know, a knight in shining armor. When I asked my mom about it, she said he was doing just that; studying to be her knight, her champion, so that he could take better care of the queen of his castle. Cool, huh?"

Sharon's eyes had grown soft as she listened to him.

"Very cool," she murmured.

"I know a lot of people think I'm just a big buffoon out there having too much fun, but I'm actually on a quest, you know?" He stretched his arms up over his head, then laced his fingers behind his neck, his white t-shirt stretched tightly over his chest. He seemed very relaxed at the moment; quite different than he had a few moments ago when he'd spoken of Kelly. "Only here's the thing: I'm looking for dragons to defeat, and battles to win, and a damsel in distress to rescue, but this place seems in short supply of all three. Dude, I want to be a champion but there seems to be little demand for them these days."

Sharon stood up and came around her desk and planted her petite form right in front of Gavin, suddenly very serious. Even though he was sitting, they were almost eye-to-eye. "Listen to me, young man. Don't you *ever* give up that quest, do you hear? There is a girl out there waiting for you to rescue her. She may not realize it yet, but inside of her there's that little girl your mom told you about, who's longing to be fought for, to be chosen." She reached out and poked one of his elbows, the least offensive spot on the guy's body she could think of, Juliette was certain. "I like you, Gavin," Sharon stated. "I just didn't know why until today."

Gavin grinned, then glanced past Sharon to the girl who'd appeared in the doorway. He straightened in his seat, running a hand over his hair. "Hey, Kelly."

"Hi, Gavin." She smiled shyly at him. "Did you turn your stuff in?"

He beamed proudly. "Yeah. And Juliette didn't believe it was my work."

"Oh, it's his, all right," Kelly turned to Juliette. "He's been working really hard at it for the last several days now."

"I couldn't have done it without your help, though."

"You did most of it on your own. I just showed you how to organize it."

"Yeah, but you have to admit, I'm pretty unorganized."

"Okay. You are unorganized."

"Um, hello?" Juliette interrupted. "Did you need something, Kelly?"

"Oh. No. That's okay. I didn't mean to interrupt. I have to get to the library anyway. They're holding a book for me, and I told them I was on my way."

Gavin jumped up. "I'll walk with you." And the two of them headed out into the hall without so much as a goodbye.

"I just caught a whiff of romance in the air." Sharon strode back to her own desk and eyed Juliette across the room. "Is that what you had in mind when you paired them up?"

"Actually, no. I thought she was all but married to her guy, and I would never have pegged Gavin as her type. After listening to him today, though, I think he might even be *my* type," Juliette chortled. "So, honestly, were you at all surprised by what came out of his mouth?"

"Uh, yeah. Completely blown away. Wow."

Juliette stuck out her bottom lip. "I want a Gavin, Sharon. Not *Gavin,* Gavin—I feel dirty even saying that—but a man who thinks that way. I want a champion so badly it hurts, Sharon. I want a man to rescue me, to choose me, a man who will claim me and make me his queen. I know I sound completely backward in this modern age we live in, but Gavin's right. What happened to chivalry?"

"No word from Victor, hm?" It wasn't a question, not really. It had been weeks, and she'd heard nothing from him.

"Nope. I kissed the guy, and he ran for his life." She'd

gone over the events of that night too many times to count, trying to figure out what she'd done wrong. "He said I made him crazy, so maybe that really is the problem. Maybe I just scared him off." She rubbed her dry eyes, scratchy from fatigue and frustration. "I guess I just thought he'd fight a little harder for me, for us."

"Maybe it's not completely his fault," Sharon suggested quietly. "I mean, sometimes we women don't believe we're worth fighting for. And if we don't believe it, then why should they? Gavin made another good point when he said that no one wants a champion anymore."

Juliette looked sharply at her friend, a question in her eyes. "Is that what you think? Do I put that message out?"

"I don't know, Juju. I haven't seen you with Victor. But I do know how you were with Mike, and you catered to him as though he was the only one who counted in your relationship." Sharon shook her head. "It wasn't like that at the beginning. I remember him fighting for you, even going toe-to-toe with Phoebe several times."

Juliette remembered a few of those encounters, too. Where did that Mike go?

"But then Mike stopped fighting. He made you pick up the weapons instead. And when a man stops fighting for something, or someone, the value of it diminishes in his eyes. Men like Chris, and like Gavin—Wow. Did I just call Gavin a man?—are prepared to fight for the long haul. Their weapons are an extension of themselves, and they never let down their guards."

"Well, Victor isn't like Mike, that's for sure. He's definitely the champion sort. He's just not fighting for me, that's all." Juliette sighed. "At least he didn't take ten years to make up his mind."

"Juliette."

"So why won't these guys fight for me?" She was desperate to know what was wrong with her that she wasn't worth fighting for.

"Think about what he said, Juju. Maybe he actually is scared *because* you push him to fight for you. Maybe he hasn't had to do that before. Maybe you need to remind him of why you're worth fighting for."

"I don't want to have to remind someone to fight for me." Juliette shook her head. She straightened the items on her desk and ran a tissue over the screen of her monitor.

"That's not really fair, is it? Every man needs to be reminded of why he's fighting, and what, and who he's fighting for, even the best of them. That's our part of the relationship; to encourage, to empower, to offer sanctuary. Real relationships aren't one-sided."

"I have Tootles now, you know." Juliette quipped.

"You do have Tootles."

"Although I would have preferred a champion without fur and a wagging tail that knocks things off the coffee table. Or one who whines all night when I lock him in the garage. Not that I'd lock my champion in the garage. That wouldn't be right."

"No, that wouldn't." Sharon eyed her across the room. "So have you been back to Saturday church at all since Peterson Pie Night?"

"No," Juliette picked up Gavin's folder and leafed through it again. "Victor knows where I live."

"Juliette Gustafson, you are the most stubborn person I've met in my life." Sharon laced her fingers together and leaned her elbows on her desk. "Maybe he's afraid that *you're* having second thoughts. Maybe he's been sitting in church, watching for you, waiting for some sign that you'll say yes again. In fact, I'll bet you a million Twinkies—"

Juliette couldn't stop the tears that welled up and spilled over. She didn't think she could be any more heart-broken than she'd been over Mike, but Victor's silence was crushing her, and she couldn't bear the thought of going to church to look for him, only to have it confirmed he was intentionally avoiding her.

"I'm sorry. I'm a jerk." Sharon shoved away from her desk and came around to perch on the edge of Juliette's. "But maybe this guy *is* your champion, Juju. Maybe you're just not giving him the chance to slay any dragons for you." Sharon patted her hand where it rested on the desk. "Go to church this Saturday, Juju. Go before it's too late for both of you."

~ ~ ~

JULIETTE stayed up as late as she could, doing everything she could think of to wear Tootles out. But the problem with her plan was that she was wearing out much quicker than the dog. Before long, she was sprawled on the couch, staring glumly at the dog chasing his tail in the kitchen. "What? Did you sleep all day while I was gone? No. Bad Tootles! Bad!"

He scampered across the room to her and licked her shoulder. She sighed, grabbed a hold of the collar around his neck, and headed out to the garage with him. She dropped down onto the blanket that was now his, and pulled the dog down beside her. He let her scratch his belly while she talked quietly to him.

"Okay, Tootles, here's the deal. I need some sleep tonight. No whining, or barking, or trying to break down the door, okay? It's only for two more nights and then I'll fix the gate and you can sleep in the kitchen again, I promise." She'd ordered a replacement part online at lunch, and paid more for 2-day air shipping than she had for the hardware itself.

It was to no avail. The moment she pulled the door closed behind her, Tootles began to whimper. Hardening her heart, she covered her ears, and hurried to get ready for bed.

She could hear him through both the garage door and the bedroom door. "You lived on the streets!" she wailed. "My garage is a mansion compared to what you're used to!"

An hour later, Tootles was still at it. Periods of promising silence would erupt into long, gut-wrenching howls that ended with forlorn yapping, and she could stand it no longer. She pushed herself up and made her way in the dark to the garage. Tootles came bounding inside, rubbing up against her, licking her hands and knees in his relief at seeing her. She headed to the couch and plopped down, throwing her legs up on an armrest, a pillow behind her head.

There was a knock on the door, and the dog began to bark ferociously, lunging at it.

"Tootles! Stop it! Down! Quiet!" The string of commands was completely ignored, and he seemed frantic to get at whoever was on the porch. Juliette pulled aside the curtain at the window and peered out.

Victor Jarrett.

CHAPTER TWENTY-NINE

JULIETTE couldn't believe it. "Look at him," she railed under her breath as she eyed him through the peephole. "Standing there like…like nothing's any different than it was the last time he stood there!" She couldn't believe how angry she suddenly was.

She flipped on the porch light and yanked the door open after getting a good grip on the dog's collar. "What have I done this time?"

Victor squinted a little in the sudden brilliance of the bulb over his head, but remained calm even as the dog tried to rip Juliette's arm off to get to him. "Good evening, Ms. Gustafson."

So it was back to Ms. Gustafson. Two could play that game. "It's not evening, Officer Jarrett. It's morning."

"Good morning, then. I'm here because of a noise complaint." He spoke in clipped tones that made her blood boil. Juliette pressed her lips together and peered up at him, knowing exactly what noise he referred to, but waiting for him to explain anyway. Her anger suddenly dissipated, replaced by shock and concern.

Under the light, he looked awful. The skin under his eyes was deeply shadowed, almost bruised, and his jaw was tight. He looked like he needed a nap, a shave, and a good, hot meal.

"Are…are you all right?" she asked before she caught herself, leaning forward just a little to be sure it wasn't just the light playing tricks on her.

"I'm fine." His curt reply made her step back, and he glanced down at the pad he held in his hand. "We've had a complaint about—" He stopped and rubbed his eyes with his thumb and fingers. "It says here you have a pack of wolves locked in your garage. Is this," he indicated the agitated Tootles. "One of them?"

"A pack of wolves? Are you serious? First I'm a call girl, then I operate a motorcycle gang, and now I'm zookeeper? Mrs. Cork is certifiably insane, okay? But then, so are you because *you*, Officer Meanie Man *Jerk*ett, actually believe her!" She let go of the dog. "Bite him, Tootles."

But Tootles defied her yet again, and threw himself against Victor's legs, thumping him with his tail, and burying his nose in all the inappropriate places, lavishing wet kisses all over his boots and kneecaps. Juliette rolled her red eyes and groaned.

"Oh, great. We've got a dog whisperer on the force." She was beyond caring how she sounded. He was here in the middle of the night, accusing her of housing wild animals, and acting as though the most incredible kiss in the whole world hadn't taken place only inches from where they were standing. "Apparently my dog likes you a whole lot better than I do."

"Not getting much sleep?" he asked gently. "You look exhausted. I take it he's new." The man was trying to be nice, but she wasn't having any of it.

"I'm not getting any sleep right *now* because I'm standing here in the wee hours of the morning, warding of friendly neighborhood defamation charges from a man who has spent way too much time on my front porch. Go away, Officer. I'll keep Tootles quiet. You can assure Mrs. Cork that he won't disrupt her beauty sleep anymore." Juliette grabbed the dog's collar and glared up at the officer. "And just for the record, you don't look so great yourself. Maybe you should get some beauty sleep, too."

Victor studied her, his expression sympathetic. Finally, he tore off the top page from the pad in his hand and held it out to her. "Just a warning this time. The next call regarding a noise violation will warrant a ticket, okay?" He hesitated a fraction of a minute before continuing. "And please understand, Ms. Gustafson. I don't want to have to visit your front porch any more than you want me to. Just keep him quiet, okay?"

His voice was soft, weary, but his words sank like a stone to the pit of her stomach. Victor reached down and ruffled the fur of the dog standing between them. "You're a good watchdog, aren't you, buddy? A little loud, but you'd scare off a bad guy."

"Oh, yeah." Juliette rolled her eyes again, crossing her arms against the chill in the air. "Look how scary he is. What kind of watchdog licks kneecaps and drools on the bad guys' boots?"

"I'm not the bad guy, Juliette," Victor said, straightening up and hooking his thumbs in his pockets, but not taking his eyes off the dog.

"The verdict is still out on that one, remember?" She wasn't joking this time.

Victor grimaced, then tipped his head to meet her eyes. "Does that mean there's still hope for me?"

Now it was her turn to stare down at the dog. She didn't know what to say to him. He'd kissed her, and abandoned her without so much as an explanation, and now he stood here on her front step asking her to believe he was one of the good guys? Who was he kidding?

Finally he cleared his throat and took a step backward. "I'm happy to see that you have a dog. It's good to know I have a little help when I can't be everywhere at once."

He really did look awful, and now she saw something in his eyes besides fatigue. Was it regret? Her traitorous heart softened just the tiniest bit.

"Well, he's clearly happy to see you, too." She clung to her recalcitrance, but her tone was kinder. "You two make a good team, keeping me up all night long. I should make you take him with you, since you seem to get along so well."

She pushed the dog inside, then turned around to face him, pulling the door nearly closed behind her so just the dog's nose stuck out between her knees. "Look, I'm terribly tired and Tootles is terribly not. We'll figure it out, I promise. If I survive." She took a deep breath and let it out in a huff. "Can a person die of sleep deprivation?"

"It's a slow and painful way to go." He sounded like he was talking from personal experience.

"Lovely. Thanks for giving me something to look forward to."

The corners of his mouth twitched a little, but that was all. He simply stood there for several moments, just long enough for her to wonder if she should speak, then he cleared his throat again. "I, uh, haven't seen you in church lately."

She shook her head. "I haven't been the last few weeks. Sorry."

"You don't have to apologize to me. I was just saying I'd noticed. I'm glad you're okay. I'll stop worrying now."

"No, I'm fine. You don't have to worry about me." But the thought of him thinking about her made her feel a little light-headed.

"We didn't scare you away, did we?" His voice became even quieter. "Did I?" Juliette looked up at his face, surprised at his genuine concern. Maybe Sharon was right after all.

"Scare me away? No! Michelle and Tom were wonderful, and I don't know if I even thanked them. Or you. You went out of your way to be kind to me, Vic—Officer. Most people just turn and look the other way when they see someone hurting. You didn't. So thank you."

"I'm not most people." He didn't catch her stumble over his name, or it no longer mattered.

"No." She shook her head. "You're not, are you?"

The silence that followed gave her little hope, and she pulled the edges of her robe closer in a subconscious effort to protect her heart. The night was chilly, and the darkness that settled just outside the circle of light from her porch felt unfriendly and cold.

Victor tipped his head toward the dog. "You know, Michelle is really good with dogs. I know she'd enjoy helping you with … well, with … your dog."

"Tootles."

"Yes. Anyway, she—"

"His name is Tootles." Why wouldn't he say the dog's name? "Too-tles." She said it slowly, as though teaching him a new word.

"Right. Well, Mich—"

"You can't say it, can you? Tootles." She was beginning to smile, teasing him. "What's the matter? Is it not tough enough for you?"

"I'll just call him Bob."

"But his name is Tootles! He won't come to Bob."

"Sure he will. He knows a real man's name when he hears it." He grinned.

She rolled her eyes again.

"Let's test my theory, then." He moved several feet down the walk before turning back to face them. He spoke firmly, but not loudly. "Bob. Come here!" She stepped aside, and Tootles charged down the steps, hurtling himself at the man. Victor looked up at her, his eyes challenging.

"Tootles! Come here, Tootles! Come to mama!" The dog had suddenly gone deaf. It continued to circle the policeman, panting and licking, leaning into the man's legs and whacking him with its tail. "Hey! I'm the one who feeds you! Come here, right now, you little turncoat!"

"He's not a turncoat," Victor chuckled, as he and the dog came back up the steps together. "He just doesn't like that 'I was named by a girl. Come beat me up!' name you gave him."

"Ha! And you won't say it, will you? A big, hunk of a manly man like you can't say Tootles!"

"Big hunk of a manly man? I thought I was Meanie Man Jerkett."

"You are!" She jabbed a finger into his chest, but he caught her wrist. With his thumb, he uncurled her fingers and brought her hand to his chest, covering it with his own, holding it there the way he had before, pressed flat over his heart. She stared at their hands, the way his covered hers so only the tips of her fingers could be seen.

Then she remembered to breathe and suddenly, everything wrong with the night seemed to right itself. Her shoulders relaxed, and the crease between her eyebrows disappeared. She lifted her gaze to Victor's face and forgot to breathe all over again. He studied her, his storm-gray gaze wandering over her features; her own misty eyes, the curl of her hair around her ears, her parted lips. Tootles stood between them looking back and forth, trying to choose which one he should lean against first.

"He doesn't even look like a Bob," she whispered.

At that moment, Mrs. Cork's front porch light flipped on. Victor released Juliette's hand and took a step backwards, and Juliette reached for Tootles' collar just as her neighbor stepped outside. She did not look happy.

"Mrs. Cork." Victor called out softly, nodding in her direction.

She glared at them, obviously waiting for some kind of explanation. Juliette pulled the collar of her robe up with one hand, covering her flushed face, while the other held tightly to Tootles' collar. At that moment, Mrs. Cork's little dog catapulted from her arms, charged down the front steps, and across the adjoining lawns. Tootles lunged forward, dragging Juliette to her knees, but she held tight to his collar. Mrs. Cork began to wail, flapping her arms like a scrawny chicken.

"Mr. Bobo! Mr. Bobo! He's going to eat Mr. Bobo!" She reached for the handrail on her porch and hitched her way down the steps, the old lady slippers on her feet making her descent rather precarious. "Do something, Officer! Call the police! Mr. Bobo!"

"Bob!" Victor's booming voice cut through the shrieking, and brought everything to a standstill for one breath of a second, even the dogs. It wasn't much; just long enough for him to grab Tootles' collar and help Juliette right herself, and then Mr. Bobo was on the porch. The two dogs were all over each other, sniffing and licking, pawing and circling, like long-lost relatives at an overdue reunion.

Victor crossed the lawn to Mrs. Cork, who was making her way over the dew-dampened grass. He offered her his arm and she looked up at him. "I don't think he's going to eat Mr. Bobo after all."

"No," said the officer, "I don't see that happening. In fact, I think Bob is missing his wolf pack, and is happy to find another man around." Juliette stifled a giggle.

"They do look like they want to be friends." Mrs. Cork's tentative tone, usually so curt, made Juliette's eye widen in wonder. Victor was an old lady whisperer, too! With a tight grip on Tootles' collar, Juliette led the dog down the steps to the lawn, Mr. Bobo frolicking playfully between the big dog's legs.

"Yes, it does. Maybe you and Juliette should arrange some play dates for your boys. It looks like Mr. Bobo might enjoy spending time with a young pup, and we all know Bob is still learning to adjust to his wonderful new life."

Juliette narrowed her eyes to glare at the policeman.

"Well," Mrs. Cork shook her head slightly. "I'm awfully busy, and Mr. Bobo usually just follows me around all day. I don't know how he'd do going to visit someone else."

"But it's not just anyone else he'd be visiting," Victor protested, patting the hand she had curled around his bicep. "It's Bob. And practically in his own backyard, too. Besides, you'll never know until you try it."

Now Juliette was getting perturbed. Who did he think he was, trying to orchestrate a relationship between her and her crabby-pants neighbor? "I don't know, Officer," she hemmed. "That might be tough with our schedules."

"Well, maybe we could work something out." Mrs. Cork stepped forward and reached down to touch the top of Tootles' head. The traitorous hound looked up and licked her fingertips. "What do you think, Bob? Would you like to play with Mr. Bobo sometime?"

"His name is Tootles," Juliette corrected.

"What? Oh. I thought...." Mrs. Cork's voice trailed off as she glanced from Victor to Juliette and back. "Tootles? That can't be right. He doesn't even look like a Tootles! I'm sure I heard you calling him Bob."

Juliette looked up at the policeman who had his hand up covering his mouth, as though he were pondering something of vast intellectual consequences. "You know, Mrs. Cork, I think you're right. He really looks like a Bob, doesn't he?"

"Yes, he does," the older woman nodded emphatically. "Bob. See? He likes it, too." Juliette shook her head in utter amazement. The dog looked up from chewing on Mr. Bobo's ear because the woman was paying attention to him, not because he liked the name Bob.

"But he's my dog, and I named him Tootles," she declared, feeling a pout coming on.

Mrs. Cork shook her head vehemently. "Oh no, Juliette! You are Bob's person, not the other way around." Then she actually chuckled, shocking Juliette into silence. She'd never heard the woman laugh in the four years they'd shared the two halves of the condominium. "The sooner you figure that out, the sooner you'll find out how wonderful it is to be loved by a dog."

"Ladies," Victor interjected. "And gentlemen." He reached down to scuffle Mr. Bobo's ear. "Duty calls and it's late. I'm sorry to have kept you up so late, but I hope the four of you will be able to figure out a way for your dogs to interact in the future. Mrs. Cork? May I see you to your door?"

Juliette snorted as he once again held out his arm to the old lady who scooped up her dog and smiled up at the officer like a blushing schoolgirl. Juliette glared at the dip between his shoulder blades as he escorted the ridiculous woman and her Mr. Bobo across the lawn and up to her own front stoop, where Mrs. Cork held out her dog for the nice officer to pet. He obliged. Then Mrs. Cork did something she'd never done before. As Officer Jarrett made his way off her porch, she looked across the street lamp-lit lawn and waved, calling out, "Good night, Juliette. Good night, Bob!"

Amazed, Juliette waved back and turned to go inside, wrestling Bob in ahead of her.

"Juliette. Wait." Victor stopped her with a hand on her shoulder and she jumped.

"How did you get over here so fast?" she gasped, having assumed he'd go straight to his car.

Grinning, he held both hands aloft in surrender. "Sorry I startled you. I didn't want to call out and wake up the neighborhood."

"Um, between Mrs. Cork screaming that my dog is going to eat Mr. Bobo, and you showing off your dog whisperer skills, I think it's too late. The other neighbors are probably calling the cops as we speak." She pulled the door nearly closed behind her again, but this time Tootles seemed content to stay inside. She looked up at Victor with narrowed eyes. "You know, that was pretty slick back there. Mrs. Cork and I haven't interacted that much in the entire time I've lived here, no less in one sitting. I think she's actually considering having a neighborly relationship with me now. I don't know whether to hit you or kiss you."

His eyebrows went up and his smile broadened. Juliette blushed and rushed on. "Sorry. Like I said, I'm ridiculously tired so I can't be responsible for what comes out of my mouth. Was there something else you wanted?"

He hesitated, as though choosing his words carefully. "I'm glad you have Bob." That was what he wanted to tell her? Juliette couldn't prevent the swell of disappointment in her belly.

"Tootles," she quipped, a little too brightly.

"Tootles," he nodded, saying the name for the first time, his deep voice tight with resistance and humor.

Juliette's brow furrowed. "Oh dear." She shook her head, a grave look on her face.

"What is it?"

"You're right, Officer Jarrett. That's just wrong in so many ways. It was really cute when we girls were calling him Tootles in our high, squeaky voices, but when you say it? Eek! Total emasculation." She snorted. "Of the dog, not you. Your manliness just highlights the girliness of his name."

"I think you just called me manly again."

"That's not what I said. Well, that's not what I meant. I mean, you are manly, but I didn't mean to point it out." She put a hand up to cover her eyes. "I just said it again, didn't I?" She began backing through the door, then hid behind it, only her eyes peeking out to look up at him. "Officer, I'm going to call it a night."

"I liked it better when you called me Victor." Hadn't she said those exact same words to him so many weeks ago?

"Well then, goodnight, Victor," she murmured.

"Goodnight, Juliette. Sleep well." He saluted and turned to leave. Halfway down the walk, he stopped and looked back at her. "Maybe I'll see you in church on Saturday."

She grinned. "Maybe you will."

CHAPTER THIRTY

HE WAS in trouble.

This time, Sarah refused to hand the paper over until Victor gave up some information. They were both putting in extra hours because of a flu bug going around, and everyone who wasn't sick was covering for those who were. It was a slow night, and for that they were both grateful, but when Sarah answered Mrs. Cork's disgruntled complaints with barely restrained laughter, Victor saw it in her eyes that her curiosity would no longer be denied.

"Whoa," Sarah said, sitting back in her chair after he finished giving her what he thought was a very objective debriefing of his on-the-clock encounters with the now infamous Juliette Gustafson. He left out the pie date with the Petersons and the line-backer take-down. That was none of Sarah's business. Besides, he'd sworn off thinking about that night during work hours. "No wonder you've been wandering around here looking like you've been hit by a Mack truck."

"What do you mean?" He'd been stupid enough to ask.

"Oh, man. Denial, too? It's worse than I thought. Hoo-ie!"

Sarah shook her head and took another call while Victor glared at her. She handed him the call report and shooed him off with a grin and a wave. He went, feeling like a flushed-cheek kid, glancing down at the paper she'd handed him. She'd written in big block letters across the top, YOU ARE IN T-R-O-U-B-L-E!

He knew it was true the moment Juliette barged out her front door to greet him with her contempt. Even in her disheveled and pink-robed state, she was radiant, making him ache at the sight of her. He fumbled with his notebook, pretending to read words that weren't written there, collecting his thoughts enough to speak coherently.

Sarah was right. He was falling for Juliette, the wild girl. The wild girl with the out-of-control sisters. And the out-of-control friends. And the out-of-control neighbor. And now the out-of-control dog named Tootles.

Bob.

He could no longer deny it. For three weeks he'd waged war in his heart; praying, thinking, contemplating, imagining, wondering how he could even consider having a relationship with her, then wondering how he could go on breathing without her. Each Saturday night in church, he watched for her, hoping his reaction to her would be different when he saw her, hoping his heart wouldn't feel like a jackhammer trying to punch a hole in his chest. And each Saturday night she didn't show left him feeling more uncertain than ever.

But tonight, instead of more turmoil, the sight of her was like a cool drink of water to his thirsty heart. When she poked him in the chest and called him manly, hope flooded through the rest of him, sweeping away the murky shadows of fear. Pressing her hand to his heart, he'd felt anchored, connected. And when he pulled away from her curb just now, he felt like he was leaving home.

"I am in trouble," he said, a hand on the back of his neck, his fingers massaging the stiff muscles. He played things over in his mind, from the beginning, back to his very first encounter with her, speeding because she was hungry. He could see the chagrin on her face as he stood over her explaining why he was giving her a ticket, like she was a child. How ridiculous he must have seemed to her. Her tears the second time—tears that seemed to come from nowhere, but now he knew better—were the tears of a broken heart, of someone taken for granted and tossed away. He welcomed the surge of anger, quickly followed by the longing to protect her from the kind of man who would treat her so dishonorably .... Then he heard her weary voice say, "I spent way too much time trying to figure out what I'd done to make you treat me so unkindly. Well, I get it now. I know your type too well."

His foot slid off the accelerator, and his car slowed to a crawl on the empty, past-midnight street. "I am that man. I'm the type of man who would treat her so unkindly, so dishonorably." He hadn't contradicted her when she said those things about herself; his reticence must've led her to believe he agreed.

Couldn't she tell how violently she stirred his senses? Didn't she see how alive he felt every moment he spent with her?

Of course not. Because he questioned her integrity every time he had the slightest opportunity. And when he finally did acknowledge feeling something for her, he panicked and ran, abandoning her to her doubts and questions of self-worth.

To add insult to injury, she'd taken his rudeness and insensitivity like a trooper, like someone accustomed to doing so. She remained authentic and transparent, while he pushed, insulted, and assaulted....

That kiss. His gut tightened in response.

She called him manly, not once, but several times tonight. He felt her hand beneath his, curled around his heart, and he brought his fist up to his chest even now. He loved how everything she was thinking and feeling could be seen in her dove eyes. He loved that she didn't wear masks. He loved that she said what she was thinking. He loved that she didn't pretend to be something she wasn't. He loved—

"I love her."

He swerved abruptly off the road and thrust the cruiser into park. His chest felt like it was caving in. His vision actually blurred and he thought he was going to be sick. Climbing out of the car, he stumbled to the sidewalk and started pacing, back and forth, breathing deeply, in through the nose, out through the mouth. With those three words everything seemed to fall into place, like a combination lock to his heart, and he thought he might just be consumed by the rush of emotions that crashed through him. He wanted to turn around and fly back to her, to sweep her into his arms, and tell her everything that was bursting out of his unlocked heart.

"Oh, God," he moaned, bending over with his hands on his knees, feeling his world spinning out of control. "Help me," he begged. "Help me know what to do with all of this. It's more than I can hold on to right now."

Then let it go, son. Stop flailing and kicking and resisting. Give it to Me. Let me take your heart of stone and give you a heart of flesh.

~ ~ ~

"'MAYBE you will,' Tootles, that's what I said. Very clever and mysterious, don't you think?" Juliette actually twirled, the thick socks allowing her an extra half spin. Tootles-Bob ran a circle around the living room, launching himself up and over the back of the sofa. That brought her dance to an abrupt halt.

"Tootles! No, no! Bob!" Juliette laughed and plopped down on the sofa, letting the animal figure out it was time to settle down. Finally, she got up, found the leash Ren had given her, and brought the dog's blanket into the living room. "Looks like we're sleeping on the couch tonight. At least I am. You're sleeping on the floor. Tied to me." She held up her arm indicating the handle of the leash looped around her wrist.

She made a bed of blankets and pillows for herself, got the dog settled on his, and they both fell asleep without further ado.

The next morning came much too quickly, and with it, a flood of doubt that her fatigue could not fend off. Why would someone like Victor choose someone like her? Of course he was glad she had Bob; now he didn't have to feel so guilty about not calling her.

Juliette dragged herself off to work, arriving nearly ten minutes late.

"Oh good. Now I can stop worrying!" Sharon quipped as Juliette stumbled through the office door, the toe of her shoe catching on the carpet because she wasn't picking her feet up. "Ooh. Maybe I shouldn't stop worrying after all. Bad night with Tootles again?"

Juliette dropped into her chair, her purse falling to the ground with a thunk at her feet. "You won't believe who came to my house at one o'clock this morning."

Sharon gasped, "No! Are you serious?"

"I was so mad. And to make matters worse, he was being so nice." She rubbed her burning eyes. "And Bob loved him."

"What? Who's Bob?"

"Tootles. He changed Tootles' name to Bob, and Bob is much happier. I just have to get used to calling him Bob now and I'm not very happy about that."

"You let him change your dog's name? What is wrong with you?" Sharon actually looked angry. "And I thought that dog had more sense than that! Did you let him in?"

Juliette squinted at her friend across the room. "No, of course not! Why would I do that?"

"But you let him stay long enough for Tootles to decide that he liked him?"

"Bob. Loved, not liked. Bob *loved* him. It took less than five seconds to determine that."

"Oh my goodness, Juju! You let that man sweet talk you in the middle of the night, didn't you? Please tell me you didn't do anything stupid." Sharon was appalled.

"Besides telling him he was manly three times? No."

"Juliette Gustafson! You didn't!"

"Don't worry. He was very polite about it all. He didn't even mention it the first time. The second time he teased me a little, and the third time I was so embarrassed, he just left."

Now Sharon looked confused. "He didn't take advantage of you?"

"Sharon! No!" Juliette burst out laughing. "Take advantage of me? Woo-hoo! You should have seen me all dolled up in my pink fluffy robe and woolly socks, and crabby as a housecat in the bathtub! I'm surprised he didn't run screaming!"

"I'm surprised, that's all. It just sounds like something he'd totally use to his advantage. And I wouldn't think he'd care what you were wearing, especially showing up at one in the morning like that. What was he expecting? A ball gown?"

Juliette eyed her friend. "Wow. That was pretty harsh, don't you think? I was under the impression you liked the guy."

"What? What on earth gave you that idea?" Sharon's voice rose sharply and she stood. "I haven't cared a lick for Mike in a very long time, Juju."

"Mike?" Juliette's sluggish mind was unable to comprehend the abrupt shift in the direction of their conversation. "My Mike? What are you talking about?"

They stared at each other for several seconds before Sharon cocked her head and asked, "Juju-bee, who came to your house at one o'clock in the morning?"

"Officer Jarrett."

"Oh, my sweet pile of jellybeans!" Sharon collapsed back into her chair. "You freaked me out! I thought Mike came over last night, and I thought Tootles fell in love with Mike, and I thought you called Mike manly three times— " Sharon paused in the middle of her tirade and narrowed her eyes. "Wait a minute. So you're saying that Victor Jarrett came to your house in the middle of the night, won the heart of your dog, and you called him manly, not once, but three times?" She pushed back from her desk and rose, coffee cup in hand, and came around to sit in the chair just across from Juliette, relief turning to delight on her face. "Oh, this is good. Do tell."

Juliette crossed her arms over her chest and stared at

Sharon, understanding finally sinking in. "I can't believe you thought I was talking about Mike!"

Sharon waved a hand of dismissal in the air. "I don't care about stupid old Mike. I want to know what happened last night!"

"No. Just for thinking the worst of me, I'm going to let you wonder for a while."

"Well, it does sound like something he might pull, doesn't it? Did you ever change your locks or does he still have a spare key?"

Juliette didn't answer right away.

"See? So I have a very valid excuse for thinking you were talking about Mike. Besides, you said you were mad."

"Well, I was! I was mad at Bob for not letting me sleep, I was mad at Manly-Man for never calling me, I was mad at Mrs. Cork for calling the cops again, and I was mad at myself for not owning one of those silky robes that doesn't make me look like I raided my grandmother's pajama drawer."

By the time Juliette had filled her friend in on the events of the night, she was feeling a little better. It helped that Sharon kept plying her with coffee.

"So he still wants to take you out."

"He didn't say that."

"Yes, he did."

"He said, 'Maybe I'll see you in church.''

"I know what words he used. But he *meant* he wanted to see you." Sharon rubbed her hands together gleefully. Then she paused, her lips pursed. "I wonder why he's not married yet. I hope he's not a weirdo."

"Oh, don't say that! I'm running out of nicknames for weirdo men. Although I did call him Officer Meanie Man Jerkett."

"You called him what?" Sharon gasped, choking on her coffee.

"I know. I'm an idiot." She shrugged. "But I don't think he's a weirdo." Juliette swept her hands across her keyboard, the gentle clatter of the keys comforting her with its familiarity. "I think he's probably just super careful. I get the feeling he knows what he wants and won't settle for anything less. Like me. He's so far out of my league, Sharon. He's got his whole life in order; a career he loves, a great circle of friends, a church. Not weird. Perfect. And I don't do so well living up to perfect. Just ask Mike."

"Stop talking, Juliette. You're starting to tick me off." Sharon set her cup down on Juliette's desk and leaned forward so she was looking her friend in the eye. "You listen to me. Mike is not the measure of a man. Nor is he something to measure other men by. He is a fool, do you hear me? Why can't you get this?" She stood up and started pacing the room, then stopped, her back to the office door, both hands on her hips.

"Just because Mike treated you like dirt, doesn't make you dirt. Just because Mike didn't respect you, doesn't mean you don't deserve respect. Just because Mike didn't lift you up, does not mean you have to lie down and get walked on by everyone else. And just because Mike couldn't see the real you, doesn't mean you're not royalty. You're a princess, Juliette Gustafson, and you deserve to be treated like one. That's the way God sees you so why should you or anyone else see you any differently? You are *not* out of anyone's league, do you hear me? Stop settling for less!" She took a deep breath then let it all out in a whoosh of air. "Now I need to go to the little girl's room."

"Oldest escape route in the world," Juliette muttered

under her breath. She turned toward her window overlooking the manicured campus lawns. She knew her friend wasn't trying to get away from her. So why did her bolstering words feel more like flying fists today?

CHAPTER THIRTY-ONE

SHORTLY after Juliette arrived home from work, Mrs. Cork was knocking on her door, a covered dish in hand. Juliette had to force her jaw not to drop—Mr. Bobo was on a leash! Tootles-Bob launched himself out the front door between Juliette's legs, and he and Mr. Bobo did their meet-and-greet dance all over again.

"I brought you a casserole," Mrs. Cork said, stepping adroitly over the leash as Mr. Bobo ducked between her legs. "I hope you like chicken and broccoli."

"Mrs. Cork, oh my!" Juliette was at a complete loss.

"Well, I thought it was the least I could do to help. I know how difficult a new dog can be, and I wasn't very understanding last night. I'd like to try to make amends, and food often opens closed doors."

Juliette could hardly believe her ears as she held open the door for her neighbor and her food. And the dogs. Unsure what the protocol was for this awkward, albeit hopeful situation, she said, "Well, the thought of cooking was giving me a headache. In fact, I was just getting ready to call Mr. Chen Yu over at The Green Dragon." She paused for just a heartbeat. "Would you like to join me for dinner?"

"That's all right. We've already eaten. But thank you just the same."

"Oh. Okay. Um, would you like a drink? I just put on some tea water."

"That's all right," she said again. "We're going to call it an early night ourselves, aren't we, Mr. Bobo?" The little dog was nowhere to be seen, having followed Tootles-Bob into the kitchen, and the muscles around Juliette's heart squeezed a little over the thought of how lonely the woman must be. Was Mr. Bobo her only friend?

"Well, maybe another time, then." An idea popped into her head, and before she could reconsider, she said, "Mrs. Cork, would you like to go to church with me this coming Saturday night?"

The light that came on in the woman's eyes was something to behold. "Oh. Well. I haven't been to church in a long time. I—I think I'd like that."

"Then it's a date," Juliette smiled weakly. "Church is at seven so if you come a little early, we can get there in time to choose our seats. And of course, Mr. Bobo is welcome to stay here with Tootles. Bob. Will that work?"

"Yes. I think that will be just fine. Thank you." Mrs. Cork turned toward the sound of scuffling dogs in the kitchen and called for Mr. Bobo. The fur-ball came bounding in, panting and happy, and she scooped him up in her arms. "We'll see you Saturday then, if not sooner. Bye-bye, Bob." And she headed out the door without looking back.

"Well!" said Juliette to herself. Tootles-Bob licked her foot supportively. Neither one of them knew quite what to think of Mrs. Cork's and Mr. Bobo's visit, but Juliette was glad it had been brief. All she wanted to do was eat, and shower, and go to bed. Or, rather, to couch.

~ ~ ~

BY THE TIME she clocked out on Friday, Juliette was ready for some down time. Between the nights spent sleeping on her lumpy sofa, and a last-minute induction into a planning committee for a new exchange student program, Juliette wanted nothing more than to lose herself in a chick-flick and chocolate marathon. She didn't really want to spend it alone, but she knew Sharon and Chris had a busy weekend planned. Phoebe hated chick-flicks unless they were foreign films with or without subtitles, and Ren hadn't been an option since her wedding night. But perhaps Gia would be game.

Her little sister was thrilled and suggested they start early, making it an all-nighter. "I brought my *Eden Rising* movies!" Gia held up the box set as she walked in the front door. Since Juliette hadn't seen any of them, they watched them, one right after the other, with only a dinner run to The Green Dragon in between the first and second movie. They also made a quick stop on the way back at Mona's, to stock up on sticky buns for breakfast, and a few chocolate essentials to keep their energy up throughout the night.

Tootles-Bob was in heaven with the attention of not one, but two Gustafson girls, and he rewarded them by being on his best behavior. By the time the credits rolled on the last of the series, all three of them were burrowed down into Movie Night Pillowland, a mass of pillows and blankets on the floor in front of the television. Juliette woke up just enough to hit the power button on the remote.

Saturday morning started out with a face-wash, courtesy

of Tootles-Bob, and Juliette sat up and hollered, "Agh! I've been kissed by a dog!"

"Good morning to you, Lucy," Gia chortled from under the blanket she'd pulled up over her own face to protect it from Tootles-Bob's lavish adoration. "I'll make the coffee if you want."

Juliette shoved Tootles-Bob off her blanket. "Since when do you drink coffee?"

"I started a new job a few weeks ago. At Café Rico," Gia said proudly, standing and stretching.

"I didn't even know you were looking. Congratulations!" Juliette hugged her warmly, a bit surprised at how grown up her little sister felt in her arms. She stepped back and looked at her, pushing a red corkscrew curl away from her eyes. "So what happened to Katie Girl?" Gia had been working part time after school at a children's clothing boutique for nearly two years, and Juliette thought she liked the job.

"I'm still working there. I needed more hours but my boss couldn't give me any, so I took the job at the coffee shop, too. According to Rico, I can make a mean cup of java."

"Is that a good thing?" Juliette teased, placing Mona's sticky buns in a glass casserole dish and sliding them into the toaster oven. She opened the slider to let Tootles-Bob out back.

"I don't know," Gia admitted. "All coffee tastes mean to me. I just paid attention to what people said they liked the first several times I made the coffee, then tried to brew it the same way the next time."

"Clever girl, Clarice."

"Ugh. I hate it when you quote that movie." Gia shivered, scrunching up her face.

"Habit. Sorry. I don't know why I used to like it so much.

How about this one? 'If you brew it, they will come.'"

"Clever girl, Clarice."

"Touché, Gia." Juliette turned away quickly, not wanting her little sister to see her blush as she remembered Victor saying the same thing to her.

Soon the whole house smelled like French roast and cinnamon, and the girls salivated as they straightened the living room. They decided to eat out on the back patio so Tootles-Bob could run around and sniff Mr. Bobo through the fence while they enjoyed the crisp fall morning. Still in their pajamas, they bundled up in blankets, foregoing the formality of robes, and headed out with their morning victuals.

"Is it all right if I thank God for Mona's buns?" Gia smirked, but bowed her head in agreement while Juliette said a simple prayer. "Lord, thank You for this time You've given me with Gia. Thank you for Mona and her delicious baked goods, and thanks retroactively for Mr. Chen Yu at the Green Dragon since I forgot to pray before dinner last night. He really knows how to cook a noodle." She dropped her voice to nearly a whisper and added, "And help things to go well with Mrs. Cork tonight. Amen."

When Juliette raised her head, Gia whispered discreetly back, "Your neighbor?" But her face was filled with curious questions.

Juliette nodded and broke off a dripping chunk of cinnamon roll. "I'll tell you about it when we go back inside," she mumbled, then shoved the piece into her mouth. When she finally managed to swallow the bite, her voice was filled with awe. "I don't know how Mona does it."

After breakfast, they gathered up their dishes to head back inside. "Tootles! Bob!" Juliette called, and Gia eyed her curiously. "That's part of the story. Inside." They quickly and companionably washed up after breakfast, and Juliette fixed herself another cup of coffee. "Barista Gia, Rico is right. This coffee is *sans imperfection*; perfect."

Gia poured herself a glass of milk. "Do you want to see how I drink coffee?" Then she added a splash of coffee to the top of her glass, and a heaping spoonful of sugar, and stirred. Taking a sip, she nodded, and said, "*Sans imperfection;* perfect." They settled into either end of the sofa and Gia prompted her for information. "So? Mrs. Cork?"

Juliette squinted against the morning sun pouring through the front window. It warmed the room, so instead of closing the blinds, she turned more fully toward Gia. "Believe it or not, she and Mr. Bobo—her dog—brought me dinner Wednesday night, so I invited her to come to church with me tonight."

"Okay. Wow. What happened?" Gia's eyes were wide, a glass blue made brighter framed by all her copper curls. "I mean, the last time I was over here you weren't even speaking to her and now you two are hanging out and you know her dog by name!"

Juliette smiled as she told Gia about her midnight mediator. "And now you also know how Tootles became Tootles-Bob."

"So this is the guy you were telling us about at the last G-FOURce?"

"It is." Juliette grinned. "Anyway, so now Mrs. Cork and I are being nice to each other because Mr. Bobo and Tootles-Bob want to be friends."

"You might as well just call him Bob, Jules. Tootles is a cute name, but it seems to me that Bob likes Bob, not Tootles."

Juliette sighed resignedly. "I know. I think I'm just resisting because of some weird control issue. My dog; I should get to name him, right?"

"I can totally see that." Gia was nodding her head, a strange look on her face.

"What?" Juliette asked, nudging her with her socked foot.

"You're just different somehow, Jules. I mean, you bring home a dog, you hardly ever talk about Mike anymore, you go to church, you speak up for yourself, but it's not in a mean way, you know? And now you're making friendly with the neighbor you've hated for eternity. And you even called me to come over here and hang out with you for no reason except to…to…hang out. You used to just do stuff alone. Or just with Sharon. It's like you're *freer* or something. Not so careful and worried all the time."

"Really? Actually, I do feel more … more awake, I guess."

"See? You're still the old you, but it's like you're all wrapped up in a new version of you." Gia cocked her head and looked sideways at her sister. "I loved the old you, don't get me wrong. But whatever is going on with you is pretty cool."

"And I have you to thank for it."

"Me?" Gia pressed a hand to her sternum. "What did I do?"

"You put Trevor on the Monday ManDate list."

"Who?"

"Trevor. Taz."

"Oh, yeah. I always forget his real name is Trevor." Gia reached over and flipped Bob's ears back, turning them inside out. Bob just shook them back into place and licked her toes.

"He helped me see Jesus in a way I'd never seen Him

before and I'm telling you what, Gia. It's changed the way I see almost everything. And everyone." Suddenly she heard Sharon's rant from earlier that week echoing in her mind. *That's the way God sees you, so why should you or anyone else see you any differently?* "Except for the way I see myself," she frowned, the words rocketing through her as she said them. "Ow. That kinda hurts."

"What's wrong?" Gia looked concerned.

"I'm fine," Juliette whispered. "I'm just a little overwhelmed. By grace. By God." She wasn't quite sure how to explain it to Gia.

But to her surprise, the girl nodded, her own eyes glistening in sympathy. "I know what you mean. Sometimes, out of nowhere, I'll think about something God's done for me, and I'll just start crying like a baby."

Juliette stared at Gia, stunned by her words. "What? You're a Christian, too?"

Gia shrugged, and dropped her gaze to her lap where she was picking at her cuticles. "Yeah."

"Why didn't you say anything when I told everyone about me at our last G-FOURce?"

"I kinda didn't want Phoebe to feel too awkward, you know? She'd be the only one *not*."

Juliette shook her head, amazed at what she was hearing. She'd learned so much about her sisters these last few weeks, things she should have known long ago had she been paying attention to anyone but herself. And the fact that Gia tried to be so sensitive to Phoebe said a lot about the youngest Gustafson girl. Juliette reached over and squeezed her hands.

"You're something else, little girl."

The girl rubbed her foot down Bob's side. "That's what Grandpa always says."

"He's right. You are." Juliette had an idea. "Hey. Do you want to go to church with me and Mrs. Cork? Officer Jarrett is supposed to be there, too. If he is, I'll introduce you."

Gia's eyes lit up almost as much as Mrs. Cork's had. "Are you serious? I can meet Officer Hot on Your Tail? That's what Ren calls him," she explained quickly.

"If he's there, and we run into him, yes. I'd love to get your opinion about him."

Gia leapt up and danced around the room, followed closely by Bob. "Ha! Ren will be green with envy! Yes, I want to go!" She flopped over the back of the sofa and lay sprawled on the cushions. "He's a friend of Taz's, right? I wonder if Ricky knows him. I should call him and find out!" She hopped up again and reached for her purse, but Juliette stopped her, laughing at her exuberance.

"Don't you dare call Ricky, you little nut! All I need is for it to get back to Victor that I'm stalking him and—"

"Victor? You're on first-name bases with him now? Woo-hoo!" Gia jabbed Juliette in her side, and Juliette responded by thumping her with a cushion.

"Pillow fight!" Gia shrieked, jumping up and launching the pillow she held at Juliette.

~ ~ ~

THEY ARRIVED almost ten minutes early for church, but sat near the back for a speedy getaway. Mrs. Cork worried about leaving Mr. Bobo too long, even though he was hanging out with his new best bud, Bob. Although the plan to duck out quickly dashed any hope of lingering long enough to scout for Victor, Juliette was surprised by how much she was enjoying herself with the other two women.

Right at seven o'clock, the musicians made their way on stage. A young man in blue jeans strapped on his guitar and stepped up to the microphone. Without any introduction, he began to play. The rest of the band and singers joined in, and the chattering around the sanctuary died down as the congregation began to sing along.

Juliette wondered how Mrs. Cork was receiving it all; the casual crowd, the full band on stage, the modern worship songs. She stole a few surreptitious glances at her, but the woman seemed attentive and receptive.

Pastor Eric, in true form, preached a wonderful message from Psalms, and before long, Juliette was swept up in what he was saying. After the last chord of the night was strummed, she turned to her seatmates and nodded, signaling that she was ready to go when they were.

"Well, that was lovely," Mrs. Cork stated as they passed through the sanctuary doors and out into the chilly fall evening. "I didn't want it to end."

Gia reached over and put her arm around the stooped shoulders of the older woman. "I didn't either. That was a wonderful message, wasn't it?" Juliette just grinned proudly, still bemused both by the disclosure of Gia's faith and Mrs. Cork's personality change.

"Juliette!" The sound of Victor's voice brought her up short, and she stopped mid-stride. Was she imagining it? Her eyes met first the question in Gia's, then the delight in Mrs. Cork, who turned and waved demurely at the man rapidly approaching them.

"Hello, Officer Jarrett," the older woman called out.

"Officer Jarrett? *The* Officer Jarrett?" Gia grabbed Juliette's hand, whispering loudly. "Is it him?"

Juliette squeezed her sister's hand, nodded, and grinned

helplessly. They both turned around to wait for him.

"Oh, my." Gia's impressed reaction made Juliette blush.

CHAPTER THIRTY-TWO

HOW ARE you, Mrs. Cork?" Victor didn't act at all surprised to see the woman at church with Juliette.

"I'm fine, Officer. You look very different in your clothes, Sir."

The silence that followed Mrs. Cork's startling statement was palpable. Gia snickered, then ducked her head to hide behind a curtain of hair. Victor cleared his throat. "Yes. I prefer not to wear the uniform when I'm not on duty." He looked down at his long-sleeved gray shirt and blue jeans. "Helps me blend in with the crowd."

"Don't be silly, Officer. You're too good-looking to blend in anywhere." Mrs. Cork nudged Juliette with her elbow. "I love a man in uniform, but doesn't he look nice in his street clothes?"

Mortified, Juliette dropped her gaze to the pavement. "Yes, Mrs. Cork. He does."

"Thank you, Juliette." She couldn't look at him but she was pretty sure he was grinning like the Cheshire cat. "And thank you, Mrs. Cork. You look very pretty yourself." He turned to Gia, and offered her his hand. "I'm Victor Jarrett."

"I'm Gia Gustafson. Juliette's little sister."

"It's good to meet you. Are you the one who knows Trevor Zander?"

"Taz?" Gia's eyes widened. "Yes! He's my friend's cousin. He's awesome! Do you know him, too?"

"I do. We go way back about ten years or so."

"Cool."

Another awkward silence settled around them while they all exchanged expectant glances. Finally, Juliette couldn't stand it any longer. "Was there something you wanted, Officer?"

"Victor, please. I saw you come in and just wanted to say 'hi.' I'm glad you ladies made it tonight."

"Thank you," she nodded, disappointment bursting the bubble of hope inside her heart. "It was a wonderful service."

"I love the passage your pastor spoke on tonight," Gia added, trying to help things along, but Victor only nodded. Juliette thought he looked like he wanted to say more, but when he remained silent, she spoke, keeping her voice light.

"Well, you two, we should get going. We've got the kids waiting for us at home."

Mrs. Cork glanced down at her watch, worry lines forming in her forehead. "Oh yes. Mr. Bobo must be wondering where I am." She looked up at Victor and explained. "We left the two dogs together in Juliette's back yard, and I can only imagine the kind of trouble they'll dream up if we leave them alone much longer."

"Of course." Victor dipped his head briefly, as though to excuse himself. "You should go. I'll look for you next week, okay?" He took a step back, but Mrs. Cork put a hand out.

"Officer Jarrett, I may be old, but I'm not blind, and I can see the way you're looking at our Juliette. Why don't you invite her out for coffee? Or mocha latte twice removed, or whatever it is you kids drink now-a-days."

"Mrs. Cork!" Juliette wanted to dissolve into the pavement right where she stood. And Gia? She was no help either, her hand over her mouth, giggling like a schoolgirl. "I think it's time to go home, ladies. Now." She spun on her heels and began to walk away.

"Juliette!" Gia cried. "Wait!"

"Juliette!" Mrs. Cork scolded. "Come back here, honey."

But it was Victor's voice that made her falter. "Juliette." Why did her name sound like a caress when he said it? And then his hand was on her elbow and he was walking beside her.

"What do you want, Off—Victor?" She was growing weary of the rollercoaster of emotions she experienced when she was around him.

"Mrs. Cork— " He began.

"You want Mrs. Cork?" Now she was getting belligerent, and she didn't care.

"No!" His hand tightened on her arm. "I want you."

~ ~ ~

THIS WAS not going at all the way he'd planned. He was used to hoofing it in uniform; running down miscreants was part of his job description in this town. But running down three women in a church parking lot didn't sit well with his ego. Then Mrs. Cork's awkward comment about his clothing, followed by her not-so-subtle attempt to coerce a compliment out of Juliette, made him feel even more out of his element. When Juliette made the decision to round everyone up and go home, he was almost relieved to be off the hook. Mrs. Cork, however, having none of it, threw the gauntlet at him with both hands. Even then, as Juliette turned and fled the scene, he might have chickened out, but one look at her little sister's face and he was done in. The pleading in her eyes was the proverbial kick in the pants, and he straightened his shoulders with renewed determination. He wasn't going to back out again. He was taking Trevor's advice; he was picking up the bat for real this time.

And swing away, he did; a solid strike. *I want you?* How could he let those words fly out of his mouth? Why did he always make such a fool of himself around her?

Well, at least she'd stopped walking.

"I'm not doing a very good job of this, but would you at least hear me out?" She nodded but didn't look up at him, crossing her arms and staring straight ahead at her car. He imagined she wished she was already behind the wheel, a million miles away.

"I meant to say that Mrs. Cork was right. I wanted to ask you out tonight. I'm sorry it all happened the way it did, because I had it planned so differently. I was expecting you to be alone." He shrugged self-consciously. "It would have made things a lot simpler."

"Well, I'm sorry I made things difficult for you. I'm sorry I didn't follow your plan." She kept her face averted. "But I'm not just a lonely old maid sitting in the back of church, pining away for Prince Charming, you know."

"Good grief, Juliette! I didn't mean it that way either!" He stepped back and ran frustrated fingers through his hair. Was she making this hard on him on purpose?

"How did you mean it, then?" she asked, finally turning to glare up at him. "I wish you'd make yourself a little clearer, because I can't figure out from one day to the next whether you're coming or going. What is it you want from me, Officer Jarrett?" She ducked her head, her words coming out harsh, frustrated. "And why am I always asking you that?"

He shoved his hands in his pockets, and his jaw muscles tightened. It seemed like everything he said she took the wrong way. But she had a point, didn't she? Hadn't he sent her some pretty mixed messages over the last few months?

When he didn't answer right away, she shook her head. "I'm tired. I didn't sleep much last night, so I'm sorry if I'm being rude. I need to get back to my dog. He seems to be the only one I don't inconvenience, let down, or scare off these days." She took a jerking step forward. "Goodnight."

Her words were like sword thrusts to his gut and he thought he knew exactly how she felt. His whole life he'd been a let-down to the people he loved. His father who never came for him, his mother whom he couldn't save, and his sisters who didn't *want* him to save them. He'd finally found his place on the police force, settling for 'just the facts' so that he knew exactly what was expected of him. As far as his relationships with women, who was he kidding? He hadn't forgotten the look on Amanda's face when she told him it wasn't enough, that *he* wasn't enough. He'd seen the disappointment and hopelessness blocking out any love she might have felt for him.

And he would eventually do the same to Juliette. Those tears building in her eyes were red flags. He would let her down, too, just like he let down everyone else.

Run, man. Run.

"No!" The word clawed its way past the tightness in his throat. He launched himself in front of her before she could get away, reached out and grasped her upper arms, stopping her in her tracks. He was aware he might be being too forceful—belatedly, he prayed she wouldn't misconstrue his intentions and cry out for help—but he threw caution to the wind. "No. Listen to me, Juliette."

He took her chin, gently, but intentionally, and turned her face toward his. She didn't resist, but stared past his left ear. "Listen to me," he spoke more earnestly, but let go of her. "Please look at me, Juliette."

When she finally did, he nearly stepped back, almost unable to bear the burden of what he saw in those gray windows. He took a deep breath and let it out in a disgruntled sigh. "I have made a jerk of myself at every opportunity with you, and if not a jerk, then a fool. I have gone about this whole thing wrong from the very beginning. When Trevor told me to...to ask you out, I should have jumped at the chance." His brows formed a jagged line above his eyes. "But you make me feel uncomfortable in my own skin, Juliette, and I don't like it at all. You make me question everything about myself; my plans for the future, what I thought I knew about women, even my feelings toward sisters in general."

"Trevor told you to ask me out? Why on earth would he do that?"

He raised his hands, impatient with her interruption. "I don't know. I suppose he thought it would be good for me, for us. I don't know, Juliette!" Is that all she heard? Didn't she care that he was baring his soul to her? Man, he was losing it, big time. "And then when Michelle and Tom made me—"

"They *made* you?" Juliette looked aghast. "Is that why you asked me over for pie? Because they *made* you?"

"No! It's not like that at all. Let me finish, please. They

made me face some things about myself that I didn't want to face. It was like they held up a mirror and made me take a real good look at myself." He sighed, wishing he could find better words to explain his behavior, but no matter how he said things, he looked bad, even to himself. "You're not making this any easier for me, you know."

"Oh, really?" She narrowed her eyes at him. "Well, while you were discussing your life with the man in the mirror, I was wondering what was wrong with me. First you patronize me like I'm some bubble-headed little woman, then you think me the worst of the dregs of society. You apologize, practically break down my door to kiss me, then you disappear into the night like I'm some kind of a...a *pariah.* And now you want me to make this easy for you?"

Victor shook his head and muttered, "I can't win with you, can I?" Everything she said was true, yes, but he wanted to make things right. She, however, wasn't going to give him an inch, and he was no longer sure he wanted it.

She shook her head. He didn't know if she was agreeing with him or just frustrated in general. He decided to try one more time.

"Michelle told me I was a fool for not pursuing you."

"Well, I don't know about that, but you're a coward for leading me on. I gotta go." She turned away to leave.

"Please don't go yet." His voice was harsh with misery and he wished with all his might that he could take back the last three weeks and do them over again. "You're right. They're right. Juliette, do you know why my friends all think I should pursue you?"

She just stood there, her back to him.

"Because being around you makes me act like this," he grumbled. "And they all think it's funny."

Now she did look up at him, just from the corner of her eye. "What does that mean?"

"They think—"

"No. I mean, act like what?" she interrupted. She turned around to face him now, her arms still crossed tightly over her chest.

"Like a fool. Like a jerk. Like a…a coward." The word did not come easy.

"So let me get this straight. They want you to pursue me because they think it's funny that you act like a jerk toward me? Why do I suddenly sympathize with Elizabeth Bennet, Mr. Darcy?"

Victor rolled his eyes and stepped back, hands raised again in surrender, having no clue who Mr. Darcy was and not really caring. "I give up. I give up." He called out to the two women who stood at a distance behind them, "I give up!" Then he turned back to her and bowed his head mockingly, pretending to doff a hat. "I'm sorry for disturbing your evening, Miss Gustafson. I will leave you in peace."

He spun on his heels and had taken three long strides when she spoke. "My sisters think you should ask me out, too."

He didn't turn around, but her words jump-started his heart. "They do?"

"Yes. And they haven't even met you yet. Well, except for Gia. But she thought so before tonight. So does my friend, Sharon."

"And now your Mrs. Cork…."

"Yes. She seems to be suffering from the same madness as everyone else. It's as though the world is conspiring against us."

Victor turned around and faced her from several feet

away. "Or *for* us."

"Hm."

"Juliette—

"Officer Jarrett—" They both spoke at the same time.

"Victor," he corrected again, his voice harsh with need. He wanted to hear her say his name. He needed to hear his name on her lips. He needed her to *want* to say his name. "Go ahead."

"Victor. Yes." She looked down at her feet as though directing them to move. She took two tentative steps toward him and raised her eyes to meet his. "I'm sorry I snapped at you. But the fact is, since we're being honest here, I feel like I'm on a rollercoaster when I'm with you. And I don't really like rollercoasters. It's a control thing, or so I've been told. I like order. I like predictable. And I don't like surprises. I know you'd probably never guess all this about me, considering my state of mind whenever you're around me, but it seems to me that you, sir, are the one who brings the wild-child dingbat out of me. I'm boring by nature. I'm sensible and steady. I wear practically the same thing almost every day—ask my sisters! I'm a color-inside-the-lines kind of girl, Victor Jarrett, except when I'm around you."

She smiled then, and he felt his shoulders relax. He moved a little closer and hooked his thumbs in his pockets, a slow grin spreading across his face as he watched her internal struggle playing out on her face.

"I wear *me* out when you're around. I can only imagine what I do to you." She snorted softly, a sound he was beginning to really, really like. "See? I don't even think that made sense."

"Actually, it made perfect sense to me. I was just thinking the same thing." If only she really knew what she did to him. "Except I wouldn't call it wearing me out. More like wearing me thin. Wearing me down. Wearing me—"

"Ok. Ok. I got it." She flapped a hand in front of her like she was shooing a fly away. "Look, it's getting late, and I did promise to get Mrs. Cork home right after church." She took a deep breath and let it out slowly, then looked up at him with a sad, half-smile. "I think we should call it a week, Victor, okay? I need to go home."

He didn't want to let her go. A quick glance over his shoulder, however, told him that Mrs. Cork was indeed getting anxious, and he had to admit that Juliette looked exhausted. *Lord, why is there always someone or something getting in the way?*

"Sure," he agreed out loud, even though his insides were resisting with every fiber. "I understand. You look like you could use some rest." As soon as the words were out, he knew he'd stepped on her toes again, and he wished he could suck them back in. "Sorry. That didn't come out right. You look great. Fantastic. Beautiful."

"Flattery, Victor, will get you nowhere. I know what I look like. Gia and I had a chick-flick slumber party with Bob."

"Lucky Bob," he interjected.

Juliette snorted rudely. "Needless to say, I didn't get much sleep. And unfortunately for you, that seems to be the way you always get me." She turned toward Gia and Mrs. Cork, and called out, "Come on, ladies."

Mrs. Cork eyed him quizzically as she approached, but she wisely didn't say anything. Victor was glad. He felt roughed up, almost like he'd been brawling, and still unsettled about a lot of things, especially his feelings for Juliette. He didn't need anyone rubbing things the wrong way right now.

He held Mrs. Cork's door open for her, then came around to Juliette's window. "I am glad I caught you tonight, regardless of how badly I handled things. Go get some rest now, okay?" Leaning in the window he smiled at the girl in the back. "Nice to meet you, Gia." With one last wave, he stepped back. Juliette started the car and backed out, then drove away. He could just make out Gia's face in the rear window as she turned to wave at him.

"What else was I supposed to do?" He voiced the question to himself first, then to God. "Force myself on her like I did last time? You saw her. She looked exhausted." He shook his head and made his way across the parking lot to his car.

"I don't want coffee," he muttered as he settled into the driver's seat. He leaned his forehead on his fingers where they gripped the steering wheel and closed his eyes. "I just want Juliette."

CHAPTER THIRTY-THREE

THEY made it almost all the way home before Gia asked, "So? Did he ask you out?"

Juliette smiled and shook her head. "No. We talked about it. We both agreed that it was silly how everyone and their dogs...and sisters...and neighbors...think we should date, but that was it. He kinda pulled a Mr. Darcy on me and I wasn't very nice about it. I'm tired and crabby anyway, so we agreed to let things lie."

"He pulled a Mr. Darcy on you? You mean, the 'I love you even though you're beneath me' scene?"

"That's the one." Juliette grimaced. "But without the 'I love you' part. He said I make him act like a fool and a jerk and make him feel uncomfortable in his own skin." She felt the prickling of tears at the back of her eyes and clenched her jaw to keep them at bay. "What was I supposed to say to that? I'm honored? Delighted? Take me now?"

The car fell silent as the others absorbed Juliette's words.

"So, he didn't ask you out." It was more of a statement than a question. Gia wasn't stupid. But she was clearly trying to decide if Victor Jarrett was or not.

Mrs. Cork chimed in. "Well, there's a thick-skulled man if I ever did see one. We practically threw you at him."

"Mrs. Cork!"

"What? Sometimes the best wine comes from a little extra pressing. I was just giving you a little extra press."

"Is that true?" Juliette didn't really feel like talking about Victor anymore.

"Is what true?"

"About good wine and extra pressing."

"How would I know? I don't drink."

Juliette laughed, appreciating the woman's tart candidness, and wondered, not for the first time this evening, why she hadn't made the effort to befriend her neighbor long before now.

When they pulled into the garage, she turned off the engine, but didn't get out immediately, instead turning slightly in her seat so she could look at Mrs. Cork. Gia sat quietly in the back, accustomed to girl-talks in the car. There was something about confined spaces; some of the best talks between the Gustafson sisters took place in cars.

"Mrs. Cork, I'm sorry I haven't been a better neighbor to you." Juliette shook her head. "What am I saying? I haven't been any kind of neighbor to you. I'm sad about missing out on all the years that we could have been friends."

"Well, I feel the same way." Her abrupt statement didn't fool anyone; Mrs. Cork couldn't hide the catch in her voice.

Juliette opted for full disclosure, not to justify, but by way of explanation, pitiful though it might be. "I recently broke up with a man who was my everything, something I've learned in the last eight or nine months is simply not healthy. You might remember him. He brought red tiger lilies and I gave them back, none too gently."

The corner of Mrs. Cork's mouth turned up just a little, a smile threatening to burst out. "I do remember him, in fact."

"He consumed me, but only because I let him. It wasn't until we broke up that I realized how much of life I was missing. It's as though I've worn blinders for the last ten years, so unaware of anything or anyone that didn't directly affect me. I'm sorry, Mrs. Cork, and I hope we can start fresh. I can also speak for Tootles—I mean, Bob—on this; we're glad you and Mr. Bobo are our neighbors."

Mrs. Cork reached over, patted Juliette's hand and nodded, but only said, "Speaking of Bob and Mr. Bobo, I think we'd better check on them, don't you?"

"Of course!" Juliette smiled.

The dogs, bless their furry little hearts, were ecstatic to see their mommies, and their mommies were ecstatic to see that everything looked just the way it did when they left.

Gia, her stuff all packed up and ready to go, kissed both puppies goodbye and gave Mrs. Cork a warm hug. "I'm so glad I got to meet you. Thanks for letting me come with you to church, too. We had a good time, didn't we?" She pulled open the front door to let herself out but turned to say one last thing. "And I'm really glad I got to meet the mysterious Officer Jarrett. Ren and Phoebe will be green with jealousy, won't they? I think he's *fantabulous*, Jules, amazing. I don't know if I've ever actually met a guy who fits 'tall, dark, and handsome' before, but your guy? Wowzer! You need to marry that man as soon as you can."

Juliette had stopped listening, her face growing warm with the blush creeping up her neck and flooding her face. Bob came hurtling through the foyer to charge outside in a cacophonous volley of barking, throwing himself at the knees of the man standing on the front stoop, arm raised to knock, frozen in place as he listened to Gia.

"Why, hello there, young man." Mrs. Cork scooped up Mr. Bobo who was tugging frantically on his leash and handed him to Gia, pushing the rattled girl ahead of her. "Walk me to my place, will you, Gia? Mr. Bobo seems so heavy tonight." And the little entourage brushed past the tangled mass of leaning dog and grinning man.

Mrs. Cork turned with one last wave. "Goodnight, Juliette. Goodnight, Officer Jarrett."

"Juliette," he said as he straightened up from ruffling the fur of the adoring dog pressing into his shins. His smile hadn't faded. Neither had her blush. She tried to think of something clever to say.

"Hi." Very clever.

"Just in case you're curious, they're both inside and I think I can see two silhouettes at the window—yep. The curtain just moved. They're spying on you."

"On me?" Juliette peered around him at her neighbor's house. "No one spies on me, Officer. You're the one they're ogling."

"Ogling? And it's Victor."

"Sorry. *Victor,*" she corrected herself. "Yes, ogling. Gia thinks you're fantabulous marriage material, and Mrs. Cork loves a man in uniform, remember?"

"But I'm not in uniform tonight."

"No, you're not. Mrs. Cork made sure we knew that, too." She tipped her head and looked up at him. "Okay. Since you're not in uniform, I'm going to assume I'm not in trouble with the law. So then, why are you here?"

"Actually," he said, hooking his thumbs in his pockets, "I came to ask if you'd like to go out with me. Just you and me."

"Oh." Clever *and* brilliant.

"Tonight, if you'll have me." He cleared his throat. "I know you said you were tired, but watching you drive away tonight just didn't feel right, like unfinished business. I had to come see you."

"Unfinished business? Is that what I am?" She didn't want to make things easy for him. Not because she didn't want him in her life, but because she didn't want someone hanging around until they figured out what they wanted, especially if it didn't include her. If he wanted to pursue her, he'd better be ready to fight for her.

"No."

She waited, hoping he'd expound without prompting from her, staring down at the dog who'd collapsed in a lovesick heap between his feet. Every sense became heightened, picking up on things usually unnoticed: the thwapping of Bob's tail against Victor's pant-leg, the mosquito-buzz of the porch light over their heads, the smell of wet grass mixed with the sandalwood scent of Victor's cologne. Even the car driving by seemed to move in slow motion as it passed on the road behind him.

"Juliette." He reached out and touched her arm just above the elbow, his fingers gently stroking. She didn't mean to, but she flinched, and he withdrew. "I'm sorry I've been such a fool these last few weeks. Can we start again? Will you share a cup of coffee with me tonight? I'd really like that."

Try as she might, Juliette couldn't resist him; the genuine longing in his eyes. She could think of nothing more she wanted to do at that moment than share a cup of coffee with this man. Tonight. "I'd like that very much."

"Okay?" He straightened, clearly surprised by her ready acceptance.

"Okay." She did smile now, and looked up at him. "Can

we go somewhere that serves French fries?"

Victor grinned back, taking it all in stride, "Do you like The Griddle?"

"Excellent suggestion." She knew for a fact that The Griddle served both good coffee and good fries and an excellent house dressing to dip them in. "Um, do you want me to drive my own car?"

"No, I don't. I'm driving. That's how dates work." He motioned toward the black Toyota parked across the street.

"So this is a date?"

"Yes, it is." He crossed his arms over his chest and turned his very pleased expression on her. "This is a date." She felt her knees go a little weak.

"Could you do me a favor? While I put on my shoes," she pointed down at her bare toes, "will you go next door and let them know? I don't think they'll survive if we leave them hanging much longer."

"Of course. I'll be right back."

She watched him for a few moments as he crossed the lawn toward the neighbor's house, shoulders back, purpose in his steps. Bob trotted along behind him, his nose bumping at the back of Victor's knees as though urging him to hurry. A new and heady sensation filled her heart and her whole body felt flushed, fingertips and toes tingling with anticipation.

"Eep!" she squeaked, her giddiness wiping away all vestiges of the fatigue she'd felt earlier. When Victor disappeared into Mrs. Cork's home, Juliette turned and headed to the kitchen for her purse and shoes, leaving the door open for his return.

~ ~ ~

"COME IN, come in." Mrs. Cork welcomed him with a disarmingly wide smile, Mr. Bobo clambering to greet Bob, whom he hadn't seen for at least five minutes now. Victor thought that maybe the woman just wasn't accustomed to smiling and the motion was difficult to control. But when he looked across the room, and saw a similar expression on Gia's face, he had to laugh.

"You ladies all right?" He stood in the foyer; a mirror-image of Juliette's, and eyed the two of them.

"Of course we are, aren't we, Gia?" Mrs. Cork reached out and patted his forearm. "Just tired, that's all. It's been a long day and it's getting so late."

But Gia was already tired of being coy. "So?"

"So," he repeated, knowing exactly what she was asking. "I'm taking Juliette out on a date tonight. Just thought you two should know."

Gia collapsed backward into the cushions of the yellow and blue chintz sofa, shooting a fist in the air. "Yes!" she whispered. Both Bob and Mr. Bobo leapt up beside her, vying for her attention.

"Oh dear. Isn't it a little late for that?" Victor couldn't tell if Mrs. Cork was serious or not. "I mean, she did have a sleep-over last night. And I'm sure she has to work tomorrow. Early."

"I'll have her back in plenty of time to get some sleep, Mom," he teased. "It's just coffee. And French fries."

"Oh dear," she said again. "Just tell me to mind my own business. I'm too nosy for my own good."

Gia popped up and came over to stand beside her. "I don't know about that, Mrs. Cork. I'd say your nosiness was actually a good thing in this case. Isn't it your fault that

Officer Jarrett has been tormenting my sister for the last few months?" She softened the prickles of her words with an arm around the old woman's shoulders.

"Tormenting?" Victor's eyes narrowed. "Is that Juliette's word or yours?"

"Mine. But you have tormented her, you know. This whole wishy-washy-can't-make-up-your-mind thing isn't cool." Victor's shoulders straightened at the verbal comeuppance from the young girl. Her boldness surprised him, and apparently Mrs. Cork, too, who stood by with eyebrows raised in anticipation. "That being said," Gia stepped forward and peered up at him, her eyes still smiling, but a serious note in her voice. "Exactly what are your intentions with my sister?"

"Yes, Officer. What are your intentions with our Juliette?" Now Mrs. Cork moved closer, too. Victor instinctively stepped back.

"Because I won't stand by and let some lamebrain—my word again," Gia clarified. "Break my sister's heart like the last one did."

"And neither will we." Now even Bob had joined the ranks, and was sitting beside Mr. Bobo at Mrs. Cork's feet.

His intentions? His mind went blank to all but the truth. "I suppose I'm going to break some relationship law by telling you before I tell her, but the truth is, I love her. I love Juliette." His own words shook him to the core, but he kept on. "I have no intention of breaking her heart. And I never meant to torment her."

Gia clapped her hands together, once again the fun-loving teenager. "Oh, goody! Because I like you, Officer Jarrett. I wouldn't mind having a brother like you."

Victor beamed, but held up a hand. "Let's see if the two

of us survive coffee and fries before we start talking marriage, okay?"

He turned to the older woman beside Gia. "And she's right, Mrs. Cork. Thank you for being—" He was cut off by a volley of barking from Bob and the accompanying yips of Mr. Bobo. The dogs went into a tailspin, charging around the room barking and whining, back and forth from the door to the big window in the living room that faced the street, and back again, as though trying to find a way out.

"Bob!" Victor spoke with command, but the dog ignored him, his desperation evident.

"Jules!" Gia's eyes widened with fright as she said her sister's name, then she lunged past Victor and reached for the door just as the same terrible thought occurred to him. He thrust her aside and threw open the door. Unable to get a grip on Bob, the dog flew out between his legs and was across the lawn before Victor was down the front steps. He quickly scanned the street. Sure enough, a blue sedan was parked a little too close to the back of his Toyota.

"That's Mike's car!" Gia cried out. "What is he doing here?"

"Trouble, I think. That's the first fellow I called the police about," Mrs. Cork declared, after scooping up the whimpering Mr. Bobo who'd been left behind.

"Call 9-1-1. Now! And both of you stay there!" Victor commanded over his shoulder before sprinting across the lawn.

CHAPTER THIRTY-FOUR

BENT over in her chair, Juliette was buckling the strap of her sandal when she heard his footsteps in the front entry. She was a little surprised Victor would come right in without an invitation, but she straightened up to greet him anyway.

"Hello, Julie."

Mike. She stared open-mouthed at him. He looked terrible. His hair was rumpled and his shirt untucked, nothing like the pressed and put-together Mike she knew.

"What are you doing here?" Her voice shook slightly, but her words came out sharp.

"It's good to see you, too," he smirked. "You planning on going somewhere?" He leaned against the counter a few feet away from where she sat and thrust his chin toward her blue toenails. "Cold feet?" He snorted his derision. "And lipstick, too. My, my. Aren't you looking extra special tonight?" He crossed his arms and grimaced, almost as though in pain.

Juliette's heart was pounding against her ribs as she stood up. She didn't like the way he was looking at her, and fear was beginning to send cold tendrils up the ridges of her spine.

"You need to leave, Mike." She had to be brave. Surely Victor would be back for her any minute now.

"No, I need to stay, because we need to talk. You said so yourself."

"Not like this. You should go home." She reached for her purse on the counter, but he lunged for her, grabbing her wrist and jerking her around to face him. She cried out as pain shot up her arm and into her shoulder.

"There was a time when this practically *was* my home," he ground out through clenched teeth.

"You're hurting me." Her voice shook. "Let go of my arm!"

He immediately released her wrist, only to wrap his arms around her and drag her up against him, holding her too tightly, too close. "I don't want to hurt you, Julie. I never want to hurt you." Then he bent down to kiss her. She turned her head.

"Stop it, Mike! Stop! What are you doing?" She tried to pull away, but he pushed her up against the wall, pinning her there with his body, one arm around her, holding her own arms tight to her sides, the other braced against the wall, palm flat, fingers spread. He ground his mouth into hers, and she struggled and twisted, her body bucking against his as he pressed into her. He felt like a brick wall, unmoving.

She wrenched her mouth from his and screamed, an ear-piercing cry for help. "Victor!"

His eyes, mocking before, now burned with something carnal and fierce as he covered her mouth with his hand. "Who is Victor?" he growled, thrusting against her hard. "Is that who had his hands all over you out front for all the world to see? Is it? Is Victor your new boyfriend, Julie?" He lowered his face until she could see her reflection in his glassy eyes. "I don't think so. You're mine." He leaned back a little, his eyes roving over her, from her eyes, to her mouth, then her breasts. "You gave yourself to me long, long ago, and I'm not letting anyone else move in on my territory." He brushed his fingers across her lips, down the side of her neck, along her collarbone, then followed the curve of her scooped neckline. "You're mine," he said again, his voice suddenly softer, gentler. "Tell me you're still my own Julie."

Ferocious barking preempted the hurtling mass of fur that burst through the front door and charged into the kitchen. Mike yelped as the dog lunged at him, then he shoved Juliette in front of him.

"Call him off! *Now!*" He shook her so hard her head bobbled, blurring her vision for a moment. "Get him off!"

Too shocked to do otherwise, she stuck out her hand to Bob, and he came to her, licking her fingertips, whimpering and growling simultaneously. He must have sensed her fear, she thought, noticing the dribble of urine he was leaving on the floor. "Bob, come here. It's okay. It's okay." The fur standing up along the dog's back began to flatten as she stroked his head, scratched his ears. *Where is Victor?*

"Put him in the garage." Mike's grip tightened and she moaned; there would be bruises on her shoulder. "Put him in the garage!" he repeated, his voice husky, grating in her ear.

She did as he commanded, taking the dog by the collar, and pulling him toward the door at the end of the kitchen, Mike still pressed against her back, walking in step with her.

She couldn't believe this was happening. She couldn't believe this was Mike. Her Mike.

No, this was not her Mike. This was someone else. *You*

are not my Mike, she screamed in silence. Opening the door to the garage, she pushed the dog out. "It's okay, baby. It's okay." Her voice was high and tight, her throat locked in the grip of her terror.

Where is Victor? The dog fought fiercely, desperate to stay inside with his mistress, until Mike kicked him in the side, slamming the door as Bob thumped up against the front of Juliette's car.

"Bob!" She cried out, straining to break away as Mike pulled her back across the room, switching the light off as they turned into the short hallway. He stopped, out of breath, and leaned a shoulder against the wall. "Lucy," he said quietly, his voice taking on a nasal quality that sounded nothing like Ricky Ricardo's. "I'm home!" He grinned down at her, a caricature of himself. "No wait. Here's a line you haven't used in a while. 'Take me to bed or lose me forever.' Name the movie, Julie. It's one of your favorites."

When she didn't answer he chuckled. "Do you remember my line? Come on, Julie. Just like old times. Show me the way home, honey." He bent down to kiss her again, this time more gently, a hint of tenderness in the way he held her. She fought hard, making Mike grunt with the effort to hang on to her.

Suddenly he stiffened and let out a low groan, then dropped his forehead to her shoulder. Surprise made her pause long enough to hear the breath hissing between his clenched teeth. He sounded like he was hurting; maybe she'd landed a well-aimed knee after all. She felt dampness on her neck; was he crying?

"Let me go," she begged him. "Please, Mike, we can talk about all this tomorrow, I promise." Her voice caught in her throat as he brought his head up suddenly, his eyes glazed as he stared at her in the faint glow from the bathroom night-light spilling into the hall beside them. His jaw clenched, he shook his head, moving once again toward the bedroom.

"Not tomorrow. Now. We need to...talk." He was gasping the words out, short of breath and trembling. "Julie, don't be afraid, please, baby. I didn't mean to scare you. I just want to talk. I...I need to sit down for...a...minute." He wasn't making any sense. He pushed open the bedroom door and dragged her into the room. The lamp on her bedside table was on—she always left it on when she was away at night. She'd never quite gotten over her irrational fear of the boogie man from childhood. She looked up at him as he kicked the door closed behind them and her eyes widened in shock. He looked even worse; his face was pasty, and his lips pulled tight across his teeth, just two thin lines pressed together. She could see beads of sweat on his forehead, pooling in the creases around his eyes, dotting the curve of his cheekbones, his upper lip.

"Are...are you okay?" She couldn't believe she was asking him that question, but in a moment of clarity, she realized something was terribly wrong, something much worse than an aggressive ex-boyfriend. Fear for herself was suddenly overshadowed by fear for Mike.

"Juliette!" Victor. Her body went limp, her legs nearly giving out as relief washed over her.

Mike, who'd been leaning into her, stumbled and went down to his knees, taking her with him. He grunted as the weight of her body fell against him, and when he toppled over, she cried out. But Mike's hand clamped down over her mouth.

"Don't...shhh. Don't let him in. Please. He won't understand. I...just want to...talk." He stared at her with terrible eyes and she nodded. He pulled himself back up to his knees and stopped to catch his breath.

Juliette watched him struggle. "Mike, you need help. Let me call an ambulance."

"No! I just need to catch…my…breath." He was grimacing again but managed to stand on his own two feet. "You're quite the little fighter, you know that?" Then another groan emanated from deep inside him and he started to sway. She leapt to her feet and tried to steady him, but he was too heavy, already falling, going down like a rock. He slumped against her bedside table sending the lamp crashing to the floor, and the light went out. As she groped for him in the dark, his head fell forward, colliding with her mouth.

"Help!" she screamed, the shock of pain giving her a voice.

CHAPTER THIRTY-FIVE

HER FRONT door stood open and Victor stepped into the darkness, his ears straining to pick up any sound. For a moment, all he heard was Bob's frantic barking, muffled, as though from behind closed doors. Then came the sounds of a scuffle, a grunt, Juliette's pleading voice.

All the lights were off; whether Juliette had turned them off in preparation for heading back out with him, or this Mike fellow had turned them off, he didn't know, but he didn't like the way it made him feel.

No light usually meant dark intentions.

Pausing at the doorway between the living room and kitchen, he listened again. Bob barked and howled from the door at the other end of the kitchen. Most likely the garage—the dog should be safe there for the moment, at least until Victor figured out what was going on.

Victor turned and moved quietly, swiftly, in the other direction, through the little hallway, past the bathroom and a tiny office or guest room, to what he assumed was her bedroom at the end of the hall. The door was closed, and he held his breath, listening. There was only silence.

His heart pounded and a bead of sweat trickled down his spine. Where were the police? Should he wait for them? But what if the man was hurting her? Or worse? His hand scrabbled for his holster...*no gun!* And his phone was in the console in his car. What was he thinking, barging in here like this, unarmed and alone? He was only putting both of them in danger. *Wait for back-up, man.*

That's what his head told him, but his heart wasn't complying. "Juliette?" he called through the door.

Then he heard movement again, a loud crash, and a scream. Instinct kicked in, caution exploded into fear, and he turned the handle and thrust his shoulder into the door, sending it flying open. He stepped back quickly, just in case, and paused long enough to realize the only sounds he heard now were desperate cries for help.

She was on the floor, crouched near her closet doors, her curved back reflected in the full-length mirrors. She leaned over a man who lay on his side on the floor, clutching his chest, his eyes large and anxious. A faint keening sound came from between his clenched teeth. He didn't seem to notice when Victor turned on the light, but Juliette flinched as though struck.

Victor crossed the room and knelt beside her. "Juliette." She turned frightened eyes up at him, and a pain so intense it scared him pressed in on his heart when he saw the blood dribbling unchecked from her split lip.

"Call 911," she stammered. "He needs help!"

"The paramedics are coming. Let's get you out of here." He reached for her but she pulled away.

"No! I can't leave him alone." Her voice faltered, but she placed a trembling hand on Mike's chest where his own were clenched in agony. "Mike, can you hear me? I'm here." Then she turned back to Victor, desperation making her voice high-pitched and sharp. "Don't just stand there! Call 911!

The accusation in her voice surprised him, and he spoke more harshly than he intended. "They're already on their way, Juliette." He saw her flinch and he reached out to put a hand on her arm. "But you're hurt, too."

She shrugged his hand off her arm. "I'm fine, Victor. Leave me alone."

Victor stood up and stepped backward, hating the way her words took him back to his childhood, making him feel helpless, worthless, useless. Staring down at her, he tried to get his emotions in check. She needed him to be strong right now; she was obviously not thinking clearly. He circled the man on the floor and crouched down in front of him.

"Sir? Can you hear me?"

Mike nodded. "My chest. Hurts." He spoke through clenched teeth, one hand lifting to grab his throat. "I can't. Breathe."

"Sir, the paramedics are on their way. They'll be here any minute now."

Mike nodded and turned his gaze back to Juliette. "Did I...do that?" His voice was tight, barely more than a whisper, and then he was crying, tears streaming from his eyes, his breathing shallow and rapid. "Oh, Julie. Did I hurt you?"

Juliette shook her head adamantly, and tried to calm him down. "No, no, Mike. Don't worry about it. I just bumped it. Shh."

He lifted one hand toward her, his palm cupping her face. "I'm so sorry, Baby-doll. I'm...so sorry." Then he grimaced, and clutched at his chest again. Juliette choked back a sob.

Victor put a hand on Mike's shoulder, trying desperately

to keep his thoughts and feelings in check. Sorry? The man on the floor was an animal. Anyone who could hurt a woman one minute, then apologize for it in tears the next, had no soul. "Sir, you need to focus on me. Pay attention to me, please." He waited until Mike's eyes met his. "Mike, right? I want you to think about your breathing. We need to calm down a little, okay? Slow it down. In through the nose, out through the mouth. Breathe with me, okay?" He didn't know who would benefit more from the exercise; him or Mike. "In through the nose, out through the mouth."

It seemed to be helping. Mike relaxed his jaw a little but there was still fear in his eyes. "I feel like I'm falling," he gasped. "Like…everything is shifting." He reached out and grabbed Victor's hand, clutching it so hard the bones ground against one another.

Victor glance at Juliette. Her tears trickled down her face into the gash at the corner of her mouth, making the blood thin and flow again. Her sleeve was smeared where she'd used it to dab at the worst of it; the front of her pale blue shirt was streaked where blood had first fallen unchecked. He felt himself splintering into two people; the one who hated, and the one who helped anyway. "Hold on to me, Mike. Help is coming. Try to relax, okay? We're here."

Without looking at her again, he asked, "Are you hurt anywhere besides your mouth, Juliette?"

"No." It came out a whimper, then she said it more firmly. "No."

"Where's your phone?"

"In my purse on the kitchen counter."

"Go get it for me. Now." She needed commands; he could see it in her eyes. Fear was driving her, and he needed to be louder and stronger.

She stood up and scurried out of the room, returning shortly. "Dial Gia's number for me, then give me the phone."

While the phone rang, he studied her, watching as her fingers tenderly smoothed the hair back from Mike's face. His heart ached to see her so distraught. She obviously cared deeply for this man, but why? How? How could she love someone who treated her so badly? Why did women love men like this? As far as he was concerned, a heart attack, if that's what Mike was having, seemed just desserts.

Gia answered, her voice small and frightened. He reassured her as quickly as he could, then barked a few instructions for her, hung up, and waited, his eyes on Mike's face again. He was unable to bear what he saw in Juliette's eyes anymore.

A few minutes later, Gia slipped into the room, bringing with her a bag of frozen vegetables wrapped in a damp kitchen towel. She knelt down and offered it to Juliette, who took it wordlessly and pressed it to her mouth. There were tears in Gia's eyes, too, and Victor didn't think he could tolerate one more woman weeping over the man on the floor.

"Gia, will you go out front and wait for the paramedics?" he asked. "They should be here any minute. In fact, I think I hear sirens."

She returned shortly with a whole team of emergency staff, and Victor stepped back, letting the experts have access to both patients. He was familiar with most of them, and he didn't miss the curious looks on their faces as they went about their business. A female officer pulled Juliette aside while a medic did a quick evaluation of her condition. He knew the procedure; they'd be asking her some very personal questions about what had gone on between her and Mike before they arrived. He kept his distance, giving her privacy.

When they seemed satisfied she was okay, they rejoined the cluster around Mike, leaving her alone in the corner of the room, her back to the wall, a new disposable ice-pack pressed to her face.

Victor took a step toward her, then faltered, seeing the way she watched her ex-boyfriend, how she put aside her own suffering for his. He saw how badly she was hurting because Mike was hurting.

It tore a hole in his gut as memories washed over him. His mother holding an icepack to her eye—one he'd made for her with a bag of frozen peas and a pillowcase--crying and apologizing to another man for whatever it was she'd done wrong. Bruises on Sasha's arm, fingerprints clearly defined, and the sick pleasure she took from forcing him to put his small hand over the marks, teasing him that his hands weren't yet big enough to leave bruises like that. Memories of tears in the night, his own, wishing he was man enough to offer his protection, but too afraid to get his ten-year-old body out from under the bed to stand between the blows and the women he loved.

At that moment, Juliette's head came up, her gaze searching the room until she found him. Her face crumpled and she dropped the ice pack as she slid down the wall to the floor, her arms hanging limply at her sides, her eyes never leaving his face.

He had to get her out of here. Now. But just as he started forward, a hand on his shoulder stopped him. He turned around to face a colleague from the force.

"Vic? You got a minute?"

"It'll have to wait," Victor stated. The policeman frowned but stepped aside to let him pass. Victor's eyes went back to

Juliette's crumpled form as he circled the crowd to get to her, but Gia made it there first.

CHAPTER THIRTY-SIX

THE NOISE was overwhelming, like clanging bells, but she knew she was overreacting. No one was panicking, no one was shouting, everything seemed to be under control. Everything except her. Mike was getting hooked up to all kinds of wires and lines and monitors, and people were moving around the room with purpose and focused intent. The icepack she'd been given seemed to have effectively numbed her whole body on the outside, but her insides felt like she'd swallowed broken glass.

Victor. He'd come for her. Her champion.

Where was he? Her eyes scanned the room—there. He stood near the opposite wall, watching her, his expression as turbulent as her thoughts. What was he doing so far away? Why wasn't he here, by her side, his arms around her? A deep, wrenching sob surged up out of her lungs, and she felt what little control she had slip away. Her legs gave out, and she slid to the floor, wordlessly begging him to rescue her from all of this.

Instead, he turned away from her to speak to the police officer who'd approached him. Forgotten, she dropped her head into her hands and closed her eyes, willing the nightmare to end.

Who was she kidding? There was no champion in her story. She was alone.

"Jules?" Gia crouched down beside her. "Come. Let's get out of the way." Gia helped her up with an arm around her waist, and they made their way out into the hallway.

"Is Mike—?"

"The paramedics are taking care of him."

"I shouldn't leave him," Juliette whispered, as she watched the man being strapped onto a gurney.

"We'll just be in their way. Come on." Gia led her into the kitchen and pulled out a chair for her. "Sit."

Juliette collapsed into the chair and let her forehead drop to her crossed arms on the table. "You should go let Mrs. Cork know I'm okay. I'm sure she's frantic."

"I'll stay with you. One of the officers can—"

The sound of frantic barking brought Juliette's head up. "Bob!" she cried, pushing up out of her chair. She pulled open the door and slipped out into the chilly darkness of the garage. She didn't turn on the lights, just went down on her knees and let Bob lean into her, nuzzle her, assure himself that she'd come to rescue him from his banishment. Gia poked her head out.

"Go." The light from the kitchen shown on Juliette's upturned face as she gave Gia her best 'big-sister's-the-boss' look. "Bob's here. I'll be okay until you get back."

Gia hesitated just a moment longer, then pulled the heavy door closed again. The inky stillness settled around her, comforting, soothing, peaceful.

"Oh, Bob," she moaned, and sat with her back to the door, hugging the dog to her, burying her face in his coarse fur.

Bob pressed against her, panting his joy in being reunited with her.

~ ~ ~

VICTOR stopped a few feet away and watched as the two girls stumbled from the room. It was best, he told himself. Leave her be. She'd made her choice quite clear tonight. If Mike was the kind of man Juliette wanted, then Victor wanted to be as far away from her as he could possibly be. *That's right, man. Don't get sucked into that woman's chaos.* He heard the words in his head and spun on his heels, as she and her sister disappeared down the hall.

He scanned the room for the officer he'd spoken to earlier; he'd give whatever information they wanted from him and go home. He didn't see the man, but he'd just wait here for him. That way he wouldn't accidentally run into Juliette again.

A few minutes later the medics wheeled the more alert but still highly agitated Mike out of the room, and the majority of the crowd followed along behind the gurney. Still Victor waited until the room emptied completely, nodding at the last young man who'd slipped in to grab a mislaid clipboard before dashing back out again. Obviously, the officer had gotten whatever information he'd needed without having to question Victor.

He looked around the room, encased in the stark quiet that follows such a commotion. There were scraps of sterile equipment wrappers on the floor, a discarded glove, a plastic bag, even a length of plastic tubing that must have been dropped in the fray. Victor collected the trash, stuffed everything into the plastic bag, then dropped it into the basket by her nightstand.

Carelessly tossed across Juliette's bed was her pink robe. He reached out to touch it, the texture soft under his fingertips. Her fragrance drifted up to him, something he didn't know he recognized until now. He bent down to pick up the fallen lamp and returned it to the bedside table, letting his eyes wander over her things: her alarm clock, a beaded necklace and two bracelets, a pen, and a notebook opened to a list entitled *My Champion*.

Patient (like Gia's sunflower)
Loyal
Faithful
Committed
Hot
Impulsive
Daring
Brave
Gentle
Funny
Kind
Believe in God

The last item on the list was circled and an arrow was drawn up to the top of the page as though to insert the word at the beginning of the list instead of the end.

At the bottom of the page was a new list, the last three words all capitalized.

Must Like (or at least tolerate):
Being organized
Having a plan

Chinese food
Chick flicks
Black pants
Blue toenails
My crying

Must Love:
GOD
BOB
ME

Victor sighed, his heart hurting for Juliette as he read it all again. For a moment he wondered if heart attacks were contagious as he rubbed his chest. "Sympathy pains," he murmured, not sure who he was feeling sympathy for. "Not Mike," he clarified to the empty room. He reached out and touched her pillow, somehow knowing that if he bent over, he'd be able to breathe in that glorious fragrance again, and he almost gave in to the temptation, his longing for her was so intense. He cleared his throat and was just about to turn away when something caught his eye.

Protruding from beneath her pillow was the corner of a business card. He reached for it, knowing even before he saw it, whose it was. Officer James V. Jarrett. His card. Under her pillow. Looking very well handled.

He flipped it over. There on the back, printed in tiny block letters, was written, "Mrs. Juliette S. Jarrett" directly over his name on the other side of the card. He remembered seeing her middle name on her driver's license; what was it? Sonia. Sarah. No, Simone. That was it. Juliette Simone Jarrett.

"Gustafson," he corrected aloud, hesitant to consider the implications of what she'd written on his card. He glanced down at the list on her nightstand again. Was he all those things? Is that what made up a champion? Were those traits what Juliette wanted in a man?

Then why was she chasing after a creep like Mike? Why did so many women fall for the Mikes in this world? He shook his head. "You're nothing but a dreamer, man. Leave it alone." He leaned over to put the card back the way he'd found it.

There was that fragrance again. This time he didn't resist. He picked up her pillow, brought it to his face, and breathed deeply, drinking in her scent like a parched addict, miserable with the knowledge that this may be the last time he....

Suddenly he thrust the pillow away from him, dropping it like it was burning his hands.

"What am I doing?" he muttered, his face flaming. "Who's the creep now?" But as he went to straighten the pillow, he felt something else begin to stir inside of him, something that felt like resolve, strength, determination. He thought of her list. Well, he definitely was a believer; that he had no doubt about. But was he loyal? Faithful? Committed to her?

No.

Yes! Yes! He *could* be those things to her! He *wanted* to be those things to her. He *wanted* to be brave and patient, kind and gentle. He *wanted* to be funny, and daring and impulsive for her. *With* her.

"Am I hot?" he asked his reflection in her mirror.

He couldn't let her throw away her life on Mike. He wouldn't. He curled his fingers around the card again then tucked it into his back pocket. Let her wonder where it was. He was going to keep it as a beacon of hope. As far as he was concerned, it was her personal invitation to him, and he wasn't ready to turn it down, not without a fight.

He had to find her, to find out for himself. He had to stop running.

He hurried out of the room and down the hall, poking his head into the spare room, then the kitchen, and the living room. The whole place was deserted. He charged outside to where a small cluster of people stood together, Gia and Mrs. Cork among them. Clearing his throat, he asked, "Where's Juliette?"

Gia started across the lawn toward him. "In the garage with Bob."

He turned and loped back into the house, pulling the door closed behind him. He didn't mean to offend anyone, and he knew it was just a deterrent, but he needed some time alone with Juliette.

He tapped gently on the garage door. "Juliette?"

There was an answering bark and he took it as permission granted. He turned the handle and eased the door open, ever so slowly, just in case she was leaning against it. "Juliette?"

She lay on her side in the darkness, her head on a pile of neatly folded towels, her body curved around Bob's, one hand buried in the fur of his shoulder. She'd pulled another large towel over the top of her to ward off the chilly November air, but she wasn't wearing a jacket and the concrete floor, even with the rug beneath her, had to feel like an ice-block.

He knelt down, dodging the wet welcoming tongue of her dog, and brushed the hair from her face. He cupped her chilled cheek in his hand, careful to avoid the swelling around her mouth. "Juliette," he murmured again, realizing he would never get tired of saying her name.

She stirred, opened her eyes, and gazed blankly up at

him for a few moments, the light from the kitchen illuminating their faces. Like a storm cloud moving in, he watched her memory come back, leaving in its wake despair and misery. She closed her eyes again, as though to shut everything out, to shut even him out.

"I'm so cold," she shivered, not opening her eyes. Bob cranked his head around and licked her chin.

"Let's get you inside, okay?" He reached down and scooped her up into his arms, standing carefully. She was a little heavier than he'd expected, and the last thing either one of them needed right now was for him to look like a wimp. "I've got you," he reassured them both. "Now put your arm around my neck so I don't drop you." He felt her smile against his neck, her head cradled on his shoulder. Hope stirred in his belly.

He carried her into the living room and set her down in the corner of the sofa, his gestures tender as he reached for an afghan from the back of a chair nearby. He draped it across her body, tucking it in around her, but he could see she was still shivering. Then her teeth began to chatter.

"I c—c—can't get w—warm."

Was she going into shock? "Are you nauseous? Light-headed?"

"No. Ju—just so c—cold."

Before he could reason his way out of doing so, he sat down beside her and pulled her into his arms, her body facing his, her head tucked into the curve of his neck again. He pressed her knees up against his side and urged Bob up on the sofa, too.

"Bob, come here, buddy. He lifted the edge of the afghan and the dog snuggled in, the two of them sandwiching the woman between them. Victor tucked the afghan around all three of them, trapping as much heat as possible beneath it.

It took several minutes for Juliette to stop shivering and even longer for her to begin to relax into him, but he didn't mind. Neither did Bob, who periodically bumped his nose against Victor's knee or Juliette's elbow beneath the blanket. He held her gently, not speaking, and not expecting any words from her, focusing on keeping his breathing steady even though he was sure she could feel the thudding of his heart.

This was where she belonged. This was where he belonged, his arms around her, her cheek resting against his chest.

The front door was flung wide by a woman with a long, jet-black ponytail pulled through the back of a baseball cap, her eyes blazing as she strode into the room. Her gaze landed on the three of them snuggled on the couch, and she stopped suddenly, making the woman behind her plow into her, nearly knocking her off her feet.

"Phoebe!"

"Sorry, Ren. You stopped too quickly. Where is she?" The second woman wore a flowing gown that fluttered around her as she moved, some kind of Greek costume. Long, black curls cascaded over her shoulders, gold bands spiraled around her upper arms, and she looked like she'd just stumbled off an ancient Greco-Roman frieze. She turned mysterious charcoaled eyes on Victor. Under the scrutiny of both girls, he was suddenly defensive, on guard.

"Who are you?" the first woman in the baseball cap demanded.

"You're Juliette's policeman, aren't you?" The goddess answered for him, her voice like rich cream. "Officer ...?"

"Jarrett. Victor Jarrett. I'd shake your hand but..." He

shrugged carefully.

"Yours are a little full," she quipped, then crossed the room to kneel on the floor in front of them. An exotic fragrance swirled around her and he found himself holding his breath as she lifted the corner of the blanket to find Juliette's hand. "I'm Phoebe and that's Ren. More sisters," she stated as she sized him up with her Liz Taylor eyes. "Jules? We're here now."

CHAPTER THIRTY-SEVEN

VICTOR knew Juliette was aware the moment the door opened; he'd felt her tense against him. Was she hoping they'd think she was asleep and leave her alone? Did that mean she felt safe in his arms? The thought made him feel insanely protective.

"She's pretty tired. It's been a brutal night," he said, hoping they'd get the hint and not bother her too much.

"Poor baby." Phoebe slid onto the sofa beside Bob who worked his nose out from under the afghan to greet her.

"I'm taking her home with me," Renata declared, dropping her purse into a chair. "And just why are you here, Officer Jarrett?"

Taken aback by the woman's aggression, Victor was momentarily at a loss for words. Finally, he simply said, "She needed me."

Renata reached up to tighten her ponytail. "Well, we're here now so you're free to go."

"Renata! Don't be so rude." Phoebe scowled up at her sister then turned back to Juliette and Victor. "We should be thanking you, Officer Jarrett, not dismissing you. I'm so glad you were here. Gia told us you were quite the hero tonight."

Her words made his gut ache. No, he'd been nothing like a hero tonight. He hadn't been here to keep Mike from hurting her. He hadn't been here to hold her, comfort her, and support her during the ordeal of paramedics and police reports. He hadn't been here when she collapsed, all alone, on the cold garage floor, with only her dog to keep her warm.

He'd been too busy sniffing her pillow.

Well, he was going to change that. Right now. He wasn't going to run anymore, not even from scary sisters.

"I'm no hero," he stated. Then he looked up at Renata. "But I'm not going anywhere unless she wants me to. And I need to hear it from her."

"Stop talking about me like I'm not here." Juliette's voice was muffled because her face was still pressed to Victor's chest, but no one misunderstood her.

"Sorry, Jules." Phoebe grinned and reached over to squeeze her big sister's foot.

Just then, Gia and Mrs. Cork burst through the front door, coming to an abrupt stop at the sight of everyone gathered in the living room.

"Everyone's gone now," Gia stated, as though she could think of nothing else to say. "How is she?"

"She's tired, Georgia. I'm going to take her home with me." Renata was still standing, shuffling a little now from foot to foot.

Juliette lifted her head. "Rennie, sit down. Please. And again, please stop talking about me like I'm not here." Her voice sounded like it was coming from far away, but it was firm, decisive.

Surprise raced across Renata's face, quickly followed by

indignation, but she did what Juliette said and sat primly in the chair, propping her purse on her lap. "I was only answering Georgia's inquiry about you."

"I know. It's okay." Now Juliette pushed away from Victor just enough to be able to see everyone, but she stayed pressed up against his side. He smiled with satisfaction and pleasure. If she wanted his protection, even from her own over-bearing sisters, he was glad to give it to her. It certainly didn't hurt that she seemed to fit so perfectly against him.

"Oh my goodness!" Renata gasped. "Your face!"

"It's just a fat lip."

"Just a fat lip! Why didn't you go to the hospital?" Renata glared accusingly at Victor, as though he'd somehow prevented Juliette from seeking necessary medical treatment.

"I'm fine, Ren. It'll be gone in no time; you know how quickly I heal." Juliette lifted a hand and gingerly brushed her fingers over the corner of her mouth, wincing a little. "And although I know you're trying to be nice to me, I'm not going home with you. I'm staying here. This is my home and I have Bob."

"Bob? Who's Bob?" Renata glared at Victor again. "I thought your name was Victor."

"Not him, Ren." He felt Juliette tense beside him, but she didn't pull away. "Bob is Tootles. Tootles is Bob." The dog's tail thumbed the sofa cushions at the sound of his names.

"Tootles? What do you mean, Tootles is Bob?" Then Renata flapped a hand in the air. "Oh never mind. I don't want to know. What I do want to know is where he was when Mike broke in?" Renata wasn't happy about being denied. "Some protector Tootles—"

"Bob." Victor pressed his lips together to keep from smiling as Juliette corrected her sister on the scruffy dog's name.

"—Bob is," Renata finished lamely.

"Bob was next door with me," Victor answered for Juliette. "We walked Mrs. Cork home and were only gone a few minutes."

"A few minutes?" Renata's eyebrows rose in disbelief. "It only took Mike a few minutes to practically rape my sister?"

"Hey!" Phoebe shot a warning look in Renata's direction. "Let's be a little more sensitive, shall we? *Etre agréable,* Ren."

"This is no time to be nice, Phoebe! We're talking about a crime here! Why is everyone taking this so calmly?"

"He didn't practically rape me, Ren." Juliette sighed, shaking her head. "He just came to talk." Victor felt his insides twist as he listened to her defend the abusive man, but he said nothing. "I thought...well, I was afraid at first, because I thought he was acting so strangely, but he had some kind of a breakdown, right?" She looked up at him, her eyes large, smudges of fatigue creating half-circles beneath them.

"That's what they believe, yes." He confirmed her story, although he didn't necessarily believe it himself.

"He looked awful," Juliette continued. "When he first came in I thought he'd been drinking or something. It was like something in a movie. He was suddenly just there. I was so surprised."

"Well, why didn't you scream bloody murder? Run?" Renata was still sitting, but just barely, her backside perched on the very edge of the chair. "Why did you let him in at all?"

"It was Mike, Ren. I didn't think there was any reason to scream. And just to clarify, I *didn't* let him in. I left the door open for Victor and Bob, and he just walked right in. In fact, I told him he had to leave and that made him angry."

"Is that when he did that?" Gia interjected, her voice still a little tremulous from all the activity of the night. She put a hand over her own lip in the same spot where Juliette's was split.

"No! This is Mike we're talking about."

"Yeah." Phoebe was calm, but the way she said the word made Victor straighten up and look at her over the top of Juliette's head. "This is Mike we're talking about. He's a bad seed, Jules. So if he didn't hit you, where'd you get that fat lip?"

"He started to fall and I went to catch him. His forehead slammed into my mouth."

Momentarily relieved, Victor gave her a little squeeze where his hand rested on her shoulder and upper arm. Juliette winced and he immediately lifted his hand.

"What's the matter?" He eyed her warily. Obviously, she wasn't telling them everything. "Are you hurt?"

"No, it's okay—ouch!"

"Liar," said Phoebe smugly, who had reached over and poked Juliette's shoulder. "Take off your shirt. Let's see."

"I am not going to take off my shirt." Juliette sat forward, slipping out of the circle of Victor's warmth. "Look. The guy was in pain, okay? He had a death-grip—literally!—on my arm at one point because he could barely stay upright."

"Liar," Phoebe repeated, sitting back into the sofa and crossing her arms. Victor couldn't stand it any longer.

"If this Mike guy's visit was so innocent, why was Bob locked in the garage? And why were the two of you in the bedroom when I found you? With the door closed?"

Juliette turned and stared at him for a long time, her eyes glistening with unshed tears of betrayal. Then she pushed herself up, swayed a little, but waved his helping hand away.

"*Et tu, Brute?*" He lifted his hand toward her again and she took a shaky step back. "Don't touch me. You're just as bad as they are." Then she turned to face the rest of the room. "Why don't you all go home now. I'm going to bed. Come on, Bob." She patted her thigh and the dog leapt off the couch and came to her side.

She made her way across the living room and paused in front of her neighbor and the uncharacteristically silent Mr. Bobo. "Good night, Mrs. Cork. Thank you for coming to church with me. I'm glad we're friends." She hugged her quickly, squeezing a little yip out of the dog, then turned back to face the others. "Goodnight, empresses. This unofficial G-FOURce is officially over." She nodded once at Victor. "Officer."

He closed his eyes and clenched his teeth together as she exited the room. Some kind of champion he was turning out to be. Why was he always so ready to think badly of her? And even worse, let her know it? Faithful? Committed? Loyal enough to believe in her? Ha! Not once in the weeks—no, months—since he'd met her, had she tried to manipulate, lie, or coerce him into doing, or being, or thinking anything that he shouldn't. Why was he so afraid to simply trust her? He felt a hand on his forearm and opened his eyes to find Phoebe leaning toward him.

"Why don't you—"

"Please," he interrupted her, pushing himself up off the couch. "Please don't tell me what you think I should do, okay?" The costumed woman sat back again, eyebrows arched.

"Well, then, what *are* you going to do?" she asked, sarcasm and challenge dripping from each word.

"For starters, I'm going to send all you ladies home." He

pointed at the spot he'd just vacated. "Then I'm going to crash right here on this sofa for the night."

"Excuse me? Send us home? Who do you think you are?" Renata was aghast. She turned to Phoebe for support, but Phoebe's eyes were glued on him where he stood in the middle of the room.

"Well, so far tonight, I *haven't* been the champion your sister needed, but that's going to change, starting now. Which means I'm staying here to look after Juliette, and you sisters," he eyed Renata in particular, "are going to have to deal with it."

"You can't just waltz in here and tell us what to do!" Renata was on her feet now, too, pointing a long finger at him.

"I can and I just did." He, in turn, pointed at the door. "It's time for you to go home. Your sister needs her rest."

"She told *all* of us to go home. You, included. Why on earth would we leave you, a complete stranger, here alone with her?"

"Because she needs me." He ignored the stranger comment.

"Oh *please*." She rolled her eyes. "Juliette doesn't need you, she's needs us. She needs her family. She's coming home with me, whether she likes it or not. It's the best thing for her."

"But she doesn't want to go home with you," Gia stated, matter-of-factly, making Renata gasp in outrage. "I can stay overnight. I don't have to work until 9 tomorrow."

Mrs. Cork reached over and patted her hand. "I know your sister would appreciate you staying, sweetie. But I vote for Officer Jarrett." She looked over at the other two sisters. "In fact, I'd feel better knowing he was here."

"I'm sorry, Mrs. Cork," Renata interjected. "That is your name, right? I don't mean to be rude, but I don't see how this is any of your business." She glared at the older woman with steely eyes, but Mrs. Cork wasn't having it.

"Of course you mean to be rude, honey. I know because I behave just as badly when things don't go the way I want them to go. I still think Victor here is the best man for the job. He'll take good care of your sister for you."

Renata stood in stunned silence and Victor nodded his head in gratitude. "Thank you for your support, Mrs. Cork." Then he stuck out a hand toward Phoebe. "Let me help you up."

Phoebe eyed him for a few more tense moments, the two of them sizing each other up, then she grinned and grabbed his hand, pulling herself up to stand in front of him. "My, my, but you are a big boy." She tipped her head coquettishly and batted her eyelashes a few times, but he chuckled, understanding that she was teasing him, not flirting with him.

"Big enough to handle your sister when she finds out I'm still here." Phoebe sashayed past him toward the door, but something had transpired between them and he knew he had an ally in her. Now all he had to do was convince Renata to like him. That, he supposed, was going to be the real challenge.

"You guys! We cannot just let some strange man sleep on Juliette's couch! She's already been traumatized enough!" Renata clenched her fists and stomped her foot and Victor burst out laughing, the memory of Juliette looking just as flustered and indignant, making fists and stomping her own foot, washing over him, easing the tension from his shoulders just a little.

"I'm sorry," he choked out, when he caught his breath. "I wasn't laughing at you, Renata. But I think we're going to be friends, you and I."

"Well, I don't *think* so!"

"Maybe not tonight," he conceded, still smiling, "But someday. Someday, we'll be like this." He held up two fingers squeezed together, then laughed again as Renata's face blanched. "Now." He took a deep breath and raked back his hair with both hands. "It's time to say good night."

"I'm not leaving." Renata stood by her chair, arms crossed, chin out. "You all can go Judas on your sister, but I won't abandon her."

"Go Judas on her?" Phoebe repeated. "What on earth is that?"

"Betrayal, Phoebe. Something you know all about."

"Let's go home, Renata." Phoebe became serious, her voice firm. "Now."

"No." Renata dropped back to the edge of her seat and plopped her purse in her lap. "If he's staying, then so am I."

"No, I'll stay." Gia took a step forward. "Renata, I know you want to go back to your boys."

"But you can't stay here all alone with a strange man, either, Gia."

"Now you're being ridiculous, Ren," Phoebe piped up. "I don't think he's all that strange, and technically, Gia won't be alone with him. She'll have Juliette."

"And Bob," Mrs. Cork added.

"And Bob." Phoebe repeated. "So you and I are going home, Renata. Mrs. Cork," she turned to the neighbor. "If you see any suspicious behavior going on over here, will you call the police?"

"I'm especially good at that," the old woman chuckled.

"Haven't you heard?"

"Oh, I give up!" Renata rose to her feet and started across the floor. Then she stopped, turned around, and marched right up to Victor. She jabbed a finger into his chest, and it was all he could do not to laugh again, so like Juliette she was. "If you make her cry, so help me, I'll kill you. Yes, I know you're a police officer. And yes, that is a real threat. My husband has a gun and I'm not afraid to use it." Then she stormed out of the house, not missing the opportunity to throw a shoulder, hard, into Phoebe, as she passed her.

"Ouch!" Phoebe exclaimed, but she was smiling. She turned her flashing eyes on Victor. "I like you, Officer. And I'm pretty sure our Juliette does, too. But," she reached out to take Gia's hand. "I want you to know that I *love* Juliette. We all do. And we Gustafson girls stick together. If Renata has to kill you, we'll be right there with her. Got it?"

"Got it." These girls weren't so bad, he decided.

Mrs. Cork sidled up next to Gia and the goddess. "Count me in, girls."

Phoebe put an arm around the old woman. "You're in, Mrs. Cork." She leaned down and planted a kiss on Mr. Bobo's head. "So are you, you little pooper."

CHAPTER THIRTY-EIGHT

HER ROOM welcomed her, in spite of the horrible ordeal that had taken place within its four walls. She was surprised to find it looking so normal, and if she didn't know any better, she might have thought the whole thing had been just a nightmare. But the muffled voices in the living room confirmed it was real. And the fact that Bob, overwhelmed by his good fortune, was sound asleep on the pillow next to hers, his bed on the floor in the kitchen a rapidly fading memory.

She pulled the lapels of her robe tighter around her, still unable to get warm. As she lay there, the blankets up under her chin, tears began to well up again. She'd thought she was all cried out, but they were back. How desperate Mike had looked tonight; and how terribly his desperation had made him behave. She didn't want to think about what might have happened if Bob hadn't shown up when he did. She shuddered as she recalled Mike's fingers tracing her neckline, but she still couldn't quite believe he'd intended to hurt her.

She thought about Victor, how he'd come bursting into the bedroom, how he'd raced to her side. Her relief at the sight of him was so great that the rest of the ordeal began to blur together in her memory.

Victor. She thought he'd abandoned her. She thought he wasn't going to rescue her after all when he turned away from her. And when it was Gia, not Victor, who helped her up and out of the room, she thought she'd be alone for the rest of her life.

But then he found her in the garage with Bob, and she awoke to the sight of his face, his eyes full of concern, looking down on her as he murmured her name.

She curled into the memory of how it felt to be swept up into his arms, cradled against his chest, her cheek pressed to the rhythm of his heart. She breathed in through her nose trying to coax her olfactory nerve endings into remembering how he smelled.

Then her sisters showed up.

Her sisters. Oh, how she loved them. But tonight she just wanted to crawl under her covers and not face any of them. She wanted to go to bed, and not get up again until everything upside down in her world was put to right again.

"Juliette Gustafson sat on a wall. Juliette Gustafson had a great fall. All of her sisters and all of her friends couldn't put Juliette together again." She whispered the Mother Goose rhyme, replacing Humpty Dumpty's name with her own, the soundtrack to her pity party.

She pressed her face into her pillow, afraid one of them might hear and come in asking if she was okay.

Juliette was not okay. She hadn't been okay for a very long time. She felt shattered into a million pieces, just like she'd felt after her parents were killed.

"I'm so tired of feeling broken, God," she whispered. "I just want to be whole again."

Juliette heard the front door opening and closing, once, twice, then a third time. Then all was silent. Bob's head came up briefly, his nose sniffing the air, then he flopped back down on the pillow and stretched luxuriantly. Good. They were gone.

"Come on, Bob. Let's go make sure they locked it. I don't want any more unannounced visitors." She pushed herself up slowly, and sat on the edge of the bed with slumped shoulders, trying to work up the energy to move.

Her head snapped up. Footsteps in the hall. Bob's tail thumped the bed a few times.

"Juliette?" *Victor.* Her heart sang out his name.

"I thought I told you to go home," she retorted. She wasn't really angry at him. In fact, she wasn't really angry at any of them, not even Mike. But she was weary, oh, so weary, and needed to decompress without everyone watching.

"You did." She could hear a smile in his voice.

"Are the others still here, too?"

"Just Gia and me. Well, she's next door saying goodnight to Mrs. Cork. But she'll be right back."

"Oh." That wasn't so bad.

"Juliette?"

"Yes?"

"I just want you to know I'm here. In case you need me. Or anything." She smiled at his choppy sentences, sensing his uncertainty.

Weren't they a pair, she thought, all elbows and knees, bumping into each other's hearts with awkward gestures and even more awkward words. How badly she wanted to throw open the door and dive back into his arms. Why couldn't she just let go and trust him?

But I don't want to fall and break again. "Okay. Thanks."

"If you need anything, just ask me. Or Gia, of course."

"Okay. Thanks," she repeated.

"I'm here. I'll be right here when you need me. I won't leave you alone, Juliette."

She remained quiet, but his words made her chest ache with pleasure.

Bob had other ideas. Letting out a delighted bark, he leapt off the bed, and sauntered over to the door, snuffling along the crack at the bottom. He turned and came back to her, licked her knee, then went back to the door again. Two more times he did this. She might as well let him out. Maybe he wanted to go to his own bed. Besides, she needed a drink.

She sighed. "You're not fooling anyone, Jules," she said out loud. She needed Victor, she admitted to herself.

She got up and padded across the floor, tying the robe belt tightly around her waist. "Okay, Bob. Let's go have a look at Officer Manly-Man, shall we?" She pulled open the door and the two of them started down the hall. The bathroom door was closed and she could hear water running.

"You'd better not be using my toothbrush," she called out. She heard a strangled yelp of surprise right before Bob nosed the unlatched door, nudging it open. Juliette gasped, her eyes wide as they took in the shirtless man reflected in the mirror above the sink in her very girlie pink and white bathroom, a foaming toothbrush—not hers, thank goodness—jutting out of his mouth. His hair was damp around his temples and neck like he'd just washed his face, and a wonderful aroma of balsam and sandalwood filled the tiny room. He stared at her in the mirror as she stared at his reflection, both of them startled into temporary immobility.

"Oh! I—I'm so sorry. Bob!" She reached out and grabbed at the dog's collar, jerking him back out of the bathroom and closing the door quickly. "Oh Bob! How could you?" She turned and fled back to her room, the dog, thinking it all a game, chasing after her. She slammed her door and leaned against it, her heart pounding. She could feel the blood pulsing in the veins of her neck and she put a hand up to her cheeks, certain they would be flaming. Bob leapt up onto the bed, barked playfully, then crouched down, hind end up in the air, ready for the next game.

Juliette snickered, still a little in shock. "Wow," she muttered. "Wowee-wow." The image of his broad chest, the dark line of hair trailing a line down the middle of his torso, was scorched into her memory. "Did you see his face?" she asked the dog. *Did you see his chest?* "I think you surprised him, Bob."

She let out a squeal of surprise when a knock sounded on her door.

"Are you all right in there?" Was he smiling? Angry? As embarrassed as she was?

"Yes!" she called. "I'm sorry about busting in on you like that!"

"No harm done," he assured her. "And that was my toothbrush, by the way. I keep an overnight bag in my car for emergencies. I'm one of those overly-prepared types." He chuckled. Good; at least he wasn't angry. "And now I'm rambling."

"That's okay. I am too. Overly-prepared, I mean," she said, leaning her forehead against the door as she spoke. "You should see my pantry. Or my garage. In fact, you could have had your choice of toothbrushes from my stock. And now I'm rambling, too." She giggled.

After a few moments of silence, he spoke again, this time with a gentle urging in his voice. "Uh, Juliette? Do you think you could come out here so we don't have to talk through the door?"

She pulled the collar of her robe up around her hot cheeks. "Um ... I don't think .... I'm too embarrassed."

He guffawed. "You're embarrassed? What about me? I'm the one you walked in on."

"You're a guy," she reasoned. "You can handle it."

"That makes no sense whatsoever. Open up."

"Okay. But you can't look at me." She stood up and opened the door a tiny crack. She was relieved to see he had his shirt back on.

"Not that again." He studied her one eye.

"Promise me."

He crossed his arms and rocked back on his heels, not taking his eyes off what little he could see of her. "Juliette Simone Gustafson. I *want* to look at you." He stepped toward her, the look in his eyes making her tremble, but she didn't close the door. "I *want* to see you." He braced one hand on the door jamb and ducked his head so that his eyes were level with hers. His voice dropped until it rumbled in his chest, a sound like the tide, sweeping over her. "Open this door and come out here so that I *can* look at you."

Then he held out his hand to her.

She hesitated only for a moment, then stepped out into the hallway, and placed her hand in his, where it fit so perfectly. He led the way down the hall and into the little kitchen. "Gia put on some coffee. Would you like some?"

He held a chair out for her, and she sat, watching him fill the empty places in her kitchen, the way he was doing in her heart. "That would be nice."

He pulled two mugs from the cupboard. "Coffee." He chuckled low in his throat. "You know, you went to a lot of trouble tonight to avoid having coffee with me."

"A *lot* of trouble," she agreed, reaching up to touch her swollen lip.

"I'm not going anywhere. I won't leave you alone, Juliette."

She felt heat spread up her neck to her cheeks at his words and she reached down to scratch Bob's head. "You said that already."

"I'm glad you were listening."

"And," she didn't look up at him. "I'm glad you're not going anywhere." She couldn't explain, even to herself, how glad she was.

"So how do you like your coffee? Cream? Sugar?"

"Just cream. There's milk in the fridge." She watched as he filled the two mugs. "What about you? How do you drink your coffee?"

"Black. Just the way the good Lord created it." He pulled open the refrigerator door and found the carton for her. "Why do you ask?"

"Thought it might be good to know in case I get to make you a cup of coffee someday." He just grinned as he poured a dollop of milk in her mug and gave it a quick stir. Maybe it was because she was wrung out, she didn't know, but she felt emboldened by his attentiveness. She opened her mouth to say what was on her heart, knowing if she didn't speak now, she might chicken out.

"Victor?" He stopped and looked over at her, still smiling. "Thank you. Thank you for…I don't even know where to begin. For everything. For chasing us down in the parking lot at church just to tell me—" Her forehead wrinkled. "What did you tell me?"

"If I remember right, I told you that you make me uncomfortable in my own skin. And that you're beautiful." He shook his head, his grin faltering a little. "It wasn't exactly what I had planned, but that's what we ended up with."

"Yes. I remember. You pulled a Mr. Darcy."

"A what? Is Mr. Darcy a duck, by any chance?"

"Pride and Prejudice? Elizabeth Bennett? Jane Austen?" She could feel her own eyes widen with each question, appalled at his lack of literary awareness. Oh dear. She must do something about that deficiency and quickly. But not tonight. "No, he's a man, not a duck. Although Lizzy might have disagreed at one time." Juliette shook her head. *Focus, Jules.* "Anyway, thank you. And thank you for not taking no for an answer, and for coming over tonight anyway. Thank you for being here."

"So you're one of those girls who mean 'yes' when they say 'no.'" He picked up the two mugs.

"I am not!" She snatched a packet of soy sauce from a bowl in the middle of the table and threatened to throw it at him. He ducked his head instinctively, but didn't spill a drop of coffee. "Usually I know exactly what I want. And then I make out a perfect plan of how I'm going to make it happen the way I want it to happen." She shrugged. "Just not lately."

"I see."

"So, thank you," she finished lamely.

"You're welcome." He set the two steaming cups down on the table and pulled out a chair beside her. "But you're only making what I have to say to you more difficult."

"Oh. Sorry." Self-doubt washed over her. Maybe she'd said too much. Maybe she'd misunderstood him and his intentions. She stared down into the creamy liquid in the cup between her hands.

"I have a confession to make."

"Oh dear," she muttered, afraid of what she might see in his eyes if she looked at him.

"I should have come clean weeks ago, but I was too chicken. Juliette, I know we haven't spent much time together." He set his cup down and leaned back in his chair. "You know, this all sounded a lot better in my head."

"It always does," she grunted derisively.

"Come." He pushed himself up and reached for her hand, pulling her up beside him. "Let's go outside. I'm feeling a little claustrophobic." He led her out the sliding glass doors to the little patio where she and Gia had eaten breakfast earlier that day—*was it only this morning?*—their blankets still piled on the patio chairs. Victor picked one up and draped it around her shoulders, then threw the other around his own. They stood side-by-side, hand-in-hand, staring up into the midnight sky filled with wispy pre-winter clouds against a black background pin-pricked with stars. They were silent for so long Juliette wondered if he'd forgotten what he was going to say.

"I think I'm falling in love with you." His voice was gentle, just like his touch. There was no preamble, no beating around the bush. "No, I *know* that I'm falling in love with you."

When he didn't continue, she peeked up at him. He was still gazing up at the sky, but she was pretty sure he was professing his love to her and not the stars.

"It seems I've known it for a long time, maybe even since the first night I came here and you met me at the door in that robe. But it was after having pie with you and the Petersons that I finally realized I needed to do something about it. Then when I didn't see you at church again, I thought maybe I'd come on too strong and scared you off. The way I felt was pretty terrifying, you know. To me, at least. Now I realize what a fool I've been, waiting until...until—" He turned so that he was facing her and took hold of her other hand, pulling her just a little closer, cupping both her hands in his and pressing them to his chest.

"Juliette, I don't know what I was waiting for. Maybe a lightning bolt from God, or a flashing billboard sign that said, 'Go get her, man.' But I'm sorry I waited. And I'm so sorry about tonight and the way things happened here. I wish I hadn't gone next door. I wish I hadn't taken Bob with me. I—I even wish Mike had done things right by you tonight, instead of showing up here in the state he was in." Even in the shadows, she could see the regret in his eyes.

"I wish I had done things differently tonight here, myself, Juliette. I shouldn't have left your side, not even when the officer questioned you." The urgency in his voice made her hold her breath. "But I can't change what happened here. And I can't change the way I've handled things up until tonight. All I can do is ask you to forgive me, and let me try to change things from here on out." He took a deep breath and continued before she could speak. She couldn't find her voice anyway.

"And, um, here's the other half of my confession." He looked away then, out over the small back yard, the small square of grass bordered by colorful flowers still blooming valiantly in the Southern California mild fall weather. Beneath her hands he still held pressed to his chest, she could feel his heart beating at least as raucously as her own, and it made her smile despite her trepidation over what he might say next.

Finally, he looked back down at her, his gaze steady. "I read your list tonight, the one on your night stand. I shouldn't have, but I'm glad I saw it. I have a lot of work to do, Juliette, but I want my name to be at the top of that page. I want those things to be about me, not just some guy you're looking for. I love you, and I want to be your champion, Juliette." He dipped his head until their foreheads touched. His voice was little more than a whisper. "Please tell me if you think you could ever love me, too."

Her throat was so tight it almost hurt. She pulled her hands from his grasp, not missing the catch in his breathing as she did. She dropped the blanket from around her shoulders and did what she'd been longing to do all night. She stepped into his arms and pressed her body close to his as he enveloped her, wrapping them both in a cocoon of warmth. Her cheek rested against his chest and she listened to the pounding of his heart, the sound of his love for her.

"I don't think, Victor," she murmured. "I *know* I love you, too."

Next door, the slider door swished closed gently, followed by muffled yapping. "Your neighbor is still a nosy busy-body." His voice rumbled in his chest against her ear.

"I think she probably fancies herself a matchmaker, too." Juliette smiled and tipped her head back to look up at him. He brought his hands up and gently cupped her face, kissing first one cheek, then the other, then ever so tenderly, the un-bruised side of her mouth.

CHAPTER THIRTY-NINE

JULIETTE and Victor were nestled together on the patio bench in their blankets, talking quietly over their coffee, when Gia finally made an appearance.

"I'm going to jump in the shower, Jules. Do you have an extra toothbrush? I can't find mine anywhere."

Victor guffawed and Juliette got up to show her where she kept her stock. When they were in the hallway, Gia grabbed Juliette's hand. "Oh. My. Gosh!" she whispered, her eyes all lit up. "We were outside talking while Mr. Bobo did his thing before bed, and you two came out. What were supposed to do? So we just shushed each other and listened, not wanting to break the mood. Oh. My. Gosh!" she said again. Then she pulled up short.

"Jules? Are you okay? Did Mike--?"

"I'm fine, Gia. I promise." Juliette leaned forward and planted a kiss on her little sister's cheek. "I'm a little battered, both body and spirit, but I'm okay. I have you, I have Victor, I have Bob, Mrs. Cork, Ren, Phoebe, and I have God. I'm better than okay."

Gia smiled and hugged her warmly. Juliette forced

herself not to flinch as her sister squeezed her bruised shoulder. "Victor. Wow." Then Gia brought her fists up to her mouth and squealed into her hands. "He's so awesome!"

"Yes. He is," Juliette preened. "And I'm going back outside to snuggle with Mr. Awesome now, okay? Do you have everything you need?"

"I'm good."

"Come out when you're done."

"Um, I think I'll just chill in the living room and watch a movie. You know, give you two lovebirds a little extra canoodle time, okay?" Gia slipped into the bathroom with a wink and a wave, and Juliette floated back outside.

Victor asked her several times if she was tired, if she needed to get to sleep, until she finally threatened to send him home. "I'm a big girl, Officer Jarrett. I will go to bed when I'm good and ready. You're not keeping me out here." Then she reconsidered. "Actually, you are. But only because I want you to keep me out here."

He hugged her and she winced. "Juliette. You are hurt, aren't you?"

His voice was so gentle. She looked at him with hesitance in her eyes.

"It's okay," he said. "You can trust me."

So Juliette told him about the endless twenty minutes she'd spent alone with Mike.

Then Victor kissed her and told her about his sisters and about how afraid he was of *her* sisters.

Juliette laughed and felt the pieces of her life beginning to fit back together.

When it got too cold, they moved inside to the sofa. Gia, lulled to sleep by the trailer music of the movie she'd had every intention of watching, was curled up in the over-sized armchair, Bob sprawled at her feet.

Juliette turned off the television and tucked a blanket around her sister, who didn't stir, then tucked herself into the arms of the man who looked at her as though she was the center of every breath.

She told Victor about Angela Clinton, and how everywhere she went, the Lord seemed to be whispering the girl's name in her ear.

Victor told her about knowing his real name but not his real dad.

Juliette kissed the spot over his heart and whispered, "Poor little James." Then she told him about her motorcycle ride with Trevor and the moment she gave the broken pieces of her life to Christ.

Victor frowned and said he'd better look into getting himself a bike. Juliette grinned and said, "I'd ride with you any day, Mr. Manly-Man."

Then he told her about his mother and promised to protect her from the dragon queen, Loreena. "I am your champion, after all."

Juliette explained her mother's Frenchness and her father's Swedishness and assured him that Grandpa and Granny G were going to love him. "You are my champion, after all."

~ ~ ~

THE MORNING sun peeked hesitantly through the slats of the blinds at the front window, gently nudging the two love-birds on the sofa awake. Juliette looked down at the hard pillow she'd been sleeping on and remembered that it was Victor's chest. Victor looked down at the wild disarray of black hair spilled across the front of his shirt and remembered that it belonged to the most beautiful fluffy pink—and black and blue—duck he'd ever met.

A light tapping on the front door roused them, and Bob leapt to his feet, untangling himself from the blankets. He charged the door, barking his greeting, and Victor followed him, his hair rumpled and his shirt crooked. Stepping back to allow Mrs. Cork and Mr. Bobo inside, he closed his eyes and breathed deeply of the aromas wafting in with them.

"Slumber party?" she asked, as she passed through the living room into the kitchen, eying Juliette who still lay curled beneath a blanket on the sofa. She was awake, and smiled gingerly.

"Good morning, Mrs. Cork!" Gia called from the bathroom where she was already up and getting ready for work. "Mr. Bobo!" she cried, as the little dog raced down the hall and into the bathroom to find her, Bob scurrying after him.

Mrs. Cork set her things down on the counter. "You two know this is the last time you're allowed to spend the night together until after you're married. I'll not tolerate lascivious behavior in my neighborhood." Gia and the dogs scampered into the kitchen. "So? Did they behave themselves last night, Gia? Or are we going to have to call in the big guns?"

"Please don't. Renata scares me." Victor had followed Mrs. Cork into the kitchen and tried to reach around her to lift the lid off the casserole. She smacked his wrist with the dishtowel she held.

"Hands off, Mister."

"I'll have you know, Mrs. Cork, that woman in there wouldn't keep her hands off of me all night long. I'm exhausted from resisting her wicked charms. I need sustenance." He reached for the casserole again, but Mrs. Cork shook her head.

"Not working. And don't bother trying to make me blush either. I'll have *you* know that I was a very happily married woman at one time. You've got nothing on Mr. Cork, son. Hubba-hubba."

"Mrs. Cork!" Gia gasped, breaking into giggles. "Hubba-hubba?"

While Juliette and Victor washed up, Gia helped Mrs. Cork prepare for breakfast. Victor leaned against the bathroom door jamb and watched Juliette's reflection in the mirror.

She met his gaze, her eyes telling him everything words could not.

Over an egg and sausage casserole to die for, Juliette assured everyone that she was all right. The swelling around her mouth had indeed gone down, and although there was a nasty gash on the inside of her lip where it mashed against her teeth, the split itself wasn't as bad as the amount of blood had indicated.

Mrs. Cork gave her a tin of homemade salve. "I'm an old lady and I know all about dry, cracked skin, Juliette. I make this myself because it works better than anything I've ever found over the counter. You try it on that lip of yours; it'll heal in no time. You'll see."

Satisfied her sister was well-looked-after, Gia hurried off to work shortly after breakfast, ready to whip up some excellent coffee for Sunday morning church-goers and weekend warriors.

Victor and Mrs. Cork straightened the kitchen and living room while Juliette showered and tried to make the best of her bruised face. Mrs. Cork's balm felt heavenly on her lips;

whatever was in it, the woman knew what she was doing. Then the three of them headed out to the patio to enjoy the morning sunshine and a second—third, in Victor's case—cup of coffee, while the dogs chased each other in circles all over the back yard.

"Thank you again for breakfast, Mrs. Cork," Juliette sighed contentedly from inside the circle of Victor's arms. "I can't believe how hungry I was. It was delicious."

"Thank you, Juliette. And I really wish you kids would call me by my first name, if that's not too presumptuous."

"Well, I suppose if you'll stop calling me Officer Jarrett and try Victor instead, we've got a deal. What shall we call you, then?" Victor asked.

Mrs. Cork nodded in agreement. "My name is Angela."

CHAPTER FORTY

DEAR ANGELA,

It has been fifteen years since my parents were taken from me. My life shattered into a million pieces that day and I thought I could never be put back together again. But I still had my sisters. I still had my grandparents. I still had my friends. I still had a life ahead of me, regardless of how I chose to live it.

It has taken me fifteen years to realize that you also lost your parents on that terrible day. But you lost so much more, didn't you? You lost your brother. You lost your friends. You lost your future. I can only pray you did not lose your faith. I seem to remember you were a believer and I hope you have held on to Jesus all these years.

It has taken fifteen years for me to invite Jesus into my own life and He is ever so gently gathering up all those broken pieces and putting them back together again. Angela, you are one of those pieces. I am sorry for your terrible loss. And I am sorry for the wasted years I've kept both of us chained to my anger, my bitterness, and my unforgiveness.

I forgive you for what you did to me that day. Please forgive me for what I have done to you every day since.

FORGIVENESS. It was like pulling slivers of steel from under the skin. Bitterness, resentment, yes, even hatred, had become familiar pain to him without him even realizing it. As Juliette shared with Victor her own journey toward forgiveness—of Angela, of Mike, even of her parents for abandoning them—his eyes were opened to all the things he'd harbored in his heart against his father, his mother, his sisters, all those who should have had his love. He didn't have to agree with their behavior, he didn't have to participate, but God had called him to be a light in their lives, not to be absent from their lives altogether. Rebuilding burned bridges was difficult; he had his work cut out for him. But he also had Juliette beside him, dealing with the past and facing the future with him.

Juliette's decision to open her heart to Angela had been easy for him to encourage and support. Honored that she'd asked for his help, he'd pulled some strings to find out more about where Angela was and how she was doing. So far, the news was encouraging, prompting Juliette to move forward with contacting her old classmate.

Her decision to forgive Mike, however, had all but done him in. When she asked him to go to the hospital in her place the day after Mike's assault, Victor had almost refused. But after an afternoon of angry prayer, and a terse phone call to Tom and Michelle for accountability and more prayer, he'd agreed. He wasn't happy about it, but he would go—in uniform—and bring back a report to Juliette.

When he entered Mike's hospital room, the nurse who was studying the monitor looked up with a scowl. Her patient's heart rate began to accelerate, and just for a moment, Victor was glad.

He took off his sunglasses and said what he'd come to say. "Mr. Wilson, I've come on behalf of Juliette Gustafson. I'm here to make sure you're going to live." Well, that wasn't exactly what he'd planned, but the effect those words had on the man in the flimsy hospital gown was probably more to his liking than the polite drivel he'd rehearsed in his head.

Mike's face fell. "How is she? I hurt her, didn't I?"

"Yes, you did."

Mike pressed his fists to his eyes. "Is she going to be okay?"

"You messed her up pretty badly." Not willing to give the man answers he didn't deserve, Victor crossed his arms and widened his stance, taking up as much space as he could. He was enjoying this.

The nurse's scowl had changed to a blank slate. He thought she was working hard not to show her newly acquired distaste toward her patient.

Mike looked up, his eyes filled with what Victor could only guess was supposed to be remorse. "She's going to be okay though, right?"

"No thanks to you, she is," he stated.

"Oh God, I'm a monster." Mike laid his head back on the pillow and closed his eyes, a single tear making a track down the side of his face and into his carefully combed hair. Without looking at Victor, he asked, "What happens now? Are you here to arrest me?"

It took every ounce of control Victor could muster, but somehow he got the next words past his lips. "Against everyone's advice, Miss Gustafson is not pressing charges, because for some inconceivable reason, she believes better of you than what you gave her. Grace, Mr. Wilson. You don't deserve to be let off the hook." He took a step closer and waited until Mike looked at him. Victor saw the flicker of fear in his eyes, and he felt the echoing flicker of satisfaction in his own heart.

"However, Mr. Wilson, if you ever, *ever* lay a hand on my woman again, I will personally come for you. And believe me, charges will be pressed, the kind that you will never find a way out from under." The nurse hummed softly to herself, jotting notes down on the monitor feed. Victor was very aware that the flickering green line spiked a little higher on the screen; so was the nurse. She took note of it, but she didn't seem too concerned.

Mike nodded, wiped at his eyes with the edge of his sheet, and said, "Whether you believe it or not, I was once a good guy. My pride nearly killed me, though," he waved his hands around, indicating the room where he lay. "And I was ready to take Juliette down with me. I'll always be ashamed of that. But her kindness has given me a second chance, and I won't take it for granted. Please tell her thank you for me."

Victor didn't say anything at first. *He needs forgiveness, Victor.* He wrestled with her words. He fought. Hard.

Then he nodded. "I'll tell her."

Mike let out his breath in a whoosh and turned to look at the nurse. "You can stop pretending you're not thinking horrible things about me."

She returned his gaze, her eyes softening a little, and said, "I don't know what you're talking about, Mr. Wilson." She reached over and checked the electrodes stuck to his chest, adjusted the oxygen monitor on his finger, and patted his shoulder, perhaps a little harder than necessary. "Your doctor says you'll probably go home this afternoon. Who knows? You might come out of this a better man." Then she scooped up her things and wheeled her little cart out the door ahead of her.

Victor turned to go, too, but Mike called out after him. "Officer? Thank you for what you did, too. I can only imagine how hard that must have been for you. She deserves someone like you. I'm glad—"

"Don't," Victor cut him off. "For one second, presume to tell me what Juliette does and doesn't deserve, Mr. Wilson." He stood in the doorway, fingers flexing at his sides. "You've been forgiven, and you've been offered grace. What you do with it is up to you. But you no longer have access to the woman who gave them to you, do you understand?"

When Mike didn't answer, Victor took an aggressive step towards the bed. "Do you understand what I'm saying to you, Mr. Wilson?"

"I understand."

"Good." Victor turned and left the room.

He climbed behind the wheel of his car, pulled out of the hospital parking lot, and didn't stop until he was standing at Juliette's front door, listening to Bob's exuberant greeting on the other side of it, and desperately hoping she'd answer his knock in her fluffy pink robe.

THE END

Keep reading for an excerpt:
RENATA & THE FALL FROM GRACE
The Gustafson Girls Book 2

ABOUT THE AUTHOR

Becky Doughty is an award-winning author and the voice behind BraveHeart Audiobooks. She writes Women's Fiction with strong elements of romance, Contemporary Romance, and Coming of Age novels. Some of Becky's books include the best-selling *Elderberry Croft Collection, The Gustafson Girls Series, The Restoration Series,* and *The Fallout Series.*

Becky is married to her champion of more than 30 years. They have three children, two of whom are grown and starting families of their own, and they all live within a few miles of each other in Southern California. They share their lives with too many animals, a large vegetable garden, and a strange underground concrete room they're certain was built for dark and sinister purposes….

Connect with Becky:
www.BeckyDoughty.com
www.Facebook.com/BeckyDoughtyAuthor
www.Twitter.com/BeckySDoughty

More Books by Becky Doughty

PEMBERTON MANOR: A Serial Novel
Ten Episodes

ELDERBERRY CROFT: A Serial Novel
Twelve Episodes

ELDERBERRY DAYS: Season of Joy
The Elderberry Croft Sequel

THE GUSTAFSON GIRLS SERIES
~ Juliette and the Monday ManDates
~ Renata and the Fall from Grace
~ Phoebe and the Rock of Ages
~ Gia and the Blast from the Past

THE FALLOUT SERIES
~ All the Way to Heaven
~ A Light in the Dark
~ A Long Way Home

STAND ALONE NOVELS
~ Waters Fall

DEVOTIONAL
~ Life Letters

RENATA & THE FALL FROM GRACE

An Excerpt...

CHAPTER ONE

"SO, JULIETTE darling, what diabolical deed could you have possibly committed?" Phoebe wound a black tendril of hair around her forefinger as she glanced pointedly at the clock on the wall. "Whatever it is, make it quick. I've got a date tonight." The dark-haired artist was resplendent in a scarlet kimono dress paired with thigh-high stiletto boots. A pointed toe dipped up and down in time to the music playing in the background, one of Juliette's beloved 80s' movie soundtracks.

"What on earth is there to do on a Tuesday night in this town?" Renata asked from across the room. The question was out before she could stop it. Phoebe liked nothing better than to flaunt her wild lifestyle, and Renata had just given her leave to do so.

Phoebe's smile became sultry. "I don't think you want to know, Rennie. Let's just say it probably isn't your cup of tea." Then she raised both her bangled wrists above her head and did a slow and sensual gyrating motion.

"You're going to hell, Phoebe Gustafson."

"Oh, I'm well aware of that, thank you very much. You,

on the other hand, may be headed for the pearly gates, but at least I'm having fun along the way."

"Hey, you two. Cool it." Juliette's soothing voice cut through the mounting tension, and Renata took a deep breath, hating the tightness in her chest when Phoebe mocked her faith. But Juliette didn't look very happy, either. "What time do you have to leave, Phebes?"

"You've got me for thirty minutes. Brandon is picking me up at my place at six and I still have to fix my face."

"What's wrong with your face?" Gia asked, her back to the entertainment center, her fingers buried in Bob's scruffy fur. Bob, once Tootles, was the beloved dog Juliette had rescued from the park with Renata's help last fall. Although she brushed him regularly, Juliette had given up on taming her dog's coat.

"I can tell you what's wrong with her face," Renata quipped unkindly.

"Please." Juliette held up a hand, an uncharacteristic scowl on her face. "If I had known we only had half an hour, I would have waited to call a G-FOURce. I have something pretty serious to talk to you about."

"That's not for like two hours, Phebes. You look fantabulous already. Do you really need that much time?" Gia asked, her curls spilling down her back in a riotous waterfall of autumn hues. The youngest of the four sisters, she was the only Gustafson girl who still lived at home with Grandpa and Granny G, but she'd obviously forgotten the epic Battle of the Bathroom that took place every morning when they'd all shared the same room.

Renata rolled her eyes. "Don't be silly, Georgia. It only takes her ten minutes to actually get ready. The rest of the time she's just admiring her own reflection." She was feeling especially snarky today, and Phoebe had been on her nerves since Christmas. Besides, for various reasons, January was always a difficult month for her. Putting away holiday decorations and giving the house a thorough cleaning gave her a satisfying sense of accomplishment, but it never lasted. No matter how hard she tried, within weeks, she'd broken all her New Year's resolutions, particularly the resolutions involving coffee, gummy bears, and the cookie dough in a tub she kept stocked in her freezer year round. Once the boys were off to school in the morning, she could hear the little chocolate chips calling her name.

Not that she would have thought of that herself, but right before the big family Christmas meal last month, Phoebe had been sent out to the garage freezer for a bag of ice. She'd taken four-year-old Judah with her, the two of them chattering away about how much lizards and aliens look alike. They returned shortly, a bag of ice in Phoebe's arms, and one of the chocolate chip cookie dough tubs in Judah's.

"I didn't ask for cookies," Renata sighed. "Just ice. We're almost ready to sit down."

"I know. But the poor little chocolate chips were calling us, weren't they, Jude-Dude? Their tiny sad voices cried out, 'Phoebe! Judah! We're so cold in here, so c-c-cold.'" Phoebe peeled off the lid and began chipping away at the frozen lump with a fork from one of the beautifully-set places around the table. "We knew just where they'd get nice and warm very quickly."

She winked at the little boy and they both shouted gleefully, "Belly-town!"

Phoebe's fork slipped and a huge chunk of dough plopped onto the clean, white tablecloth and rolled a few inches, leaving a discolored smudge in its wake. "Oops!"

Before she got to it, Judah reached under her arm, snatched it up, and popped it into his mouth, then dove under the table so Renata couldn't get to him. Phoebe laughed out loud.

"Great. Thanks for spoiling his appetite." Renata grumbled. She didn't want to fight with Phoebe, not today of all days, but it seemed inevitable no matter how hard she tried not to.

"Did I just make you lose your appetite, Jude-Dude?" Phoebe lifted the edge of the tablecloth and peeked underneath at the boy. Judah chortled gleefully, but shook his head, then crawled out to prove that everything, including his hunger, was still intact. Tell-tale brown streaks ran down the front of his white shirt as he stood in front of Renata.

"I'm starving, Mommy! I'm starving for salad, and smashed tater toes, and ... and turkey bird, and corn." He continued to list the items he could see as he craned his neck to get a better view of the dishes on the table. "My appetite didn't get lost. It's right here." He patted his tummy, leaving even more smudges.

"Oh, dear. Let's go wash up and change your shirt, shall we, little man?" Phoebe shoved the tub of dough in Renata's already packed refrigerator and grabbed the boy's hand. The two of them disappeared down the hall, and Renata frowned after them.

Now here she was, sitting across from Phoebe, picking fights with her again, and it occurred to her that she was breaking yet another resolution: I will not fight with Phoebe. "Sorry," she muttered. "That wasn't nice."

"Maybe not, but it's true." Phoebe wasn't going to allow her to be gracious. "I practice my pucker, my blink, my surprised look." She put both hands on her cheeks and shaped her mouth into a perfect, scarlet 'O.' Gia grinned at her antics from her spot on the floor and Renata wished the girl wasn't so easily impressed with Phoebe. "I even practice my 'come hither' look because there's always a chance I might meet Hither while I'm out and about."

"Cute, Phoebe. But enough. I really do need to tell you about something," Juliette cut in. "I just don't want to feel rushed." She shifted in her favorite corner of the beige-toned sofa. She'd added some new throw pillows, Renata noticed, in plum shantung silk and a gorgeous apple green. She saw traces of the same colors around the rest of the room, too. Even the black and white Ansel Adams prints on the walls were now accented with pieces that looked like some of Phoebe's artwork; bold, swirling colors against serene blue backgrounds. Renata had to admit she approved.

Juliette continued. "Nor do I want anyone to leave until we've talked things through."

"Fine," said Phoebe from the other end of the sofa. "If it runs too long, I'll just call Brandon and make him wait. It'll be good for him. He's getting a little too comfortable." Phoebe took a long sip of her iced tea and turned to Gia.

"Get on with it, little sister!" As the youngest member, it was Gia's job to begin the pledge. "Welcome Empress Juliette, Empress Renata, and Empress Phoebe." She pressed her hands together in a prayer-like manner and nodded her head to each sister accordingly.

"Welcome, Empress Georgia." The other three spoke just as somberly, nodding back at her.

They clasped hands, formed a circle, and began the G-FOURce pledge, a time-honored tradition that had somehow survived adolescence into adulthood.

Let the words of our mouths
Be necessary, kind, and true.
Let the secrets we share
Be kept safe amongst us few.
Let the decisions that we make
Be brave, noble, and wise
Oogie-boogie-doggy-loogie
Wiggly-jiggly-fries!
G-FOURce unite!

They didn't collapse into giggles the way they used to, but none of them was quite grown up enough to give it up. The pledge was like an unbroken cord weaving through their lives, binding them together. They released hands and settled back into place, and Phoebe turned laughing eyes on Juliette.

"So? Does this have anything to do with our favorite police officer? Has he put you on house arrest?" She wiggled her ring finger in the air. "Did he ask you to marry him, yet?"

Juliette didn't smile, and a sense of foreboding settled around Renata's shoulders at the look in her older sister's eyes. She laced her fingers together in her lap and waited for Juliette to speak.

"No," Juliette shook her head in emphasis. "He doesn't have anything to do with this. Not exactly, anyway."

Renata took a sip of her tea, relieved. Juliette had fallen madly in love with a local police officer, Victor Jarrett, last year, and although Renata could see how happy he made her, she still wasn't so sure about the man.

Sometimes, when Officer Jarrett looked at her with those foggy-morning gray eyes, it felt like he could see right through her, making her self-conscious and uncomfortable.

Her boys adored him, her husband thought he was the best thing that had ever happened to Juliette, but Renata had butted heads with him from the very beginning, and he'd made her feel silly and foolish and incompetent, all things she didn't like feeling. She couldn't find anything wrong with him except for how he made *her* feel, and she wasn't against Juliette loving him. She just didn't want to be around him, herself, any more than she had to be.

"What is it, Jules?" Gia brought her knees up, resting her chin on them. She wrapped her arms around her legs, and Renata thought maybe her little sister felt the same wariness Renata felt. When Juliette raised her eyes again, they were glistening with unshed tears.

"It's about Angela. Angela Clinton. I wrote to her a few weeks ago. And she wrote back."

CHAPTER TWO

"YOU WHAT?" Phoebe's hushed voice cut through the silence like a dull knife, ripping and tearing, rather than slicing cleanly, the way it usually did. Her tone, in spite of its brevity, held accusation, anger, betrayal, and something else Renata couldn't quite place. Fear? "You did *what*?" she repeated. Then she turned on Renata. "And you? Were you in on this, too?"

"No!" Renata held up her hands. "I knew nothing about it." But she did know something about it, and Phoebe must have read it on her face. That day in the park, when Juliette had rescued the starving Bob from under the hedge, she'd seen Juliette's notebook open to the page with Angela's name scrawled at the top. She'd asked her about it, and they'd talked briefly about how difficult it was to just write the girl's name.

She did not, however, know that Juliette had succeeded in moving past the salutation to the actual letter itself. And she'd had no reason to believe her sister would actually send it.

In fact, had she known of Juliette's intentions, she would have done everything in her power to prevent that letter from going out. Short of committing criminal acts, that is, lest she be forced to deal with Juliette's policeman.

"She didn't know, Phebes," Juliette swiped at a lone tear that tracked down her cheek. "I didn't talk to anyone about it except Victor—"

"Victor? Officer Jarrett? You talked to him about writing to Angela before you talked to us?" Now it was Renata's turn to raise her voice. "What business is it of his? And just how long have you two known each other now?" Little currents of electricity sparked behind her eyes, making it difficult to connect her thoughts together.

"Ren, please. Don't make this about Victor."

Phoebe was on her feet. "Uh, *you* made it about Victor, Jules. Not Ren." She began pacing the floor between the back of the sofa and the arched opening into the kitchen. "What were you thinking? And why didn't you talk to us before you did this?"

"I—I couldn't. I couldn't talk to anyone about it."

"Really? Because I don't remember you having any trouble talking to me about it last year," Renata retorted. "And you obviously felt you could talk to Victor." His name curled her lips into a sneer.

"So you did know?" Phoebe stopped pacing and glared at Renata.

"No. I mean, we talked about *thinking* about writing to her a long time ago. But I had no clue she'd actually go and do it." Renata glanced over at Gia and sighed. The girl had her forehead resting on her knees, her folded legs hugged tightly to her. She turned back to Juliette. "Why didn't you just talk to us first?"

Juliette took a deep breath and pushed her long, dark hair away from her face with both hands. "I'm sorry I didn't. I should have. But it was such a strange process. I tried so many times to write to her. I'd start with her name and then...*nothing*. I did that countless times." She looked pointedly at her and Renata looked away. She, too, had experienced the same struggle and had admitted as much to Juliette. "But then, when the whole thing with Mike happened, and then his meltdown—"

"His assault, you mean," Phoebe interjected.

"Phebes, please. He wasn't himself."

"Right. He has that wolf disorder." She rolled her eyes. "Apropos name, I'd say."

"Wolff-Parkinson-White syndrome," Juliette corrected quietly.

"Stop making excuses for him," Renata said. She could tell Juliette was trying to remain calm, but how could she defend the guy? How *could* she after he'd broken into her house and hurt her? Renata was still appalled at his behavior. She'd always liked Mike, at least until he'd broken Juliette's heart, but Renata wasn't in any hurry to let him off the hook because of some obscure diagnosis.

Juliette clamped her lips shut for a few moments, her fingers toying with the strings of a tassel on the cushion she held in her lap. Then she straightened her shoulders. "I'm not trying to excuse him, but it doesn't matter anyway. The point I was trying to make was this. Something happened when I chose to forgive him. It was like a light got turned on inside of me, shining into the corners of all these locked rooms in my heart. Rooms that harbored all this ugly stuff, you know?"

Renata made a real attempt not to roll her eyes. Ever since Juliette had climbed on the back of Trevor Zander's motorcycle, she'd turned into a Christian cliché queen.

Light shining in the darkness. All things made new.

Forgive and forget. Washed clean. God's will.

Whatever. Renata had heard them all. She'd used them all—in fact, she still did among certain circles, and sometimes just to goad Phoebe—but she knew each word and phrase for what it was. A nice way to say, "Life is hard, but now that you're a Christian, suck it up." She tuned back into what Juliette was saying.

"In a way, forgiving Mike freed me to forgive others I never thought I could." Juliette took a deep breath and let it out slowly, hugging the cushion to her chest. She spoke firmly, but she didn't make eye contact with any of them. "It was like this dam broke loose, and suddenly the words just came out of me in a rush." Her eyes were bright, still fixed on something just above Gia's head.

"That's all fine and well, Jules," Phoebe stated. "But why didn't you talk to us then? Why couldn't you wait and talk to us before you sent her anything?"

Juliette blinked twice, slowly, then shrugged, looking more like the noncommittal Juliette they all knew. "I—I guess I was a little afraid to tell you because I had no idea how this would all turn out. And," she chewed her lip, then continued, her voice dropping to just above a whisper. "We've never really discussed Angela before, you guys. And...and I didn't want anyone trying to talk me out of writing to her."

"Well that's exactly what we would have done," Renata exclaimed. She stood up and crossed over to where her youngest sister sat on the floor, her head down on her knees, long red hair spilling around her like a veil. Renata dropped down to sit beside her. "You okay, Georgia?" Renata had a difficult time using the nickname she preferred, Gia. There was a part of her that wondered what was so wrong with the names they'd been given. Why change them? Juliette was Juliette, not Jules, not Juju like her best friend, Sharon, called her. Just Juliette. Phoebe was Phoebe. Not Phebes, but Phoebe. And Georgia was Georgia. 'Gia' sounded like the name of a Victoria Secret model, or something racier, and it bothered her calling her sweet baby sister by a name like that.

Gia lifted her head and nodded. "I'm fine."

An awkward silence settled over the group, and although she was no longer pacing, Phoebe didn't sit down. She stood with one shoulder against the wall, almost as though she were separating herself from the rest of them.

Finally, it was Gia who spoke. "Do you have her letter with you?"

"Of course. Would you like to read it? Or I can read it out loud."

"I want to know what you said to her first." Phoebe pushed away from the wall, and to everyone's surprise, crossed over to the two sisters on the floor and sat down on Gia's other side. Four against one, Renata thought; even the dog stayed curled up around Gia's feet.

Juliette must be dying inside, but Renata wouldn't look at her, not directly. Out of the corner of her eye, she watched her sitting all alone in her spot on the couch, not moving, not speaking, just studying them, sizing up the situation. Renata knew that if she were in Juliette's shoes, she would be on the verge of kicking everyone out. Juliette wasn't like that, though. Although she was stubborn and a little stand-offish when she was hurting, she would do everything in her power to make sure the rest of them were all right. Which is what made this whole situation so surreal.

"Well," Juliette began slowly, testing the weight of each

word. "I told her I forgive her for what she did to me. I didn't speak for anyone else. And I asked her for forgiveness, too."

Another long silence, then Phoebe's husky voice asked the question the others longed to. "For what, Jules? What did you ever do to her?"

Juliette snorted softly, a sound so derisive that Renata did look at her now. "I think a better question would be 'What have I *not* done to her?'" She set aside the pillow and leaned forward. It was just a coffee table and a few feet of floor space between them, but it felt like a chasm to Renata, with Juliette on one side, the look on her face raw and ferocious, the three of them on the other, disbelieving, betrayed. "I have run her down, run her over, shoved her off the Golden Gate Bridge, thrown her into an abandoned well. I have left her stranded in the middle of the Mohave Desert. Naked." She clamped her mouth shut as though to put a halt to the litany of atrocities spilling out of her. Her nostrils pinched as she breathed in, then said, "I have spent the last fifteen years hating her, wishing she was dead, and coming up with a million ways to off her. That, my sisters, is what I've done to her."

Renata was shocked. She shouldn't be, because she'd struggled with her own feelings about Angela, but this was Juliette. Sweet Juliette, who wouldn't hurt a fly. Literally. The girl would rather shoo one out the back door than break out the flyswatter. Yet here she was admitting to contemplating all forms of murder for Angela Clinton.

"I have wasted so much of my life wishing her dead, you guys," Juliette's soft voice was loud in the stunned silence. "And it has kept us both trapped by that horrible night. Not just Angela, *both* of us! I've had her locked inside the jail in my heart, and every time I thought of her or heard the name

Angela or Clinton, I'm back in that dark place, standing on the other side of those bars, *hating* her. Wanting to kill her was killing me."

Juliette's eyes were overflowing now, the tears falling freely as she reached for a tissue from the box on the coffee table. "It's as though my life stopped that night. I've just been walking around like the living dead, waiting for satisfaction so that I could go lie down and die for real."

Renata could feel her throat tightening as Juliette bared her soul to them, but she would not let herself cry. The others needed her strength; even Phoebe, although she'd never admit it. Renata cleaned up the messes and held the pieces together. It was her role in their little circle, and she did it well. They didn't always love her methods, but she was the go-to-girl when it came to getting things done. She was the backbone of this little family of orphans.

She looked around at her sisters. Juliette was the level-headed glue, the oldest, Gia, the peacemaker, the youngest. Phoebe, not quite two years younger than Renata, shared the middle sibling slot with her, so she resisted being categorized. If nothing else, she brought the entertainment, the fuel, the fire. Phoebe gave them a reason to kiss and make up.

It had been this way since they were children, even before Gia showed up, a bonus baby late into Maman's and Papa's parental careers. When it was just the three of them, it was always Phoebe who pushed first and hardest. Renata would rage and tattle and pout until Juliette stepped in the middle to sort it all out.

When Gia was born, Renata seemed to find her place in the family at last. She loved being a little mother and she doted heavily on the baby who responded with sweet coos and slobbery nuzzles. Gia was the kind of infant who smiled and chortled far more than she cried, who raised her arms to anyone who looked twice at her, and wanted desperately to be right in the middle of things. While Juliette was planning her future, and Phoebe was planning her evenings out, Renata was planning out a home and family of her own.

When she and John had their first baby, Reuben, she didn't care that he didn't have tiny red curls and no eyebrows like John's baby pictures, like Gia's. He still cooed and nuzzled and wanted to be nowhere more than tucked into the crook of her arm.

Simon arrived two years and two months later, solemn and scowling, mostly silent, his brow often furrowed even in slumber. Renata loved to stand over his bed while he slept and watch his constantly moving features. One day, she just knew, when he finally figured out all the things he really wanted to say, a torrent of amazing words would flow from his lips and he would change the world.

Then Levi was born, and Renata thought if there was ever such a thing as a perfect baby, Levi was it. He smiled for the sheer joy of it. His internal clock coincided perfectly with hers, and if she didn't put him to bed by 7:30, he'd fall asleep in his highchair, his swing, or curled up in a corner of the play area, usually underneath or behind something, throwing her and John into a momentary panic.

Judah made his entrance into the world roaring like a little lion cub, and he hadn't stopped since. He was the last to fall asleep, the first to wake up in the morning. His cries were the loudest of all the boys' and his belly laughs shook him so hard he often fell over. When he was angry, he did not want to be comforted with hugs and snuggles. He preferred to crawl into a corner and complain, sometimes in irritating whimpers, other times in endless yowls, until he either got tired of tormenting everyone around him, or fell into an exhausted sleep.

It was with the birth of Judah that Renata started to wonder if God was no longer listening to her. Every time she became pregnant, she begged for a baby girl, for their own John and Renata Dixon version of Gia, and every time another son was born, she fell in love with him and agreed to wait until the next time. But four years after Judah, it was still Renata and her family of boys.

Now, as she looked around Juliette's living room, she again felt that spiraling ache, that emptiness in the deepest part of her belly, that longing for a baby girl to love, to cherish, to dress in pretty polka-dots and lacy socks.

And suddenly, an overwhelming sense of being rudderless and adrift washed over her, even as she sat with her hip and arm pressed against Gia, her feet tucked under the warm body of Juliette's dog. She felt alone on the outside, surrounded by her beloved sisters.

She wondered if Angela Clinton felt the same way in prison; lost, untethered, and alone.

CHAPTER THREE

ANGELA Clinton killed Maman and Papa. On the night that Angela and Juliette and the rest of their senior class were to walk the aisle and flip the tassels on their cardboard caps, Angela Clinton got plastered, then climbed behind the wheel of her classic 1970 El Camino, a sweet-sixteen present from her daddy. She drove full speed through a red light, plowing into the side of the Gustafsons' Buick Park Avenue Sedan, making Maman's head snap back so hard against the passenger door window that the impact killed her almost instantly. Papa, on the other hand, lasted nearly an hour, but not long enough for any of the girls to say good-bye. At least Grandpa had gotten there in time to hold Papa's hand as he slipped away to join Maman.

Renata attended the same high school, two years behind Juliette and Angela. The girls weren't friends, but they weren't enemies, either, because Angela was kind to everyone. In fact, Angela had few enemies, only those who couldn't tolerate kindness from someone as popular as she was. She was the brightest star in their school, and Renata could still remember the first time she'd seen the girl perform. The voice that flew out of her mouth was like nothing she'd ever heard before—or since—and Renata sometimes wondered if Angela still sang. What kind of opportunities did prison offer a girl who looked like a pixie with flaxen blond hair, dreamy eyes, a brilliant smile, who had a voice that brought people to the brink of euphoria?

Angela. Why, of all days, of all people, had Angela Clinton been drinking? Alone? She stated at her trial that she'd been at home in her room, drinking her bottle of whiskey all by herself. According to Grandpa and Granny G, Angela gave no real reason for her binge, only that the alcohol was available, so she took advantage of it. But what would cause a girl with so much promise to drink alone on the day of her high school graduation?

Angela had turned 18 three months earlier, so was tried as an adult. Her sentence required her to serve two consecutive sentences of 10 years each. It would be 15 years this coming June, and Renata wondered how the parole system worked, if Angela might be eligible. Did her family still live close by or did they move away to begin a brand new life where the visage of Angela wasn't hanging over their heads? And if they had stayed local, what would that mean for Angela when she was released?

What if Angela came back to Midtown? Renata shook her head briefly, not ready to think about what that meant.

But Juliette had opened a can of worms with Angela's name on it, and they were all being forced to stare at the grotesque contents against their will. Juliette sat waiting, holding a pale yellow sheet of stationery in her hands, offering to read the words Angela Clinton had written, words that would bring the girl back to life in a very real way.

Renata didn't want to know what the letter said. She didn't want to feel sorry for Angela. She didn't want to feel anything for the girl. And from the expression on her face, neither did Phoebe. For once, the two of them were in complete agreement.

"I don't know, Jules." Phoebe shrugged, feigning nonchalance, but not fooling anyone. "Honestly, I'm not really interested in what she has to say to us, to you. I'm more interested in the unbelievable fact that you took it upon yourself to contact that woman in the first place, especially without including us." She pushed herself up off the floor and brushed her long-fingered hands together, the bracelets on her wrists jingling prettily. "I need to get going. I don't think it's really fair to Brandon to leave him hanging after all. So," she turned around and held out her hands to Renata and Gia. "I don't know how you two feel about this, but I'm ready to call it a night. Come say good-bye to me."

Gia stood up, her pale skin mottled with color. She flushed in patches when she was upset and Renata could tell the girl was despairing over the way their meeting had completely unraveled. When Phoebe made up her mind, though, there wasn't any budging her, and this time, Renata didn't feel like arguing with her. This time, in fact, she agreed with her. She turned to Juliette who still sat curled into the couch, hands clasped over the letter folded in her lap.

"Phoebe's right, Juliette. You should have included us long before now. And I'm not going to let you put Gia on the spot about this. We're going to call it a night so we all have a chance to think things through a little. We can get back together over the weekend. Maybe Saturday night."

"That will work for me," Gia murmured.

"I'll have to check my calendar." Phoebe clearly wasn't ready to commit to anything yet.

"I'm sorry. I didn't mean for it to go like this." Juliette looked at each one of them, imploring, her eyes revealing the truth of her words.

Renata sighed deeply and shook her head. She couldn't imagine what had motivated Juliette to act independently of them, especially over something so pivotal in each of their lives. "I'll call all three of you tomorrow to set up a time. A good night's rest should clear the air a little." She stepped forward and reached for Juliette's hand, pulling her up to stand as well, the corner of the coffee table still between them. She still held tightly to Phoebe's hand, even though the younger woman tried to pull away. "Let's do this right, okay?"

As we go our separate ways
As we ponder what's been said
May we keep each other's secrets
Lest we all wind up dead.

It was a terribly morbid way to end this meeting in particular, in light of what had been discussed, but they brought their clasped hands toward the center of their circle then let go, lifting fluttering fingers high overhead.

"Oogie Boogie," they muttered in unison, voices flat.

"I'm outta here. Thanks for the coffee, Jules. We'll talk soon." Phoebe was never really angry with anyone except Renata, but she didn't fake her feelings, either. If she wasn't happy, you didn't have to guess why. She hugged Juliette quickly, bending over the top of the coffee table. "I just need time to process, okay? You threw me for a loop with this."

Juliette just nodded. Gia circled the table and hugged her, too, then quickly followed Phoebe without saying anything more. Renata stood with her arms crossed and watched them leave, waiting until the door closed behind them. Then she rounded on Juliette.

"What were you thinking, Juliette Gustafson? Why didn't you say anything? At least to me, so that I'd be prepared to support you." She pressed a hand to her chest. "I feel like you tried to manipulate me into backing you up. Like you thought I'd be okay with this because we'd talked about it once last summer."

Juliette didn't answer at first, and Renata momentarily regretted the harshness in her voice. But when she did speak, Renata stiffened defensively.

"I think the point of breaking up this G-FOURce prematurely was to *not* talk about this now."

"Excuse me?" Renata's eyebrows rose in astonishment. "Don't get all snippy with me. I'm not the one who stirred the pot, you know."

"No, you're not. And it isn't your job to clean up the pot, either." Juliette made quotation marks in the air as she used Renata's words. "It's your job to go home and think things through a little. Get a good night's sleep on it, remember? Those were your words." Juliette bent down and picked up the purse from the floor by the armchair Renata always sat in, and handed it to her. "I have to take a shower. Can you lock up behind you?"

Renata snatched her purse out of Juliette's hand and glared at her. "What on earth is your problem? You're acting like Ph—"

"If," Juliette interjected, crossing her arms, her eyes bright again. "If you tell me I'm acting like Phoebe, Renata, so help me, I will stop speaking to you altogether. I am acting like *me.* This is how I act when I'm not happy with how things are going. I'm not angry. I'm trying not to be rude. I love you, but I don't really want to talk to you about this right now, especially since the others aren't here, okay? Just let it go for now."

Renata was livid. No one seemed to care how hard it was for her to always be the bad guy, the one to take the hits. Phoebe could just up and walk out of a room without so much as causing a ripple, her silky voice soothing any frayed nerves, her looks intimidating everyone into compliance. Georgia? Well, no one could be upset at the girl, not for more than a second or two. But her? It was as though people looked for reasons to be angry at her. And always found them, no matter how hard she tried to keep things from getting out of hand. She clamped her lips shut, slung her bag over her shoulder, and marched to the front door.

"Fine. Why don't *you* call everyone tomorrow then and arrange the next G-FOURce. I wouldn't want to interfere with your plans. I was just trying to help, you know."

Juliette nodded, her tears gone, her cheeks flushed. Renata was accustomed to her big sister's tears, but not this dry-eyed, slightly haughty version of her. Was this Officer Jarrett's doing?

"I'll call you tomorrow, Ren. And I'll call Phoebe and Gia, too. You shouldn't have to worry about always cleaning up the messes we make. We're all big girls now. Even Gia. She can make her own decisions, too." Juliette took a step toward her. "Sometimes messy is actually a good thing, you know."

Renata let out a derisive snort, then stepped out into the cold January air, pulling the door shut behind her a little more forcefully than she'd intended.

Don't worry about cleaning up after them? About fixing things? Well, who was going to take care of business if not her? It was what she did in this family. Nothing would get done if she, Renata Gustafson Dixon, didn't take the bull by the horns and deal with it. Phoebe would walk away, Georgia would dissolve into the floor-boards, and Juliette would curl into a fetal position, bawling her eyes out. Someone had to be responsible, and that left only her. They needed her. They just had no clue how badly they needed her.

CHAPTER FOUR

"THEY TAKE me for granted." John could tell Renata was trying not to give in to the tears that were making her eyes glisten. "They have no clue how much I do for them. They have no idea how hard I've worked to keep things together all these years. They think I'm bossy because I like to be, but if just one of them would step up and stop acting like selfish babies, I wouldn't be forced into this role. Then I could be self-centered and ridiculous like them. Georgia, at least, has an excuse. She's still practically a kid."

Across the table from her, John just nodded as he methodically cut and ate uniform bites off the baked potato in front of him. He knew better than to contribute to her rant. Anything he said could be used against him when she got this way.

"Have you heard anything I've said?" She glared at him, her eyebrows raised. Clearly, not saying anything could be used against him, too, but at least it was the lesser of two evils.

"I heard you, Mom. You're bossy, and they don't like it." Simon, nine years old, expressed himself in short, declarative statements that often left those around him deflated. It really bothered Renata who thought he was too young to be so opinionated. But Simon's directness was refreshing to John. It reminded him of Renata—how, at least in the early days, he'd never had to guess what she'd been thinking.

"Actually, no, you clearly did not hear me, Simon." She turned toward her son. "I said they *think* I like being bossy, but I'm not. It's because of them that I constantly have to step in. They force me to take charge because if I didn't, nothing would ever get resolved in this family." She turned narrowed eyes on John and he knew what that look meant. *Why aren't you defending me?*

The thing was, John did defend her. Everyone knew better than to say a negative word about her to his face. When she was being attacked, in any way, shape, or form, he was there by her side, at the ready, the moment she needed him. But more often than not, he'd step in too early and then get yelled at for treating her like a child, or worse, like an idiot. He never intended to do either, and he didn't like being accused of it. He would lay down his life to defend her, to cover her, to protect her, but she made doing so the biggest challenge in their relationship. Lately, he'd opted to err to the side of caution, so he often kept silent, waiting for just the right moment to step in…and inadvertently leaving her high and dry and on her own. It was a fine line to walk and he constantly listed to one side or the other these days, according to his wife.

She plucked the napkin from her lap and tucked it neatly under the edge of her plate. Did that mean she was leaving the table? Her food was barely touched. John sat back and studied her, waiting for her next move. It never ceased to amaze him the inner workings of his wife's mind. On the outside, she was beautiful, incredibly sexy with her sleek black hair and a mouth God shaped for kissing, eyes the color of summer rainstorms. But what went on behind those eyes, well, sometimes it was like standing at the edge of the bottomless Loch Ness and wondering if the creature in its depths was a timid gentle Nessie…or a beast that would swallow him whole if he looked too closely.

When they'd first met and early into their marriage, she'd burst into bloom under his affection, a flower so exquisite he was sometimes afraid to touch her lest he bruise her very soul. But somewhere along the way, something had bruised her anyway, and like a cactus blossom at the end of the day, the delicate petals folded in on themselves, leaving nothing exposed but prickles.

Oh, he knew her heart was breaking for a baby girl. He understood. He, too, had dreamed of a pink-cheeked daughter, chubby fingers reaching for him, a miniature of Renata. But it was more than that. His wife held on to things like no one else he know. She didn't give second chances. Not even to herself.

He looked around the table at their boys, studying each one for a moment or two. Reuben, suddenly a tween, was listening to music in his head. He didn't need wires hanging from his ears to hear it; it came from inside of him. When he wasn't doing homework or playing soccer, he was working on a song. Usually it was someone else's music, but more often now, when they asked him what he was humming, he'd answer vaguely, "Just a song I'm writing."

Levi watched everyone with that half-smile he had yet to outgrow. With his big gray eyes and coal-black lashes, his coloring was the most like hers. Even his hair, straight and thick, grew as quickly as his wife's did. They called him Harry Potter sometimes, which he didn't mind, because as soon as Renata trimmed his hair, it seemed to grow back the very next day.

Levi was like him in his temperament; tolerant, patient, and quiet. The kid said only good things about people. His favorite new saying was "You slay me!" and even though John didn't think he knew what it meant, it was pretty funny coming out of the gap-toothed mouth of a grinning seven-year-old.

Judah. Well, all that could be seen of him at the moment was his hand gripping the edge of the table. There was more food spread in an eight-inch swath around his plate than could be credited to what had originally been on the dish, and his cup lay on its side, thankfully all but empty. How could one child create so much chaos? The rest of him was rooting around underneath the table where he was either retrieving runaway food or trying to sneak away so he wouldn't have to eat the orange Jello melting on his plate. He didn't like the stuff, but for some reason John couldn't fathom, Renata felt compelled to keep trying to convince Judah otherwise, and served it to him every time she made it.

Simon, still stoic and often scowling, always seemed to be listening. Always alert, aware of what was going on around him, even when they were certain the conversation topics were over his head. They'd learned the hard way that they couldn't talk freely around him; he had the embarrassing tendency to ask questions at the worst possible time, especially when Renata's sisters were around. John was pretty sure he did it intentionally, just to be cantankerous. And because his calculating little mind knew exactly what went on in his mother's head when he did.

Sometimes Renata admitted to John that she wondered if Simon did stuff like that just to be mean to her.

His eyes fell on his wife, having made a full circle around

the table, and he smiled at her, hoping she'd soften and stay. He wanted to tease her, but he didn't dare. She didn't use to mind when he did. She use to blush and bury her face in his neck. But lately, she often accused him of ridiculing her, of thinking she was just a silly girl. He'd pull her close and kiss her until her knees gave out, reminding her that the best gift she ever gave him was laughter. She couldn't argue with that, but she did anyway.

"John?"

"Hm?" His eyebrows went up in question. Dang it. He'd forgotten the question.

When she pursed her lips and raised her own eyebrows, waiting for a response of *any* kind, he swallowed and took a sip of his iced tea. "You'll figure it out, Sweetie. You girls always do."

~ ~ ~

RENATA lay in bed, her back propped up against her pillows, reading the latest Ella Robbins novel. She was a fan through and through. Ella could craft a story like no one else, maybe not even her beloved Agatha Christie. Of course, she'd never admit that to anyone. Ms. Christie's books were classics. They were Literature, with a capital L. Ella Robbins' novels, on the other hand, were purely Pleasure. With a capital P. They were predictable stories that started with a bang, roared through the pages at a heart-thumping, break-neck speed, included plenty of passionate entanglements between the heroes and heroines, and ended with earth-shattering revelations Renata could see coming from the very first page. She loved them anyway. In fact, she loved them because of that. Ella wasn't going to pull the rug out from under her feet. Ella wasn't going to surprise her with anything but a happy and blood-pounding, climactic ending. Yes, Ella's love scenes included rather explicit details, but Renata tolerated them for the sake of the story.

Granted, she wouldn't want John opening one of the books to any of those scenes—or anyone else, for that matter—which is why she kept her collection tucked neatly into shoe boxes in her closet, amidst the myriad of other shoe boxes…containing shoes. Besides, she really didn't have to worry about John. He knew she read them, but he never bothered to open one. He didn't read anything except hunting, fishing, and various other outdoorsman magazines.

He also read the Bible, she admitted, and more often than she did, eyeing the worn leather-covered book sitting on his bedside table. Although he rarely read in bed, he kept it there for the morning when he'd slip out from the cocoon of their 1200 count Egyptian cotton sheets, scoop it up, and pad off to the kitchen. While waiting for the coffee to brew, he met with the Lord. Then he'd return to their bedroom with two steaming mugs and warm wake-up snuggles.

She loved those languid morning moments with him, before the world around them stirred, before the boys awoke and realized they wanted something immediately. Lying in the circle of his arms, curled against his solid man-strength, the faint bergamot of his aftershave still lingering on his skin from his shower the night before. Sometimes they talked about the day ahead, or of some other pressing matter, other times, rather than words, they communicated with the whisper of flesh and bone.

On nights like this, especially, when the sink of dinner dishes seemed bottomless, and the boys' bedtime rituals lasted far longer than they should, Renata wanted nothing more than to escape into someone else's story, preferably one with an idealistically happy ending.

John, too, seemed quieter, deeper, like still water, and Renata tiptoed around him, not because she didn't want to disturb him, but because she wasn't so sure she wanted him to disturb her.

She heard the bathroom door open and peered at him over the top of her book, watching him as he crossed the room to their bed. His short hair was still damp and rumpled from drying it with a towel after his shower. He wore only his boxers and socks, his chest and limbs pale with the winter months. Come summer, he would absorb the California sun into his skin, turning every exposed part of him a golden brown.

He noticed her eyes on him and winked, then did a slow soft-shoe shuffle toward her. She smiled appreciatively, but waved her book at him, held open in her right hand.

"You already know how it's going to end, Renata." When John was especially tired, his voice took on a husky quality that made her skin tingle. She let her long hair fall forward a little to hide the blush.

"No, I don't. This one is brand new." She turned the page purposefully, even though she couldn't remember a thing she'd just read.

"I wasn't referring to the book. I meant the competition." He eased himself under the blankets and slid over beside her, snaking an arm around her middle, jostling the book in her hands. "Who will make your heart race tonight? Will it be Ella Robbins and her paperback pirates? Or John Dixon, in the flesh?"

"In the cold flesh!" Although she knew he was like a furnace and would be hot to the touch in moments, his skin, even through her nightgown, was chilled after his shower. She tried unsuccessfully to nudge him away. He reached up, took the book out of her hand, then tossed it over his shoulder. It landed on the floor and slid beneath the tapestried slipper chair in the corner of the room.

"Hey! You shouldn't treat books that way." She stuck out her bottom lip and crossed her arms, feigning petulance.

"I love that glint in your eyes when you don't get what you want." He leaned over and braced his hands on the bed on either side of her, his face mere inches from hers. She could see the goose-bumps on his skin, feel the fine reddish hairs on his forearms stiffening beneath her fingertips as she ran her hands up to the smooth curve of his shoulders. She laced her fingers through the damp hair at the back of his head and pulled him toward her, the book forgotten for the moment.

"Who says I'm not getting what I want?" She whispered the words against his mouth.

The Gustafson Girls Series is continued in…
RENATA & THE FALL FROM GRACE
The Gustafson Girls Book 2

Made in the USA
Lexington, KY
14 July 2018